Till I'm Laid to Rest

Garfield Ellis

©2007

Nsemia
PUBLISHERS

First Edition February, 2010
Published by: Nsemia Inc. Publishers (www.nsemia.com)

Edited by: Margaret Brito
Cover Concept Illustration: Abel Murumba
Cover and Layout Design: Danielle Pitt

Note for Librarians:
A cataloguing record for this book is available
From Library and Archives Canada

ISBN: 978-0-9810362-8-1 Paperback

For Joan Masters: Life Fan
The Feelings Never Change

The title, *Till I'm Laid to Rest*, is inspired by the chorus in Buju Banton's song of the same title.

'Til I'm laid to rest
Always be depressed
There's no life in the West
i know the East is the best
All the propaganda they spread
Tongues will have to confess

I'm in bondage living is a mess
I've got to rise up alleviate the stress
No longer will I expose my weakness
He who seeks knowledge begins with humbleness
Work 7 to 7 but I'm still penniless
All the food upon my table Massa God bless
Holler for the needy and shelterless
Ethiopia awaits all prince and princess

The first chapter in the book appeared as a short story in titled Shirley's Temple in the collection *Wake Rasta and Other Stories*, Tallawa Press (2001).

Acknowledgements

I would like to express deep gratitude to Carol Reid for inspiring the project.

I am grateful for the honesty of good friends who read the early drafts and gave their dispassionate opinions: Sonia Mills who has been there from day one, Carmen Tiplin who had critical words, Bob Vassell & Trevon Garvey, who gave practical advice and Patricia Saunders who fell in love with it from the first word.

Endless love and appreciation to my children: Garfield, Fiona & Odane who inspire me to rise every day; and Doreen who has been a constant support even through her own trials.

I was wondering if I could find myself
all that I am in all that I could be;
If all the population of stars
would be less than the things I could utter;
And the challenge of the space in my soul
be filled by the shape I become

. . . . .*Martin Carter (Poems of Shape and Motion)*

Forward

Till I'm Laid to Rest is Garfield Ellis's third novel and like the characters that inhabit his other novels, Shirley Temple Brown is a reflection of the seldom heard but often felt realities of everyday Jamaicans whose voices are often hidden or suppressed. However, unlike his previous two novels, *Such As I Have* (2003) and *For Nothing At All* (2005), which feature the voices of Jamaica's youth through memorable characters like Headley, Pam Wesley, Skin, and Stevie; Shirley Temple Brown is a young woman who has survived some of the hardest social and political times Jamaica has seen. But now she is finally tired of just surviving, she wants to thrive and she knows she must leave Jamaica in order to do so. *Till I'm Laid to Rest* situates women's experiences and voices at the center of the cultural landscape, rather than at its margins. To be sure, several women writers have represented the complex experiences of migration that women have had to contend with. *Till I'm Laid to Rest* places Garfield Ellis solidly among this tradition of representations once thought to be the purview of women writers. In Shirley Temple Brown Ellis has created a protagonist that will surely take her place among the many unforgettable characters that are part of the tradition of migration narratives in Caribbean literature.

When we meet Sam Selvon's Moses, Tolroy, Captain, Big City and Galahad ("the boys") in Lonely Londoners (1956), they are struggling to live out their modest dreams in London. Leaving Jamaica, Barbados and Trinidad, one might imagine that their dreams were wealth and comfort, but sometimes for "the boys" these dreams amounted to a few pounds a week, a meal and a warm female body for the night, preferably one that did not come with a price. Instead, what they met were the mean, cold streets, boarding houses and hostels of the Empire and work that barely paid them enough to live, let alone prosper. Selvon's characters belong to a long tradition of young men (also present in the works of George Lamming, V.S. Naipaul and later, Austin Clarke) who left the Caribbean to take a chance Britain, only to arrive and discover that as the sun was beginning to set on the British Empire, not all of its subjects were accorded an equal share of belonging.

A few years later Paule Marshall's Brown Girl, Brownstone (1959) introduced us to another perspective of the immigrant experience, this time through the eyes of a community of working class Caribbean women in the U.S. When we are introduced to Silla Boyce, her family, and the women who reside in the brownstones of Brooklyn, we immediately notice the difference between Silla and Selvon's protagonists. She is not a subject of the American empire, and those who are subjects/citizens (Black Americans) were still treated like unwelcomed guests in "this man country. Marshall's protagonists are dealing with what it means to be black, female, mothers, single and (during World War II) at the lowest rung of the social and economic hierarchy. And yet, they scrub floors, fight unrelentingly to make a way for themselves, their families and, at times, one another. Nights filled with laughter and drinking are few and far between as theirs is a life of hard work and hardship and those who dare to refuse to embrace this reality cast out of the community as is the case with Suggie and Deighton.

Till I'm Laid to Rest and Shirley Temple Brown, are proud heirs to both of these traditions of Caribbean migrant narratives. Set in Miami, affectionately known as "Kingston 21" (a social and cultural annex of Kingston) to many from Jamaica, the reality she encounters in the mean streets of Miami is contrary to what her story-book name prepares both her and us for. Like her predecessors, Shirley leaves Jamaica [for an opportunity to "make it big" and she is prepared to face the difficulties that appear repeatedly like a soldier ready to do battle. The only things between her and success are a green card, a job that pays her a living wage while allowing her to keep her dignity in tact, and a safe environment

viii

in which to live; no small order by any measure. She had known the comfort of a concrete house in Spanish Town, living with her mother and father; she had also felt the pain of the poverty that ate at her sense of well being when they were evicted and took up residence Sufferers Heights, an impoverished settlement in Central Village. Life for Shirley Temple Brown was beginning to look up, she was experiencing a new level of comfort; living with a wealthy businessman, working a very good job in a bank and possessed all of the material markers that distinguished her from her peers as a woman who was "going places." But when her comfort and future are threatened, she makes the decision to leave Jamaica for a new start in Miami.

Enthralled by the bright lights and shiny veneer of this tropical city, she quickly learns that sometimes, the things that shine the brightest are nothing more than a fool's gold in disguise. Not long after arriving in Miami, she begins to see what the glare of the sun and the bright lights have kept hidden: elderly American retirees living out their last days in the warmth and comfort their youth never afforded them, while being cared for by complete strangers; drug dealers hungry for their slice of the American dream, sexual predators, con artists and murderers. Miami – the cellophane wrapping which brightens and preserves the colors of tropical flowers, large malls, night clubs and expensive cars – is a willing accomplice in the drama that seems determined to dull the shine of Shirley Temple Brown's star. Alone in a place where standing still is sure death, Shirley learns the ropes from a community of Jamaicans who have gone before her and made hard beds as comfortable, as best they know how. *Till I'm Laid to Rest* is inhabited by a host of memorable characters who, no matter the depths of despair and desperation, create small envelopes of trust, friendship and love; at times within themselves and, when lucky, in one another. Shirley, Queeny, Tiny, Moet and Chef all navigate her way through the fast paced life of this tropical city against the backdrop Caribbean rhythms that become the soundtrack to their complex lives. By the end of this novel it is clear that these characters want the same things those who continue to leave their homes, families, communities and even their countries want: to improve their futures. What separates us from these characters are the lengths to which they are prepared to go in order to improve their circumstances.

Patricia J. Saunders
University of Miami
April 2010

PART I

There Is Something
Better Somewhere

Chapter One

It was Friday evening and close to five thirty when Shirley crossed the threshold of the Mutual Security Bank into a humid New Kingston evening and caught up with Dawn a half a step ahead. Knutsford Boulevard was a hive of after-work activities. The other banks and insurance companies were emptying and people jammed the pavements as they waited for pickup. Bumper-to-bumper traffic jerked forward. The two women paused near a mini garden at the side of the building and Shirley rested her bag along its unkempt edge. They had hardly stopped when a brand new Honda halted in front of them and the tinted window slid noiselessly down. A smiling face pushed through. "Taxi?"

Dawn looked strangely at him. "You are a taxi?"

"No, but anywhere you ladies going this evening, I will take onoo there right now."

She turned away in disgust.

"What a nerve," Shirley laughed as he drove away.

Dawn looked her up and down at the baby pink dress that flowed along her figure like a second skin. "You caan' wrong the man to stop?"

"Is you him stop for," Shirley chided back.

Dawn laughed. "Me! Ah boy, when Mister Mark see you this evening him must get heart attack."

They were two strikingly beautiful women. Shirley was half Indian with olive, smooth skin and wavy curly hair that fell to her shoulders. Her lithe sensuous figure had the effect of being poured into something. Had she been a few inches taller, she could easily have modelled. Dawn was full Negro with large eyes, a dimpled smile, and a face that would have been round had it not been for high cheekbones that gave it a constant glow when she smiled or stared too long. Where Shirley was elegant she was voluptuous and where Shirley was poised, she was relaxed and

3

mischievous.

"You called a taxi?" Shirley switched topic.

"We getting a ride."

"Berto come back in the picture?"

"Berto? If I see him now I spit on him." Dawn put her bag on the extended edge of the garden so that she was facing the bank and Shirley was facing the street.

"So where you get ride?" Shirley asked.

"Barnes." Dawn dropped his name as if Shirley was missing the obvious.

Shirley eased backward until they were staring into each other's eyes. "Barnes! I must drive in Barnes's car?"

"Lord man, is just a ride. We just going Jonkoono Lounge down there so. Why we must pay a hundred dollars on taxi when we can get a free ride?"

"Me! Next thing people see me leaving his car going into hotel and start talk things."

"Things! What kinda things?"

"I am not driving in his car."

"Lord, Shirley man." Dawn began to apply some lipstick. "What him going do, rape both of us?"

"Play with puppy and they wan' lick you mouth."

"Play! Who a play with Barnes? Much less lick. What him going lick? You going give him something to lick? Him can lick anything? Him mouth big like jester pot. What him going lick?"

"Him too nuff."

"Lord, missis, relax. You not even spending five minutes in the car and you worrying. Relax yourself, man. I just see a fool and using him. Something wrong with that?"

Dawn had hardly put her lipstick away when Barnes's old Toyota appeared in front of the bank with its extra large wheels. Shirley sighed as the handsome supervisor with his toothy smile and presumptuous barefaced stare, reached across to push the door open. The rear door also swung wide as if pushed by an invisible hand. Shirley shivered in disgust – they had already been paired.

Inside, the car was clean and smelled of cheep perfume and furniture polish. Luther Vandross blared from high-powered speakers. Shirley nodded civilly to Orville, the nervous teller on the other end of the rear seat, as he shifted to allow her entry even though he was already pressing against his door and had left three quarters of the seat vacant for her.

The back seat was spacious, so Shirley crossed her legs and leaned back into its faded leather pretending not to see how uneasy Orville got as he watched her skirt ride up and down her thighs. As she leaned her shoulder into the corner, she looked unconcerned through the window at the after-work traffic of New Kingston and wondered what she would do with someone like Orville.

Poor. Just out of school. Just left his parent's house for a little room somewhere. Ambitious, no doubt, but right now bracing himself for that long spell of drought and hardship that would come with his first set of furniture, his first car loan, his first real rent and food bill. Poor, just like her. Ugly too. She could have a million like him at any given day. They infested Sufferer's Heights, like ants, stopped at the bus stop every morning to offer her rides, rubbed up against her on the bus, sent her notes and letters every day. But what would she do with someone like that? Can hardly help himself. Can't help her. A piece of poverty just looking out to latch on to another piece of poverty and make one big hell.

At least Mark had money.

She cracked the window a bit to let the fresh air in. Mark was a fresh-air man – a lover of garden restaurants and beaches.

They had met six months before on a bad morning inside the bank when he had slammed his hand on the counter and shouted at a girl whom she supervised, shouted so loudly the whole bank stopped and looked around. At least that was what Shirley thought. He, like most of the country, trying to come to grips with the new foreign exchange restrictions, was demanding why, if he had just banked ten thousand US dollars, he could not get five hundred back in kind. The young teller had done all she could and the slap on the counter had been Shirley's signal to step in.

It turned out that the girl had misunderstood the nature of the rules. Shirley quickly cleared up the matter and the big-belly white man got his money and was on his way. The next time he came to the bank, the foreign- exchange teller glanced over to Shirley and indicated that the feisty white man was there.

A junior supervisor with a reputation for diplomacy and good judgement, Shirley did not hesitate, nor did she show the disgust she felt for the young cashier's apparent lack of quality. Every customer was a valued one. The cashier would not get far. Shirley smiled and invited the gentleman to sit by her desk while she finished attending to something.

Two weeks later, he called from Miami and asked if she could perform a transfer of funds for him. Though company procedures dictated that he be present, she acted on her instincts and did his transfer based on a telephone conversation and a one-paragraph fax. Not only did she save the gentleman a trip to Jamaica but she earned him some money as well. His next deposit to the bank was nearly a hundred thousand US dollars.

On his next visit to the bank, he brought her a little red Gucci bag, Ray Ban sunglasses and Elizabeth Taylor shampoo. He wanted to say thanks. She accepted gracefully and told him he did not have to, she was only doing her job. But gradually, her relationship with the no-nonsense white man grew. Soon, the broken-down dresser she had in her room at home began to acquire an expensive array of perfumes and accessories.

One day, he asked her out. "Make we take a drink one evening when you not so busy," he had said, "I not doin' anything Friday."

She promised she would think about it. As soon as he left she reviewed his accounts. His records listed him as into tour sales. Shirley was not sure what it meant but figured and later learnt that it had to do with the selling of tour packages to the island. She also confirmed that he had more money than she would ever hope to see in twice her lifetime. The next time he asked her out she said yes.

There were no apologies about him. He was a big Jamaican white man with a sharp aggressive nature and an impatient no-nonsense manner.

He spoke with a strong insistent tone that seemed to give orders all the time. A haphazard sampling of grey sprinkled his unruly, curly hair and placed him farther past forty than he really was. A half-sized belly, more due to neglect than beer, moved freely when he strutted.

Though she had planned to see him for only a few times, Shirley insisted on a discreet arrangement, she did not want her friends or her colleagues at the bank to see them and think they were dating.

On their first evening out, he took her to Heather's, a quaint and quiet garden restaurant in the middle of New Kingston. There, the waiters wore red and white plaid shirts and black pants, balanced trays on their hands, bowed and whispered and called her ma'am. He introduced her to shish kebab, and steak with creme sauce and expensive Italian wine.

"A woman like you don' belong here," he said as they ate.

"Pardon?"

"A woman like you wasting you time working in a bank like that."

"Oh." She smiled in relief.

"I bet they don' pay you nothing."

"You are right about that."

"Woman like you belong in America, where you can maximize you potential."

That momentarily took her back to her father and his gruff beard scratching her face as she sat in his lap when she was little. He would say, Shirley my movie star. Shirley my movie star. And as he said this, she would close her eyes and dream that she was made for something special. It was strange how Mark always make her feel that way, as if she was wasting time not being more.

Yet she had not wasted time. She had only left high school three years now, and though the job at the bank had been her only one, she had not been stagnant there. She started as a teller, and was so quick with her hands that in less than a year they moved her to the drive-in window. After six months of that she went to Loans, then on to Foreign Exchange. A year later she was Senior Teller and now she was Junior Supervisor, the only junior in the whole Mutual Security chain. They created that post for her because she was too young to be given a full

Supervisor, but Shirley did not expect the bank would hold that against her for too long.

"Boy, I tell you," he continued, "some o' those people in that bank... how them get job in bank God He knows. You know what is wrong with this country? You don' get good service any more."

The waitress glided to the table and gave half a curtsy. "More wine?"

"You want more wine?" He looked at Shirley.

"No, thanks. A fruit punch."

"Just another glass for me, and bring her a nice fruit punch."

The waitress slipped away.

"Is you save that bank, you know. I was going to take my business and leave. Damn people, caan' get good service these days." He lifted the shish kebab and bit it savagely, dragging meat and vegetables from the stick which bent slightly under the weight of his assault. "What happen, you not eating you shish kebab? You 'fraid to bite it?" He spoke through a careless chew.

"No." She lifted hers and gently pulled the meat at the end.

"Eat it, man. You know this is a famous Indian dish?"

She thought about it and put the shish kebab on her plate. She removed the food with a fork and placed a suitable piece in her mouth. They were poor but her mother had taught her well.

"How you like it?"

"It's OK."

"You never have it before, no?"

"Not really."

"Oh."

After a few outings with Mark, she told Dawn about him and regretted it immediately, because Dawn kept teasing her, asking if he was good in bed. But she had never slept with Mark and had no intention to. Sometimes she barely liked his company and condescending conversation though she liked the wonderful places he took her to, and she loved the gifts. He had an air of power and arrogance about him that was attractive at times, especially when he was half drunk and his face became ruddy and his eyes sort of glazed. But she hated the smell of alcohol and food that went with the dangerous cherry high.

Yesterday, he called from Miami, said he would be in Jamaica today, and invited her for drinks at the Promenade deck of the Wyndham Hotel.

"OK," she had said.

They had never met in a hotel before though he always stayed in one. He did not have a car in Jamaica but he would always send a taxi to pick her up and would be waiting at the front of the hotel when she arrived. After an evening out he would leave the taxi at the front of the hotel, stuff the driver's hand with money and bellow: "Take her home for me, my dear sir. And don't let nothing happen to her." She would have been a fool not to expect that one day he would invite her in.

She hung up the phone. The day had come.

She decided to wear her baby pink dress that Friday because it had a jacket that suited work and could be stowed for an evening out, and also because he had bought it for her, placed it in her hand, almost shoving it at her "Is things like this you must wear." Now she was wearing it, to look nice for him, and tell him no.

She did not expect that she would break his heart. Hers, she knew, would remain unmoved. Saying no was one of the first things her mother taught her to do. He was nice, she would tell him. She liked him, she would say, but not in the way he wanted. She would make him understand that taking the relationship to another level would compromise her professionalism and their friendship. And if it got sticky, she would just flatly say she had thought about it and did not think it would be a good idea.

The ride in Barnes's car had been short and uneventful, and that was good enough for Shirley. Now they stood at the entrance of the Jonkonoo Lounge to part company , Dawn to the after-work jam inside and Shirley, to the other side of the hotel and the classy Promenade deck where the talk was quiet and the piano played unfamiliar tunes.

"Monday," she said to Dawn.

"Mr. Mark time now."

"It's not like that." She tried to counter the suggestive sound in Dawn's voice.

"Don't bother kill him." Dawn spoke mischievously.

"It's not like that and you know it."

"Well, when him see you in that dress, you can't tell him no tonight."

"No. We'll have dinner and talk, that's all."

"Well, him mus' be board man or something."

"You gwaan – you only have one thing on your mind all the time. You better go inside to Barnes."

"That," Dawn laughed, "is not like that."

"Who knows, you must be glad I'm going. Now you can give him a dance."

"Me, missis? Next thing you know, him wan' fresh himself or something, wan' grind up himself on people."

"I'm sorry for you this evening. No you ride?"

"You better go 'long, don' keep the gentleman waiting."

"True."

"Later."

"Monday."

She was on time, he was not.

She entered the Promenade deck, sought a table near the window that looked out on to New Kingston through tinted glass, and sat elegantly into an expensive green floral sofa. A waiter appeared at her elbow. He was as elegant as the room, with a voice tilted just above the soft floating music of piano. She ordered a glass of Bristol Cream Sherry.

The waiter placed the drink on her table and disappeared. She sipped it as the piano's unfamiliar tunes reminded her of an evening when Mark had taken her way up on some steep hill to another garden restaurant called Ivor. He had looked out at Kingston and commented on how beautiful it was. "Ever see no scene so pretty?" and then he had gone on to talk of the many places he had visited in the world and how beautiful they were and how "places in Acapulco would lick this for six".

But all the time she was thinking that the view from her home was just as good. And that the road to her house, though not as steep, led to a hilltop too, and the dinners were outside most of the time, and they could see as many stars, and the breeze was just as cool. Only it was on Sufferer's Heights, in a poverty-stricken place, where she had not even had the guts to invite Dawn to the shack not more than a room and a half that she shared with her mother who worked tirelessly cleaning a hospital. And she wondered how different the same things could be, depending on who one was with. She had sighed, and he caught himself at the end of a soliloquy on some rainforest in Dominica and said, "me talk too much, no?" She smiled. "Depend on how you look at it." He laughed. "Bwoy, you bowl me with that answer, you learning too fast." She looked at him softly and said: "Nothing wrong with talk. Talk all you want." For she wanted to compare how far she had come and how far she would go as she moved from hilltop to hilltop, stars to stars, view to view and elegance to poverty – depending on who she was with.

"Hi" Mark dropped easily into the sofa beside her.

"Hi."

"You waiting long? Sorry. I had to take care of something." He stared at her. "The dress really looks nice on you."

"Well, thank you, sir. And how was your trip?"

"Same old, same old. The damn people them almost crush up me things." He beckoned to the waiter.

Mark seemed mildly uncomfortable, as if nervous about something. There were no gifts that evening. She wondered what that meant. He had never come empty-handed before. She hoped he did not have one of those small boxes in his pocket. She felt too good to deal with something like a proposal now.

"Are you OK?" she asked.

"Fine. Fine," he said, too quickly. Then: "That will take care of it?" he asked the waiter, handing him some money.

"More than enough, sir."

"All right then, keep the change."

"Aren't we having a drink?" She looked curiously at him.

"No, I don' feel like it."

"Where are we going? You seem to be in a hurry."

He was like a schoolboy, looking nervously at her. His brow was damp. "I look like I in a haste, no?" he said sheepishly. "Sorry."

"So where are we going?"

He leaned across the table to look at her seriously. "Well, we can go anywhere you want tonight. But first I have something I want to show you."

Her drink was three-quarter way through and the ice had almost melted. Shirley held the glass by its rim and twirled it on the edge of the wet circle it had created. She was not sure what he meant and how that fitted into her plan for the evening. She strategized for a minute.

"Where is this something you want to show me?"

"Upstairs in the room." His forehead sweated some more. But she did not think he was nervous; anxious maybe, but not nervous.

"Why you didn't bring it down with you?"

"It too big."

She leaned back into the cushion, pushed the drink aside, and gave a suspicious smile. "Are you up to something?"

"What I could be up to?"

"You tell me."

"Come, man." He began to rise. "Come."

"OK." They stood up together.

As they entered the dim room she immediately saw a basket as large as half a drum in the centre of the bed. It was wrapped in shining silver dotted by little hearts that spelled Victoria's Secrets. A red ribbon was tied around it and a card was attached.

"You bring that from Miami?" she squealed.

"In a big box. The damn man them nearly crush it."

"But why? I mean, what occasion?"

"Which occasion that? That necessary?"

"It's beautiful."

"Yeah, well, call it birthday or something."

"But it's not. What's in it?"

"Look, no. Is yours, you know. You can open it."

"It's so big," she said excitedly, tugging the ribbon undone. She reached in beneath the candles and candy to find the first fabric. White laced silk, light as baby's breath, fell against her hand. She pulled and it unfolded like silver drifting smoke.

She hardly felt him behind her as his encircling arms obstructed her momentarily. "Shirley, I like you bad. Don' tell me no this evening."

A negligee came loose from the basket. She dropped it onto the bed and reached inside once more. She fingered more lace, more silk. Then she felt the strap of her dress against her elbow. He was undressing her. She froze. "What you doing?" she whispered.

His voice was hoarse against her neck. "Don't tell me no this evening, Shirley. I beg you."

"We need to discuss this." Silky laced panties filled her hand. "We need to discuss this."

"Anything you want, Shirley, tell me. I give you anything." He began to push the other strap of her dress down her arm.

"It's not like that," she breathed. "It's not like that." But soft silk weighed her to the spot.

He pressed forward to gently pull her hand from the bed and through the strap.

"What are you doing?" She made to turn and stumbled against the bed. He pushed her onto it and she fought him back. But he was heavy and big, and though he held her lightly his grasp was firm.

"Mind you scrape youself on the basket," he said huskily.

"Stop," she whispered. "Mark, stop a little. We have to discuss this."

"Mind you head," he said, as he tried to shove the basket away. "Mind you head."

She struggled with him for a while but he held her down and managed to slip both her hands through the strings of her dress. She pressed herself backward against the bed to squeeze her dress to her and prevent him as he tried to pull it down the length of her body. She felt the cold of the room on her bare skin as he succeeded in exposing just her breast, felt his asthmatic pant as he caught his first look at the soft flesh bulging against her clean white brassiere.

He was a confusion of movement and caresses. "Shirley," he groaned, "you think I would do so much for you if I never love you?"

Shirley fought vainly against him, but not hard enough. She should have expected the moment would come, and now, lying there, beneath his panting groping self, she could not see the sense in running from the inevitable.

She pushed against his side. "Mark."

"Shirley, don't tell me no."

"OK, Mark, but wait. Mind you tear the dress."

He paused. "What?"

"OK, but let me take off my dress."

"You not going run?"

"Run? Why? No. Just let me do it."

She stood and let the dress fall around her. Snapped her bra, and saw the sweat trickle down the side of his face. She walked to the bed. "Help me with this."

He helped her remove the oversized basket from the bed.

She slipped beneath the sheets and watched him as he began to undress, pulling his shirt excitedly over his head while it was yet half-buttoned. His stomach fell like a weighted breast against his waist.

"Turn off the light," she said.

Chapter Two

Six months later, Shirley left her mother's house to live with Mark. That day it rained so hard she could hardly see the old zinc fence from the veranda.

Shirley hated Sufferer's Heights, and when it rained her hate rose like bile and her whole sensory system became sensitive to every scent the showers brought down. And she would be afraid to open her door because she knew the dogs and hogs from the neighbours would leave filth in the yard, and all the dead fowls that washed down from the hill would somehow find their way there too, and the mud and the muck would be so high, she would sink to halfway up her thighs before she got to solid ground; and the filth would last for days, and the scents would linger for over a week.

But that evening, she did not mind the rain. She would be out of Sufferer's Heights before the mud settled or the filth gathered in the yard. And what was more, Shirley thought the rain would be a good excuse to tell her mother, Miss Ivey, that she could not come to help her set up house.

She had wanted her mother to come, but Mark had surprised her by returning from Miami to help. Shirley had no intention of having her mother meet him. Whatever she did, she could not have her mother know she was leaving to live with a man. An older man. An old white man at that. Miss Ivy would drop dead on the spot.

Shirley turned from facing the water at the sound of her mother's shuffling behind her. She was placing her old hospital issue raincoat atop one of Shirley's suitcases that was lying there.

"You no 'fraid you catch a draft no?"

"Just little rain, Ma." Shirley tried to avoid meeting her eyes. It was not going to be easy to tell her. They were almost finished packing. The rain fell harder. Dawn was to bring the van any minute now.

"I wonder what is keeping Dawn and that van?"

"Dawn! Why you worry bout Dawn? Is van she driving."

"You right," Shirley smiled painfully as her mother left for another bag, and wondered why a simple thing like leaving home had to be so complicated.

She wished there were some way around it. Maybe she could move another day, but she killed the thought immediately as it came. If she did not turn up at the apartment that evening, Mark would come and find her, and that would be worse.

But how do you tell your mother she cannot come to help you set up house? When both of you have struggled for so long together in the broken-down house since your father left some years before. When she has taken care of you all your life, cooked for you every evening, washed almost every stitch of clothing you ever wore.

She was born the last day of Cancer in the Spanish Town Hospital and christened Shirley Temple Brown because her father said she was born to be a star. She grew up in Greendale on the outskirts of Spanish Town in a three-bedroom house with concrete stairs leading to the roof railed as a large balcony. Miss Ivy was a nurse's aid at the Spanish Town Hospital and her father a supervisor at the Ariguanabo textile factory. She remembered her father as a gruff fat Indian man, always half-drunk and jovial, with a thick, coarse beard he would rub constantly in her hair. And she remembered snuggling up to him till his beard would scratch her face and her nostrils would be filled with the mellow smell of white rum, and twisting the hair on his belly, while he called her his movie star. She remembered waiting at the gate or on the house top for the sound of his bike as he rounded the corner so she could run down to circle his bike for a lollipop she knew he would always bring. She had a brother, Carlton, five years her senior, a younger version of her father who was the brightest in his class, always neatly dressed.

When she was ten years old, her mother joined the Pentecostal church in Spanish Town and became so dedicated to God that she began to come home late at nights, shut her father from the bedroom; insisting through their half-opened door, night after night, that her body was the temple of the Lord. Then she would pray so loudly the neighbours would wake up to her wailing for God to forgive her and purge her for being unequally yoked together with an unbeliever.

After that, her father began coming home later. Many times Shirley would wait on the roof for him and her mother would call her down to bed long before he showed up. Sometimes on weekends he would not come home at all until early the next morning. Then he would be dirty and smelled of stale rum. His hair would be unkempt and scattered over his head and his eyes would be red, glaring with a fogginess that hardly seemed to recognize her. One morning he went to work and did not come back. After a month, her brother went to school and did not return either. The next day, her father rode by to tell her mother that Carlton was living with him now. She remembered that last hug he gave her and the last lollipop as he asked her if she wanted to come with him. And she remembered how the yes had frozen on her lips as Miss Ivy had snatched her away from his embrace and shoved him and his ungodly hands away.

Two months later, unable to pay the rent, Shirley and her mother were evicted to a one and a half room lean-to at Sufferer's Heights, the poorest part of the impoverished settlement of Central Village. She hardly saw her father after that, except on holidays when she would visit him. Carlton came by regularly, and when he had grown and joined the police force he would bring his friends by the house for food and to see his sister, Shirley Temple, the movie star.

Her relationship with her mother had never been one of long conversations or sophisticated notes on the kitchen table. It was one of silences and grunts and dropped words. Feelings were never openly expressed, hardly came out to air. They had come to understand each other's mumbles and mannerisms: which tone meant that the next word would start a war or which smile was a closed door.

Sometimes they hardly saw each other, because Shirley worked late and Miss Ivey was mostly on the graveyard shift at the hospital and worked overtime on her weekends or filled in for some friend or the other, doing missionary work. All day Sunday was spent in church. But the evidence of her care was there, in the food freshly cooked on the stove or the clothes freshly ironed and placed on Shirley's bed, the sheen of polish on the floor or clean curtains in the window.

Shirley turned from the rain and wiped the water from her face. As she passed through the doorway, she wondered if the wooden side of the house would hold. Something told her it would. She knew that, no matter how she thought she felt, she was going to miss the house. She had lived through many struggles in that old place. When they got there it was just a thirty-foot-by-fifteen-foot wooden shack that sat awkwardly on the hill, not facing any particular direction, built with no sense of design except for the sloping zinc roof that caused the rainwater to run off quickly. It seemed the rest of the world and the village it looked out on were built in concentric lines while it stood strangely skewed. There was a front door in the centre of the broadest side that faced downhill, and another door in the side that met the rising sun. It had three windows: two on either side of the front door and one to the left of the side door so that the front was an open-faced smile and the side a profile of a grin.

When they moved in, her mother used heavy curtains and the placement of the sofas and tables to partition off a bedroom on one end and a small kitchen on the other, leaving the middle to serve as a living, dining, sitting and any other room.

Then Hurricane Flora came. It rained for three days and halfway through, the side of the house that faced the sun collapsed. It just fell away like a large door that someone had left wide open. The rain came in and battered them, wetting everything beyond repair. After the storm, as they stood together in horror looking at their soaked belongings, part of the front wall fell on its side with a large bang and took half of the front of the house with it. The neighbours and members of the church came to help, but the wall had torn away so badly that it was impossible to lift it back into place. So they used what could be salvaged of the fallen walls to partition off the section that was still standing. The house was transformed then into a one-room affair. The condemned section, now outside and bare except for portions of a wall, doubled as veranda and kitchen.

Later, they built a two-room concrete structure adjacent to the wooden one with the intention of tearing the old house down. But Miss Ivy had grown so accustomed to the old house, she continued to sleep in the wooden section and allowed Shirley one of the concrete rooms as her bedroom. They used the other concrete room as a living and dining room.

Shirley watched her mother as she moved busily in the room, a little woman who had grown almost portly and neat, skin the colour of ripe mango with a cute nose and small lips, and thick black hair almost always in a bun. She wondered if she had to pick a fight to do it.

Shirley did not want an argument. She had not gotten over the last major quarrel they had, nor did she feel the wounds had sufficiently healed.

It happened one Sunday when her mother had stayed home from church to ask her why of late she had been spitting so. Shirley had been taken aback, for she too had noticed that since she had become intimate with Mark, she had indeed been spitting quite regularly. Dawn had noticed it too. So Shirley had purposefully avoided her mother for nearly a month or so, hoping it would wear off. But she should have known better. For though they had figured out how to keep out of each other's way, they shared a special bond, and any change in pattern in one was immediately noticed by the other.

When Miss Ivy raised the subject, Shirley was sarcastic, and told her mother that she was not pregnant, so Miss Ivy need not worry about holding her head up in church. Miss Ivy looked up from the rice she was picking. "You not pregnant, or you not pregnant any more?"

They quarrelled as they had never quarrelled before. Everything came out that day, all the feelings they had kept inside as Shirley grew through adolescence in the hills of Central Village without her father or brother.

Everything came out that day.

Shirley blamed her mother and her church for chasing her father from their lives till he rode his bicycle, drunk, one evening and was killed by car; and condemning them to the hell hole on the hill in the middle of what was perhaps the most violent political constituency, in a broken-down half-concrete half-wooden shack of a house of which she was so ashamed she hardly ever invited friends over; the one bank manager who asked her out, never called her again after he took her home and saw where she lived.

Miss Ivy attacked Shirley's lifestyle, her staying out late at nights and what the neighbours were saying. She had given Shirley rope, even allowed her to have a TV in her room so long as she kept the volume down – though it was forbidden by the church for her to have one in the house. And what of all that stuff in Shirley's 'palace': where did she get all of it from? She knew her daughter had a good job but she noticed that the money in her bankbook rose steadily while she got more and more fancy clothes and jewellery and perfumes. Something was rotten in the house; something was sinful: there was some iniquity that she could not pinpoint.

When they were done, Shirley locked herself in her room and did not eat. Then, for the first time in her twenty-two years, she placed a padlock on the door to her room.

The lock stayed for two days. By the time she cooled down and removed it, it was too late. Apart from the washing placed carefully at the front of her door, there was no evidence that Miss Ivy ever entered her room again.

And now the day had come for her to leave.

Shirley knew her mother felt the quarrel was responsible for her leaving. And Miss Ivy had softened when Shirley informed her. Their relations had normalized to the point where Miss Ivy even visited her room one last time to help her pack. Shirley knew this was her mother's way of reaching out to her.

Now she had to tell her that she could not come and help her set up house. Now she would have to place another padlock on another door and she did not know if she would be able to open it again.

"You know you should take the bed," Miss Ivy said heavily. "It makes no sense having this good bed and buying a new one. It is not as if you married or something. Dawn buying new bed too?"

Shirley had lied to her that she would be sharing the apartment with Dawn. "Why you bothering about the bed, Mama? You don' see it old. Suppose a want to visit, where I sleep? You can use it. Move in here and throw away that old coyer one you have."

"You girls will need this dressing-table."

"Yes, I'm taking that."

Had Shirley moved six months ago, all she had would have barely filled two bags. But now she needed a suitcase just for all the perfumes and gifts.

She felt her mother's eyes on her as she lifted the basket Mark had brought from Victoria's Secrets. She had kept it intact with all its finery of silk, satin and lace. As she took it from atop the wardrobe, her mother left the room. "Let me see if the rain wetting up the things," she said.

Every time Shirley looked at the basket it left her breathless. She had never worn a single garment from it. There had never been an occasion special enough.

Sometimes, lying in her bed and looking up at the basket, she wondered how good it would feel to be in her own home – a place with her man for whom she could wear Victoria's Secrets every day. A man like Richard Channing from her favourite soap opera, Falcon Crest.

Mark was not as beautiful as Richard Channing, but when she suggested that since he was in Jamaica ten days a month it would be more practical to get an apartment rather than waste his money in hotels, he did not hesitate. He immediately told her to look. She found a little place in Oxford Manor in the middle of New Kingston, but he laughed at her and rented a one-bedroom apartment in Embassy Apartments with a living room almost the size of the whole house in Sufferer's Heights.

The keys were dropped off for her at work. Then in his flamboyant style, he called a friend who owned a furniture store she had never heard of before. By mid-week the man had come, looked around the apartment and by Friday, there was a truck filled with furniture there.

She did not know how far it would go, and who was to say that it would last? Maybe one day when she was ready, when she had all she wanted, he would turn out to be married or something. And then she probably would be free in a place of her own filled with clothing from the catalogues of JC Penny, Macy's and Bloomingdale, with furniture from Modernage, undergarments and negligees only from Victoria's Secrets.

She left her special basket on the bed and dragged the last bag through the open door. On the concrete roof the rain was constant murmur, and as she neared the board side, it sounded as if someone was bawling as it hammered on the zinc. She dropped the bag close to the door next to those her mother had already left there.

Shirley sat down heavily on the old sofa which was covered with sheets to hide the dirty worn fabric. The cushions were deep and rounded to the shape of their bottoms. She watched her mother as she fussed clumsily among the many glasses in the old cabinet that rested against the concrete wall. "I wonder if Dawn going to make it through the rain," she said, just to do something about the silence that was coming on.

"She will come," Miss Ivy said. "She must leave town by now, so the rain probably catch her halfway."

Miss Ivy turned carefully as she spoke, lifting a large silver tray with a perfect little crockery teapot and five perfectly fashioned cups. It was the first time Shirley had ever seen that whole tray removed from the cabinet except for cleaning. She had only touched them once when, fifteen years old, she tried to clean the set and had broken one of the six cups. Her mother was so sad she was unable to find the strength to beat her for it, but had sat speechlessly on the sofa picking up and dropping the pieces on the floor as if trying to put them together again.

And now Miss Ivy was pulling them from the cabinet to give to her.

Shirley knew she could not take those paper-thin cups from which no one had ever drunk, that had been passed on to her mother from her mother, who had received them as a gift from the great Mrs Withinworm, for whom she worked as a maid on The Great Plantation in Linstead. It had been a twenty-five-year anniversary gift brought all the way from England. Now she was passing them on to Shirley. "Here, I want you to have these."

There was something about those cups that made her mother's efforts over the years to speak proper English, especially to strangers, seem so appropriate. Miss Ivy held the tray to Shirley, then thought about it and laid them easily on the table. "At least you girls will have something decent to entertain with."

"But Mama, we won't be having anyone over for tea."

"Take it. I'm not asking you."

And then they sat there and waited while the rain shed its pain upon the roof and the water ran down the columns of the old veranda like unending streams of tears.

"You not going church tonight?" Shirley finally asked.

"Depend on what time I come back."

"You ever miss Sunday night church yet?"

"Why you worrying about that? That is between me and the Lord."

"I just don't think you have to come," she blurted. "I mean, if you going to have to miss church." Neither Shirley's shifting eyes, nor did her hands, combing nervously through her long black hair disturbed miss Ivy's silence. "In any event, me and Dawn, we will be driving up and down all over the place, we might not even get to the apartment till late."

"I know you don't want me to come!"

"Mama! I did not say that."

"Then what you saying? Why you don' just say it?"

"I want you to come."

"You! I know you don't want me to come."

"I want you to. It's just that it's not convenient, look how hard it is raining and you have to go to church. The apartment is not even ready yet, all kinds of old boxes are packed up everywhere. It's just work, you don't want to come."

"Since when you know what I want, Shirley? Since when?"

"Ma."

But Miss Ivy was rising from the corner of the old sofa. She passed Shirley, going onto the old veranda through sheets of rain misting in, and turned the corner to her room. The sound of her door closing was loud and piercing even above the thundering rain.

Dawn came during a lull in the weather. Not wanting to brave the rain, she had parked at a shop in Central Village to wait. Shirley told her that her mother was asleep. When they had finished packing and they were ready to leave, Shirley knocked at her mother's door. There was no answer. She knocked loudly as the rain began again, but Miss Ivy did not answer. The door was never locked, so Shirley turned the knob and entered. Her mother was lying on the bed, propped up by a pillow. She had her Bible in her hand and reading glasses sat studiously on her nose.

"Ma'am, you don' hear me knocking?"

"What is it, Shirley?"

"I leaving now. I'll come and see you tomorrow."

"Mmmm."

"I'll come and see you tomorrow. I'll come for you, I promise."

Her mother raised herself slightly on the bed, closed the Bible and lowered it into her lap with one finger holding the page, then removed her reading glasses. "Don't make any promises you cannot keep," she said. Then she returned the glasses to her face and lifted the Bible from her lap. Shirley had never seen her look so sad.

As the van's engine caught, she turned her head to take one last look at the old house, half-wood and half-concrete, and saw her mother standing sadly there. They had been through hell and high water, fought off gunmen and survived only because her brother was a policeman. She stood alone on the veranda, her glasses held in one hand and her Bible in the other. Shirley wished life had given her a better way to leave her.

A little old lady, skin the colour of mango, hair greying, always in a bun, cute and almost portly. Shirley felt as if a part of her had died.

Chapter Three

Shirley was refused the promotion to full Supervisor of the Foreign Exchange department. The bank brought in a woman of ten years experience in foreign exchange from another branch. They said that the personnel choice was due to the new government policies on foreign exchange, and that the bank had to display a solid and mature management team. But Shirley knew it was not that. She knew it was because she had gone out with the bank manager and he had taken her home that night to Sufferer's Heights even though she had given her address as Greendale. He had seen where she lived. A lie was on her file. Even though she had moved it made no difference. They had summed her up, weighed her in the balance and found her wanting.

Shirley was certain the position was hers because the manager had told her that it was only her age and experience that had prevented her from getting it. He said they had created a Junior Supervisor post as an apprenticeship for the full post. Now the vacancy had come and they had given the job to someone else.

She pretended not to mind, but it bothered her. It was not the money, for it would have added little to her paycheck, which she barely saw these days anyway as it went straight to her account. It was not the movement from a desk in an open space to a desk in a cubicle with her own filing cabinet – she was not fooled by platitudes and pats on the back. It was because she did her job well and deserved the promotion. She was elegant and classy, efficient and sharp. If she did not bring business to the bank, she kept it there.

They had no reason to hold her back.

Shirley did not ask the manager why. She kept her disappointment to herself. But no matter how far down the road she looked, she could not see a promotion for another two years. And that was not the timetable she had sketched for herself.

Mark called one day.

He hadn't been in Jamaica for nearly a month. Usually he would come once per week or three times per month, spend two or three days each time and then he would be gone. If he stayed away longer than a week he would call, and always before he came he would call to tell her and find out if she needed anything. In addition there was the weekly call to the bank to have some financial business done. That was enough for her. She liked it when he was away. And usually, as soon as he arrived, sex was the first thing he wanted. She could never understand what Dawn was so excited about; sex had never been anything special for her, and now Mark had made it almost repulsive.

When he was not there, she not only had the place to herself, she had herself to herself. She would have her slumber parties and play queen and have Dawn over. Sometimes she would invite her mother but those visits never turned out as well as she wanted.

Today she was glad to hear from him because she was not sure how much of the pre-paid rent was left, and she did not want to embarrass herself by asking the manager.

Mark wanted to have some money transferred to him in Miami.

"You send the fax?" she asked, removing the diamond studded earring he had given her as a birthday gift.

"I send it this morning."

"You know you should send it one day before."

"Lord Shirley, take care of it for me, man."

She called a young clerk and asked her to find the fax in the communications room. The young lady left with the information scratched on a sheet of paper.

"When you coming home?" Shirley curled her fingers behind her neck and combed them through her hair, pulling the long locks aside and over her left shoulder so the telephone could fit better against her ear.

"Any day now, baby. I just have to take care of a few things up here."

"Sometimes I wonder if you forget about me."

He laughed. "You not easy at all."

"If is up to you, they kick me out of the apartment."

"I take care of that, man. I take care of that. The rent pay till August."

"You did not tell me that."

"I don' have to tell you that. The fellow who owned the place is my friend, man. I take care of that. Is that what you worrying bout?"

"Me? I'm not worrying about anything, just wondering when I'm going to see you, that's all."

"You think it easy for me to stay away? You see me 'bout next week."

"Blow wow!" Shirley's eyes almost popped out of her head as she looked at the fax the clerk had placed on her desk.

"What that now?" Mark asked.

"You moving the bank, man?" Shirley exclaimed.

"You find the fax?"

"Yes."

"How soon I can get that?"

"As soon as I authorize it. Business is good? Hold on a little." She got the paperwork together, signed the authorization form and gave it back to the girl. "Ask Benny to do it before two."

The girl nodded and left.

"Business good?" She restarted the conversation.

"Could be better."

"I miss you."

"You think you is the only one? You will see me next week. You take care of the thing?"

"Yes, you should get it tomorrow morning first thing. So when you coming?" She began to wind down the conversation.

"You know, maybe you should leave that job and come to rahtid. If you come here with your talent and so, you set in less than a year."

"Yes?" She began to reset her hair.

"How you mean? Even in the same kinda job. And like how you love school and so ..."

29

"You sound like you giving up on the country." She laughed at her joke.

"I tell you to rahtid, Shirley, that country not going anywhere. I bet you that in six months the tourist industry crash."

She paused with her earring halfway from the desk.

"You know, I even have to look at other markets," he continued. "Maybe Barbados or Trinidad and so. Carnival is always good business. I went to Dominica last week. Them have good tour possibility. Them have a good-looking forest there."

"Mind how you talk," she said cautiously, the words coming slowly so that she could hear every reaction he made to every word. "People might take you the wrong way."

"You know, I don't care much these days. Them boys messing up the place down there. Damn fool them. In another year nobody won't be coming to Jamaica for tourism. Damn fools."

The earring dropped from her hands. Something clicked in her head as she remembered a night not long ago when his actions had jolted her similarly. At the time it didn't seem important, but now it all began to make sense. She felt a cold finger run down the back of her neck.

"Is something wrong, Mark?" she said. "Are you all right?"

"Aw, boy," he grunted. "Shirley, I have to go now."

"No! Hold on! Is something wrong?"

Is something wrong? That was exactly what she had asked him that evening. They were watching TV in her bedroom. They had just finished having sex and she, having gotten used to his belly and the smell of him, was lying with her head in the crescent where his stomach bulged away from his waist.

The news was on and she had just pushed his waving legs away so she could see properly. The announcer was discussing the opposition leader's return from a Miami visit.

"He could have been a movie star if he wanted," she said.

Mark had smirked. "Then what you think him is now?"

They had become quiet as the man took the stage and began to defend comments he had made about his intention to renew his links with Cuba once he became Prime Minister again. It was an election year; the polls had been showing him ahead by two thirds since January. The calls for election were coming fast and furiously from all sides, the campaign had unofficially begun and every word spoken was important. She remembered as he spoke how still Mark's waving foot had become. She remembered that when she turned to look at his face, it was white and still as stone. She had propped quickly onto her elbows and stared at him. "Are you all right, Mark? Is something wrong?"

"Is the seventies all over again to backside," he had whispered softly staring at the screen as if the blood had frozen in his veins.

"Hello, Mark?" The phone had slipped and she had missed his last sentence.

"Yes? I'm here. I said I have to go now, Shirley. I see you next week, all right?"

"Mark! You did not answer. Is something wrong?"

"I talk to you, Shirley. Next week I talk to you, all right?"

"OK."

"Later. And thanks."

The phone went dead.

Shirley placed the phone quietly back on the desk, lifted the diamond studded earring and clipped it gently to her ear. Then she rose a bit too casually and passed beyond the door of her new supervisor's cubicle.

The clerk, eager to please, approached her. "I finished the transaction, Miss Brown."

"Thanks. You updated the cards?"

"Yes."

"You have them with you?"

"No, I put them back."

Shirley left her without another word. She entered the section of the bank that held all daily transaction cards before they were double-checked and stowed, pulled down the stack that held the cards for the last hour and searched through them until she got to a small bundle stapled together with Mark Delores typed boldly at the top. As she looked at the card her stomach turned.

Mark's accounts showed that, whereas in the last month and a half he had made five large withdrawals, he had not made a single deposit. In less than a month the balance in his account had dropped to below half.

She went with Dawn to see Rambo III that evening. She had not wanted to go because the day had made her pensive and she felt that she needed some time by herself to think. But Dawn was a Sylvester Stallone fan and they had developed the habit of seeing certain big movies on their opening.

But she hardly enjoyed the movie. After ten minutes her mind wandered off to consider her future and the possibility of life without Mark. She was not normally a worrier, but something about the day's events caused her to take stock of herself and her life. She wondered what would happen if Mark called tomorrow and said he wanted all his monies transferred to his Miami account. What would happen if he never returned to Jamaica?

Clues began to come back to her, small hints he had made that she should have seen as warnings, had she not been so complacent, like the day he came back haggard, declaring that he would never fly Air Jamaica again because of the higglers. They clogged up the airport with their dirty selves, ugly raucous ways, and huge bags and barrels of goods as if the airplane was a market truck, each having ten pieces of luggage though the airline stipulated only two. Ugly. Dirty. Smelly. Shoving their extra bags at passengers who had few, saying: "Check this in for me," cussing those who refused. "They killing the tourist business, damn higgler them. The government should charter a plane for all those old niggers," he had wailed.

Then there was the time he wanted to discuss the threat America had made to deport 300 hardened criminals and posse members to Jamaica. He insisted that crime would increase and that the tourist industry would be damaged without repair. He slammed the Gleaner down on the table at the Hot Pot restaurant, spilling Shirley's orange juice, to point out to her the headline where the Tourist Minister had said that tourism would be down this year.

"May as well them call the damn election and done," he had fumed, "and that might even be worse with the violence that our elections bring."

Shirley played her hands through her hair. She had not been as worried as she should have been.

Growing up in Central Village made her accustomed to violence. It was always around her in some form, from gang wars to bad men on the streets giving her the eye. She had accepted it as a part of life because she could do nothing about it. But this familiarity with the violence and death may have caused her to take Mark's point of view too lightly, underestimate how much it frightened people like him.

Perhaps she had been living too much in the moment, day by day, issue by issue. Now, taking all the various issues and comments and piecing them together, they seemed a frightening whole, and it was difficult to find a reason why Mark should stay at all.

And what would she do if he left? Her salary could not support her lifestyle. It could not pay half the rent of that place. She could not go back to the old life, or move to some cheap side-of-a-house in some god-forsaken housing scheme.

Later, while sitting on the small patio at Burger King, Dawn asked about her mood.

"Is the stupid Supervisor job you still worrying about?"

"Not really," Shirley said. "But lately nothing seems to be going right for me."

"Yeah, right," Dawn laughed, looking Shirley up and down, then pointing at her designer blouse. "That's how I want things not to go right for me."

"Clothes is not everything."

"Cho Shirley, I know you – is that job you worrying about. You young, you bright, you pretty, you can do anything. Leave the bank if you want, get another job, spite them. But get over it, man, for I can never respect a woman who say clothes is not everything, especially you."

"Now you start sound like Mark."

"Maybe you should listen to him."

Maybe I should, Shirley thought without answering. Maybe I should.

"Tell me about America," she asked as she lay against the flab of Mark's belly the night of his return. "Tell me what it is like."

"Just shut you eyes and dream," he told her. "Rights, freedom, opportunity. Just dream, man, anything you want life to be."

"Anything?"

"Anything."

"And all you need is a visa?"

"That's all you need."

"Job easy to get?"

He kissed his teeth. "Job? That is the easiest thing. What you think all them people who buy visa every day do? There is always something to do there. One thing you, have to work hard no bitch. But there is work. The Miami Herald employment section bigger than the whole Sunday Gleaner to rahtid."

"And school?"

"Don't even talk 'bout that. That is what build America."

"I need to ask you something." She ran her fingers along his thighs till they caught in the thick hair of his bent leg. "I need to ask you something and you need to be honest with me."

"What that now?"

"Are you - are you planning not to come back?"

He shifted himself to set the pillow beneath his head and his arm beneath it as if to prop and steady himself. "Boy, Shirley, I tell you the truth. The way things going, I am not even sure myself."

"But would you tell me if you decided?"

"Tell you what?"

"Tell me if you not coming back."

"You wouldn't have to worry 'bout that."

"But I do."

He sighed, rose from the bed and headed to the bathroom. She rolled aside and watched his back as he padded across the floor. The light flicked on. The water ran and stopped, flushed, ran and stopped. He emerged naked and ugly through the door, unconcerned and powerful in his demeanor. He began to search for his underclothes on the bed.

"What you want me to tell you, Shirley? I sell tourist packages. If them destroy the tourist industry I don't have anything to sell. I am a businessman and I have to go where the business is. I can't sit down and wait till them mash up the place. What kind a businessman I would be? Tourism is a business that you have to learn to read one year in advance. The tour season start one year before the tourist season. You have to project things – and right now, the projection for Jamaica is zero. Nobody not coming here next year. You can't walk in peace down the road because everybody hungry and a thief."

By now he was struggling into his underpants. He sat on the edge of the bed and looked at her. She was stretched on her side of the bed with a pillow beneath her chin, watching him silently.

"You don't see anybody with any sense selling out and leaving? In six months, nobody will be able to leave, you don' hear them talking 'bout locking down the country?"

"So this is your last trip, you not coming back?'

"Dammit Shirley! I can't tell you that. I don't know!"

"But sooner or later you'll leave? Follow the business."

"What you want me to tell you?"

"I just need to know, that's all. I need to know what you are doing. What is this we have here, a sex stop?"

She eased her body up, pulled the crumpled sheets from beneath her, almost throwing the pillow against the head of the bed, and angrily dropped her head into it.

He moved deliberately, shaking his feet as if to rid them of possible debris, before lifting them together and, almost like a dancer, pointing them down the length of the bed, as he lay down beside her. He then pulled the sheets up to his chest and folded both hands under his head.

"I will take care of things," he said.

"Mark," she said, with a voice soft and filled with darts, "I think you should go to sleep. Don't you have an early flight tomorrow?"

"So you vex now?"

"Me! Vex? Why? I just want to sleep."

I will take care of things. What did that mean? How long would he take care of things if he was in Miami and she in Jamaica? How long would any man take care of a woman he was not seeing?

Shirley had never given serious thought to leaving Jamaica before, but as she lay there and the conversation played back in her head; she began to realize that, for her, America was inevitable. Everything in her life had been telling her so; she just had not been listening.   From the moment she met him, Mark had been telling her she belonged there, but Shirley had ignored it as platitudes from a man wanting to impress her. Now he was about to pull out, leaving her in a job where people did not appreciate her, waiting for a promotion that never came - and never would come. Why should she stay in this country that was falling apart, while her man, her rich man was pulling out and leaving?

It was a long, long, time before Shirley fell asleep that night.

The day after Mark left, Shirley transferred two hundred thousand United States dollars from his account to hers and kept it there long enough to generate an impressive bank statement. She certified the statement with the bank's official seal then returned the money. Next evening, she waited after work and searched through the vault for an appropriate title held as security against a loan. She photocopied the title, returned the original, then used a blotting ink to cover the original name from the relevant section. She then typed her name over it, and re-photocopied the document.

The next Monday, Shirley presented herself to the Embassy of the United States as a woman with over two hundred thousand dollars in her bank account and fifty acres of beach-front property in St Ann's Bay. She had a freshly generated bank statement to prove it and a copy of the title with the relevant stamps.

The councilor wondered why a woman of her means had never applied for a visa before. Shirley told him traveling never appealed to her before. This was just to attend a friend's wedding. He asked how long she wanted to stay. She told him a week. He gave her a three-month one-entry visa. She could apply for an indefinite one next time.

It took all she had not to retort that he would be very lucky to see her back at that window ever again.

After leaving the Embassy, Shirley felt an urge to visit her mother. It was close to three o'clock and she was expected back at work, but somehow she felt she needn't bother that day.

It had been six months since she moved from Sufferer's Heights, and this would be only the third time she returned there. She had invited Miss Ivy to the apartment, but after the second time, her mother found excuses not to return. It seemed they could hardly find things to talk about these days.

Shirley found her fussing around the old coal stove on the broken-down half of the wooden side of the house. "You going live long," she told Shirley. "Me mind just run 'pon you."

"What happened to the oil stove?" Shirley asked.

"Oxtail don't do well on oil stove."

"You and that old coal stove."

The old house looked drabber. The kitchen-veranda seemed more like a garbage heap. Shirley sat on the edge of the long wooden bench that ran along the wall and dropped her bag on the seat beside her.

Her mother was about to remove the three-legged wrought-iron pot from the stove. Another pot of white rice was on the table with a calico kitchen towel still hanging over the cover.

"You expecting visitor?" Shirley asked, motioning to the pots.

"No, but sometimes you brother come. And you know he is always hungry and him always have plenty friends with him."

Shirley tried to ignore the possible meaning of the mention of her brother. If she was not careful, every word she spoke would lead her into some trap. Every time her mother mentioned her brother it seemed a comparison was drawn. Maybe her mother meant no harm. Maybe she was not upset that Shirley never invited her friends over for dinner or for anything. She tried to meet the point head on.

"How is he? He dropped by the apartment one night. Him and three of his friends."

"Them have to travel in groups."

"So him say. How is he?" she asked again.

"He's all right. I wish he did not have to carry so much guns."

"That is what stop them old hill boys from molesting you."

"The Lord protect me. If you live by the gun, you die by the gun."

Shirley reached for the offered plate laden with oxtail and big slices of tomato leaning against a mountain of white rice. "I can't eat so much food."

"Eat! You don' see you losing weight? Even your hair losing color."

"Is shading. I put the color there."

Her mother paused as if she was slapped. There was a small silence and then she passed a glass of lemonade to Shirley, collected her own plate of food, and sat next to her on the bench. She was obviously contemplating the next statement.

These last days were like that.

They trod carefully around each other like a babysitter around a sleeping child. They spent so little time together that Shirley wished those times would be more precious. But one evening together could not open the issues and rectify them. Too much needed to be resolved before they could ever be fully reconciled to each other again. So they tiptoed around themselves trying to steal a human moment by small talking on subjects that did not run too deep. But now things were so bad, that almost any topic they touched led to trouble. In their search for peace between themselves they were running out of options. Pretty soon, Shirley knew, there would be no way of bridging the gaps that time had made.

Miss Ivy sucked an oxtail bone and tried again.

"You staying?"

"I have to go work tomorrow."

"You used to go from here."

"But I don't have any clothes."

"You still have clothes here."

"But I have to wear uniform."

"You not eating the food."

"I know. My appetite is not as big as it use to be."

Shirley wished her mother would ask her why she had come so she could shut her eyes and in one big effort spill all her worries and uncertainties to her. She knew however, that the Christian in Miss Ivy would not understand why she had to do things that might not be right or good in her sight. Shirley wanted her to understand that she did not mean to shut her out. it was out of love and respect that she had to hide things from her. But if her mother asked her right now, Shirley would spill every dream and ambition right there on the veranda. If only she would ask. But her mother sat there quietly, eating on her side of the Red Sea of Silence and waited for Shirley to stretch out her hand, say the words, open wide the way.

Shirley looked at her watch. She had told the taxi driver to return in an hour or so.

Her mother noticed but did not comment on it.

Shirley wanted to use the bathroom, but could not bring herself to go to the old wooden latrine that sat at the back of the house. She decided to wait.

"How is Dawn?" Miss Ivy asked. "Say hi to her when you go home."

Shirley shrank. With each piece of conversation Miss Ivy challenged her to lie. "She is all right. I will." She felt condemned. Her mother was deliberately driving nails into her coffin.

"Yes, she is a nice girl."

So they went on, dropping one word here, another there, till even the droplets of conversation ceased and Shirley was forced to eat all her food for want of something to occupy her mouth. Meanwhile, Miss Ivy finished her meal and busied herself cleaning the torn-down kitchen, straightening out the utensils, and putting away the excess food in case her brother passed by with his friends.

When the taxi climbed the hill, Shirley was on her feet before it stopped at the gate and blew its horn. She had a feeling nothing had been accomplished by her coming, yet a million things had happened. She was still not sure why she had come, yet she felt her mother knew exactly why. One thing was sure: they were both relieved that the awkward silence had been broken. Shirley had leaving to do, and her mother could be relevantly occupied with the business of goodbye.

When she got home, she called Mark in Miami.

A woman answered the phone.

"Is the maid," he said when he came on. "Where you get this number?"

"You gave it to me."

"I did? Anyway, what happen now?"

"I have a visa."

"You what?"

"I have a visa."

"But that's nice, Shirley," he said slowly after a short pause. "What kind?"

"Just a three-month. How you sound like that?"

"How I sound?"

"You don't sound too excited for me. Mark, is everything all right?"

He paused for a minute and seemed to be speaking to someone off the phone. There was click and some scratching and then he returned. "Yes, Shirley, you still there?" His voice boomed and he seemed normal now.

"Yes, I am here. How you sounded like that?"

"It was the blasted maid, man. I'm all right now. So you get visa?"

"Yes, I did."

"Now you want to come sample America?"

"I was thinking about it."

"When you planning to come?"

"I don't decide yet," she lied. "I have to think about it. I may not even use it."

"Use it, man! If is even for a one-week visit, use the damn thing."

She paused strategically. "OK. I probably will."

"All you do," he said, "if you coming, when you coming, make sure you give me plenty notice. Remember I am a man have plenty plans to make."

"I know," she said. "So how things going otherwise?"

"Could be better. And you?"

"Not too bad." She eyed the half-opened passport on the bedside table. "Not so bad at all."

That night, lying naked in her bed, she contemplated how far she had come from Sufferer's Heights in such a short time.

She was only twenty-three and she was poised on the brink of success, on the edge of real life. She had money in the bank, she was young, she was beautiful and she had a visa to the United States of America. She had no doubts as to the next steps in her life. At the end of the month she would resign from her job. She would give up the apartment, sell everything in it except her clothing, and collect the remaining rent from the landlord. She would convert all her money into US dollars and give her mother a couple of thousands or so. For when she bought that ticket for the United States of America, and when she boarded that plane at the Norman Manley International Airport, she had no intention of ever coming back.

PART II

The Promised Land

Chapter Four

She arrived in Miami on a summer night that was lit and sparkling like a Christmas tree. She wore her baby pink dress. Mark was there to meet her, his belly bulging under a loose-fitting polo shirt, his hairy legs bold and strong, jutting out from a pair of white shorts that was almost tight. He chucked her luggage into a large shiny car without the slightest complaint.

"How the flight? All right?"

He slammed the doors, wound the windows down and eased the car into the traffic.

"OK, I guess," she said.

"Feel just like Jamaica. Hot same way." He piloted the car adroitly amidst a maze of underpasses and meandering highways.

She wound her window halfway up and cut Miami in half. He said something about how nice she looked but she hardly heard. She sat agape and astounded as they sailed above the glimmering city as if she sat on a bed of stars. She closed her eyes momentarily so she could open them again to the magic around her and confirm it was not a dream.

Kingston had buildings. Kingston had lights. But to see the beauty of it, one had to be in the hills as the streets all ran at ground level. Here in Miami, the highway took them through the centre of the shining city, not just horizontally, but vertically too.

"You eat?"

Mark's words brought her back. "What?"

"You eat on the plane?"

"No."

"OK. Let's go on the beach."

"Now? Like this?"

He laughed teasingly. He had deliberately worded the suggestion to have a double meaning. "Don' worry, we just going to eat."

"The place pretty," she sighed.

"You don' see nothing yet."

Later, when asked what she remembered most about her first nights in Miami, Shirley Temple Brown said, 'The lights.' Those that lined the vast cruise ships from stem to bow as she passed the causeway, the ones that ran up and down the vast cranes reaching into the skies and guarding the port of Miami like sentinels, the big blue sign of the Miami Herald that appeared to her left as the draw-bridge approached, and Miami Beach emerging as they crested onto the bridge, prescribing the rim of the dark waters like a jewelled arc.

And when they got to the beach and cruised along the strip looking for a place to park, there were more lights blazing on buildings – hues of blue and red and purple and neon green; pink, and hazel and orange too – buildings with names like Avalon, Olympiad, Majestic. Lights everywhere. Lights strung through trees, running along the sidewalk, on bikes, on people's backs, on skateboards and skates.

This, she thought, was heaven on earth.

They walked by a club that spewed calypso music onto the street, paused momentarily at the expensive French boutique next door to feel the fabric and test the hundred-dollar perfumes, then took a seat in a sidewalk café with Latin music floating gentle from inside. In the midst of the crowd throbbing casually around them, they ordered lobster and wine from a waiter dressed in formal black and white, who bowed to serve a clientele that varied from tanned bodies in the skimpiest of bikinis to men in wrinkled business suits and women in gowns shimmering like ashes flecked with glass.

"Miami Beach." Mark sighed. "You like it? Never see nothing like it, eeh – bet you?"

She nodded happily as she watched a half-naked man slip his skate in and out of the traffic and blow a kiss to a couple seated on the back of a convertible.

Even as the waiter laid the food before her, the lobster's back split and bulging with stuffing and cream sauce trickling down its side, she was in a daze. Everything had happened so quickly she hardly had time to catch her breath. Four hours ago, she was in the dry sweltering heat of a dusty Jamaica, dodging in and out of traffic in an old car without air-conditioning, as a sweating, cussing driver manoeuvred his way along the Palisadoes strip towards the airport. Now she was sitting in a sidewalk restaurant in paradise eating lobster.

"Don't fraid to break off the claw with your hand. Is Miami this." Mark was busily working his way through his lobster. It was so big. She reached for a fork.

"So tell me," he said, "when you going back?"

"Not so sure." The tender flesh came easily away and she tasted the lobster for the first time. It was a bit tangy but she chewed well and washed it down with a delicate sip.

Mark pointed half a claw at her as he searched for the silver tweezers on the side of the table. "You see all these people here walking 'round you now? Ninety per cent of them is tourist. This is how Jamaica should run. Now, the trick in the business is what you call "throughput". You get them in, you show them glitter, and then by the time they squint, they gone. Like a little fairy tale. Now all the rest you see skating and going on and looking funny? Them make the landscape. Some people just come here to look at people. This is tourism heaven. I bring some of them here and they don't even know. You see how everything peaceful and nice?"

"Everything is like a big party going on."

"Yes. And so it must stay. You know election going on? You can tell election going on? You see anybody driving 'round on truck, you hear any gunfight, you hear any damn talk 'bout communist? Election going on right now. Governor election or something. November is presidential. But not a man could tell. Not like them damn idiots down there in Jamaica."

She nodded.

"So when you going back, eeh?"

"I tell you I'm not sure."

He kissed his teeth fondly. "Oh. I ask you that already no? Head going and coming."

"Old age." She smiled.

"Maybe to rahtid." He seemed a little preoccupied. He snapped his lip down on a piece of claw and began to suck the meat from it, then sighed with the pleasure of his success. He dropped the empty claw to his plate and began to retrieve pieces of shell from his mouth as he masticated; placing them along the edge of the dish. Then he rubbed his hands roughly in the napkin and swallowed a generous mouthful of wine. He was acting like a pig and to Shirley's surprise it did not bother her. The food was good, the evening was heavenly – even a pig would seem charming.

"You live near here?" She tried to push the conversation along.

"Oh?" He almost jumped. "Well, not too far really. 'Bout twenty-five minutes from here."

"How far that?"

"You know, I couldn't tell you? Twenty - twenty-five minutes. In America nobody talk 'bout distance. Everything is time. Nobody have time for 'round-the-corner distance. How long is the thing not how far. Time is money and money is time."

"Listen to you!"

"I bet you going like this place and don' want to go home."

"You think so?"

"I know so."

She ignored the claw and pressed her fork down on a mound of potato to flatten it into the sauce on her plate. She began to think of later, of going home with him.

"Listen, Shirley," he said.

She listened.

"Listen, we doing some refurbishing at the house, you see. . ."

"I am fine with that, I won't get in the way."

"Well, is not exactly that."

She paused and looked up at him.

"Well, they actually remodelling the whole damn place. Them have workers all over the house. Them Americans not easy. They doing a little remodelling and is like they quarantine the whole damn place."

"You know I can adjust easily. Why you worrying about me?"

"I not worrying about you at all. The refurbishing don't even bother me. You see... I in and out most of the time. . ."

She saw him listen for her reaction to that. "So what you worried about?" she asked him as she took a sip and levelled her gaze at him across the wineglass.

"Well, you know, my business take me in and out of town. And you come kinda sudden. I don' want you in that house with all them workmen and dust and all that. Especially when I am not there."

"So how long that refurbishing going take?"

"About another week or so."

"But that will be too much hotel bill."

"Well, yes." He began to speak softly. "Well, yes, but not to worry. I set up something with one of my cousin. She agree to have you stay with her till the refurbishing finish."

Shirley was relieved. "Then is that you sound so worried about? So you staying at your house?"

"Well, you know I have to watch the workmen them and so. Plus I am out of town sometimes. This is the slow period of the tourist season - summertime. So I have to be up and down looking business."

"You are trying to say I won't be seeing you?"

"Of course you'll be seeing me. But it's not like when I come to Jamaica and I spend all the time with you. You understand? Here I'm up and down and so on."

He was speaking slowly and carefully and she could feel his eyes searching her on the trail of every sentence. But she thought he was being unnecessarily concerned. What's a week away from him? She reached across the table to pat his hand. "Don't worry about me. I'll be fine."

The house sat on the edge of a busy street.

Mark pulled into the fenceless yard and stopped on the short driveway that sliced a quarter from the nicely cut lawn. The house was dark except for a few lights on the underside of the roof and in the grass at each corner of the building. There was a detached cosiness about the place.

"She work out most of the time," he said, as he began to pull the suitcases from the car. "As a matter of fact, she only come home on weekends. Won't even bother you at all."

"What part of Miami is this?"

"Miramar. Is a nice area, but too much Jamaicans moving in now."

"Oh?"

"Yes. If much more come here, I would recommend she move. They drop the value of the place."

"Oh? She is not Jamaican?"

"Yes, she live here since seventy-six, but that don' matter. Come."

Shirley followed him to the side of the house where he opened a door into an apartment. She had thought it to be the garage, but it was an apartment similar in structure, she could tell, to the concrete half of the house at her mother's place. They entered a living room separated from a small kitchen by an L-shaped counter. On her left, as she walked in, was a white cloth sofa. There was no table. A passage led to what she later discovered to be a small bedroom beyond.

"Have its own bathroom too." Mark sighed, dropping the first grip. "Her son use to live here. Boy turn man once him start go college, so she fixed this side of the house for him. Him move to New York now, say him studying music or some stupidness like that."

"Well. It's not so bad." She dropped her handbag onto the sofa and made her way into the bedroom. It was half the size of the one she left in Jamaica and the bed was smaller and pushed against the wall. There was a window with a long blue curtain and a doorway that led to the bathroom. It, too, was small but clean and adequate. There was a dresser with a small mirror that matched the hue of the bed. Shirley sat on the bed and kicked her shoes from her feet.

"Food should be in the fridge," Mark said as he entered the bedroom. "The door near the kitchen lead into her house but you don' even have to worry 'bout it. I will bring you a TV tomorrow."

She looked up at him standing there. "I'll be fine, I'll be fine. How you worry so much? Sit down."

He sat next to her on the bed. "You don' want to hear where everything is?"

She kissed him, caught him by surprise. She had never initiated romance before, but tonight, she was heady from the magic of Miami. She kissed him hard and deep while he was still on the edge of the bed. He began to slip from the edge and struggled to steady himself, but she pressed against his shoulders and kissed him down till they were both on the carpet. She reached under his polo shirt and ran her hand into the mess of hair on his chest. He tasted of fish and stale wine.

He buried his face into the V of her dress where her breasts showed.

She fell aside and pushed him flat so that he lay there dishevelled and surrendered. And as he lay there, she removed her baby pink dress, saw his Adam's apple bob. She kissed his mouth, his face, his neck, trailed her tongue along his earlobe. He responded with passion, pressing his lips hard against hers, his tongue searching the hollow of her mouth. He moved from her mouth to her breast in one quick, hungry motion, then from her breast, to her navel and then between her legs. Shirley surrendered to his charge, gave way to his hungry groping mouth. Then she felt his hardness against her face, went drunk on the smell of stale sweat and foul, musty maleness. She pressed her lips against him and opened to the once unthinkable. Then she heard him moan loudly, and shout her name, felt him quiver, tasted him explode.

Shirley woke alone early the next morning and was so excited that without washing her face she went outside to have her first real look at Miami. There wasn't much to see. The house sat directly on a four-lane street and cars ran busily up and down. Across the street were similar houses separated by hedges. The houses were of average size and structure. The cars that pulled out of them were average too, no different from many she saw in Jamaica. There was an intersection a few blocks to her left with large lights hanging in the air. There was a gas station and shopping mall.

She returned and looked around the apartment. That did not take long. It was much smaller than she had become accustomed to. The kitchen hardly had cupboards, the carpet was cheap and unclean, and there was no bath in the bathroom. She was glad it would be temporary. The middle door was locked so she could not examine the larger side of the house. She thought of unpacking and changed her mind. She thought of food, found the fridge stacked with orange juice, vegetables and other groceries which would have to be cooked. She thought of taking a bath, but finally ended up lying lazily across the bed thinking how un-American America felt.

Shirley slept.

The ringing of a phone woke her. She found it in the living room on the bar-like counter. It was Mark. "What happen, you don' wake yet?" he asked

"What time is it?" she yawned.

"After one. You want drive out today?"

"Sure."

"A bringing you TV too."

"Thanks. What time you coming?"

"See you in half an hour."

He came in forty minutes and it could not have been sooner. He placed the large TV on the counter in the living room and began to set up the antenna. The picture was not too good. He fussed with the antenna for a while then slapped his head. "Oh, you know what? You probably not connected to the cable system."

"So?"

"So, the reception won't be too good."

"How you mean?'

"If you connected to cable you would see the difference. Now make I see." He began to switch the channels. "You know what? You will have to settle for the ordinary network channels for now."

"How much is that?' She stood beside him.

"Three."

"Three! Only three channels?"

"Well, you can get more, but you have to connect it to the cable."

"Well, connect it."

"Well, that not so easy. You have to pay for that. Like how you not staying so long it might not make a difference. But I will ask Tiny about it."

"I am hungry."

"You don't eat from morning?'

"I couldn't bother to cook." She shrugged.

"Well, I can take care of that."

She grabbed her bag. "I thought you were working today."

"Yes, but I took the afternoon off."

She felt lust in his eyes but ignored his intentions. "Come then. I am starving."

The first week ran quickly. The events were on and off. Mark had to work so she saw him only in the evenings. She had arrived in Miami on a Wednesday night. She saw him Thursday but she did not see him on Friday at all. He came by Saturday morning and they packed and drove to Orlando to see Disneyland. After spending three hours in the sun waiting for a half-hour ride, they agreed that the place was for kids. They spent the rest of the time touring the grounds hand in hand, enjoying the scenery with other couples. Later they danced in the club of their exclusive hotel. They got back late Sunday night and Mark stayed with her till just before morning. She did not remember to ask if the refurbishing of his house was complete.

She slept all that day. The next day she walked to the end of the street to see the mall near the gas station. Among the large stores were a K-Mart, a Publix and a Home Depot. She walked around for a while, went to the Burger King a half-block further down and sat and ate while America happened around her. Down the road she saw an Acura car dealership with flags flying around it. She went to have a look. She stood outside in her faded jeans looking tentatively at the sea of cars that filled the lot. "Are you interested in a car?"Asked a bright and handsome young man.

Shirley said she was not sure.

"Which car do you like?" He asked.

She pointed to a cream Acura Legend that was parked in the centre of the drive.

"Would you like to feel it?" he asked.

"Yes," Shirley said.

He got the keys, flung the door open and told her to get in. She sat and sighed as the rich leather seat folded around her. She let her fingers play along the dashboard and the beautiful wood of the interior.

"Would you like to take her for a ride?" the young man asked.

"I can drive it out?" she asked, bewildered.

"We can take her for a spin."

"You drive," she told him.

The young man took the luxury car around the block while she leaned back in the seat and closed her eyes. Shirley hardly heard anything he explained about the car. All she could hear resounding in her ear were the words Mark had spoken nearly a month ago: Just shut you eyes and dream. America, land of opportunity.

The car stopped and she realized that they were back. She opened her eyes, smiled at the nice young man and told him thanks. "I'll bring my boyfriend later," she said. "I'll see what he thinks."

She stepped away from the lot, afraid to look around any more and get totally intoxicated. Though she had made up her mind in Jamaica, that ride had convinced her. This was her country. She would never leave it.

Next day, she decided to explore a bit on her own instead of waiting around for Mark. She checked the directory and called a taxi. She wanted to go downtown.

"Where downtown?" the driver asked.

"To the shopping centre," she told him.

"To the Omni?" he asked.

"Is that downtown?"

"Well, not exactly. It is a mall."

"Isn't the mall downtown?"

An experienced taxi driver, the old Cuban man summed up the situation. "You wanna go shopping?" he drawled in his funny accent. "You wanna go shopping or you wanna go downtown? There are many malls."

"Which is the biggest?"

"The one closest to you is the Aventura. I'll take you there."

"Fine."

When she saw the Aventura mall she was so startled at its size and beauty that when the driver asked her what shop she wanted to visit, he had to ask her twice. But she had no hesitation after that. "Just drop me anywhere," she told him.

"You call me when you are finished," he told her giving her his card. "You ask for Louis."

She did not leave the mall until seven o'clock that night.

When she got home, Mark was parked outside pacing worriedly up and down in front of the house. "Jesus Christ, Shirley, you had me worried!"

"Why? I just went to the mall."

"So you should tell me, man."

"How?'

"Leave a message on the door or something."

"How did I know you'd be coming around?" she asked testily.

It was then she realized that she had to tell him soon about her plans not to go back. She had hoped to wait until she moved into his house but the way things were going, she wondered if the refurbishment would be completed in time. Mark did not seem in a mood to continue the conversation and she was tired. So she gladly decided to wait for an appropriate time.

Next day he brought her an answering machine. "If you going anywhere, just leave a message on it. I will retrieve it." he told her.

"I'll just call you at work," she told him.

"I might be on the road," he said.

"Well give me the mobile number."

He did. A little reluctantly, she thought.

But she had no real intention of calling him there. She was a free spirit. She liked to have him worry at least a little. Keep him on his toes.

Next day she called Louis.

"Where you wanna go today, Shirley?" he asked.

"Downtown," she smiled, bounding into the taxi.

Chapter Five

The owner of the house, Mark's cousin, drove up that Sunday in an old Chevy Citation. She did not resemble Mark at all. Shirley watched through the window as the woman stepped from the car, retrieved a few bags from the back of the car, placed them on the bonnet then returned to lock the doors.

The woman was much darker than Mark, darker than Shirley herself, about five feet six or so, with an overly made-up face and hair poorly done hanging to her shoulders. Shirley had seen her before in her mother and other Jamaican women who left their homes every Sunday morning in their best dresses and trudged to church. She must have searched through every store in Miami to preserve that Pentecostal look, Shirley thought unkindly. And sneakers too. She must be the maid. Walk proud, though.

About half an hour later, Shirley heard a knock on the inside door. The woman had obviously showered, and her damp hair was slicked back. She now sported a bright pink tracksuit, complete with hood hanging behind her head. Up close, she seemed darker, with deep-set eyes that were searching and wise.

"Good evening," she said in a voice that almost squeaked. "I never too sure anybody was here. Tiny is the name. Everything all right?"

Shirley opted for diplomacy and perfect English. "Hello. My name is Shirley. I was wondering when someone would show up around here."

"Yes. Well, yes," said Tiny sheepishly. "I work out, you see, so I am hardly here. That's why. I did tell him."

"You mean Mark? Yes, he told me."

"Oh. I see you start shop already." She looked past Shirley into the messy room with shopping bags strewn all over the place. "If you need any help or anything like that, I know a few places. Next weekend I not doing anything."

"Would you like to come in?" Shirley asked.

"No. You come." She turned slightly. "I was just going put on something. You eat yet? You mus' be hungry."

Tiny obviously wanted to show off her home to Shirley. "Them call this the Florida room," she said.

The little rectangular room was carpeted in beige, with matching drapes that blocked the light from the rear of the house. Faded sofas were neatly arranged around a centre table and faced a TV at the far end. A large kitchen and dining area were to the right. To the left the house opened up to a large living room with low cosy lighting and new carpet and furniture. Tasteful oak coloured tables and a cabinet filled with glassware and silver took up one wall. The chairs were thick and firm with a wonderful floral design that would have lightened the room had they not been covered by thick dull plastic. Shirley knew the plastic was to protect the material and keep them clean, but it also made the room dull, and once the light was turned on, they shone like cheaply polished tiles. She wished people would learn that it was safer and better to let the furniture breathe.

"You can sit down anywhere," Tiny said as she disappeared into the bedroom off to one side.

Shirley sat. The plastic squeaked beneath her.

"When you come? Wednesday or Thursday?" Tiny emerged from the bedroom, her hair tied in an oversized floral kerchief that showed the FL&O of Florida. The rest of the word disappeared in the folds.

"Wednesday night."

"I planning to put on something. What you want to eat?"

"Actually, I have eaten."

"Well, you can't too full. I put out the chicken already. I going microwave it. They microwave everything in this place, you know mi dear. Microwave everything. Not like Jamaica with them big ol' fireside."

Shirley smiled to herself. She had owned a microwave at Embassy

Apartments.

"Come roun' here so no," Tiny shouted halfway to the kitchen. "What you one doing roun' there?"

Shirley rose and the plastic squeaked. "I like your home," she said. "You have some good furniture."

"Thank you," said Tiny. "I put in one piece of chicken for you and set everything for fifteen minutes. What you want to drink?"

They settled into the Florida room. Tiny brought Coke on a tray and served it in large flamboyant glasses. She then collected her remote, sat theatrically across from Shirley and made a great show of pointing and clicking the television on. "Everything remote and so in this country, mi dear," she quipped.

Shirley almost rolled her eyes. The last thing she wanted was to be petted by some lonely never-see-come-see old woman with a motor mouth.

"So tell me," Tiny said. "When you going back?"

"Well, I am not sure." Shirley sipped her Coke.

"When you going down, I have a box I want you to take down for my sister, you hear? See it over there. It half-pack. I still have some things to put in it."

Shirley's eyebrows rose.

"You have a bag already packed for me to take down?"

Tiny waved a dismissing hand. "Not really you. Anybody. Every time I go shopping I put something in there. I don' even remember what in there now. But every time I put something in, and if I know somebody going down, I ask them. I pay the freight and duty and everything."

"Oh. So Mark has been taking things down for you?"

Tiny smiled. "So him tell you no? So tell me," she continued, "tell me what you been doing since you here. What you do a daytime? You know what you should do? You should get a little job and save back you plane fare. Buy few things to go down and sell. You know how much people do that? Caan' waste time these days. So what you been doing?"

"I have been going to the mall."

"Lord, them big eeh? Big!"

"Yes, they really are." Shirley smiled and glanced at the TV. An ad for a telephone was on.

"Which mall you go?"

"Oh," said Shirley, "I have been to a few. I have been to Aventura, Omni, I have been downtown. I plan to see the Saw Grass Mall. I have heard so much about it."

"My dear, that's the one you mus' see. It bigger than all of Kingston."

"That big ? ugh!" Shirley finished her drink.

Tiny had barely touched hers. Had barely even watched the TV. She sat on her chair and stared across at Shirley as if afraid she would disappear any minute.

"So you alone go to the mall?"

"Yes."

"Oh, that nice. I don't even remember the bus route."

"I don't take the bus."

"Oh. Him take you?"

"No. I take a taxi."

"Oh. But that mus' be a lot of money."

"No. Twenty-five or thirty-five sometimes."

"That's too much, Shirley. You could buy a lot of things to take home with that. Thirty-five dollars a day on taxi?"

"No. That is one way. It comes up to about seventy dollars plus tip."

"Tip? You tip the taxi man too?"

"I always tip my taxis."

"You mus' be rich, man," Tiny said, her eyes narrowing. "What kinda work you do in Jamaica?"

Shirley smiled almost condescendingly. "I work in a bank. I am a supervisor in a bank."

"You know, from I see you I know you not any ordinary girl. Bank supervisor. Who is Indian in you family? You mother or you father?"

"My father."

"You hair really pretty."

"Thanks," Shirley said.

"You really a nice girl," Tiny said almost sadly. " You hear the microwave click? It suppose to click when it stop. You hear it click?"

Shirley shook her head.

"Make me check it. Sometimes the TV so loud you can hardly hear anything." She rose and made her way into the kitchen.

The lemon chicken was nicely done. Tiny served it with mixed vegetables from a tin and baked potato with a thick slice of butter stuffed into its gaping side.

They ate and Tiny talked into the evening. She talked so much Shirley was unable to pursue the family ties with Mark. She figured it would come up in time and in any event, it was not her business. People didn't have to resemble each other to be related. Maybe she was a distant part of the family. Mark was obviously of a much higher cut, but Tiny was nice in a homely, country sort of way. By the time Shirley finally retired, she had begun to like her. She hoped that when she moved in with Mark, Tiny would come and visit sometimes.

On the evening of her third Saturday in Miami, Shirley told Mark she would not be returning home. They were having dinner in a little café at Bayside and he was in the middle of eating a three-layer Italian sandwich. He hardly reacted, but his eyes narrowed slightly and his chew became more careful.

His silence made her uneasy.

As she watched him chew, it came home to her how little she really knew him. Since that fateful evening in New Kingston she doubted that their total time together was more than six months. He had shared her bed, pampered and kept her, yet she was sitting across from him unable to predict his reaction to her very important announcement.

"What you mean by that, Shirley?" he finally asked at the end of the long chew.

She shrugged. "I'm staying."

"What kind of visa you have?"

"A three-month one ."

"How long immigration granted you to stay on this visit?"

"Two weeks."

He sighed. "Shirley, you making a big mistake, if you were serious."

"I am serious."

Mark thought for a while and spent another strangely silent minute. He then pushed the paper plate with the half-eaten sandwich aside and pulled his glass of Cola to him. He did not drink from it but rather rolled it back and forth on its heel making a wet arc on the plastic table.

He looked up at her frankly and open-faced, his grey eyes serious. "Shirley, this thing come at a very bad time for me." She sensed a mood of negotiation.

"What do you mean?"

"I mean I have a lot of things going on now. I have to do some travelling."

"So?"

"So is not a good time for you to be here now."

"I can take care of myself when you are away. I have been doing fine so far. You only come in the evenings now. Sometime you don' come at all."

"It better you go home now."

"Why?' she asked. "Don't you think I am old enough to know what I want?"

"Shirley, if you know what is good for you, you better go home."

"I can't."

"How you mean you can't? What you mean?"

"I can't. I gave up the apartment and everything."

He leaned back in his chair and rocked back as much as he thought was safe for his overweight frame. "Next thing you going tell me, you resign your job."

"I did." She wished he would seem surprised, make a loud exclamation or something like that, but he sat there calmly, his tone patient and clinical.

"I thought you had more sense than that. You could have at least asked my opinion."

"You are the one who told me to come. You are the one who told me to come and live here."

"Shirley, I never told you to leave you work."

"So what? What difference does it make? I am here with you."

He dropped his chair and leaned forward as one having made up his mind about something. "It is more complicated than that."

"I don't see any complications," she said.

"You don't see a thing. I could be a married man, to rahtid. I could have wife and children. And now you just do something like that."

"Are you married?"

"Does it make a difference?"

"Are you sitting there and telling me that you have been married, Mark? All this time married and you didn't tell me?"

"Look, I did not say so."

"Are you?" she shouted.

"Look, Shirley, you are missing the point. The point is that you have made decisions in your life that include and affect me and you did not ask me. You did not check what kind of plans I might have."

"You have not answered the question."

"Married or not, it does not matter, Shirley."

"You should have told me, Mark. You should have told me."

"You! It would not have made any difference to you whether I am or whether I told you or whether any damn thing! You knew what you were getting into."

"And what is that?"

"I don't know. I tell you is a bad time. I have to travel out of town for two weeks or so. I have been putting it off until you leave. I must go now. I can't wait any longer."

"So what will happen now?"

"I have to think 'bout the whole thing. All this thing so sudden. I have to work out something for you."

"I did not ask you that. I can take care of myself. Are you married?"

"Shirley, I tell you, I don't know."

"What the hell you mean, you don't know?!" she asked loudly, ignoring the turned heads of the tourists around her. "You don't know if you married or not?"

"That's not what I meant," he said calmly. "Come." He rose and dropped some money on the table.

"Mark, you need to answer me now." But her voice broke and revealed her fear.

"Come," he said. "We will talk about it in the car. Come, don' bother make a scene, Shirley. We talk about it in the car."

But they never talked about it in the car. Though her mind told her she needed to get answers from him, the weight of her emotions stilled her tongue. When he made an effort to open conversation she shook her head and raised her hand. "Please, just take me home, I'd rather not talk now."

She would always remember the sad patient look he gave her when she told him good night that evening, and slammed the door.

Shirley did not see mark for two weeks, but she remembered that he had said he would be travelling. When time went on and she had had no word she fought her pride and searched through her book for the number he had given her for his office. A recording told her the phone had been disconnected. She tried not to panic. Maybe he had switched the phone off till he returned. Maybe he had returned, but had not had time to have it reconnected. She waited until night when she thought he would be home, and called the number she had only used twice. The message that the number had been changed to an unlisted one was like a blow that swept her spirit away. But her mind had not stopped working. Things would turn around. She was living at his cousin's house. Tiny would give her directions to his home. She would find him. She would compromise. He would make arrangements for her.

Saturday morning, she awoke to knocking on the inside door. She felt elated. Tiny was just the person Shirley wanted to see. She jumped from the bed, whipped her silk robe around her and ran quickly to the door.

"Come in," she said. "I was just thinking about you."

But Tiny stood her ground tentatively, still dressed in her church dress and running shoes. "Sorry to bother you," she said. "Me wan' catch you before you leave out. You see, is almost a week now."

Shirley sighed and smiled a knowing smile. Tiny, too, had not heard from Mark. "Almost a month, you mean," she chuckled weakly.

"No, the gentleman take care of the first one." Tiny nodded to her. "Him give me before you come."

"What are you talking about?" Shirley asked.

"The rent," Tiny said. "It due one week now."

Chapter Six

Shirley rose from the hot seat at the bus stop and stood next to a sign that said she could rent the space for less than one dollar a day. She was going to be late for her interview. She had called the metro bus and had them send her the schedule of bus routes. She had readied early and took a leisurely walk to the bus stop four blocks from the house. But after half an hour of sitting there, the bus had not come, although Tiny said they usually ran on time. She waited calmly.

Miami's sun was already up and burning. There were no trees to shade her no clouds to block it, just the open sky. The bus stop was a lonely, unsheltered place, and the heat a constant thing that baked her face, milked the sweat from her armpits and settled into her long black hair, steaming perspiration from her scalp to make sauna at the back of her neck.

Shirley saw the progress of the morning as another incident in a chain of disappointments, a penance she must bear, like another throb to a toothache she had caused by sinking a bad tooth too readily into a joint of hard sugar cane. Inside she felt strangely serene. Everything would be alright. She had to believe that. There was nothing else she could do.

Mark had not returned to her. He never called again. After Tiny had asked her for rent that morning Shirley did not bother verifying whether she was his cousin or not.

Mark was not her whole world. He had entered her life for a purpose, and even if he had not served it to the extent of her expectations, he had done a lot for her. Through him she was in the United States with a place to live. It would have made no sense dwelling on his absence or the possibility that she might have cared more than she thought she did. She had cried and moped for a couple of days after she realized he would not be coming back, but she dared not sit around much longer. All her bridges had been burnt so she had to make her way forward.

Shirley assessed her finances and found a little over eight hundred dollars. She paid Tiny three hundred and fifty dollars for rent and utilities. There was some food in the house so she did not have to worry about the supermarket for a while.

Then she began to buy the newspapers. Mark was right about one thing. The Miami Herald had an employment section that was bigger than the major newspaper in Jamaica. There were no shortages of jobs that suited her qualifications. It should not be difficult to land one. She was young, beautiful and bright, and she knew how to write an application and make a resume.

So she forced the past behind her and began to send out letters of applications. She did not know how long these letters would take to get where they were going, but after a week she began to make follow-up phone calls. Two weeks after she sent the first letter, she got her first response. In another two days she had scheduled five interviews for the next week.

Now she was on her way to the first one.

She had been tempted to take a taxi, but knew she could not afford the sixty-dollar bill back and forth from downtown Miami. Plus, this was America and here, she knew, bussing would only be for a time.

The bus finally came. Shirley looked through the window as it pulled away toward the 163rd Street mall where she would transfer to an express that would take her to downtown Miami. They had told her on the phone that the interview would be downtown, but if accepted, she would be placed at a branch of the bank that was much closer to where she lived. So she was not bothered by the extent of the journey. She sat quietly in a corner and tried to remember the last time she took a bus. She had told herself when she left Sufferer's Heights that she would never take the bus again. It seemed that unwanted experiences were part of being in America. At least the bus was clean and there were no sour conductors bawling and haggling over fares or bus seats.

When she reached the mall, she discovered that the 9:45 express had already left. She made a call to the bank to apologize for her lateness. The pleasant woman on the line showed understanding, and told Shirley she should come anyway. Anytime before three would be fine.

Downtown, Shirley found she had miscalculated again. The Brickle building she was trying to get to was an hour's walk from the bus terminal. Though she now had time, she knew she would not endure such a walk, so she bit her lips and paid the seven dollar taxi fare. The cab dropped her at the foot of a large building that shimmered in the sunlight like polished glass and shot a hundred stories into the sky.

The familiar commercial setting made her relax. Here she knew how to handle herself. She went straight to the bathroom, washed and cleansed her face of the morning's dust and dead skin, applied a thin layer of moisturizing lotion and combed her hair.

A minute later, she presented herself to the receptionist.

She met a friendly, professional, approving smile and took the proffered application. "Anything you can't fill out now, just leave vacant."

Shirley smiled, sat on the sofa and filled out the form to the best of her ability. She knew that applications were less than ten per cent of the reason people were employed. It was the interview that mattered. Personality and presentation were the key factors.

She was to be interviewed by a distinguished-looking young woman a little older, she estimated, than herself. Shirley was pleased to see that. They entered a tastefully furnished office that was separated from the work floor by tinted glass. She sat across the black lacquered desk and crossed her legs professionally.

The woman opened her file and began to peruse and compare her application with her resume. "Oh!" she exclaimed almost laughing. "You forgot something."

"And what is that?" Shirley's tone diction and pronunciation equalled or surpassed hers.

"Oh, just your social security number." The young woman pushed the application form quickly across the desk and continued to peruse the application. "Just jot it at the top."

"Ah, what?" Shirley stopped short of sounding as if she did not know what a social security number was. The woman's tone suggested that she should. "I don't have it with me," she said.

"You don't have one." The woman placed her paper carefully down.

"Well, not really."

"Oh, you are from Jamaica." The woman smiled. "You just got here?"

"Yes," Shirley smiled, relieved. As soon as she left, that was the first thing she would get.

"You haven't gotten it yet." The woman reached across the desk. "Well, I realize that these things take time. It's OK for now. Your alien registration number would do."

"My what?"

The woman straightened and placed the papers down, her eyes narrowed slightly. "Your green card. You do have a green card, or work permit?"

"Well," Shirley countered, "I am qualified for the job, am I not?"

But the folder across the desk was already closing, and the woman had not even attempted to retrieve the application form that was between them on the desk. Her expression was already hardening to that of a busy executive annoyed at having had her time wasted. "You do know it is illegal to seek employment without proper immigration authorization?"

Had it not been for the word "illegal" Shirley would not have found the strength to rise from the chair and stagger from the room.

Shirley didn't gave up. Every morning she rose early, dressed in another beautiful dress and made her way to another interview. And every evening after another rejection, she came back home to make her follow-up calls to the companies she had not heard from. Then she would scour through the papers to circle another ad. First she tried for jobs in banks as supervisors, then as tellers. When those did not work out, she tried for secretarial positions, and administrative assistants. Then she tried for receptionists. She even replied to an ad for English teacher. In another two weeks, she was down to office help. No one would employ her, not for her qualifications, not for her perfect English and precise pronunciations, not for her beauty and sophisticated air. Yet she continued seeking. She never failed to get up every morning to try.

It was near the end of the month and she had little over four hundred dollars left. Her rent was due, and after she paid that, there would be less than a hundred. She had no food in the house, she had no toiletries, yet she dared not touch the money for fear the time would come when she would have to choose between her needs and bus fare to jobs she knew she would not get. Soon she began to wake up in the nights to the horrible sound of a million voices in her head: green card – social security number – Drivers Licence – Florida ID.

One morning she awoke, showered, fixed her hair and was halfway through the door before she realized she was still in her silk underwear and silk Victoria's Secrets dressing-gown. She returned in a daze to the bedroom to dress and collapsed on the bed.

When Tiny came home and found her that Friday evening, Shirley had been there for three days. She had slept and awakened several times in the same spot she fell. Tiny discovered her draped halfway onto the bed like a garment carelessly thrown aside. She could have been praying had it not been for the lifeless droop of her body; her face down on the mattress, her arms spread wide while her feet were curled under her on the carpeted floor. There was a foul, stale smell about her. Her hair was dishevelled and tangled around her neck as if to strangle her. Her mouth seemed glued by days of inactivity and she was hardly able to speak. The silk she wore was wrinkled and dead. She was too weak to stand and when she tried, she lunged across the room, staggering out of control.

Tiny tried to hold her up but she sagged lifelessly; she slapped Shirley's face but she mumbled incoherently. Finally, Tiny dragged her into the bathroom, hauled her into the bathtub and exposed her face to the full force of the shower. Slowly she revived and began to shiver as the wet silk shrunk around her in a cold wet embrace.

"What happen to you?" Tiny inquired, her high-pitched voice wailing mournfully. "What happen to you?"

Shirley blinked as the last of the water fell from the shower, and pulled her hair back away from her face. She stepped slowly from the tub and took the towel Tiny offered. Then she walked past Tiny without a word as if searching for something, wandered around the room for a few seconds, then plopped unto the bed and covered her head with the towel.

All the time, Tiny watched her carefully, following a step or so behind, talking continuously. "Is sick you sick? How you feel? No, Shirley! You caan' stay like this. What happen to you?"

Shirley finally removed the towel from her head and looked up at Tiny as if seeing her for the first time. "What happened?" she inquired.

"I am asking you that. How you look so?"

"What time is it?" Shirley began looking around suddenly, reaching for her dress, upon which she had slept for three days.

"Is after six."

"After six? I am late! Jesus, I must have overslept!"

"Where you going? You caan' go anywhere like this. That have to stay. Wherever you going have to stay, man."

"I have an interview!"

"Interview? What you talking 'bout? How you mus' go interview on Friday evening?"

"Friday!"

"Then is how long you sleeping ? Oh God!" Tiny moaned sadly and sat beside her on the bed. No, Shirley, you can't let yourself go like this. Tiny helped her to stand and removed the wet silk robe. In an open closet she found another. She put that around Shirley and helped her across the room, through the adjoining door. Tiny placed her in the Florida room on the long sofa with two pillows under her head and covered her with a light comforter. She left her shivering while she prepared a bowl of chicken broth and fed her like she would a sick child. As soon as she finished the soup, Shirley fell asleep. Tiny tucked her in right there and pulled the comforter to her chin.

Around seven o'clock, Tiny heard her sneeze and came running from her room. Shirley seemed focused and alert. She was sitting and though her hair was still dishevelled and her clothes were rumpled, the robe was pulled tightly and neatly around her.

"Oh, you wake up." Tiny sat across from her. "How you feel?"

"I'm fine. What happened? How did I get here?"

"Me! I bring you over. It look like you faint way in you room."

"Faint away? Are you serious? I have never fainted before."

"Well, you faint 'way though. Even talking foolishness, a mix-up the day them."

"Really? How you mean?"

"You think today was Wednesday."

"Then what day is it?"

"Is Friday, Friday evening."

"Friday? How can three days just disappear so?"

"But them things happen, Shirley. Take it easy. Rest little. Them things happen. Is Miami, time disappear all the while."

Chapter Seven

Shirley felt the presence cross the threshold to invade the space of her room; she knew it was Tiny with kindness on her mind, but somehow she wished she would go away. Shirley was not being ungrateful - she just did not want to see anyone right now. Not even the images on the TV before her that she dared not switch off for fear of being alone in the room where time disappeared when she closed her eyes.

"I going drive out you want to come?"

"I don't want to impose on you," Shirley said. "I will stay"

"The fresh air will help you. It not good for you, to just stay in here like this."

"Tiny, I need to think, be alone for a while," she replied faintly. Hoping by her tone, that the very kindness and sensitivity that made Tiny come to see her would let her know she wanted to be left in peace.

"Come, man, is Friday night. Who want stay home Friday night? I have a place I want to show you."

Shirley did not respond to that, for fear of the memories the topic would evoke - of the home she had abandoned; of Dawn to whom she never wrote; of food in abundance; of friendships and old and happy times.

"Come, Shirley, come." The voice changed slightly, now a light no-nonsense coat was layered on it. " I not leaving you here. Plus the food good there."

It was at that point that Shirley accepted that America had defeated her and she would be returning home. For at the mention of food, her mind lost control to the reactions in her body. Her stomach growled, her pulse quickened, her mouth watered and she found herself searching for a way to graciously accept the invitation without seeming too desperate to eat. It must be the lowest point of shame she could ever attain in her short life, when a stranger could try and manipulate her decisions with food. And that knowing this was so, Shirley with all the will in her could not say no.

It was a cozy little steakhouse affording a distant view of the buildings of Miami Beach. Inside, the lights had a dim, yellow glow, and soft music drifted under the subdued conversation like dust barely disturbed from the floor.

"I come here once a month," Tiny said as they were seated and the waiter placed the large burgundy napkins across their laps. "When I get pay, I make sure treat myself even one time. Order anything you want, wine - anything."

Shirley sat for a while and for some unknown reason was almost brought to tears. Who was this uneducated, clumsy never-see-come-see old woman sitting in front of her?

"You can eat any amount at the salad bar, you know, any amount and them have everything there. Come, but save space for the food, the steak them big. Come."

"Thanks," Shirley whispered

The salad bar had an abundance of the freshest fruits and wonderful cakes that Shirley could ever remember; the New York Strip was a slab of steak almost as thick as her wrist and twice the length of her palm; the baked potato was a fist and a half. The wine, Merlot was close to black.

Shirley ate.

Tiny talked all through the meal. And Shirley was glad for this. She was hungry, but the occasion for some reason had made her emotional. Every time she opened her mouth to speak or to answer, she was happy that a few words of acknowledgement sent Tiny off into another story . . . After a while, as Tiny spoke and the food filled her and the mood softened, the anguish inside her subsided and Shirley began to enjoy the moment for what it was.

She regarded Tiny across the table. Who was this woman, so unassuming, simple - so kind?

It was as if a different person was seated in front of her. Not transformed : she still gripped the stem of her wine glass as if it were the handle of a large mug, and her utensils were held as awkwardly and strongly as if the meat before her required more than just the gentle laying of the blade to it. She was master of her surroundings but not through breeding or upbringing; it came from deep within her - deep inside where dreams and ambitions grow.

Halfway through the meal, Tiny motioned with her fork and took a gulp of wine. "I have something to show you, almost forgot." She rummaged in her bag and finally brought out a photograph and pushed it along the side of the table to Shirley.

"Lot 44 Tamarind Place, Eltham Gardens."

It showed a medium-sized blue and white house built like a hexagon. It was nicely done with grey and white trimmings. The fence was made of whitewashed wood designed in small hexagons. "It's very nice," Shirley said.

"Is my house. I moving down one day. My sister fixed it up for me. I send her the money from here."

"Your house?" Shirley was almost at a loss for words. The simple, out-of-date woman had a plan.

"You like it?" Tiny smiled.

"It is nice, really." Shirley was sincere. "It is really nice."

"Lot 44 Tamarind Place - all my friends them tease me 'bout it all the while. Every other weekend or so we gather over one another house an' they tease me. Every body know the name now, is like a recitation Lot 44, Tamarind Place."

"You are going back, you are going home to Jamaica?"

"Yes, mi dear. Going back one day."

"But why, when you can have this, when you life going well?"

"Foreign, America, look like everything, Shirley, but is not everything."

And now, as the meal concluded and Tiny paid the bill, and they slowly drove westward to Miramar, it was not so hard for Shirley to accept the decision that had plagued her over the past week or so. It was not a bad or disgraceful thing to return to Jamaica and her home.

"It is as if Jamaica tied to us, Tiny, as if our navel string cut there and we have to go back no matter what we do."

"Must be so," Tiny sighed and cornered into the centre of Miramar. "Must be so, mi dear. Everybody lonely up here."

"All the while?" Shirley asked.

"Well, not all the while, but you know how it go sometimes." Then she caught herself. "What me saying? Lonely, yes - all o' *we lonely*. We go on like we happy but we very lonely."

Shirley did not answer.

"That's why me going home. Is fifteen years now me live here. My house finish, I going rent out this one and go home. As next year come so." Tiny brought the car to a halt in the driveway. "Well," she said, "we reach back safe."

"Yes," Shirley said. "Thanks."

For some unknown reason both women sat silently in the parked car in the dark driveway and stared through the windscreen. Shirley felt she had to say something. She turned to the little woman who had shown her so much kindness. Tiny had invited her to dinner for a purpose; so she could see something. And now she had opened to her, we lonely, as if she wanted to drive home an important lesson.

"Thank you," Shirley said again. "Thank you for everything."

"Lord," Tiny said shyly. "Thanks for what?"

"For everything."

"All right. All right."

Shirley turned, clasped the handle of the door and opened it.

"I know is not my business," Tiny paused uncomfortably. "I know you know what you doing an' so... but. . ." Tiny shook her head.

Shirley stopped halfway through the open door. She turned back to Tiny. "Is all right," she said. "I kinda understand what you trying to say."

Tiny smiled gratefully. "You understand though?"

"I better," Shirley said, and alighted from the car.

"Shirley?"

Shirley paused and turned around. Tiny had alighted from the car on the other side.

"Listen." Tiny dipped into her bag and produced a small folded piece of paper. "I don't know if you interested or not. But like how you soon go home and so, you may need a little money." She twisted the paper in her hand, then she spoke rapidly. "Anyway, Babs, one of mi good friend, tell me 'bout a little work you can do if you want. You can make a money to buy something to carry home for you friend them and so."

Shirley snapped to attention. "Work!" She touched the top of the car.

"Yes. Well, you don't have to take it or anything. Me know you work in bank and so, but since you here not doing anything. . ."

"Work!" Shirley repeated. "What kind a work?"

"Well, is little babysitting. Some people have two children. Them want a babysitter for a few weeks. Is live-in if you want or you can just go during the day."

"Oh, I see." Shirley hesitated. "Well, I don't know. . ."

" You don't have to take it," Tiny said, all the time staring kindly across the top of the car.

"I didn't say that," Shirley said. "Babysitting, you say?"

"Yes," Tiny said. "It pay about two-fifty a week, but you know Babs have to get her twenty or so, because is her job. But it better than nothing." She pushed the paper across the top of the car.

Shirley took it slowly. "I'll think about it," she said.

"Yes." Tiny was sober. "But tell me if you don't want it, so me can tell Babs."

"OK," Shirley said. "I will."

"All right then," Tiny said, as she turned towards her door. "Well, all right. Me gone in. Me gone in."

Shirley could not find the words to say to the disappearing back.

Chapter Eight

Monday morning, Shirley Temple Brown presented herself at the modern guardhouse of the Coral Estates Golf and Country Colony and asked to be directed to the home of the Williamsons. She was given a computer printout with directions and twenty minutes later, she followed a wide driveway that sliced through immaculately cut grass to a massive white door of the largest house she had ever seen. She rang the bell, saw a curtain move and the excited face of a blond child peeping through.

The curtain fell and she heard a patter of little feet and an excited scream. "Mommy, mommy, mommy, the new maid is here!"

Minutes later, a slim white woman with her head wrapped in a towel opened the door for her.

"You are early," she said.

"Yes."

"I am just getting out of the shower. Hi – my name is Nicole, and you are Shirley?"

"Yes," Shirley said.

"Come in and wait in the dining room, I'll just be a minute."

The dining room in which she stood was all glass except for the chairs, which were metallic and high shining silver. The table was glass and the places were set complete with napkins finely folded as in a five-star restaurant. There were stools around a small bar – silver stools. Large paintings hung on the huge walls including one of a big warship. Pictures were arranged on a table: of children; of Nicole by herself and in groups and of a tall handsome man in military uniform. There was a feeling of space and luxury about the room that reminded her of her favorite soap opera, Falcon Crest.

Five minutes later, a little boy came down and stood where the dining room opened into a large living room. He stared at her without speaking. He just stood there, dressed in white shirt, navy blue pants, and tiny shiny shoes; his eyes wide open as if he had not learnt to blink.

"Hi!" Shirley said. "What's your name?" She stepped toward him and he turned and fled through the archway.

Nicole returned with her husband beside her and the little boy pulling at the side of her silk dressing gown. Macy's Allure Collection, fall 88, Shirley made a mental assessment.

"This is my husband, Tom." Tom was tall and lean, with thick graying hair and gentle eyes - a softer version of the military man in the picture. He reminded her of Richard Channing from Falcon Crest. He smiled and took her hand. "Hello, Shirley," he said.

"And this one, acting shyly," the woman pulled the little boy from behind her skirt, "is Brad, my three year old."

"Hi, Brad," Shirley said.

"Say hi to Shirley," Nicole urged him but all the boy did was stare at her.

"Let's talk in here." Nicole led them through the vast living room, done in lavender with a glazed floor and large white leather couches, into a smaller sitting room that was much more cozy. Shirley sat, turned down the offer of coffee and tried to size up the very cordial couple in front of her.

Nicole was about five feet seven with blonde hair that fell to her waist. She walked as if she dragged her feet but did not; it was more like the flat-footed stroll of a ballet dancer. Shirley later discovered that she had indeed done some ballet at high school.

Tom, the husband, sat quietly and sipped his coffee. He was dressed in a solid blue shirt with a blue and white tie. His jacket was thrown carefully across the back of a chair that held a stuffed leather briefcase. He's on his way to work, she thought.

Nicole was the one in charge, or wanted to give that impression. She did most of the talking. Tom stayed long enough to satisfy himself with whatever scant assessment he wanted to make. Then he looked at his watch, placed his coffee cup on the table and reached towards his wife.

"Honey, if I am to take Brad to school, I must go now." He kissed her cheek. Shirley noticed for the first time that he was old enough to have been Nicole's father.

He regarded Shirley. "Whatever you decide, whether or not I see you when I return – it was nice to have met you."

Shirley rose slightly and took his hand. "Same here," she said.

"Have you ever babysat?" Nicole asked.

"Yes," Shirley lied. What could be hard in babysitting? Every Jamaican is a natural mother. "I thought there were two children."

"They are," Nicole said. "They are asleep upstairs."

"They are upstairs?"

"Yes, twins; I have twins. You won't have to worry about Brad. He goes to a private school and is hardly here."

Shirley was already feeling better. She wasn't sure she wanted the task of trying to win Brad over.

"So tell me about yourself," Nicole asked. "How long can you work for?"

"What do you mean?" Shirley watched her closely.

"How long? A week, a month?"

"How long do you need a babysitter?"

"I need a fulltime babysitter. The salary is two hundred dollars a week; you have your own room and board." Nicole cut right down to the bottom line.

"Two hundred? I heard two-fifty," Shirley remarked carefully.

Nicole shook her head slowly and held her stare. "No, I don't remember giving that impression."

"What would my duties be?" Shirley asked.

"To take care of the twins, see to it they are fed and clean, maybe assist around the house as required. Would you like the job?"

"Would I have to live in?"

"I would prefer that. But if you are able to get here by seven in the mornings, that is fine with me."

"I could," Shirley affirmed. "I don't live far from here." She had no intention of relinquishing her apartment at Tiny's.

It did not sound like much work to Shirley. How hard could it be to feed and watch two children? In any event, she was in no position to bargain because she needed the money. "I could give it a try. Yes, I'd like to try." What is more, she thought as she watched the relief in Nicole's eyes, she could seek a job from there by using her free time to make local calls. There was nothing to lose; if by the end of the month nothing worked out, she would have money to buy her ticket back home.

Nicole rose and pointed to the stairs. "Let me show you around." They crossed the marble tiles and climbed carpeted stairs. Nicole paused outside a half-opened door and then quietly pushed it open. "Here they are," she said with a smile. "Here are my babies."

Shirley entered a well lit room complete with baby wallpaper and cute pink and white curtains. There were two large cribs in the room and in each crib was a small bundle sleeping quietly.

"They're just babies!" Shirley exclaimed.

"Two and a half months," Nicole said, leaning into the pink crib.

"I thought they were older." Shirley hesitated.

Nicole rose. "Is there a problem? If you are unable to do it, now is the time to say."

"I did not say I was unable to do it. . ."

"Well then, that's that. This is Christopher and this is Christine. They should be bathed and fed by eight o'clock and every two to three hours after that. Their feeding is here with all instructions. . ."

"Feeding!" Shirley exclaimed. "Feeding at two and half months old?"

Nicole turned to her. "What do you mean?"

Shirley paused and searched for a tactful way to tell the young woman before her that, as far as she knew, babies were to be breastfed for at least eight to twelve months. "Well, I guess early weaning fosters independence."

"Pardon me," Nicole's voice took on an edge. "I don't think you should worry about the feeding they get. Let us leave that to my judgment. If you follow instructions, everything should be fine." She turned to go. "If you change your mind about staying, your room is across the hall."

At that moment, a baby woke up and began to scream. The next second, another scream pierced the morning. "Right on time, every morning," Nicole sighed. "Well, I guess your job has begun, Shirley." They re-entered the room and attended to the screaming children.

It took Shirley one minute flat to realize that even without experience, she was the expert in the room. Nicole seemed hopelessly lost, lifting Christine and shaking her madly. Her face became red with confusion as the child refused to stop and hollered much louder. They were both wet, dirty and hungry, and it did not take a genius to see that.

The room was equipped like a five-star hotel, with its own bathroom and large tubs specially designed for the babies. She helped Nicole bathe and change them, after which they quietened. Then Shirley dropped the side of one of the cribs and placed them side by side as she powdered and prepared them. This made them happy and they began to coo playfully.

At this, Nicole, her silk robe wet and covered with powder, excused herself with a quick, "Ooh, they seem to like you, Shirley. Will you take it from here? I must leave. I have to get dressed. I have an appointment I must make."

And that was the last time Shirley remembered ever seeing her touch those twins in that way.

Someone must have changed them during the nights when Shirley had gone home. But she could never be sure whether it was Nicole or husband, as even the Velcro clasps on the diapers were never put on straight.

After the twins had eaten and gone back to sleep, Shirley was not sure what to do next. The babies were resting and there was not much else to be done for them except to wash their tiny garments and straighten their room. She did this, then walked around a bit and passed through a side door to a large pool. She sat there for a while and looked across the vast manicured fairways of the golf course and the people driving up and down on golf carts, hitting balls and driving after them again. American people don't have a thing to do. Bored, she walked back through the house into the kitchen. There were dirty dishes in the sink. She was in a good mood so she washed those. The cleaning woman must be having the day off.

Around three or so, Tom returned and to her surprise, changed and went into the kitchen to cook. She sat with the twins and watched as he whistled and sang his way around the kitchen. This was an activity he obviously enjoyed. She later learned that he had been a cook in the navy and that the kitchen was his domain. He was now a lawyer and partner in a very large firm. His routine, however, was set around the kitchen. He would get home around three o'clock or so, cook and relax by the pool till around five or five-thirty when the family had dinner. After dinner, he would relax for another half an hour and then return to the office. Two or three times a week he would go for a walk on the golf course and not return to the office at all. Sometimes he would take his clubs but when he went after dinner he would just walk out with the evening and then at times return to his large study and work till late into the night. He was a quiet business-like person. That first day he whistled and cooked and Shirley attended to the twins and they hardly exchanged a word.

The next day was just as uneventful and Shirley began to think it was not so bad. She could handle it. All she had were the twins, Tom was hardly there, Nicole was hardly there and Brad, she understood, would only be home on weekends.

On the third morning after she had finished bathing and feeding the twins she came downstairs to find Nicole dressed for the road. Shirley was heading toward the washing machine with the few garments that the babies had soiled overnight.

"You are doing a very good job, Shirley," Nicole remarked, as she followed Shirley into the large space that held the washing machine. "The babies never cry when you are around."

"Thank you," Shirley said.

"With me they cry all the time. I don't know, I seem to wear a sign or perfume or something that says: Here is mommy, time to cry!" She was trying to be funny and Shirley humored her.

"No, I don't think so. You are a good mother."

"Do you have any children?" she asked Shirley.

"No," Shirley said as she poured the softener.

"I tell you one thing, I am glad I had those twins. That Tom will never come near me again, I tell you."

Shirley laughed.

"Anyway," Nicole smiled back, "I have to run, but could you do me a favour?"

"What?" Shirley asked.

"While you are washing, could you just check if there are other things that may need washing in our room, and just drop them in for us."

"Sure," Shirley said.

"Tom and I really appreciate how clean you have been keeping the kitchen."

"That's nothing," Shirley said. "It's always clean anyway, I just hate a dirty kitchen."

"Me too."

"The cleaning lady has not been here for two days. Is she on vacation?"

"Who?"

"The. . .," Shirley gestured around, "you know, the maid, to clean the house."

"Oh," Nicole bounced away. "I wouldn't worry about her if I were you."

As she bounced through the door, the garbage truck pulled up outside. A minute later Shirley heard a large bang as the empty garbage pan was flung carelessly back into the yard to slam against the side of the house. A baby screamed from upstairs. A second later another voice joined the chorus. The twins were awake.

Chapter Nine

The next evening, Shirley had just finished feeding the babies on the patio and was burping Christopher while Christine cried in the play pen. It was close to the pool and Shirley liked sitting there and looking across the vast acreage of the golf course.

Tom stopped by on his way back from disposing of the garbage to coo at Christine through the transparent plastic of the playpen. "Daddy's hands are a bit dirty now," he cooed. Shirley will burp you."

After he finished in the kitchen he returned to them, but by then both babies were playing and Shirley was sitting easily in the beach chair looking out across the fairway.

"Don't be afraid to use the pool," he said, sitting down. "If there is anything around that you need to use, feel free to go ahead and do so."

"Thanks," Shirley replied, "but I can't swim well. I never enter water deeper than my waist."

"You can't swim? But you are from Jamaica!"

"Yes."

"I thought everybody in the islands could swim."

Shirley sat up and regarded him fondly. "Well, you are wrong. Funny enough, most people I know back home cannot swim."

"Well, you don't have to be able to swim to use the pool."

"Maybe," she said.

He seemed to want to put her at ease, make some sort of conversation, but it was a bit awkward. And she was not sure how to proceed either. He did not lack intelligence or the ability to make conversation – he was a successful lawyer – but he seemed to be searching for a way to address her, like a driver trying to determine which highway to take.

"Where in Jamaica are you from?" He made a swathe into the silence.

"Close to Kingston."

He was a large man – not fat, but large-boned and elegant. Shirley guessed his age to be around fifty or so. His hair was gray, not white, but a sort of dusty gray, like someone had tried to comb the brown out of it. His eyes were soft and wrinkled.

They sat there in an uncomfortable silence until they heard the alarm buzz, indicating that the front door had been opened. Tom rose, and as he did, Nicole appeared through the kitchen, shouting behind her for Brad to be careful when changing and came directly to join them. She kissed her husband lightly and looked over at the twins, then sat in the chair he had vacated. She shook her long blond hair loose and sighed how hot it was outside and how horrible the traffic was. "Shirley, could you get me some lemonade, please, I could just die." She lay back onto the chair and kicked her shoes to the floor.

Shirley looked up in surprise but before she was able to respond, Tom moved toward the kitchen. "I'll do it, dear," he said. "I'm already standing."

"Thanks, darling," she said. "What did you cook this evening?"

"Chicken a la Crème. Shirley, would you like something?"

"No thanks," Shirley said. She was still trying to understand why Nicole would walk past the refrigerator and then ask her to go into the house and bring her a drink.

Tom returned with the drink and handed it to his wife, then went back to the house. Nicole drank half her lemonade and then inquired how the twins had been.

Shirley told her. They had cried a lot but she figured they were probably teething as they took the pacifier rather eagerly. Christine, she thought, did not seem to like bottled vegetables. Besides that they were fine.

"They really seem to like you," Nicole said. "That other Latino woman we had here, I couldn't understand a word she said, and they did not seem to understand her either – they cried all the time."

"Thank you," Shirley said.

"Tom and I were saying how well you seem to be working out," she remarked.

"Thank you," Shirley said again, "but I have only been here a few days."

"Ahh, but we can tell." Nicole drank some more and looked for a place to put her glass.

Shirley moved toward the playpen. "Well, I'd better take the twins up to their room." She was not sure how she would respond to another lemonade request. She was the babysitter, not a maid.

"Oh, they can wait a bit," Nicole said. "Stay with me awhile. It's not often that I have another woman around to talk to. I am not opposed to us being friends, you know."

"It's getting a bit late," Shirley said. "And I have to catch the bus."

"But Tom could drop you if you are late. He may be going back to the office anyway. That's all he does – work."

Shirley did not respond.

"Anyway," Nicole said, "I like to talk to you. You are so intelligent. Not like those Latinos, or Haitians. Yuck, I could never have a Haitian in my house. They are so nasty."

Shirley sighed. Well, at least they agreed on something. If someone confused her for a Haitian she would die.

"Do you have a boyfriend?" Nicole looked conspiratorially at her.

Shirley sat back in her seat. "No, not now."

"All the better. Men can be such pain in the asses sometimes."

Shirley smiled. "I concur one hundred per cent."

Nicole stretched onto the pool chair and Shirley could see that she had a fair shape. She had no fat on her but she lacked bounce. Her designer jeans did her more justice than she deserved, but her skin was clean and white – almost like cream. "I would take a swim if the damn pool weren't so dirty," she said. "You like swimming, Shirley?"

"I can't," Shirley said. This must be swimming quiz evening.

"Now you are pulling my leg."

"No, I am not."

"Well, anyway, I am sure I called the pool man. Did anyone come to clean the pool today?"

"No," Shirley said.

"I wonder why not. I am sure I called him since last week." She shouted into the house, "Tom, did you hear from the pool people?"

Tom did not answer.

"No one came to clean the house either," Shirley said. She felt comfortable enough with Nicole to bring the subject up. She knew it was not her business, she was just the babysitter and it was only her fourth day on the job, but such a big house required constant attention. It was very clean but it required upkeep at least twice per week to keep it as sparkling as it was.

"You know," Nicole looked at her fondly, "I wouldn't care if that damn woman did not come back."

"Why?" Shirley asked.

"She complained all the time. Not like you. You just do things, you know. If something is to be done, you do it. I like that about you."

"Well, she must have been doing something right: the house is sparkling."

"Yes, but she complained a lot. I hate people who complain. I mean, if there is something to be done and it is in your way, what is wrong with doing it, as long as you are being paid?"

"I agree," Shirley said.

"You see? That is what I like about you." Nicole turned toward the pool again. "I tell you one thing, we will be very careful about the next person I hire. In the meantime, Shirley," she said casually, "if you see something that needs doing around the house, you wouldn't be against doing it, would you, until we are able to hire someone else?"

"Of course not," Shirley said. "I'd be glad to help."

"I knew you would say that. Tom and I would be so appreciative. You are so willing, and so intelligent. Not like those Latinos and Haitians."

"Thanks," said Shirley.

"Please," Nicole said, "that's nothing to thank me for. Do you want me to help you take the children to their room?"

"Sure." Shirley was pleasantly surprised.

"And then you could join us for dinner," Nicole added. "We don't mind you eating with us, and Tom cooks beautifully. He won't allow me near that kitchen, he designed it himself."

"Oh," Shirley said.

"So you'll stay for dinner?"

"Sure, and thank you again." Shirley began to lift Christine.

"Oh, don't mention it," Nicole laughed as she lifted Christopher awkwardly from the playpen.

Chapter Ten

Weeks passed: days, hours ran into another and time became one continuous flow. Shirley's spirit too was tied to the blending of the days, and all things seemed right and natural around her. Thus with a sunny disposition, a willingness to please and a hint of complacency, she failed to spot the subtle changes in the pattern of the days. Deeds became tasks, wishes became commands, babysitting turned to housekeeping, till one day Shirley was startled to discover that she had become responsible for the keeping of the house.

And it took a party to do it.

During the first weeks, Shirley had not minded helping around the house. She was there, there was work to be done, and Nicole needed time to be selective in her employment of a new maid. There was no pressure on her - she worked at her leisure. While she took the twins' clothing to the laundry, she could take the rest from the other rooms. The kitchen was in her way, keeping it tidy was a cinch. She would wash one day, vacuum the next and clean other spaces as she went along. One night she even joked to Nicole that if she paid her double she could probably take care of the whole house and the kids in one – but she would need a month's vacation every month.

That was the evening she cooked for them because she had been in a good mood. Tom had brought up the subject of Jamaican food some time before, said he had eaten it once and had loved it. So one evening she decided to surprise them with a simple curried chicken. Even Brad emptied his plate that time. After that, every now and then, she would cook. At times Tom would call home from the office and ask if she could cook. She did it willingly.

She was having a good time even with all the extra work to do. Tom and Nicole had practically adopted her. She ate with them, had long discussions with them over dinner at times, and though she had to return to wash the dishes after they left she did not mind. They even had a room prepared for her, should she change her mind and decide to live in fulltime.

She was saving some money. She had even written a letter to her mother. Though she told her she was in banking school, it was a start. She felt it would do no good to tell her what she was really doing. These were good people - they had accepted her as an equal. She had introduced them to Jamaican culture and they had expressed a desire to visit the island. She had even 'forced' them to attend a reggae party at the Bi-centennial Park and they had loved it.

Once Tom even tried to teach her how to play golf, It happened one evening as he prepared for his walk around the course. She had asked him why he walked the course more than he played. And he had laughed and told her that the walk was better for his mind.

"How come?"

"Golf is better weekends."

"But these people play all the time."

"Well, that is the reason. It addicts you."

"So why live on a gulf course?"

"I play . . . I like the game. But sometimes I think I like the course more than I like the game. I like the

wide open spaces and the peace . . . and the colors of the evening." And then he had looked quizzically at her and she had noticed for the first time that his eyes were dark brown like hers. "Would you like to learn?"

"Me, I could not."

"But you could."

And he had taken her while the twins slept to the garage for a large net which he placed at the back of the yard; and he tried to teach her to hit the ball. And halfway through teaching, she fell into his arms and felt to linger there and he had guided her gently as if he did not notice and his eyes were never less than kind and never more than friendly. But Shirley did not have the flair for golf. After that there was warmth between them – somewhere, Shirley thought, between brother and father. He made her feel safe. My Richard Channing.

Then there was the party.

Tom and his partners were having a party at the house for one of their overseas clients. They had planned to have it in the large living hall but Shirley had encouraged them to have it outside around the pool. She had helped to pick the menu and set the decorations. And Nicole had told her that she hoped to see her that night.

"We know it is your night off," she had said, "but Tom and I would be so happy if you could come."

"Don't worry," Shirley replied. "I wouldn't miss it for the world."

It had been over a year since she had dressed up for anything, and Shirley was surprised to discover she had lost a little weight. But that did not matter: her baby pink dress still hugged her curves.

She decided to be a little early so she could help Nicole organize the caterers.

When Nicole opened the door for her, she exclaimed how beautiful Shirley looked. "I just love that dress!" she squealed.

"Thank you," Shirley said, thinking how good it felt to surprise people sometimes.

"Tom." Nicole called her husband.

Tom came around the corner, looking so much like Richard Channing in his suit and silk tie.

"You look very nice." He smiled a slow smile.

"So, you are here," Nicole said. "I hope we did not pull you away from your date - you did not even change."

"Yes, I hope we are not inconveniencing you." Tom looked directly at her. "Did we pull you away from a big occasion?"

"No, not at all." Shirley began to feel a weird sensation coming on.

"Well, not to matter," Nicole said happily. "The kids are upstairs. I don't want to see them. I know you do a good job, but whatever you have to do, keep them quiet tonight. And look out for that Brad. I don't want to see him down here."

"What?"

"And if you want to change your dress, just slip into my room. You may use a pair of my jeans or something."

Shirley tried not to look at Tom, gazing at her with those serious knowing eyes. She tried to regain some composure, as she stumbled across the room for the stairs and her job – the baby pink dress flowing down her curves with matching shoes and hair done up high. She had been known to overdress on occasions – especially on Fridays.

When she awoke the next morning, the house was empty. Though the party had gone on till the wee hours of the morning, her employers had already left to play golf with the guests.

Shirley stumbled to the kitchen in search of a cup of coffee and found a note in Nicole's handwriting stuck to the refrigerator door. The heading read: Things for Shirley to do: We will be back around twelve. Please have the house shining before we return. These are very important clients of Tom's and we want to give the best impression. Then there were a few additional things listed on the paper.

Shirley turned around and looked at the after-party mess in the kitchen: the dirty dishes and glasses carelessly strewn all around, the dining table yet to be cleared, the floor and carpet soiled. It would take a whole cleaning crew a day to tidy that place. And Nicole wanted it ready by noon. Suddenly Christine screamed from her room and as if on cue Christopher joined in. Shirley looked toward the stairs and a minute later the kettle joined the confusion. All thoughts of coffee left her as she saw Brad walking sleepily down the stairs rubbing his eyes.

She stood there in her borrowed slippers and crumpled baby pink dress, lifted her eyes to the skies and screamed aloud : ' when did I become the cleaner of the house?'

There was a confrontation the following week. Nicole had called her from hushing Christine, to ask if she would vacuum her room that day. When Shirley came sullenly to perform the task, Nicole had gone into the shower and left her panties in the middle of the bedroom floor.

Shirley left and gave her time to finish her shower.

But when she re-entered the room, Nicole was half dressed and the panties were still lying on the floor where she had stepped from them to take her shower.

"I'd like to vacuum now," Shirley said.

"Oh, I'm sorry," Nicole said. "Just a minute, I'm almost done, you can wait right there."

"I'll come back," Shirley said.

Ten minutes later, Nicole called to say she was done and that she would be going shopping. Shirley came quickly to see if she had removed the panties, but they were still there. She stood above the undergarment and called Nicole in the calmest voice she could find.

"What?" Nicole said. "I have to go."

"Aren't you forgetting something?"

"What am I forgetting?"

"Those," Shirley pointed at the panties. "They cannot get into the basket by themselves."

"What?"

"Those panties on the floor," Shirley said angrily, "they don't have feet to jump."

"Oh," Nicole said. "I am sorry if they offend you." She walked around the vacuum cleaner, picked up the garment and threw it into the laundry basket. "Shirley," she said, "I can't believe you called me back for that."

"Well, I am not a maid," Shirley said.

"I know," Nicole said. "But you did agree-"

"I agreed to help - till you found a new maid."

"But we haven't yet."

"Are you trying? I don't think you have been trying hard enough, Nicole."

"What!"

"I am tired of all of this. I can't do so much work and then take care of the babies."

"Are you raising your voice to me?"

"I am saying that you need to find someone to clean the house."

"But you said you would. You said you could!"

"I said I'd help."

"Can't you manage? Tell me if you can't manage, I'll get someone else."

"I can't manage," Shirley said, holding her stare. "I am saying I can't manage."

They stared at each other for a while then Nicole threw her hands into the air. "You know, I think you should consider what you are saying."

Shirley tried to control her voice. "I have thought about it, Nicole. This is a big house. I have thought about it."

"Do not raise your voice to me."

"I am not raising my voice at you," Shirley shouted.

"I cannot talk to you like this. You cannot speak to me like this."

"Nicole," Shirley said slowly, "that is not going to work."

"I am trying to get someone. What do you want me to do? What can I do if no one comes?"

"Maybe they know damn well why they don't come," Shirley said under her breath. "Such a damn bitch."

"What did you say?" Nicole hollered.

"All right, Nicole," Shirley said. "I am willing to work with you, I am willing to help, but you need to get someone to clean the house. Get someone for two days to take care of the vacuuming and the laundry and the general cleaning, and I will do the rest. But I cannot continue like this. I cannot perform my job the way I should do it."

They stared at each other again. "You know," Nicole said, "I don't think I can continue this conversation. I think we should wait until Tom gets home. And now I have to go." She spun around and stormed through the door. Shirley watched her departing back and kicked the red button on the vacuum cleaner viciously.

Shirley was determined to have the situation resolved before she went home that evening. So she sat around while Tom and Nicole locked themselves in the bedroom and argued. After about half an hour or so, Tom emerged, nodded curtly to her and raised his eyebrows slightly. It could have been amusement or weariness, Shirley was not able to interpret the expression on his face.

After a while Nicole came from the room and looked over to where Shirley was sitting in the living room. "Shirley, may I speak with you?"

Shirley rose to join her. She had calmed since the morning, but her temper was not far from her. The work was there, it did not require imagination to know it was too much. In any event she was not a maid, she was the babysitter.

Nicole closed the bedroom door behind them. "Firstly, I would like to say that I do not appreciate how you talk to me at times."

"How do I speak to you?" Shirley asked.

"You speak to me as if I work for you," Nicole insisted, trying to be calm. "With disrespect."

"But you are disrespectful to me," Shirley returned.

"If it seems so, I do not mean to be," Nicole asserted. "I do not try to offend you."

"But you do."

"Then I am sorry."

Shirley could hardly withhold her smirk. "You? Sure you are."

"See what I mean?" Nicole said. "I expect a certain amount of respect. I deserve that. This is my house and you work for me."

"If you show respect for me, Nicole, I will show respect for you."

Nicole was silent for a while and Shirley could feel the tension building in the room. She had no intention of doing anything to reduce it.

"I don't want this to become another argument," Nicole finally said. "I am willing to offer you another twenty dollars for the extra work you have been doing."

"It's not the extra money," Shirley said. "It's the work. It is too much."

"I know," Nicole said. "But this is until we get someone to do the cleaning."

"And how long will that be?" Shirley asked tiredly.

"I am asking around, but as you know, it is not easy to find good people."

Shirley laughed slightly to herself and shrugged. She could hardly believe this conversation was taking place. That she, Shirley Temple Brown, was negotiating the terms of cleaning someone's bathroom. She could not determine what was more disgraceful; to fight or not to.

But what was she to do? Though she was sure as she sat there that Nicole had no intention of hiring anyone else, she knew she had no choice. Nicole held the handle. She was broke, she needed the job.

Shirley picked up her bag to go. "If you say so," she said softly to Nicole. "If you say so." She did not even wait for Nicole to respond.

The two weeks came and went and there was no sign that Nicole would be hiring anyone. Shirley stopped complaining. It was around that time she began to talk to herself. Sometimes she would sit at the pool and look across the golf course at the golfers while the twins cried or slept, and she would try to remember when it all began: when did she become the cleaner of the house? When was the laundry her full responsibility? From where did dusting come? And garbage disposal! How was that? She could have sworn there was a time when Tom did that.

It was not as if time had changed her. She was still Shirley, she still had pride, she still stood up for herself. She still walked around with her elegant stride, still stood for her rights... and talked back too. . . She stood up.

That day when she and Nicole clashed in the bedroom, that was standing up. Did she not tell her off? She would vacuum and she would wash but she was damned if she would walk behind her and pick up her panties. She had told her off. And even though Nicole continued after a while, to step out of her panties and leave them right there on the ground, she, Shirley, did not pick them up; she used a piece of stick or the mop stick to pick them up. She would not touch those things. After they were washed was OK, but she would not touch them dirty. And they knew that. They knew she was proud. They knew they had to speak to her softly.

And Brad the brat, he knew she was a serious woman. He knew he could not stomp naked in front of her and holler, "Shirley, I am ready for my bath!" irrespective of what she was doing. He knew he should stand quietly and wait or sit in his tub of water. And when he first called her nigger, did she take it? She did not! Did she not call the family to answer? Did she not call Nicole and tell her? And when Nicole mumbled that they did not teach him racism here in the house, what did she, Shirley Temple Brown, do? What did she say? She stood her ground! She looked Nicole straight in her eye and told her that if he brought it home from school, then it was her duty to stop it. Now they knew she did not stand for that kind of foolishness. And though Brad still called her nigger, and though she had come to ignore it, they knew, they knew. They knew she did not take foolishness.

But when did she become the cleaner of the house? When did she begin cleaning toilets and scrubbing bathrooms?

And always in the midst of these reflections she would rebuke herself with a harsh whisper: Leave then. Why you don't leave then? Leave or shut up! Most of the time she shut up. But by the time she felt she could not take any more and that she had to leave the job and make her prodigal journey home to Jamaica, she met Queeny, and her whole outlook changed.

Chapter Eleven

One Saturday morning the twins were crying so Shirley thought she would take them and Brad for a walk to get some fresh air. It was after nine o'clock when she pushed the double carriage along the wide walkway, and the only vehicles that travelled the roads at that time were golf carts. Coral Estates was a beautiful place – every house was custom-built on half an acre of land and from a distance they seemed to blend into the undulating mounds of the course itself. Each had three or four large trees near the front and some had hedges of dwarf sesame trees.

As she took the kids along the walkway, Nicole pulled the large Lincoln up to the curve and suggested they go to the mall. Shirley thought it was a good idea. She had not been to the mall for quite a while and she looked forward to going there. But it was hardly what she expected, as once they got to the Aventura, Nicole stepped ahead with her light elegant strides and left her behind with the twins in the carriage. She did not mind this because she liked strolling the mall herself. But Nicole soon turned around and beckoned to her impatiently. "Shirley! Stop lagging." Though she hated it, she found herself hastening her steps to catch up with her boss who walked the mall as if she owned it.

Brad was especially excited, and kept bothering her to allow him to push his siblings.

She finally relented. "OK, but only to JC Penny."

Brad was a picture of joy as he pushed the twin-carriage. It was a large stroller as strollers went and a bit tall for him, so he could not reach the handle. Shirley placed his hands against the undercarriage that held the baby bags, and he pushed contentedly though he could hardly see where he was going. Out of the line of his vision however, Shirley carefully guided it through the throng of shoppers. As they neared JC Penny, Brad abandoned the carriage without warning and began to play with a little dog that was nipping at the feet of everyone it passed.

Shirley parked the carriage at the closest wooden bench and waited for Nicole to finish shopping. Though it was just after ten and the mall had just opened, the hallways were busy with shoppers strolling leisurely through. An elderly couple caught her eye as they chatted and gestured to each other over the contents of a shopping bag. The woman was teasing the man over some purchase he had made too hastily at a store at the other end of the mall, and was trying to encourage him to return the goods and buy it for less at the store they were now passing. Shirley watched them for a minute with an amused smile on her face, wondering if she would ever marry and have someone to grow old with so she could tease him in a mall about his follies.

When she turned to check on the twins, the stroller was gone. She looked around in panic. There was a squeal and she turned the other way just in time to see Brad's back as he raced the carriage with the babies down the mall. Shirley could hardly see him behind it. All she saw was his little blond head and the pink blue and white ruffles of the stroller as it parted the bustle of shoppers moving up and down the hall.

She ran quickly after him. "Brad!" He was farther away than she expected.

Shirley bounced rudely against a couple, a bag fell. A woman cursed. She hardly noticed. "Brad!" He heard her, looked around, laughed and increased his pace. The large stroller picked up speed down the corridor. Shirley had to be quick and she had to be careful. If she ran at him too swiftly he would get overly excited and capsize the stroller, yet she had to catch him before he ran into someone. Then she had to hold him firmly – she did not want to risk anyone accusing her of abusing him. But most of all, she had to catch him before his hand hit the lever that collapsed the stroller for stowage. His hands were right beside it.

"Brad!" she hollered. "Brad! Stop right there!" The blond head bobbed in front of her. He was past The Gap and headed straight for a booth where a man in a pointed hat penciled portraits of passers-by. The carriage did not veer, it headed straight for the easel which flew to the side in its wake.

"Hold him!" Shirley shouted. The artist glared angrily at her as she reached after the disappearing child. "Brad!" Someone giggled. Another mocked: "Run, Brad, Run!" But Shirley paid no mind. She had to end this stupid chase now. She increased her speed and made a great lunge at him. He slid, fell, and gave the carriage a final push. Shirley tried to jump to avoid him, skidded and fell onto her bottom. The carriage continued toward another booth. She rose quickly from where she fell and made another lunge to catch the axle and stop it. It tipped to capsize, but a hand reached to grab and stop it. She in turn slammed into the foot of the booth that sold designer license plates. Shirley rose, completely humiliated, and removed a license plate that had fallen onto her chest. It said Lexus No Stopping Here.

She passed the sign to the man who held the carriage. He smiled with understanding as she replaced Brad's hand on the bar of the stroller. "Thank you," she said, too embarrassed to look him in the eye.

"Kids!" He smiled. "Are you OK?"

"Yes, thanks, I am fine." She checked the twins. Both were waving their hands gleefully. They had enjoyed the ride and would have loved another go.

Shirley walked away from the stall in a daze. She hardly even noticed that Brad had quietened and was walking slowly and guiltily beside the stroller, in apparent acknowledgment that this time he had gone too far. All around her seemed strange and distant: everything was a white blur. Her eyes burned and the tears were hot against her eyelids.

The bench appeared and she sat down. She pulled the stroller close to her knees and stared across at the JC Penny sign without seeing it. This was the limit, she would not take another day. She would resign the moment she returned to Coral Estates.

"Your bag this?"

She ignored the sound. She wanted to be alone. None should dare talk to her now.

"Is not your bag this? I hold it for you when I see you run after the boy. I keep it for you, you know."

Shirley turned and glanced to her right at the woman who was offering the handbag to her. She had not missed it, had not even remembered that she had brought it to the mall with her. But here was a woman, with her coarse Jamaican accent, orange weaves heaped high on her head and face black and open, offering it to her.

Shirley stared at her with bewilderment. "What?"

"This your bag?" It sounded like 'thiz yo' beg'

"Yes," Shirley said. "Thanks – I must have dropped it."

"I saved it for you, man."

Shirley took the bag without meeting the stare of the woman who had now taken a seat beside her. She wrapped the shoulder strap carefully and placed it on the under carriage of the stroller along with the babies' bags. She wished the woman would go.

"Children stay like that sometimes; if you follow them you get into trouble."

Shirley did not answer. Her eyes burned in her effort to control the tears that were backed up behind them. The woman sat quietly for a while. One of the twins giggled, passersby looked into the carriage and smiled. "How cute." Little Christine howled loudly. Shirley leaned over and placed a pacifier into her mouth. "You no bother start," Shirley said under her breath.

"Yardie?" the woman asked.

"What?" Shirley looked at her.

"Yardie, you sound Jamaican,"

Shirley winced as the "Jamaican" sounded like Jemaicen. "I am Jamaican, yes." She might as well be civil to the woman.

The woman dropped her half-American slang immediately. "Mi know you sound like Yardie, man."

"Yardie?" Shirley asked.

"Yeah. Yardie, J'can, Jamaican."

"Oh," Shirley said. "Yes."

"Lord, missis, them American pickney them bad, eeh? Jesus missis, them mus' give you a hard time."

Shirley softened her face a bit and regarded the woman fully. She was not in the mood for conversation, but the woman had been kind to her and for some reason would not leave. Moreover, it was some time since she had heard a kind voice. And though she tried to ignore it, the sound of another Jamaican voice warmed her like coffee in the morning.

"So, what's you name?" the woman asked.

She was black with a small neat mouth. Her clothes did not match, but they were expensive and she wore them well. Shirley noted her Versace shirt, Guess jeans and Nike sneakers, and quickly estimated that she was dressed to the tune of six hundred dollars or more. She sat with her legs wide like a tired football player. A rebel, Shirley thought, real Jamaican old nigger. The type of people she had spent her life avoiding. Shirley smiled weakly. "I'm Shirley."

The woman laughed loudly. "Them call me Queeny."

"Nice to meet you," Shirley said heavily. "I'm not being rude, you hear, but is just that sometimes. . ." Her voice wavered.

"You don' have to tell me," Queeny said, her eyes widening as if accepting a dare. "You don' have to tell me at all – me see fi myself. Them American pickney rude no backside."

"That's an understatement," Shirley said.

The woman looked blankly at her for a minute. "Them worse than any statement, mi dear, and if you touch them you gone a jail. That's why me can't bother with them little pickney," Queeny continued. "Caan' bother with them at all. The first work me get in America was to look after one little boy. One day him throw bread so lick mi inna mi face. Me just pick it up and throw it right back in him face, right in front of him mother. The last day I work there. But I bet him think twice before him throw bread pon anybody again."

"Well, they don't have to worry about that happening from me," Shirley said. "I can't take this another day."

"You planning to leave?" Queeny screwed up her face. "Lord missis, me don' wrong you. That there work must be hard. You one a take care of two twin and one bwoy. It no hard?"

Shirley had no plans to share her grief and shame with Queeny, who was acting as if they had known each other much longer than five minutes.

"All the same, is so life go sometimes. America hard, missis," Queeny continued. "Me so glad is one little old woman me have fi look after. She don' give a trouble. All me do is make sure me feed her, watch her when she go sleep, and make sure she get her medicine pon time. That's all. Plus her head go and come, so sometime she not even remember a thing – Allsimer. The only thing is that every week me bring her to the mall so she can do her hair. The woman a ninety and she have to go hairdresser at least once a week – never see nothing so yet. All when she can't remember her name, she a look inna mirror and a put on make-up and fix her hair. But me make sure bring her to the best though; every week me bring her here, make she get the best. Use to model too, you know. Use to be on magazine cover, she show me, yeah man, when her head no take her and so, she show me picture. Use to model. Now she can't even take care of herself." She paused. "Is a job like that you want, Shirley. A little old man or a old woman with couple year lef'. Me caan' bother with the whole heap o' headache. Me caan' bother hackle myself 'pon them bruck-bad pickney. My two in Jamaica."

Shirley could not help her surprise and curiosity. She looked again at the woman sitting there and wondered how she could afford a Versace shirt looking after an old woman.

Back home in Jamaica, in Sufferer's Heights, Central Village, she would never have spoken to Queeny on the street. She would never have offered her a drink of water if she asked, would never have taken one from her if she was dying of thirst. Who would regard someone with a name as stupid as Queeny, anyway? There was a baseness about it that could hardly be imagined.

Many days Shirley had seen them from her veranda, passing below, or stopping a few yards away in the middle of some tracing or fight over some man. These were women who were not afraid to carry guns and knives in their brassieres, who were not afraid to roll in the dust in the middle of the street, or drop their drawers to make a point of quality to an opponent. Women who frequented dancehalls and followed sound systems from town to town. Who lived with gunmen and sheltered them. Hard women with colorful ugly hair, changing hairstyles and colors every week, laden down with jewelry; who never seemed to have any special work. Higgler women, dancehall women, base, unkempt, raucous women: teggeregs, with three children before they were twenty, hauling behind them wherever they went. Poor and hungry, yet overdressed and overweight with all kind of fandangle.

In Jamaica, in Sufferer's Heights, Shirley – though poorer, maybe, than most of them – would never have spoken to a Queeny. And a Queeny would never talk to her. If she should pass a group of them, she would walk on the other side of the road and hold her head very high, while they laughed and threw some unkind word at her. And if their eyes should meet, it would be with open hostility and unspoken warfare. For Queeny would know exactly what Shirley was thinking, that the rabble was beneath her, but she Queeny was dying for a chance to point out in graphic detail the flaws in that perception. And the stare between them would be the only link, the only place they met. But they would both acknowledge that Shirley, if she wanted, could mix it up just as bad.

Now this day of all days, Queeny was sitting across from her, speaking endlessly as if they were friends. "So you work with an old lady?" Shirley asked civilly.

"Yes, mi dear. She inna the parlor 'round the corner. You soon see them a run come call me. But me! Me not in any haste today, missis. All like how my foot a hurt me. So you going leave the little work?" Her "work" sounded more like wok.

"Yes, yah." Shirley dropped her English. "Yes yah sah, me caan' bother. Me not even have children much less."

"But look 'pon him too no." Queeny regarded Brad who was standing quietly by. "Him must be Dennis the Menace."

Shirley laughed. "Jesus, you know you right and is same so him hair stay, you know, same way like Dennis the Menace. You right to rahtid, Dennis the Menace. Him rude same way."

"Lord, missis!" Queeny laughed lightly.

The mood lightened. Shirley began to feel a bit better. At least she could laugh. She thought she had forgotten how to do that.

"Me nah fast in you business or nothing," Queeny said, "but what a nice girl like you doing 'bout you working with people pickney?"

"Well," Shirley said, slowly. "Well, you know, I have a little vacation, and I thought I would come up and maybe work some money to take home."

"Oh, you a teacher or so? From me look 'pon you and see how you talk me know say you a intelligent, educated woman. Missis, then you don' have to take no Dennis the Menace. Leave it, Shirley. Lef' it to rahtid."

"Yes," Shirley said a bit too jubilantly, sad that she had lied so fluently, so instinctively. "Sometimes you make mistake in life."

"Well, at least you better than some a them who sell out everything and run come a United States think say is a bed of roses. Is them suffer. In Jamaica them gwaan like them shit can make patty, and when them come here, them do all kind a work to stay. At least you a teacher and so."

"Well, I work at a bank," Shirley said. Making sure she used the present tense.

"Bank! Which bank?"

"Mutual Security, Knutsford Boulevard."

"A lie! Me use to bank there, you know. But some of the gal them in there too feisty man. I don't mean you, you know. But some o' the gal them in there go on too feisty man."

Shirley smiled faintly and refused to take offence. "So how long have you been here?"

"Me go and come you know," Queeny answered proudly, "me go and come. Sometime me spend a six months or so. Me have a little dressmaking business, so me go and come. Like now, business kinda slow, so me come up fi a six months or so. As a matter a fact, this is the longest me ever stay up here. And is because me a plan to put on a hair dressing parlor on the shop. So me want buy some dryer."

"Oh!" Shirley said.

"Yes, me up here-what? Make me see." She rolled her eyes and counted. "March... 'bout six months now. Is so time fly to rahtid!"

"So you soon gone back, mi dear." Shirley was warming to her quicker than she expected.

"Well, yes, is so me did plan. But you know, things change sometimes."

"Me you a tell," Shirley sighed.

"As a matter a fact," Queeny drawled, "is yesterday I was saying to miself that, the little job so easy, and the woman look like she kinda strong. A might stay little longer this time. And just make one big thing, you know."

"So what would happen to you shop?"

"Me have a girl in there. She kinda good, and she honest. And mi husband kinda give a eye."

"So you married!"

"If you can call it that, missis." She kissed her teeth. "And is just because of the pickney them. Me have a boy and a girl, you know. But them caan' feisty like Dennis the Menace him. Yes, me have a piece of man, mi dear. Although me caan' call him my own once me leave that yard. But if I ever catch him!"

Shirley laughed. "So the men them stay, mi dear."

"Man!" Queeny said scornfully. "Man! All o' them is the same thing. Even you who pretty and so, your boyfriend still a look outside."

"Me," Shirley said, "I can't be bothered. I don't have a boyfriend."

She felt Queeny's eyes on her. Felt them scan her face and detect the lines there; felt them follow the slopes of the darkened hollows around her eyes. Saw her recognize her loneliness and misery; heard her silence, heard her voice stutter, then soften, and hated that she was wiser and sharper than she seemed to be – and sensitive enough to change the subject and prevent awkward silence from breaking the thin bond they were establishing.

"You ever think 'bout staying up here?" Queeny inquired.

"Me?" Shirley looked sternly across at Brad. "Where are you going?"

"To look at the fish," he said.

"Is your fish?" Queeny asked him. "Is your fish? Leave the people fish!"

Brad took one look at her and sat quietly.

"Is you him want," Shirley said.

"Me, ma? I don' joke with pickney, you know. Yes," she touched Shirley conspiratorially, "yes, missis, all like how you pretty and so. Why you don't get a green card, and just stay? All like you, and with your education and so. Lord Jesus! Especially how you look like Cuban and so. Missis, if me look like you me no leave."

"You just saying that," Shirley said, her pulse racing at the sound of green card.

"Lord missis, if me never have my pickney them, me would have my green card long time."

"Yes! How?"

"Lord missis, married one white man or so."

Shirley pulled up. "Me?"

Queeny laughed. "How you mean! Anyway, is joke me making." She continued more seriously: "Then you no can buy one green card, missis?"

"Buy!" Shirley repeated.

"Yes, man! Make me show you something." Queeny reached into her bag and pulled a fancy purse from it. She opened it to show about six credit cards. She reached into one of the transparent pockets and retrieved a laminated card with her picture on it. She handed it to Shirley.

"What this?" Shirley asked.

"You don' see?"

"Is a driver's license?"

"Five hundred dollars," Queeny said, pulling out a social security card from another pocket. "Same thing for this. Five hundred dollars. Me is citizen with them. Me can go anywhere and get any work me want. Get all credit card. Is just because me not getting no job to pay me the four hundred dollar a week, tax free, that me getting as nursing aid. That's why me stay. But me can do anything with them there. And is just five hundred a piece."

"Them look real."

"How you mean them look real? Them real. Is social security office mail that come give me. And I walk in and collect that in the driver's license place – like anybody else."

"But how?" Shirley asked bewildered.

"Lord, missis! How you mean how? You ever see any system that Jamaican can't beat?"

Chapter Twelve

"Go home nigger, I hate you. You better go home to Haiti where you belong."

"Whatever you say," Shirley said without emotion. "You'll still have to fix your clothes. Stay still." She drew her mouth close to Brad's ear. "Stay still or I'll pinch you so hard, you'll be as pink as a piece of pork."

The boy stood still.

Shirley finished tightening his belt and held the flesh near his navel. "Now sit quietly beside your sister."

"I'll call 911 on you." Brad looked her boldly in the eye. "I'll call the police if you pinch me."

"They can't get here before I break your neck."

He fell silent and sat on the bench beside the twin-stroller that held his siblings.

"And don't touch that stroller," Shirley warned sternly.

He sat down sullenly beside the baby carriage, then knelt on the bench to play with the plants in the wood-ringed garden behind them. She allowed him that.

They were sitting in the spectacular lobby of the Aventura Mall across from Mayors. In front and bearing left, a plethora of stores flowed along a wide hall toward Lord & Taylor; behind and to her right was the yawning passageway to the Macy's store where Nicole had gone half an hour ago. Shirley looked impatiently in front of her, past the pool in the middle of the lobby and the escalators of glass that veed to the levels above, beyond the various stalls and stands and through the throng of shoppers to see if she could see beyond to the entrance of the JC Penny where Queeny should be.

They had agreed that Shirley would either be sitting near the JC Penny or Macy's. They had met there before. This was where Nicole shopped.

Queeny knew this. But now she was late, and Shirley was anxious.

"Where are you going?"

"I'm just going to look at the fish." Brad opened his large blue eyes at her and searched for his most innocent tone.

Shirley watched him closely but did not stop him as he rose and made his way across the hall, through a few shoppers, to sit on the side of the artificial pond with its artificial waterfall. She knew that in another minute he would begin playing in the water. First he would watch, then he would lean nonchalantly as if looking closer, then his hands would creep along the sides and before one could realize, he would be trying to catch the fish. In another minute he would be wet from head to toe. And that would be the minute that fate would choose to let his mother appear from wherever in the mall she had lost herself. Such was Shirley's luck.

She looked at her watch again then checked the mall entrance. Where is Queeny? She sat back onto the bench beside the double pram and checked the twins. They were fast asleep. Shirley's face softened momentarily. She glanced sideways at Dennis the Menace, as Queeny called him, and instinctively checked that the brakes of the carriage were on. He sat innocently across the hall, his face serene, his hands in his lap, his attention glued to something in the shallow pond or on the glass elevator that moved up and down at its southern end. Shirley did not care what he looked at; she was not fooled, she had learnt never to take her eyes off him.

Where was Queeny?

For once she wished Nicole would shop the whole afternoon. She had a million chores back at the house and just by accompanying Nicole to the mall she would have lost at least four hours. But that did not matter.

All that mattered was that Queeny appeared right now. But she was late for the first time ever - today, when it was most important.

Shirley opened her bag and checked her purse for the umpteenth time. The money was in place. Eight months of her life was in that bag. Her whole future was in that bag and she was going to place it in

Queeny's hand.

And Queeny was late.

Maybe it was a sign. Maybe the man did not come. Maybe Queeny could not find him. Maybe there was no man, and Queeny was searching for any man to bring with her to lie to her and swindle her of her savings. Maybe it was all a lie and was not possible. Maybe, Shirley shook her head and rose nervously. Queeny would come. Queeny was her passport from this miserable life.

From the moment Shirley passed the documents carefully back to Queeny that afternoon, all thought of leaving her babysitting job left her head. Having actually touched them and been assured that it was possible to have them after a few short months of work, she decided to bite her lip and remain with Nicole just a little longer.

And Queeny had suddenly become her friend.

It was a relationship built on needs. First, the need for a green card. Then, after many days on the phone, it turned to something else – a refuge for two souls alone in America and up against the same system.

A week after they had met, Shirley swallowed her pride long enough to ask Queeny about her mysterious "systems man".

"Look, the boy looking me," Queeny had told her.

"You tell him you married?"

"Then that stop him?"

"Him can get for other people?" Shirley blurted quickly.

"Get what?" Queeny had asked.

"You know," Shirley felt a little tentative – a bit embarrassed. "You know, documents. For other people."

"You mean like you so?"

"Yes," Shirley said.

"That no nothing."

"Then how much it would cost?"

"Me will have to ask him, it depend on what you want."

"Him could get a green card?"

"Him can get anything. The last time me hear, a green card plus social security cost fifteen hundred in all. But I will ask him."

"So much?"

"Lord missis, that a nuff? Is something that going serve you for life. Plus how long it take you to work that?"

"Remember I have to pay rent. That would take me two years to save."

At the sound of rent, Queeny kissed her teeth and shouted across the line of the phone. "You stupid, eeeh, man. What you paying rent for? You have furniture?"

"No," Shirley replied.

"Then what you paying rent for? You caan' live in with Nicole?"

"They ask me but. . ."

"Them ask you but? Live in and give up the apartment."

"Then where I must put my things?"

"How much things you can have so? You don' say you no have no furniture."

"But mi have clothes."

"Is how much clothes that so? I will keep them for you, man. Bring them come."

"So you have an apartment?"

"Yes, me have a little place, yes. But me different - member me go and come, you know. And when me buy my things, me have to have somewhere to put them."

"You see, I don't want to put you out of your way."

"Lord, missis," Queeny said. "Bring the clothes, come and save you money. You no tired fi look after people pickney?"

So she moved into Coral Estates as a fulltime maid with only one weekend free each month. She took her things from Tiny's house and moved them into Queeny's tiny flat in Miami Gardens. Nicole surprised her and added twenty dollars to her salary. She was now earning two hundred and forty dollars per week. She continued to give Babs her twenty dollars per week until Queeny found out.

"Tell her say she must come fire you." Queeny demanded. "Ask her if is she doing the work."

When Shirley stopped sending the money Babs did not even ask about it.

"I don' know how you so damn fool." Queeny grumbled.

As time passed, Nicole piled on more chores. Shirley groaned and complained, but worked and saved. After a while she just bore the burdens with grunts and fierce whispers under her breath. She would be soon free of the slavery. Just a few months and she would have her green card and social security number.

She had hope now. She had a plan. It had taken her seven months to save the money.

Now today she would be placing it in the hands of a "system man" on Queeny's word. Shirley had insisted that Queeny bring the man with her. She wanted to see who she was giving her money to.

It was getting on to one-thirty. As a rule or by some invisible clock in her head, Nicole would never stay in a mall past two-thirty to three o'clock.

Shirley looked around her. She knew the mall by heart, knew every store on that level. Victoria's Secret was up the stairs and three doors down to her left. She could close here eyes and name every store – walk into each backwards. She remembered the first time she came there when the taxi driver dropped her at the front and she had money in her pocket. How she walked confidently into every store and bought what she wanted.

The mall was now a painful place to go to. The first few weeks living at Nicole's had almost driven her mad, and on weekends when she had the time off, she would come to the mall and walk around. Eight hours at a time. Eight hours at a time she would spend in these malls, walking around, aimlessly, till all the store clerks got to know her, and glared scornfully at her; for she would spend time in their stores examining garments she could not afford and never spend a dime. After a while, like everything else in her life, the mall had become a place she feared to return to. These days, she hardly entered the stores any more except to retrieve an unruly Brad or to bring the children for Nicole to try some garment on.

Where is Queeny?

She came bouncing around the corner through Lord & Taylor in a long Donna Karan skirt and silk shirt with oriental patterns. There was a large man beside her. They approached the bench and Queeny paused and ruffled Brad's head as he played in the water. "Dennis the Menace, you rass you. You don't stop give trouble." Brad shrank from her and pulled his hand quickly from the water.

She had a new hairstyle. Shirley did not care to imagine that she had stopped to braid her hair. She also seemed particularly bouncy and bright this morning, and Shirley did not want to imagine what caused that either.

"What happen?" she said, taking the seat next to Shirley.

"How you take so long?" Shirley inquired.

"What kind a long? No just one-thirty?"

"Yes, and we said twelve-thirty."

"Lord missis, how you so miserable? Nicole leaving Macy's for now?"

"Is not miserable. She shopping quickly today. Remember we going to West Palm Beach."

"Nicole can shop quick? Today onoo going Palm Beach?"

"Tomorrow morning," Shirley said.

"When onoo coming back?"

"We spending a week."

"You worry too much, man," Queeny laughed. She paused and looked up at the large man who stood casually in front of the bench. He wore a loose-fitting jumpsuit with one shoulder strap unbuttoned to fall across his waist revealing a large TOMMY written in red across the white T-shirt he wore underneath.

"Is Mikey this me telling you 'bout."

Shirley nodded and tried to sum him up. He smiled and sat next to her. "Wha' happen," he said.

"I am fine," Shirley said.

There was a short awkward silence as Shirley sat boxed in between them and the baby carriage in front of her.

"You have the money?" Queeny asked impatiently.

"Yes."

"Then give the man no?"

"But I have to talk to him first," Shirley said.

"Why you want to hurry the woman for?" Mikey reprimanded. "Make she take her time no."

"What kinda time to take?" Queeny rolled her eyes. "All you know, is that she give you her money and you bring her rass documents come. What kinda long argument in that?" Her tone was sharp and businesslike, Shirley had never seen her do business before.

The man rolled his eyes. "You can go on, eeh man?"

Shirley turned to him and looked him squarely. He was huge and swarthy with an assuring manner about him. She held her bag against her lap and caught his eyes dead on. "Listen, you can do it?"

"Yeah man. Who you think get you ugly friend own?"

"Ugly like you, ma," Queeny quipped.

"Yeah man," he said soberly to Shirley. "Is nothing. Queeny say you want a green card and a social."

"Yes."

"She tell you how much?"

"Fifteen hundred."

"Yeah man. You don't want a driver's license too?"

"I figured that once I got a green card and the social I could get that myself."

"Make sense."

"How long it going take?" Shirley said.

"About a week or two. The most three weeks."

"Look," Shirley said, forcing herself to hold his stare. "This is all I have. I worked seven months to save this. If you can't do it, tell me now."

"No man, is my hustling this, you know."

"But is everything I have," Shirley insisted, "Everything. Seven months."

"Yeah, man. Queeny tell me everything, man. Don' worry 'bout that. Me will take care of you man. Queeny threaten me enough."

"After him wouldn't rass mad no bring it come!" Queeny said, across them. "Him wouldn't rass mad. And you better bring it in two weeks too!" she snapped at Mikey.

He reached for the money. "You have the picture them?"

Shirley's hand jumped as the gold Rolex watch glistened on his hand. It gave her some comfort. The watch was worth ten times what she was giving him. He took the money along with her passport photographs and dropped them carelessly into the front pocket of his overalls.

"Me a go move, you know." He looked across at Queeny.

She gave him an odd smile.

"Later?" he asked.

"Awright," Queeny said.

If she were red she would blush, Shirley thought.

As Mikey left, Queeny leaned back against the bench and stretched. "Don't worry 'bout him, man. Him will bring it. Him dependable them way there."

"What kinda work him do?"

Queeny looked at her strangely. "Him is a juggler."

"Juggler! You mean him sell weed?"

"I don' know. Him juggle. I don't ask what him juggle. Is a Lexus him drive, you know."

"And wear Rolex watch."

"You know how much for that watch? I want hold two like that. That could add on a room on my house."

"So what him mean by later?"

"You too fast, man." Queeny pretended to look into the carriage at the sleeping twins, then yelled at Brad who had his hand in the water again. Shirley gave him a stern look and he finally settled away from the pool.

"You changing the subject, Queeny. But the way you talk to Mikey, if I didn't know better, I would think onoo have something going."

Queeny kissed her teeth. "So?"

"Don' tell me you gave him!" Shirley said in genuine disbelief.

Queeny kissed her teeth again. "Give him yes. And him can work! If me did know say him so good, I would give him long time."

"You slept with him!" Shirley was taken fully aback. For over the months the rebel had become her friend and she had come to respect her. Especially when she shared her dreams and spoke of her husband and children back home. Everything she earned, every insult she took, every breath she breathed seemed to be for them: her two children and the piece o' half-dead man she said she had in Jamaica. And now she was casually admitting that she had slept with someone else.

"So what happen to your husband?"

"So what happen to him?" Queen shrugged. "How me sure him not doing the same thing?"

"But that don't say you must do it. Plus you ever catch him yet?"

"Missis, who can catch a man when him want have other woman? Plus who business?"

"You are not serious!"

"How you mean, Shirley? You think him care? You think him ever ask me one day what I have to do to make money up here? All him do is send a different list every time him write me. And when me bring home all kinda clothes and things, you think him ask me how much them cost? Him just want to dress up and show off on him friends. Him don't care. If him did care, him wouldn't have me up here working in the first place.

Shirley refused to agree with her, though she sympathized. "It's not about him, it's about you. It's for you. What about your standards?"

"Is nearly a year now I don't do anything, you know, Shirley. You can take the nun life, but I not so good. Plus is him fault? Tell me, if you was a man, would you allow your wife to come up here and live like how me and you a live right now? Let your wife work with old people and clean them shit. Make people take all kind of advantage. And you, the man, not even know what you wife do, where she sleeping a night time, how far she have to go to take bus, how long she have to spend a bus stop, what she have to thief or how much law she break. Just a wait so; waiting till she bring home things to full him belly and give him clothes to wear. You would do that if you was a man? You tell me!

Shirley had no answer.

"Same thing!" Queeny almost shouted and straightened on the seat. "You can't talk. What kinda man that, Shirley? Is pimp that. Worse than dog to rahtid. And you want me to bother 'bout him! Him lucky! I could be up here selling myself on the street and him wouldn' care; wouldn' business. And when I reach home, him take the money same way, wear the clothes same way and as me walk in the house, him ready to jump on me before mi drop mi bag. Man like that a dog."

"But is your husband."

"Husband! Him lucky. Him have him friend them down there. But is me one up here. Me lonely, Shirley, man... me lonely."

Chapter Thirteen

Nothing could break Shirley's mood that evening. They returned from the store around three o'clock and she went to her chores with a lightness she had not felt since the day she was promoted to Junior Supervisor a lifetime ago at the bank in Jamaica. She approached every chore with diligence. She could see the end of them. Three weeks, he had said, the most three weeks. In three weeks she would have her green card, she would have a social security number – three weeks and then after that, no more twins to feed. Queeny had said that once Shirley got the documents, she could bounce it with her for the first month or so, till she got herself on her feet. So Shirley had nothing to worry about: after she got her papers she would hang around Nicole for another three weeks till she had set up some interviews and then no more picking up drawers.

She slammed the last drawer of the chest of drawers in Nicole's room, ran her rag against the surface till it shone, brushed the crevices where a little dirt may have been hidden. Shine now, shine now, three weeks, six the most. She reached for the vacuum cleaner and kicked the big red switch. It whirred to life. She vacuumed in wide straight swaths; the thick carpet changed color in the wake of the heavy cleaner. Brad bounded in behind a light white ball. She picked it up and tossed it back to him. Enjoy yourself, "Don't wake up the babies," she warned pleasantly. Even he looked nice today.

She stopped the vacuum cleaner and bounded to the kitchen where steam whistled from a pot on the stove, turned the knob to low and dropped the lid onto it. She flipped the oven open to check the chicken; it was on the brown. On her way back she detoured through the washroom to check the washing machine; it was tumbling. The dryer was going full strength. Shirley did a quick check to make sure the remaining wash loads were sequentially lined up. Suddenly, the dryer stopped. She reached in, checked the clothes, removed them and dropped them into an empty basket, reloaded and set to permanent press. The dryer whirred to life. The washer shook and rumbled to its final cycle; she reloaded, then headed back toward the master bedroom and the vacuuming.

She heard the sound of falling water: Nicole was in the showers again. Instinctively she walked into the bathroom to retrieve the used garments that lay on the floor in front of the frosted shower doors. The water stopped.

"Could you bring me a fresh towel and robe, Shirley? I forgot."

"OK," Shirley said. She went to the chest of drawers and returned with a towel, a terry-cloth robe and fresh underwear. She laid them on the small stool near the shower and trotted quickly out to drop the dirty clothing in the washing.

The vacuum roared as she returned to press its big red button. She had all in control, her mood was good, she knew how many minutes were left in the kitchen, how long before the washer and dryers would be ready for the next load. She knew what time the twins would awaken and be ready for feeding.

The outside door slammed. Tom was home. Dinner would be served in forty-five minutes. Shirley finished his bedroom as he entered. He gave a quick hello. She moved from room to room, checking, cleaning, dusting, vacuuming, making sure all was in order. Then she was in the kitchen again, setting all knobs to off. "Any dirty clothing, Mr. Williamson?"

"As a matter of fact, yes. How come you are washing at this time of day, Shirley?"

"We went to the mall, sir." She did not wait for an answer; she was on the move, everything was by the clock, she had things to do. His underwear, his pants, his socks: plop, plop, plop into the bundle. The washer stopped. She removed the clothing. Another bundle was ready for the dryer. It still had another half-an-hour to go. She reloaded the washer, just as the first cry came from the twins' bedroom.

Non-stop, Shirley, non-stop. But that's OK, three weeks more. Just three weeks and then maybe another three.

Baby feeding time. She reached into cupboards. She knew precise measurements. Warm boiled water was ready, feeding made in ten minutes, twins, baths drawn, twin sets of fresh clothing lying on twin beds. Non-stop Shirley, non-stop. Just three weeks more. "Come baby Christopher, come Christine, water warm enough now. Just lie still, let me change you."

Babies dry and clean, powdered and oiled. Now feeding: first Christine – she was the crier. Shirley put the bottle in her mouth and sat rocking Christopher in his rocker. He lay and stared up at her, his face clean and scrubbed. Powder showed in the wrinkles of his neck; he kicked and gurgled. I'll miss you, but life's like that; three weeks and then three more, and then you're on your own.

Babies fed and resting, she headed back to the washroom. The washer and dryer had stopped. She reloaded them quickly and pushed the switches. The machines whirred to life.

"Shirley, we would like to eat now if we can."

"In a minute, Nicole."

Now she had to change. Now she had to at least change into something clean in which to serve the food. She took a quick shower. White T-shirt and jeans skirt would do. She picked the twins up on the way, brought them to the table and placed them in their high chairs. Tom and Nicole moved from the sitting room with their wine. The chicken was tender and ready, the rice was neat, the vegetables were perfect and the salad was fresh and juicy.

"Will you eat with us tonight, Shirley?" Tom was cordial, his smile genuine. There was a time when she did – eat with them, that is. Those were the days when Tom cooked. When he took the garbage out every night, when he washed his own clothes. Those were the days when they had competed and cooked alternate days; when they complimented each other on the various dishes, before his wife accused him of fraternizing with the help. Before she ordered him to leave his clothing on the floor and leave the garbage in the kitchen.

Of course the invitation was never withdrawn and she could eat with the family as she wished, but eating took time, and she had none of that. The washing was going, the dirty dishes would be piling up. The garbage was already high. There was ironing to do. Brad would have to be bathed as soon as he finished eating. The twins would have to be put back to bed. "Not tonight," Shirley said. Shirley will not eat with you tonight. Three weeks, just three weeks more and maybe another three.

It was eleven o'clock before she entered her room again. She went straight to the shower to wash the last of the garbage from herself – the knot had not been tight on the bag, her hands had been tired. She bathed quickly, returned to her bedroom and began to walk around confused for a minute; she was not sure if she had eaten.

She turned on the TV. She would not watch it for long, but she needed it. She was so tired, she knew she would not fall asleep unless she watched it for a while.

She found her favorite black comedy show.

She paused to look, then turned toward the drawer. She needed to pack. But a handsome black man was the comedian for the night. He had on a white suit and a black hat. She watched him for a minute then turned away. But whatever he was saying had the audience in an uproar. She turned to watch him for a minute as he spoke.

. . . . . Say a white man is sick, he don' care where the medicine is, he go' get it. He don' care what it look like, or how much it cost'. He go get it.

Now say a black man is sick. You bring him a bottle of aspirin. He won' take the aspirin - he won' touch the cotton at the mouth of the bottle. (Laughter).

He won' touch the cotton but he will take the white tablet. (The crowd roar). Black man particular 'bout two special things. He won' touch cotton, an' don't call him nigger.

What's with them names? People be calling you Afro-American and be still meaning nigger.

But black folks don' care. White man can do what he want, discriminate as he want, put him in the back of the bus, move out of the city and leave skeleton buildings and no industry and shit. He don' care, just don't call him nigger. You think them white people stupid?

They on to us.

He call you Afro-American on one hand, while on the other hand you still his slave.

He remove the cotton, and give us his pills... shit.

The crowd cheered, loudly, Shirley slammed the TV switch to off and fell tiredly across the bed.

Thee weeks, and then maybe three weeks more.

Chapter Fourteen

In spite of everything, Shirley loved the twins.

When she came to Coral Estates, they were barely two months old and they had taken to her as lost calves would take to the first warm body they found. She knew everything about them: what brand food they ate, when their next vaccinations were due; she could differentiate their voices from a distance, knew which cry meant they were hungry, which told they were messy, and which were for the hell of it. There was no questioning their parents' love for them, for many times Shirley would drop by their cribs unexpectedly and see Tom, when he had the time, staring down at them with moist eyes, or Nicole on break from her shopping would, when she was in the mood, stop by the playpen and play with them a bit.

But it was Shirley that they knew and cried after. The first words they uttered were to her; the first distance they crawled was to get to her lap. And many times when she felt like leaving, it was they who made her stay in the miserable job, because somewhere in the back of her mind she felt they needed her. Few pleasures could surpass the days when she would lie in the playpen while they crawled around and over her, using her body as a drum and their toys as drumsticks, or when she would chase them on her hands and knees around the den.

Now they were having their first birthday – a massive affair. Friends and relatives were invited from all over the country. Nicole's parents were coming in from Georgia, her sisters and brothers were expected from West Palm Beach. Everyone who was anyone to the family would be there.

The importance of the occasion was driven home to Shirley when Tom summoned her to a meeting in his office. It was Friday evening, and the house had quieted down. Brad was in his room on his Nintendo machine, the twins were sleeping and Nicole had just stepped out for the hairdresser.

She had come to like Tom. He did not talk much, but he was fair and she respected him. Those days when she and Nicole would have their differences, he never took sides, but allowed them to work out their issues. He never spoke down to her, was never afraid of holding the most sophisticated conversations with her.

"Am I being fired?" she joked.

"Why would you ask that?" He sounded bewildered as he turned from his computer and offered her the large leather chair that faced his desk.

"Well, this is my first meeting in your office."

"No. Heavens, no." He reached across his desk for a small envelope she knew held her salary. His movements were careful though he was not a hesitant man. "Is this your weekend off?" he asked, playing with the envelope.

She laughed. "In this house there is no time off!"

He did his mysterious arcing of eyebrows and smiled.

"Would you like to have the weekend off?"

Had it been Nicole standing there, she would have felt that there was some ploy to manipulate her free weekend. But she had never had problems being honest to Tom. "This weekend," she said, feeling his careful stare on her, "is the twins' birthday. I can't miss their party."

He let her words fall between them and held her stare gently without speaking so she would know that those very words were the reason for his suggestions. Shirley sat in the measured silence till she felt it change as she gradually realized what the meeting was all about. He is trying to tell me I am not invited. So now he had given her this small silence, relying on her intelligence and imagination to conclude the obvious and spare his tongue the difficult words.

"Are you trying to tell me I am not invited to the party?"

"No, you are. You would be."

"Then what are you saying?"

"I'm asking if you would wish to take the weekend off."

"I see," Shirley said. "The special guests are coming, so there is no place for the hired help. The low- class people."

She saw him let that slip by and knew she should watch her tongue. He was on her side but he was fair. He would do whatever was necessary to keep peace in his household and would not hesitate if that required firing her on the spot. As she watched him pause and try to line up his words, Shirley realized he was as much a victim of the situation as she was, complying with the wishes of his wife. He was just the messenger.

"You are welcome to stay if you wish, but knowing the circumstances, I thought I would ask you."

"But why?" she said, half because she was angry and half because she knew she had nowhere to go.

He leaned back into his chair and tapped its arm with the envelope. "Why would you want to be caught in a houseful of red-necks for a whole weekend?"

So they wanted her out of the house for the weekend and the bitch Nicole did not have the guts to tell her.

"I wanted to tell you myself," he said as if he read her thoughts. "I think it would be better than having you sleep on a couch somewhere. You deserve more than that."

"So it boils down to a matter of space."

His smile was patient. He would not be drawn into making explanations of that sort. His intentions were to say as much as he could without spelling out the words – to lead her to conclusions and be able to deny the responsibility. He could do no better; that was how he was trained. Shirley understood everything then; she could see Nicole insisting that her relatives needed to use her room and that she had to sleep in the den somewhere or on a couch. And she could see him trying to say it was not fair, that her family could afford to stay in a nearby hotel. And she could see Nicole insisting that she wanted her family around her, in the same stubborn way she insisted she wanted the babies with her at the mall. And she could now see him struggling with his conscience, trying to find a decent way to cross his wife. And now he was relying on Shirley's feistiness and pride to help him, so they could pull it off together.

"Who would take care of the twins?" she asked.

He sighed. "We are the parents. I'm sure we could swing that for a couple days. Grandparents will be here, aunts and uncles. . ." His guard wavered. He almost sounded disgusted.

"So it's a matter of sleeping arrangements?" she mused aloud.

"Yes," he said quietly, painfully. "You do have somewhere to go?"

Thanks for your concern. "Sure. When do you want me to leave?"

"There's no rush."

"Is first thing in the morning OK?"

"First thing in the morning would be fine."

He handed her the money. It felt heavier than usual. She reached inside and found that there were six hundred dollars inside. Her salary should have been two hundred and forty.

She watched him read the question in her eyes. "Do something nice, on me," he said softly. "You deserve it."

Queeny did not answer her phone all night, and she was not at work, and next morning when Shirley packed a small overnight bag and slipped from Coral Estates, her phone still rang without an answer.

While she lived in Jamaica, Shirley would look forward to the weekend. She was never short of things to do or places to go. On any given weekend there would be so many invitations to go out that if she wanted quiet time, she would have to take her phone off the hook. Often times she would sift through the several possibilities, discard each as unappealing, then call Dawn and complain how bored she was.

Now she would pay a million dollars or the six hundred in her purse just to hear a phone ring and someone call her name or a voice speak to her – even to say it was a wrong number; for someone to regard her in the street and tell her good morning; a friend to worry where she went or if she would like to go out somewhere, care that she had a weekend – a precious forty-eight hours to share. The occasion need not be a special one. She did not have to be the centre of attraction; the background would be fine. Any assurance, any reminder that she existed, meant something to somebody would do.

Usually on her days off, Queeny would come and they would go to the park or if Shirley was really in the mood, they would check out one of the several Jamaican nightclubs. But the clubs Queeny frequented did not have the kind of crowd that appealed to Shirley; she felt there was too much loud sparkling clothing and studded gold teeth on show. After the first man groped her on the way to the bathroom, Shirley gave up on Queeny's clubs.

She took two buses and arrived at the Skylake Mall in North Miami and waited the remaining minutes for the dollar theatre to open at ten o'clock. She had discovered the nest of theatres some time ago that showed movies from anywhere between two months to twenty years old. She could see two-month-old movies for a dollar and if she timed it right, she could fill her day for just six dollars.

She was first in line.

She found a seat left of centre and sat down for the double bill. Later she would move to another auditorium for another double bill. She would call Queeny around four.

Sitting there alone in the dark theatre, her mind returned to Jamaica and to her mother and the old house on the hill; half wood and half concrete. She wondered how the house was. She remembered how she had planned that as soon as she left high school and got a job, she would fix up the old kitchen and veranda to look like something. But once she began working in a bank, she had spent most of her money on clothes and buying furniture on lay-away so she could get out as fast as she could.

She remembered her mother's every gesture, her every nod, her every movement or sigh; every crease in her face, every strand of hair that would come loose and fall against her forehead; the sarcasm in her voice when she called her Miss Princess and her room the palace; how she picked up her dirty clothing and washed it every day; cleaned her room when she had gone to work . . . till the day she, Shirley, shut her out.

In the year-or-so since she had been in America, she had written her mother only four letters. Each time though, she had enclosed twenty or thirty dollars. She knew that even with the Jamaican exchange rate the money would not be much, but Shirley had mentioned that she was in school and did not have much money. Her mother's responses were painful ones that showed no hint of conviction; just bland careful phrasings that had no impetus or energy of their own. Shirley realized that if she did not write first, her mother would not write to her at all. Writing became more difficult for Shirley, for not only did she have to lie in every letter she wrote but she felt that, in a strange way, she was only writing to herself.

So the words for the page dried up; just like the conversations did so long ago in Jamaica.

Sitting there in the darkness, Shirley wondered for the first time if she would ever see her mother again and if she did, if they would ever return to those days when she could look her in her eyes.

She heard a scream and looked up, surprised to see that a movie was in progress. It was Pretty Woman, with Julia Roberts and Richard Gere; a movie she had seen several times before and loved. It was already one third through. Is it the first movie? Is it the second? Did I fall asleep? Is it happening again, did time disappear on me again? She panicked slightly and pressed the luminous dial on her watch. It was still Saturday and only ten forty-five. Less than an hour had disappeared this time. Lord, how long would this continue? Another week! Another week, and then maybe three more?

Shirley left the theatre around five-thirty and headed for the phone booth to call Queeny. The phone rang for a long minute then went to the answering machine. Shirley did not leave a message but decided to call again in a few minutes. Queeny would normally be at home at this time unless she had gone shopping or something like that; Shirley wondered where she might be.

A large bus stopped a few meters away and filled the air with plumes of smoke. As Shirley stood waiting for it to leave with its growling engine, she noticed on the side the picture of a pristine and magnificent view of the Miami coastline and the wonderful towers that lined it. The advertisement said: The Miami Grand, one way to see Miami and the Beaches. She wondered what could be so grand about the Miami Grand Hotel.

As the bus drove off she had an idea. She craned her neck so she could memorize the telephone number on the departing bus. Then she returned to the booth and dialed it.

The operator answered. "Miami Grand. How may I help you?"

"I'm interested in seeing Miami from your hotel," Shirley said instinctively.

"Yes, ma'am. And what sort of room would you be needing?"

"Something that looks out on the ocean, on Miami Beach and then the city."

"And when would you be joining us, and for how long?"

Shirley hesitated, she did not even understand why she was in the middle of this call. Then she decided to take the joke a little further. "What are the rates on the rooms?" she asked.

"Well, a room such as that would start at one seventy-five," the voice said.

"One hundred and seventy-five dollars for a room?" Shirley asked.

"Yes, ma'am."

"And I'd see Miami and the beaches?"

"Would you like to make a reservation, ma'am?"

One hundred and seventy-five dollars for a night – one hundred and seventy-five. She remembered the evening in the Pegasus with Mark. She thought of the extra three hundred and sixty dollars Tom had given her. Pay-off money. Do something nice, he said.

"Hello, ma'am, are you there?" The clerk was urgent on the phone.

"Yes," said Shirley.

"Do you want to make a reservation?"

"Yes," said Shirley.

"How long would you be staying?"

"Just one night."

"May I have your name please?"

"Shirley Temple Brown."

"Pardon?"

"Shirley Temple Brown. You promised me a great view."

"Certainly, ma'am."

"And your room service is good - I can get a good steak?"

"But certainly, this is the Miami Grand."

"Book me," she said. "Book me, please."

Shirley did not give herself time to second guess what she was about to do. She hung up the phone, and hailed the first taxi she saw. "The Miami Grand Hotel," she said. She closed her eyes and blocked every scene from her mind except the one of Julia Roberts, in Pretty Woman, walking across the hall of the Regent Beverly Wiltshire. When she entered the hotel, she already knew what she would do. She paid the bill in advance at the counter, laid the rest of the three hundred and sixty dollars on the table of her room. She soaked for two hours in a tub of perfumed soap suds. Then she ordered the largest steak room service could find, and a bottle of the best Champagne her change could afford. She told the busboy he should take whatever was left as his tip. Then she pulled a chair to the patio, sat with her feet on the rail in the white robe of the Miami Grand, ate well and got drunk above the pristine sparkling view of Miami and the beaches.

Shirley returned to Coral Estates just before nightfall on Sunday. It was a fine Miami evening. Halfway through fall, the hurricane season was on its way out and its last hurrah of showers left whatever shrubbery there was, green and lush. And the well-kept Coral Estates golf course was especially beautiful that evening with the sun going down, slipping into the edge of the mauve sky, giving the grass a dark blue hue. It was a cool evening too and her long walk from the main gate to the house had barely caused perspiration.

There were still two extra cars in the driveway. She passed around toward the back of the house to use the pool entrance in order to avoid the remnant of the weekend's gathering, and by doing so walked right into it. A group was gathered around the pool. Tables were out with drinks and snacks on them. Low music floated on the evening. Brad and two other children were playing in the pool with a large old man with grey hair plastered across his face. Shirley immediately recognized him as Nicole's father. Both Nicole and Tom were seated in conversation with a younger woman. An elegant older lady she assumed to be Nicole's mother, was sampling food from the laden table. It was she who saw Shirley first.

They both stared at each other across the space. Shirley paused, wishing she had not turned the corner so suddenly. The woman froze, the morsel halfway to her mouth.

Tom noticed and turned quickly. "Oh, Shirley," he shouted. He seemed to be a little drunk. "Why are you standing there? Come on up."

Shirley passed through the small gate onto the pool deck and nodded as she was introduced to Nicole's parents and sister. Nicole's mother had a warm look about her. She reached out and took Shirley's hand with a quick-release handshake; bunching her fingers and withdrawing them against Shirley's palm as if wiping them there.

"And this is my sister, Elizabeth." Elizabeth was an older version of Nicole. She raised her glass to Shirley. "Nicole tells me what great work you are doing with the kids."

"I try my best," Shirley said. "Thanks."

"Those are my two." She nodded toward the two children in the pool with Brad. They seemed to be between eight and ten years old.

"Have something to eat," Tom said. "You must be hungry."

"Tired is more like it," Shirley sighed. "Thanks, but I think I'll go and lie down a bit."

"We made a mess in your room," Elizabeth said sheepishly.

"No problem," Shirley said, "I have seen messes before."

"Just push whatever is on the bed aside," Elizabeth took a sip. "We'll be out of here in another hour or two."

Nicole made a smart remark and Elizabeth made a face, but Shirley was already on her way out of there, heading through the sliding glass door into the house. She walked quickly up the stairs wondering what kind of mess Elizabeth may have been referring to. Then she entered the room. From the evidence of clothing and toys lying around, the woman must have shared it with her two children. It was not as bad as Elizabeth had made it sound.

Shirley dropped her bag atop the dresser, where she noticed her things had been carefully pushed to one side. She moved the clothing on the bed and stretched out on her stomach.

Then she froze.

Just as she was about to close her eyes, she caught sight of what seemed to be a piece of lace-trimmed silk protruding from beneath the long curtains at the window across the room. The patterns seemed familiar. She was sure she had garments with the same cobweb patterns; garments she knew would have no business being out of the dresser – on the floor.

The dresser had four levels of drawers. The top tier was split in two, the other three went the whole width. She knew the bottom drawer was locked because she kept her passport and important documents and jewelry there. The top drawers held mostly papers and everyday wear, jewelry and cosmetics. In the middle drawer she kept her most private garments, while the second to bottom was stuffed with skirts and blouses and general clothing. She flung the drawers open. The garments in the second drawer up were unfamiliar to her. The drawer above also was overfull and could hold nothing more. She turned slowly toward the curtains with a scream of disbelief, flung them aside. Someone had dumped the contents of her drawer – her most private things – across the room. They had tried to stuff them into a large Macy's bag but the bag had broken. In any event, it was much too small and her things filled the corner and lay along the wall.

She stood there silent for a moment, feeling shame she had never felt before as the images blurred through the tears in her eyes: every over-washed and worn-out piece of underwear – private intimate satin, delicate silk; scrubbed too often, bleached, soaped and sunned – faded, made bland, by her wanting year.

Someone had heard her scream; she looked around. Tom filled the doorway. "Shirley," he said. And then he walked through her silence, pulled the curtain aside and drew away a blushing pink. "Jesus." She sensed his eyes on her but she felt too naked to meet them and stayed huddled against the bed.

"Nicole!" he shouted. But she was already passing through the door with her sister.

"What's the shouting for?" she asked.

"Over there," he said with disgust. "There, behind the curtain. Go and look, it won't hurt you."

Nicole pulled away the curtain. Then gave a sigh of relief. "You frightened me, I thought there was something wrong."

"You see nothing wrong?" Tom asked.

"Well," she raised her hand, "I told them to put them aside. They could have done a better job of it. Elizabeth, you could have. . ."

"It was the children," Elizabeth offered lamely. "The bag broke."

"You did what?" Tom gasped at Nicole. "You told them to throw her things aside like that?"

"Not like that! To put them away. They needed space. Where should they put their stuff?"

"I'm sorry," Elizabeth offered. "I take the blame for this. I should have paid a little more attention."

"Shirley deserves an apology," Tom said.

"She did say she was sorry, Tom."

Then the silence came. And Shirley felt the weight of it as three pairs of eyes focused on her.

"She said she was sorry, Shirley," Nicole offered.

"It was the kids," Elizabeth repeated. "It's my fault, I should have supervised them."

"No," Shirley whispered hoarsely. "It's not your fault, it's mine. It's my fault - I'll take care of it."

"See how easy that is?" Nicole turned toward the door. Her sister followed her.

"Come along, Tom." Nicole pulled her husband's shoulders. "Shirley needs her privacy. She is tired."

"I wish you would not do that," Tom said disgustedly.

Shirley smiled sadly to herself as she heard Tom's annoyance; it was the angriest she had ever seen him. I wish I had the courage now to see the defiance in your eyes, my Richard Channing. But she could not raise her head before the room was empty.

She needed to pack. She pulled the drawers fully open, then she reached under the bed for her large suitcase and began to place her worn and tattered belongings into it.

After an hour of packing, she reached for the phone.

This time Queeny was in. "Wha' happen?" she said. "You try call me? Me see the machine light up but no message no leave 'pon it."

"You said if I ever needed to, I could come."

"What happen to you? How you sound so? What them dirty people them do you now?"

"You said I could come," Shirley insisted. She felt the tears welling up. She did not want to break down now.

"Cry you a cry? What them do you?"

"I can't talk about it... can't talk over the phone."

"You want me call Mikey? Make him come pick you up? Him in town. Make him come in him Lexus, make them know you a somebody too."

"Can I come?"

"Come, yes. How you mean? Pack up you things them. Come! Lef them rass people, and come."

"Thanks." Shirley hung up, reached into her purse and found an old and faded card, then began to dial for her taxi.

The exclamations, the questions, the shouts did not reach her as she dragged her suitcase through the pool house and the party, across the lawn to drop it at the foot of the taxi. She told the driver to follow her inside for the other bag and no one dared object that she was inviting a strange man into the house. When she entered the taxi, Nicole held its door and shouted at her, demanded that she not go: she was being ungrateful, forgetting all that had been done for her, forgetting the risks Nicole had taken to employ her without a green card. Shirley did not respond. She sat stonily, looking ahead without a word. She did not tell the driver to drive nor Nicole to close the door - did not respond to her shouts, to her cursing and pleading: what would she do now; who would take care of the twins; how could she take care of her children alone?

But Shirley did not respond. She was like a camper in the wilderness whose light had suddenly gone out, whose eyes were forced to grow accustomed to the darkness. Now, for the first time, she saw everything in a different light and each image was grey and indistinguishable from the one next to it. She could not see their faces: not Nicole hanging on to the door, nor Tom pulling her from the car to close it, nor Nicole's mother off to the side, astounded that her daughter was making a fool of herself over a maid, a black one at that; could not see Brad standing by the pool with two little girls dripping beside him. There were no people there. Her light had been put out and as she readjusted to the darkness, all she saw around her were forms, tilting and shifting like shadows... And she was a stranger there, who had lost her light, lost her means to distinguish, make sense of, trust, regard or care about those grey dancing images in the dark.

Chapter Fifteen

Queeny pulled her robe around her and brushed the loose weave from her hair. In the bathroom mirror she could see the bond-in was showing. The last time the stupid girl in the mall would do her hair. She would return to Razzmatazz. The wait was long but the work was good.

Queeny splashed water across her face and walked past the sleeping Shirley into the kitchen to place the kettle on the stove. She then sat on the small stool, looked across the counter at the crumpled form in the sofa bed and shook her head sadly.

What could the dirty Nicole have done to hurt her so; and still call back day after day apologizing, leaving countless messages on the answering machine. Shirley, I'm sorry, I'm so sorry. We will go to the store and buy back everything. Tom will buy back everything. Elizabeth apologized. The children miss you, Shirley. They cry all the time, I don't know what to do with them. What should I do with three children?

What could they have done to her?

This was not the woman she had met in the mall, chasing after the pram. Yes, she had fallen in the mall; yes, she had been humiliated, but Queeny could still remember how proud she was, hair so black and long, complexion half white like them Cuban, proud nose neat and up in the air, shape like them model with a little meat on her - beautiful and strong. So proud in fact that she, Queeny, had wanted America to teach her a lesson – to humble her. For it was obvious that she was not on any leave, and that she was desperate and could not return to Jamaica, for whatever reason it was. Yet even though she could not, she still walked with a haughtiness and pride that said she could turn her back on America at any time. So she had wanted America to teach her a lesson. But the more Queeny came to know her, the more she found herself respecting that dignified look and that bold exterior – realizing how strong Shirley must be, to keep on being so proud.

So they must have really hurt her bad.

Shirley came to the apartment that Sunday evening, her eyes red and her face puffy; so disoriented she could not even find her purse to pay the taxi, though it was right there in the bag that hung from her shoulders. It was Queeny who paid the fare. When she entered the house Shirley was curled into a corner of the large sofa without saying a word. It was as if she could not speak or cry – as if something inside had locked her throat.

That first night Queeny was so touched, she offered Shirley her own bed to sleep in. But she insisted on staying on the couch. So Queeny helped her unfold the sofa bed and tucked her under the covers as she would a sick woman whose illness limited her mobility.

She left her to go to work and returned twelve hours later to find her in the same position on the sofa bed. For the first couple of days, Queeny was unable to determine whether Shirley had moved, eaten or even performed the basic human functions. During that time, half the messages on her answering machine had been from Nicole. Yet there was never any evidence that Shirley had attempted to answer them.

Now it was almost a week and Queeny figured that enough time had passed for whatever cut inside Shirley to heal. She knew that a sore left unattended would take its own course. And if Shirley did not move she would probably fall into some coma or something.

True, something had happened to crush the pride in her but this was America and Shirley would not be the first or the last to touch rock bottom. And sleeping at the bottom was no way to leave it. It's OK to gather strength there, but the way to the top requires climbing, and climbing requires standing, and standing means one has to move.

The kettle whistled. Queeny reached into the cupboard for a stem of mint and dropped it into the hot water, then left it there whistling while she retrieved two cups from the cupboard and placed them on the counter. She gave the mint a few more minutes to brew then prepared two cups.

"Shirley."

Shirley did not answer. Queeny watched her for a minute then called her again. She did not answer. But Queeny saw her eyelids relax, then tighten, then relax again. She was awake and pretending.

"Come, Shirley, I have some mint tea."

Shirley did not budge.

Queeny took the cup of tea into the living room and pulled the love seat closer to the edge of the bed near Shirley's head. She then placed the tea on the floor near her nose. The steam took the fresh scent of mint right into her nostrils. "Me know you not sleeping. You wake long time. Get up and drink the little tea."

Shirley turned and rubbed her eyes. "I'm fine, I'll be fine."

"Drink the tea, Shirley, and stop go on so. Drink the tea. You think you can lie down here every day?"

Shirley opened her eyes and brushed a few strands of hair from around her mouth, then rose halfway on her elbows and looked around the room. "What time is it?"

"It matter what time? Is Saturday morning. Over a week now. Drink the tea."

"Mikey come yet?"

But Queeny would not fall for that. It had happened before. She had tried to wake Shirley and her reference to Mikey had made Queeny feel a bit guilty because they had not heard from Mikey in three weeks. Shirley had skillfully used it to stump her twice, but she was ready for her this time.

"When him come, him come."

"Is nearly a month now."

"Shirley, drink the tea!"

Shirley leaned over, picked up the cup and reclined against the back of the sofa bed. Then she lifted her knees to her chest and blew into the cup to cool its contents before taking a short sip. "Thanks."

"You right to thank me. How you can sleep so? You not answering the ugly gal, Nicole?"

Shirley's stare went hard and dead; this was to tell Queeny that the subject led to a precipice.

But Queeny was tired of the silence. "Well, I don' wrong you, missis," she said, "I don't wrong you at all, leave them rass. I wouldn't lose sleep over dirty people like that."

"Queeny, forget it."

"Them people there only wan' use people. You help them out and them think you a slave."

"Queeny!"

"Don' have no respect for nobody, you have no privacy, no nothing."

"Queeny, it's my business!" Shirley screamed. Her hand was so tight against the handle of the cup, it trembled and spilled hot tea onto her leg. "I said it's my business."

Queeny placed her cup on the floor. "Is not your business alone, you know, is my business too, because you live in my house."

"I'm sorry for the inconvenience," Shirley sighed. "As soon as I get my papers I'll leave."

Queeny looked up at her and felt her temper boil. "You know you not a nice person. You not a nice person." She rose to walk to the kitchen.

"I'm sorry," Shirley said. " You are only trying to be kind."

Queeny paused and turned to Shirley. "I not trying anything, you know. My mother never raise me to go on like me better than people. I am not trying anything. If something there to do, I just do it, I don't have to try to be kind."

"That's not what I meant."

"Well, what you mean? Talk what you want to say. Talk what you really want to say. Me and mi man take you money and fuck it out. Talk what you want to say."

"You know," Shirley said, placing the cup beside her, "I think we should forget this conversation. You are taking this way out of context and I am not in the mood for it." The cup on the floor, she curled up and pulled the sheets over her head.

Queeny shook her head sadly. "Yes! Cover up you head, you must think is so life go. You must think you can just forget it and cover up and hide. Cover up you head!" She walked toward the kitchen. "Must think is so parson get him gown."

Shirley snapped the covers from her face and sat rigidly on the sofa bed. "Don't you ever try to do that," she said. "You don't try to analyze me, OK? I know I am at your place, because I can't do better. But it was you who invited me here. OK. I was rude, I apologize, but don't you analyze me, because you are not qualified to do that."

"You don' have no more education than me." Queeny walked back over to her. "So don't come in here with that! You no have more education than me. You think you better than me? We come from same place. And where I come from better than where you come from. Is pure dutty nigger and thief and gunman come from Sufferer's Heights. So don't bother try that in here – with you stoosh self a go on like you better than people."

"Awe God," Shirley sighed. "Awe God."

Queeny hated when Shirley did that; rolled her eyes as if she Queeny was so stupid she could not understand the most basic things. "You know what?" she said. "You know what? I tell you what." She walked into her bedroom and reached on top of the closet into a stack of shoe boxes, took down a large wad of bills and waded back into the living room, counting as she went. "See you money here, see you money yah." She began to throw the bills onto the bed as she counted them. "See you money here. Take you money, take you things, and go on where you want to go. All right? And see interest and taxi fare here too. Take you things when you ready and go on. Miss Criss. Miss Show-off. Miss Better-than-people. Go on 'bout you business." She stormed to the bedroom, slammed the door and sat puffing on the bed.

Ten or fifteen minutes later, when Shirley knocked on the door, Queeny was already crying. Things had gotten so much bigger than she had imagined. She felt helpless and confused, and angry on top of it. "It open," she said as Shirley knocked softly again.

Queeny heard her enter but did not look up because she was afraid of breaking into sobs. She sat so that she could only see Shirley sideways through the corner of her eyes.

Shirley walked over to her and stood near the end of the bed. "I'm really sorry, Queeny. It is just that I was taking things out on you. I'm sorry."

"Shirley man, you mustn't say them things," Queeny began to sob. "You mustn't talk so. You make me vex, Shirley."

"I know," Shirley said. "If you want me to leave, I'll leave."

"Then Shirley, you think I really could make you walk out of the house and know you don't have anywhere to go man? You think I could really run you out? You mustn't say them things there, Shirley!"

She heard Shirley move and looked up to see her collapsing at the foot of the bed, falling against the wall. Her hand was on her head and she was clenching the money in her fists. Her eyes were tightly closed and the tears were spurting from between the long eyelashes. "I can't take it," she cried, "I can't take it no more! You think it's easy, Queeny? It's very hard. I just don't think I can take any more."

Chapter Sixteen

That Sunday, Shirley stirred. It may have been the fight or maybe all she needed was to have had a good cry; whatever the reason, instead of sleeping in that Sunday, she woke early, folded the sofa-bed into place, tidied the living room and watched TV. The next day she washed her dirty clothes and watched TV.

Tuesday she cooked.

The mood became lighter around the apartment. Her relationship with Queeny slowly returned to the point where at nights they would sit and watch TV, and make jokes about Nicole and Brad the brat. But she was never able to go into the reasons why had she left and Queeny seemed to respect that. Another piece of great news also came that Sunday. Mikey called to say he would be picking up her documents and she would have them in her hands by Wednesday at the latest.

Wednesday came and went and they did not hear from Mikey, but she did not worry about it. He had mentioned that he would be stopping in New Orleans or some place like that. Plus Queeny had won her trust and by extension she believed that Mikey would bring the documents later that week.

Thursday night Queeny came home with the news that the nurse who worked nights with Grace, the old lady in her care, was taking two weeks off to go to Jamaica. Shirley could have the job if she wanted. It paid nearly four hundred dollars per week.

Shirley hesitated for a while; she had no intention of going through a little babysitting again.

But Queeny said the work was easy. "Just give her the medicine and put her to bed. Talk to her sometimes if she feel like talking – and watch her, that's all."

Shirley remembered how quickly the little babysitting at Nichole's had turned to something else. Every job seems easy when it is being sold; but doing it is another thing.

"I do it every day, I mus' know," said Queeny, "and if you have any problem, just call me.

Just make sure she have her medicine on time; eight o'clock in the evenings and six o'clock in the mornings – And look out for her sleepwalking - every now and then she do that."

"That's all?" Shirley asked.

"That is it," Queeny assured her. "All you doing is keeping an eye on a little old lady. I will get there by eight and take over. Carry a book with you if you want, it get boring sometimes, and she don't have cable. She hardly watch TV anyway."

The manner in which Queeny spoke and the cast of her eyes made Shirley relent. The last thing she wanted Queeny to say was, If me do it, why you caan' do it? You better than me? In any event she needed the work. Yes, she would be getting her green card in a couple of days, but Queeny was right, she would need the money to buy things . . . and it would not be for long.

Grace lived on the tenth floor in a tastefully furnished apartment that looked out onto North Miami Beach. Queeny showed Shirley around the home with its large bathroom specially designed so that it could be easily accessed by an elderly person. The bedroom was huge, and the first thing Shirley noticed was that the bed had rails like a child's cribs and latches that, when released, caused the sides to fall so Grace could leave it. "Them just for safety, so she won't fall off the bed," Queeny said. "You know, once a man twice a child. Sometime me not even put them up. But for the first you may want practice, you know. For, if anything happen to her, you goose cook."

"I'll remember," Shirley said.

"Remember that her head go and come. And when it go she cause more trouble. When she all right she will call you and so, but when her head go she think she is forty or younger and want do all kind of antics."

Grace was seated in a rocker near the thick glass window of her bedroom which was at the corner of the building, giving her a choice of views: east over the Miami Beach and the coastline or north over North Miami and the intercostals. Both views were breathtaking.

"Grace, this is Shirley I have been telling you about." Shirley was a bit surprised at Queeny's precise English, though she spoke it with her normal flat Jamaican tone.

The old woman was frail with a strong gaze. Her hair was thin and the blond of it had faded to silver. It was set stylishly with a white bow to one side. Her voice had a slight shake to it. "Oh, you are so beautiful," she said.

"Thank you," Shirley smiled.

"I like her already, Melva," she said to Queeny, who looked sheepishly at Shirley. Shirley smiled. Melva, so that is your name.

"You like everybody," Queeny said under her breath. "Don't give her any trouble because she is new. I told her about the ice cream; one scoop and none after seven."

"You go on - go on and leave me." Grace waved her away fondly. "Sometimes you are no fun."

"Remember, Doctor said not too much fun."

"If I follow you I'll live like an invalid."

"If you follow us, you'll live longer." Queeny smiled.

Shirley was already warming to Grace. She liked her spirit. "Melva is just looking out for you," she told her, as Queeny disappeared inside the bathroom.

"I know. She is like a daughter to me - she is the best nurse I've ever had." The old lady punctuated the air with her finger. "The best, I tell you. But I like to give her trouble."

"Give who trouble?" Queeny emerged from the bathroom.

"You," Grace winked at Shirley. "You are always giving me trouble."

Queeny left at six-thirty. As promised, she had prepared all the food and fed Grace before she left. Even the snacks were fixed and in the refrigerator. Shirley looked around the large living room and smiled to herself. It indeed seemed an easy job. The medicine came packaged in a compartmentalized container with different times written on it. At eight o'clock, all she had to do was remove the plastic from the eight o'clock compartment and give the pills to Grace. And that was that.

Grace for the most part, sat and looked through the window quietly, lost in her own thoughts.

There was only one bedroom, so Shirley would have to sleep on one of the two couches in the living room. She walked over to the eastern end of the living room, slid the glass doors apart, and stepped onto the balcony. She was met by a view of the beach that was undisturbed for miles to the north and south.

The beach looked like a large dike with a few palm trees and mangroves running along its edge. She could see lovers sitting on the benches, huddled in corners or walking hand-in-hand in the fading light while others strolled to and from the various pubs that opened onto the sand. It had been a while since Shirley saw the beach. The sight of it made her promise herself to bring her bathing suit and take a swim one evening after Grace had gone to sleep.

"Shirley," Grace called from the bedroom.

She entered to find her standing near the edge of the bed. Her robe was hung neatly over the side of the chair she had vacated. Shirley was a bit surprised to find her there. Somehow she had expected to lift her from the chair to the bed. But Grace was obviously not an invalid.

"Could you be a darling and help me onto the bed, dear?" Grace asked.

"You want to go to sleep?" Shirley asked.

"I'm a bit tired," Grace said. "I'd like to lie down a while."

"OK," Shirley said. She held older woman by her arm and helped her onto the bed.

"I'd like to sit," Grace said.

Shirley adjusted the bed.

"Thank you, darling." Grace sighed and produced a candy from out of nowhere. "Here is a nice candy. Candy is good for your complexion, if you don't have too much."

Shirley took the candy from Grace's hand, smiled and looked up at the clock on the wall. It was just after seven-thirty.

"Sit with me a while," Grace said to her. "Sit right there on the bed. God knows it's hard enough. Sit! Tell me about yourself."

Shirley sat on the edge of the bed and wondered just what facet of her short life she could relate that would maintain the pleasant mood. "You don't want to hear my story," she said.

"Ah, I bet you have a lot to tell too, so pretty and all. When I was your age, I had a story a minute."

"Well, you were a model," Shirley said. "Models live glamorous lives."

"That I was too, that I was too," Grace said pensively. "And a fantastic one at that. I've been to every country in the world, I have. Every country, even Africa - I've been there." She nodded her head.

Shirley could not help wondering how such a beautiful and glamorous woman could end up like this. Alone, in an expensive apartment complex, telling stories to someone like her. But it was not in her nature to ask. "It's about time for your medicine," she told her.

"I know," Grace said, "and bring my big photo album when you come. The red one. I'll show you I was in Africa."

Shirley brought the medicine to her, dropped the tablets in their cup and raised her so she could take them. She then placed the large red photo album in her lap and sat beside the little old woman as she took her through the journeys of her life. She followed her pointing trembling finger through time from year to glorious year, through hairstyles and colors, through styles and fashions, from country to country, and handsome men to handsome men. "You know who this is?" Grace paused. "That's Fred Astaire."

Shirley screamed.

"Damn right it is, and this is Rome too." Grace flipped the page. "And over here Cuba. We were shooting for Vanity Fair that year. I was a redhead then." Time rolled by with the turning of the pages ."And here I was in Africa," she said. "I was almost turning thirty then." This picture was not as glamorous as the others. She was dressed casually in a white flowing dress and high top boots. Her hair was wrapped in a white sash and she sported a white scarf. She was standing on the gangway of a huge steamer, obviously about to disembark, while a bunch of half-naked natives scurried around her large trunks.

"This looks like India." Shirley noticed the turbans and facial structure of the natives.

"That is it, that is it. Yes, India it was." Grace laughed. "It took you to remind me. Have you ever been there - to India, I mean?"

"No, but I'd love to one day," Shirley said.

"Oh, you'd love it. The people are so nice and wonderful."

Shirley reached to turn the page and continued to enjoy the album till she realized that Grace had fallen off to sleep. She closed the book, lowered the bed to a flat position, laid the old woman onto her pillow and pulled the sheets up to her chin. The silken strands of her silver hair spread against the pillow and glowed in the night.

Shirley tiptoed away and closed the door. She selected the couch closest to Grace's bedroom, lay on her stomach, placed the album on the floor and began to leaf through it. After a while, she too fell asleep.

She was awakened by a stench that reminded her of an outside latrine made ripe by a hot summer sun.

Grace was shaking her. "I have to go to the store and my pants keep falling down."

She took one look at the old woman with her hair disheveled, her eyes wild and troubled, her clothes and face covered in some brown matter, and shrank away to fall onto the floor. But what was that smell? It was on Grace's hand but closer, it was right under Shirley's nose. She pulled her T-shirt around to check where Grace had held it to shake her awake and almost fainted when she realized what Grace had deposited there.

"Oh my God!" She looked up at Grace who was standing sternly at the back of the chair.

"I need to go to the store," she said to Shirley. "I told you to fire that damn seamstress. She made too few darts." Grace looked like a child who had been playing in the mud, covered from head to foot in brown muck - muck on her hands, in her hair, on her face, on the chair that she held – her clothing was more brown than white. Nicole would call this a toilet accident. Shirley wailed. Oh my God, the woman shit up herself. Oh my God!

Then she yelled at Grace. "Don't move!"

"I need to go to the store," Grace insisted.

"Yes, soon, but now don't move!" Shirley panicked. Queeny said it would be an easy job but she did not say anything about crazy. The woman could fall down dead at any minute. She could start wielding a knife. Grace began to move again. "Don't move!" Shirley shouted and began to run toward the phone.

The whole house stank. Grace had apparently walked around before waking her. There were feces on the tables, on the door frames, and on the walls; it was trailing on the carpet and on the floor of the kitchen. She had to pass around Grace to get to the phone in the kitchen. Please Lord not the phone too. Not the phone.

Shirley picked the phone from the wall. It was clean. She dialed Queeny's number. "You have to come fast!" she yelled as Queeny responded. "We have an emergency!"

Queeny's voice was urgent. "What happen? Tell me."

"The whole place!" Shirley yelled. "You never tell me say she mad too."

"Jesus, Shirley! Calm down. What happen? Take a deep breath."

Shirley took two deep breaths, but still could not get it right. "The whole place full o' shit," she said. "The whole place full o' doo doo. She walking up and down. She calling me all kinds of names."

Queeny gave an annoyed sound. "That you call me for? Me think something serious happen. She do that all the time. Just give her the medicine and put her back to sleep."

"I gave her already."

"You have one in a red bottle on the table, just give her one of that."

"But what about the doo doo?"

"How you mean what 'bout it? Just clean it up and wash her off."

159

"Me? Clean shit?"

"How you mean, Shirley? She do it sometimes. That's why you must watch her. But is long time now she don' do that. Something must get her exited. She go on like that sometimes. Say she have to go store and things. One time they find her at a bus stop just like that. Clean her off and clean up the place. Use the disinfectant."

"I have never cleaned my mother yet, much less this."

"Shirley, she is a old woman. What you expect? You have to treat her like baby."

"I don't even know where to start," Shirley said wearily.

"Jesus Christ, Shirley! Clean her off, man. Look in the bureau drawer, you see some big diapers."

"Diapers!"

"Yes, Shirley. Them look like baby own, but them bigger. She is like a baby. Just put them on her."

"I can't bother with this, you know. I thought you said the job was easy."

"Then it no easy, Shirley? What can hard 'bout cleaning a little shit?"

Strangely enough, Shirley did not know how to respond to that. Maybe at some other point in her life she would have been able to – but then again, maybe not. At what other point in her life would there be possibility of that question being posed to her? She fell silent.

"Just clean her up." Queeny's voice was hard in the receiver.

Shirley could only find one thing to say. "You don't hear anything from Mikey? Him come? Him call?" But Queeny had already hung up the phone.

Grace surprisingly did not put up much resistance. Once Shirley directed her to the bathroom, she went. She was, as Queeny said, like a child, and the process was similar to what Shirley would have undergone with any of the twins or Brad if they had a 'toilet accident'. After she returned Grace to bed and had given her the red capsule, she turned her attention to the living room. Shirley worked quickly and calmly and by eleven o'clock had restored some semblance of normality to the apartment. Now the place was filled with the intense odor of lemon and disinfectant.

Shirley walked over to the balcony and closed the glass behind her. But though the night air was fresh and crisp the stench seemed to have soaked into her and not even the breeze could remove it.

She took off her T-shirt right there on the balcony and threw it into a corner. That took some of the stench with it. She thought of doing the same with her shorts but changed her mind. Later she would bathe and scrub for half an hour, then throw the clothes into the garbage. She had brought them to sleep in but now they were beyond further use. She would have to sleep in her jeans.

But what difference would a bath make? How could bathing clean that dirt inside her; that stench of shame and failure that ran so deep it burned her stomach? Why had she become so unlucky? How could she rid herself of this bad luck... this saltness?

And what was it that Jamaican people say about bad luck and being salt? How do you cure it? A sea bath, isn't that what people do in Jamaica for curing bad luck – saltness? Half an hour bathing in the sea, that is how you cure?

She looked over the balcony.

It was strange how close the ground began to look from there – how near the sea. All she had to do was climb onto the little chair and step over onto the ground then walk to the sea. The sea would welcome and cleanse her of all her saltness. . . change her luck forever. She could jump out, have a quick dip in the sea and return in seconds. Shirley pulled the chair to her, held the rail, placed a knee on the hard plastic seat and made to climb it. Her head hovered momentarily over the edge. The ground moved as if being zoomed away by a telephoto lens, the distance increased and the twenty stories suddenly seemed a mile to the ground. People were like specks; the sand was invisible. Shirley felt dizzy. The world spun around her. She held her forehead and fell back against the wall.

What am I thinking? Is it suicide I'm thinking?

A normal bath would have to do tonight.

Shirley straightened from the wall, picked up her T-shirt, left the balcony and headed for the bathroom. She reached into the large closet for an oversized towel and tested the showers for temperature. As she went to remove her shorts, the stench of the evening's ordeal rose strongly from the disturbed garment. She shook her head. Soap and water can never remove this.

Shirley wrapped the towel around her and left the bathroom. She picked up the keys and her jeans and blouse that hung across a chair. Eleven o'clock or not, she had nothing to lose.

A sea bath it would be.

The elevator was empty and so was the lobby. She walked quickly through the back door and crossed the boardwalk through the little wooden gate onto the beach and dropped her T-shirt into the first garbage bin she saw.

It was a clear night. There were no stars, no moon, but the blue empty sky seemed to have a light of its own. Shirley walked slowly with the large towel wrapped around her and raised her face to let the night wash against her skin. The fresh air felt good.

Shirley chose a spot directly in front of the apartment. She dropped the towel, jeans, blouse and keys onto the sand and walked out of her slippers straight into the water without testing it. It was lukewarm. She did not care that she could not swim. She waded a few feet till the water reached her waist, then turned around and backed into the sea until it covered her shoulders. Shirley closed her eyes submerged, then pushed her head above the surface again.

Baptism.

She removed her bra and washed it with her hands till it squeaked between her fingers. Then she scoured herself from head to toe with it, removing each garment, letting each piece float away wherever it may – till she was naked in the water with just the brassiere in her hand. After about half-an-hour of scrubbing, her skin felt tender and refreshed. She then discarded the bra. Her clothes were right at the water's edge, and the beach sloped down, so she hardly felt exposed. She waded around for a while in the lukewarm water, feeling cleaner and lighter than she had since entering Miami that fateful night. She waded till her limbs felt heavy.

She was washed, she had taken her sea bath, she was baptized anew.

It was time to go.

At the edge of the water, she dried herself, dressed and put her slippers on. Then she thought about it and flung the slippers back into the water as far as she could. She was walking up the slope to the beach proper, drying her hair as she went, and just like that she met Vince Austin.

"Aren't you afraid to swim alone?" he asked.

"Pardon?" She was startled - terrified that he had been so close while she had performed her ritual. She made to circle his beach chair. She wondered if he had seen her as she stood naked to put on her jeans.

"Are you a model?" he asked, standing and lifting a half-filled glass of wine to his lips. He was a handsome white man. Maybe mid-thirties, but Shirley could never tell the age of white men. He was about five ten or so, his body was hard and sculptured, his blond hair fell close to his shoulders. Is he a model? "Why do you ask?" Shirley said.

"Why?" He was now standing. "Because you look like one, that's why."

"I must go," Shirley said, but she had slowed her steps.

"I'll walk with you a bit," he said. "I live in the apartment over there." He pointed to Shirley's building. "I am Vince," he switched his glass to his left hand and offered her his right.

"Shirley."

"Where are you from? You have an accent."

"Jamaica," she said.

"You live around here?"

"Yes, I live in the same apartment."

"You have never modeled?" Incredulity was in his voice.

Shirley wished he would at least be a bit more original. "I told you no."

He fished into his pocket for a small leather wallet. "Well, if you are ever interested, call my agency. Call me."

He handed her a card, she made to read it but it was too dark. "What kind of work do you do?"

"I am a scout." He shook the hair from his face. "A talent scout. I hang out on the beach and check for prospective clients – models, you know."

"What do you mean?"

He finished his wine and sailed the glass across the beach. "I look out for beautiful women like yourself," he smiled. "Fun job, isn't it?"

Shirley wrinkled her nose.

"Shirley," he said, as they approached the edge of the beach. "Just imagine what you are doing right now."

"What?"

"Just stop here for a minute and look at me."

Shirley paused and laughed gaily. "What?"

"OK, just stand there."

She stood.

"Now, do you know how many women make millions of dollars just doing that?"

"Doing what?" Shirley asked.

"Standing on the beach, with wet hair, looking just like that."

"Just looking?"

"The only difference is, instead of looking into my face, they look into a camera lens. That is the only difference. My job is to expose women to their possibilities."

"I see." Shirley resumed her walk. "But I don't think I would be interested in that."

They had now crossed the boardwalk. Shirley made sure she walked toward the front of the building and the lights. One could never be sure about anything.

"You don't believe me, do you?" He opened the main door for her.

"Oh, I do," she said. "But I am too short to be a model."

He laughed. "How tall was Marilyn Monroe?"

"You are a joker," she said. "You know that?"

They paused near the elevators. "I live on that side," he said.

Shirley sighed with relief. "OK, good night."

"Listen," he said persistently, "have a drink with me tomorrow night. Forget that I am a fashion scout. My number is on the card. I'll be around."

"I'll think about it," Shirley said as the elevator came. "Good night."

"Good night," he said, as the door closed against his handsome face.

Chapter Seventeen

The next night Shirley brought her bathing suit to work.

As soon as Grace was fed, medicated and bedded, she went to the bathroom to change.

It was the strangest thing, she thought as she stood in the bathroom, how much time and suffering it had taken, before she realized what her biggest mistake had been in the United States. She had ignored her greatest asset: her beauty. She had always been able to get any man she wanted, with just a flick of her head and a swish of her hips. And yet she had come to the United States, the land of the greatest opportunities, the most handsome and richest men, and had not used her beauty at all. Some women would die to look like her. Was it not the first thing that people always mentioned when they saw her? Tiny: You really pretty fi true; and Queeny – what did she say? If me did pretty and look good like you . . . Even Grace had remarked, Oh, but you are beautiful. But she, Shirley, had let the beauty stay idle – she had wasted it. And not only had she wasted it, but as she looked into the mirror, she realized that time had also taken its toll.

Her once-flawless face was a mess of liver spots and black blotches. Even with a good base, it was impossible to hide the bumps. Her eyes were sad and concerned; the skin beneath them dark, as if it held a thin layer of eye shadow. Her hair had lost its vibrancy because she could not afford to treat it any more. Her shape was still there, but her skin had no bounce, it was slack against her body.

She looked in on Grace. The old lady had fallen asleep as soon as she got her medicine. Shirley had contemplated giving her one of the red capsules that made her sleep so soundly, but Queeny had warned that they should only be used when she was agitated like the night before. So Shirley had made sure not to excite her; almost ignoring her and her stories all evening. Now she was sleeping as soundly as a baby.

Shirley made sure the bed rails were up and secured. She dimmed the lights, found her towel and her small purse and headed for the door. It was time she used what beauty she had left.

She had been sitting for less than ten minutes when she saw him coming towards her, from down the beach, with the wine glass in his hand.

"So you showed up," he said as he stopped by her chair.

"I thought I'd look out," she said.

"For me?"

"No. Just look out. You know, just relax a bit."

"Whatever," he smiled. "Let me buy you a drink."

"OK," she said, too quickly.

"Come," he said.

She rose and walked with him to a little bar halfway down the beach. "Wine?" He raised his glass to her as they entered.

"Sure." She wrinkled her nose as he closed the door. "It's stuffy in here."

"Yeah," he agreed. "Once we get the drink we'll walk a bit. It's a lovely night and I should be scouting, anyway."

She laughed. "Right."

Drinks in hand they began walking along the beach in the direction from which they had come. It was close to ten o'clock and the night was pleasantly warm. He paused in the sand, lifted his glass and toasted her. "To our first date," he said.

"To our first date," she humored him.

"You know, I've never dated a black woman before," he said, as they continued walking.

"I'm not black," Shirley said.

"I thought you said you were Jamaican."

"I am."

"Then you are black."

"I am half Indian," Shirley said.

"Is that like Hispanic or something? Your parents are not Jamaican, uh?"

"They are." She sipped the wine.

"So how do you mean you are not black?"

"Do I look black to you?" Shirley wanted to change the subject. He obviously did not understand.

He paused, unsure. "I guess."

"It does not matter." Shirley dropped the subject.

"Whatever," he shrugged. Then "Are you tired?" He broke the short silence.

"No, not really."

"We can sit if you like."

They were close to the water. There the beach sloped steeply down, so that as they sat on the sand, they were practically invisible from the rest of the beach.

He sat beside her and touched her hair. "Why are we touching?" she asked.

"Why are we not?" he asked hoarsely.

"Because I hardly know you."

He reached for her. She pulled away and fell against the sand. In a flash he was on top of her. His hips were spreading her legs, his torso pressing her into the sand, and his hands holding her firmly with his mouth inches above hers.

"What are you doing?" Shirley tried to fight him off.

"Don't struggle and I won't hurt you," he whispered.

"Let me go, get off me!" She tried to heave him off her by twisting her hips.

"I said, don't struggle." His voice was urgent, his eyes fierce.

Shirley ignored his order and screamed. He moved one hand to cover her mouth and she fought against him desperately. If he was going to rape her, he had to kill her first. He had to rape a dead body.

He was heavy and his hardness prodded against her. He pressed himself to her chest and smiled wickedly. "No one will hear you." As he spoke, he crossed his right hand under her chin, cutting off her air.

Shirley was trapped beneath him. She tried to scream again but could hardly find air in her lungs.

He began to pant, his hard hands fumbling with her clothing as he searched for a path for his hardness. He kissed her neck, her hair – his passion gaining intensity as she struggled against him.

Then suddenly she surrendered; dropped her hands and relaxed her legs. "Take it," she managed to say. "OK, take it, you fucking dog."

"That's more like it," he cooed. "More like it, my Shirley." He pressed his lips against hers. She felt his slimy tongue probing against her teeth, opened her mouth, and bit down so hard her teeth jarred as they met through his flesh.

His body went slack and hardness whimpered against her bathing suit. His eyes were wide and wild above her. Still holding his tongue with her teeth, she twisted her head to the right and felt warm blood against her chin. She wanted to tell him he had tried to rape the wrong woman, let him know that there was over a year of frustration and hatred in that bite, that her cup had run over and he had made the worst mistake of his life, but she could not open her mouth, dared not release him, so she shook her head and felt the flesh tear, and the blood run, and hoped he could read the madness in her eyes.

He was on his back now, sprawling hands slack in surrender. And she was above him, in charge of the macabre kiss. Her hand found a wine glass and she closed her hand around its stem and slammed it, mouth-first, square against his temple. It shattered in her hands.

Still biting down onto his tongue, she groped for her purse and towel. By the time she found them, her jaws were tired and he had crept around under her till blood and tears mixed all over his face.

She counted to five, released his tongue and made off down the beach at a dead run. But she need not have run because, as she looked behind her, she could see him curled into the fetal position with his face in his hands. But she did not stop running.

As she neared the apartment complex, she could see the flashing lights of a police car. Maybe they had heard her screams after all. She ran directly toward them. As she crossed the boardwalk she saw that there were three police cars and a large ambulance parked in front of the apartment. That was one thing about America, she thought, quick medical and police response. She did not fix her hair, nor pull the strap of her bathing suit up onto her shoulders. She wanted them to see her as she had left him, looking like a madwoman, with blood on her face, her hair awry and her clothing torn. She wanted them to know what kind of mad rapist was roaming the beach.

But the crowd gathered at the apartment was not looking in her direction, the police cars were not pointed her way. The ambulance was parked way up against the steps that led to the lobby. The policemen were pushing away the crowd of onlookers that had gathered around another car was parked on the edge of the A1A highway.

As she got to the edge of the crowd, a policeman pressed roughly against her.

"Stay back! Please stay back."

"Sir," she said.

He may have noticed the blood on her face. He squinted with concern. "Are you all, right ma'am?"

She paused and tried to catch her breath. She realized the emergency had nothing to do with her. "What?" she panted.

"Are you OK? Is that blood on you?"

But her answer was stuck in her throat. Up near the entrance, near the lobby, the police were making way for the paramedics who were about to place a stretcher into the back of the ambulance, a stretcher that held a frail figure with blond hair turned silver, hair filled with brown mess, like that of a child having played in the mud. "Grace!"

"Are you OK, ma'am? Is that blood on you? Do you know that woman?"

"What happened?" Shirley almost screamed.

"Ma'am, please step back," the officer said. "Is that blood on your face?"

Shirley stepped back from him. "What happened?!" She bumped into a large man. "What happened?" she pleaded.

"Poor old woman," the man said. "Sleepwalked out of her apartment and fell down the stairs. Why do they leave them alone? There should be a nurse or something. Somebody should go to jail for this."

Shirley saw the policeman looking closely at her as she backed away into the crowd. But that was all she saw. She was struck by a sudden, searing headache that shook her to her very core. Dropping the towel she lifted her hands to hold her hair on both sides of her head as if to tear it from its very roots. She opened her mouth to scream, but no sound came. Then she staggered away, spun around and ran wildly down the sidewalk, around the corner and along the length of the Florida A1A.

PART III

I'm In Bondage

Chapter Eighteen

Shirley sipped the rose pink wine and looked across the sparse dance floor of the Stinger Lounge where a few people swayed to the easy rock of Gregory Isaacs. Her eyes wandered over the bar to where a large TV was showing videos. The video was obviously shot at some dance hall in Jamaica, and the camera man had zeroed in onto the gyrating vitals of a woman dressed in a black skin-fitting mesh jumpsuit. She was pivoting on her heels and digging her hips along the rhythm of the music. Shirley could not hear the TV but she could tell that the song the woman danced to was hardcore Reggae and different from the one that filled the club. There was a time when Shirley would have thrown up at a video like that, but tonight she wished that the music on the speakers was the same as that of the video. Still she closed her eyes and found joy in Gregory Isaacs crooning that he had returned the keys to the front door.

It was Queeny's idea that they come to the Stinger Lounge to wait on Mikey. They had not heard from him since the day some weeks ago when he called to say he would be bringing her documents. So, tired of waiting, Queeny decided it was time to go after him and find out why he was avoiding them all of a sudden. "Him live a Stinger Lounge," she had said. "Every Friday night him and him friend them out there."

Now twenty minutes inside and Shirley was feeling much better than she expected. Something about the people casually rocking to the familiar sounds in the totally Jamaican atmosphere was lifting her. She heard herself singing along with the old songs and cheering when a new era or singer was introduced.

"I tell you, you must come out sometimes," Queeny shouted across the table. "But you want to stay lock up in the house every day."

Shirley smiled without responding. For a minute she had forgotten why they were there. She had left Queeny's apartment with purposeful strides and an angry look of determination on her face. But somehow the evening was dictating differently. The wine soothed her and slowly the tension and anger were draining away.

So what if Mikey did not come? So what if they never saw him again? She wasn't even angry at Queeny any more; his absence was probably just as painful for Queeny as it was for her.

Shirley remembered the she had seen on Queeny's face, that early morning when the police took her home. They had found her at a bus stop on the A1A. She had run until her feet gave out then collapsed on its bench, hugging herself in its farthest corner, while the world spun around her at high speed. She had not been able to speak, but the police had found Queeny's address in her tiny handbag that had miraculously survived the ordeal. Queeny did not complain or even think of rejecting Shirley, whose folly had brought the police into her circumstances.

She simply took her in as she had done before.

Shirley spent the whole week spaced out and silent. Queeny never asked about that fateful night and She never ventured an explanation. Queeny was still going to work at Grace's apartment, and somewhere through the haze, Shirley was able to learn that Grace had not died but had merely broken her leg. When conversation finally came, it was halting and uncomfortable. What was more, conversation or not, Mikey's absence hung between them like a visible thing.

So now they had come to The Stinger Lounge to find him.

The music changed to calypso. The dance floor filled. "Don't I tell you to come out sometimes?" Queeny insisted, looking onto the floor. "One thing with calypso, all who can't dance look like they can dance."

Shirley watched the dancers trying to chase the mad rhythm of the calypso with the gyrations of their hips, and agreed. "Especially under psychedelic lights."

"My dear," Queeny said.

Shirley nodded to Queeny. The music thumped from the floor, from the walls, from the tables, even through the chairs. "See the one big wood Moet there." Queeny's eyes seemed to catch fire in the dim light.

"Who?" Shirley ignored the reference to size of the man's penis.

"Mikey friend. You never see one without the other. That mean Mikey 'bout the place."

"Where?"

"Over there so," Queeny nodded toward the entrance. "The black one you see passing through the security."

Shirley followed Queeny's eyes across the club. Through the flickering lights of the dance floor, she could see two men, having cleared the security booth, making their way to a private platform right of the entrance.

"The big one?"

"Same ugly one. And the one dutty Chef. That mean you soon see Mikey; the three o' them always together."

"The two on the platform?" she asked to make sure.

"Yes," Queeny said. "The short one name Chef. Him is the cook."

"So where is Mikey?"

"Suppose to soon see him. Them always together. And if Mikey don't come, them know where him is. If anybody know - them know."

"So, let's go and ask them." Shirley's excitement stirred.

"Make we wait on the one Mikey," Queeny said. "Me and him tonight! Him goin' frighten to see me tonight!"

The men sat and spoke at length with the waitress. Shirley's stomach burned as her excitement and anxiety increased. Her mind quickly ran over the possibilities and doors that would open to her once she got her green card, then instantly reversed to explore the ones that would remain closed if she did not get it. So much of her hope had gone into that money she had given to Mikey.

Suddenly she did not want to wait any longer. She must have news now.

The man Queeny called Chef rose from his seat and began to make his way slowly through the growing crowd and across the club toward them.

"Look like him see we," Queeny said.

"How could he?" Shirley questioned.

"Probably the ugly waitress tell him," Queeny said.

But Chef had not seen them. He passed just beneath their table without so much as a glance upward, and headed for the bathroom. As he returned, Queeny waited till he was just below them and yelled, "Ugly Chef!"

He spun quickly, looked up at them and grinned.

"Where you friend?" Queeny shouted.

He motioned for her to wait, squeezed past a group of dancers on the steps and bounded up to them. "What happen?" he asked, beaming lustfully at Queeny.

"How you mean, what happen? Where you friend?"

"Which frien' that?" he inquired. "One frien' I have and you know what that." He nodded down at the front of his pants.

"Don' bother with you freshness, you ugly like. You well and know is Mikey me mean."

His smile widened. "Mikey is him own man. How I must know him whereabouts?"

"Is you friend and you well and know where him is. All o' onoo take up for one another."

"So, how come the two o' you just siddung one-away so." He glanced at Shirley.

"Don't bother change the subject. We want know where you friend is."

"Why you go on so bad, man?" The lust in his eyes increased and his reprimand sounded more like a coo. "Why you go on like you bad so?"

"Bad yes! Me know the one Mikey have him whole heap o' woman. But tell him say him don't have to hide. Is business we come to talk 'bout. We want we things that him have."

"What kinda things that?" he asked.

"Is not you business."

He is hiding something, Shirley thought. He laughed too quickly, his eyes moved too restlessly. She watched him as he flattened his palm against his chest and looked around the room, as if trying to find somewhere to put his eyes other than on Queeny while he answered her.

And when he did look at her it was with a searching hard look, as if he had mustered his courage for the stare and wanted to know if she could see through it.

"Do you really know where he is or not?" Shirley intervened.

He seemed glad that she spoke. "That me telling you frien'," he said. "I don' know where him is."

"Lie you telling," Queeny said. "You covering for him. But we not leaving here tonight till we see him."

He laughed. "Boy, you bad! Me soon come." Shirley watched him closely as he moved away and bumped into the waitress who was serving the table behind them. He helped her steady her drinks, whispered to her, nodded toward them, then slipped the waitress a bill.

The waitress smiled and nodded.

"He is hiding something," Shirley said out loud.

"Me know," Queeny said angrily. "But I goin' surprise the one Mikey tonight."

Shirley watched as Chef went back across the floor to the little platform where the other man sat. From this distance she could not discern the expressions on their faces, but she could see Chef sit and lean over and speak into the other man's ear. They talked together for a while then sat back to drink.

"What?" Queeny brought her back again.

Shirley looked around to see the waitress placing frosted long-stemmed glasses onto their table in spite of Queeny's exclamations of surprise. "I never order any more drinks." But the waitress continued to place the glasses before them. "Your friend paid for them."

"What friend?" But Shirley had already guessed.

"The guy who was standing here. He's not your friend?"

"Rass," Queeny laughed loudly. "Mean Chef buying people drinks!"

"What is it?" Shirley asked. "What kind of drink is it?"

"Champagne - Moet champagne," the waitress said.

"Lord! Champagne to backside!" Queeny hollered, then motioned to Shirley. "You want it?"

Shirley shrugged.

"Tell him thanks," Queeny told the waitress as she poured the Champagne and burrowed the half full bottle into the bucket of ice.

Shirley lifted the champagne to her lips. The lights dimmed across the club and the music fell to soul. Teddy Prendergast began screaming for someone to turn off the lights. She was hardly surprised at the way things were going. She had become so accustomed to disappointments that the conversation with Chef hardly fazed her. And what was more, the night was working on her. The Stingers Lounge, with this music, with these vibes, in a strange way insulated her from the world and its problems, and all those feelings of worthlessness that had haunted her over the past year.

Her eyes wandered once more to the TV across the room. Another woman was dancing to another rhythm she did not hear. But she could see the woman glide and grind along the beat of the bass line, as only a Jamaican could. She wished she could hear that music; she had nothing against Teddy Prendergast, but she wished she could hear the raw Jamaican music right now.

She was beginning to feel a certain pride of being she had not felt before. As if to say: Here in this club, among the ragamuffin Jamaican crowd, there is significance to my existence. Here was proof of origin of which she could be proud. She was somebody; and this place, this night, this music, these people, were here to prove it. Here, fun and significance were available to her. Tomorrow would tell her she was nothing. Here, this minute, she belonged.

"What?"

Queeny was shouting above the music to the waitress who had reappeared at the table. The woman leaned forward, spoke into Queeny's ear and then left.

"What is it?" Shirley asked.

"Them want we come over there," she said. "Over the VIP section."

"Who?"

"Moet," she said. "Mr. Moet."

"Like the Champagne?"

"That's why them call him so. Is only that him drink – is only that them drink."

"The big black one?"

Queeny shrugged. "It matter?"

"Are you going?"

"What you think?"

"It's up to you."

"Me going, yes." Queeny was picking up her bag. "Me going. I not making them leave my sight till I see Mikey tonight. Plus the club filling up and we soon can't see them from here. So come."

"OK." Shirley picked up her bag.

They got to the platform and the one Queeny called Moet rose and offered Shirley the chair to his right. He stood behind it as she sat and gently pushed it into place. She liked that he smelled good too – a man should smell good. She gave him a cool thank you. As he lifted the large champagne bottle to fill the two extra glasses, she noticed his well-kept hands and perfectly manicured nails.

He wore black. Good black. For black did not do well on very black men unless it was of the right texture, quality and cut. She took the glass he offered and nodded more in approval of his taste than regard to him.

"I don' feel Mikey going pass through tonight." He said this as he handed Queeny her glass. "The last time I talk to Mikey, him was going somewhere else."

"Like which part so?" Queeny put the drink back onto the table.

Moet leaned back into the chair and sipped his drink. "You know Mikey: things happen, and him probably decide to just stop off somewhere."

"So how you know him not coming here tonight?"

"Him never tell me him coming - and him would tell me."

"Is you friend," Queeny said. "You covering for him."

Moet placed his glass onto the table and smiled at Queeny. "Mikey not coming tonight."

There was a finality to his words that made Shirley's spine tingle. His gentle manner reminded her of the soft padding of the door of a bank vault - harmless and charming, with ten-inch-thick steel underneath. People were always rubbing their hands against the soft leather padding, as if to say it should look more severe, more rugged. But it did not have to look the part. It was there because it did not matter what it looked like. The man sitting next to her had that same kind of quiet arrogance, a cocky don't-care honesty that framed raw power. "You nah introduce me to you friend?" he asked Queeny.

"Well, that don't sound like Mikey." Queeny ignored him, defiant. "Him call me the other day and tell me him coming. And him never come, and him never call back. That don't sound like him. Something happen, don't it?"

"How you go on so?" He spoke gently to Queeny while he looked at Shirley.

"She name Shirley and she don't want nobody," Queeny said roughly.

"Is you bodyguard?" He looked at Shirley across the top of his wine glass. "You have a good bodyguard." He then nodded back at Chef and waved a hand toward Queeny "You try talk to her."

Chef raised his hands. "Is me you want she beat!"

"Out of fun and joke," Queeny said after another large sip of champagne, "I don' care if him have woman or not, because me know onoo always have whole heap a woman. This is business, man. So if you know where him is, tell me."

"All right." Moet spoke reasonably. "If is something important, maybe I can help. What you want see him 'bout?"

"You don't have to know."

"All right." He raised his hands and leaned back into his seat.

For a while no one spoke. The mood at the table was not uncomfortable. It was more like a pause as each of the four drank their wine and listened to the music. Shirley caught Queeny's eyes across the table staring intently as she worded a message to her. "Me a go tell him," she said. Shirley shrugged. She did not care any more. Anything was better than them sitting at home waiting for Mikey. If the men were as close as Queeny said, there could be nothing about the whole affair to surprise either of them. Plus he had offered to help.

"All right," Queeny said aloud to Moet.

"What now?" He leaned forward as if he had forgotten the whole affair.

"Me goin' tell you."

"Tell me what?" he asked.

Queeny ignored that, beckoned him forward and told him the whole story.

Both Moet and Chef listened intently as she spoke, allowing Shirley just a few instances to drop in a word or two. When Queeny was finished, Moet looked thoughtfully at Chef for a brief second. He then looked from woman to woman. "Is that?"

"How you mean is that?" exclaimed Queeny.

"It was all my money," Shirley lamented.

"I will take care of it." Moet was smug.

"How you mean?" Queeny asked. "How?"

"I will take care of it. Once is something Mikey working on, I can check it out." He smiled coolly at Shirley. "Can't make you lose you money."

"So, you well and know where the one Mikey is." Queeny was sounding a bit tipsy.

"How much time a man must tell you one thing?" Chef said in exasperation. "We know the system, all o' we work the same system. If Mikey not available, we can check it out."

"Relax and enjoy youself," Moet said.

"Yeah man." Chef smiled lustfully.

"You sure you can help?" Shirley stared squarely at Moet. She did not want to build up her hopes again.

"Don' worry about it." Moet's smile was confidence itself. "Call the waitress there," he motioned to Chef as he topped up the glasses on the table with the last of the champagne.

Shirley believed him. He had the honesty of a bank vault's door.

A fresh bottle of champagne came, the tension dissipated, the music returned once more to reggae. Shirley watched amused as Chef tried to persuade Queeny onto the dance floor.

"Onoo love rub up pon people too much," she heard Queeny say.

"Dance with the man," Moet said playfully.

"Why you don' dance with him?" Queeny quipped. "I don' go from friend to friend."

"Is jus' a little dance, some easy skanking," Chef insisted.

"Look how much woman in the place." Queeny pulled away her arm. But it was obvious she wanted to dance and that the music was affecting her. After a while she raised her finger, pointed into Chef 's face and ticked off a list of rules, warnings and regulations. Then she rose with him and headed for the dance floor.

The crowd roared as Shinehead's 'Strive' hit the speakers. Shirley found herself almost rocking to the beat.

"So what you doing with a friend like that?" His voice floated in to her.

"How you mean?" She looked at him. Through the haze and the mix of wine and champagne he seemed almost charming.

"Onoo don' match."

A point for Mr. Moet, Shirley mused. "She is my friend."

"But you so different, like onoo come from two different world or something."

"So?"

"I suppose." He smiled his lean smile and let his glance cover her like a blanket – a gentle floating blanket. "You nice, you know that? You really look good."

"Thanks."

"Don't drink the champagne so fast. You probably can't stand up to go home."

"I'm fine," she said.

"Just telling you, it's a creeper." He smiled and sat back, lifting one leg to lay gently on the other as if he was in his living room; leaned back and let his glance float around the club.

He handled silence well, she thought, was not bothered that she ignored him for the music - a man in complete control of himself.

The reggae beat was heavy, the selector playing rhythm by rhythm. First he would play one song which he would then merge into another with the same rhythm, and then another. After a couple of tunes, he would switch and let the different singers and DJs compete. The crowd was going wild, the atmosphere was electric. Dancers spilled into the passages, people were dancing at their tables. Shirley wished he would play them all: every reggae song that was ever made, every artist that ever sung. The DJ seemed to have heard her thoughts and tried to oblige by playing songs from the best reggae artists. So he went back and gave her Dennis Brown, then Gregory Isaacs, then Freddy McGrggor, and Cocoa Tea. Then he moved up to Sanchez, and Pinchers and Papa San. Shabba heralded the new age with 'Trailer Load a Girls' and Buju railed on about the 'Browning'. Then Beres Hammond asked all to 'Step Aside Now' - for another man would like to take over'. As Beres's vocals chilled her insides she heard herself shout; "shots."

"You can dance if you want, you know," Moet said calmly. As if dancing was his to give.

She looked at him a bit surprised – a bit flattered.

"Yeah man," he insisted. "You can stand up right here or we can go to the dance floor."

"I'd prefer the dance floor," she heard herself say.

He rose and offered her his hand. Shirley took it even as she closed her eyes and rocked her head to Beres singing; Step aside now, another man would like to take over. The trip to the dance floor expended the song but the selector kept Beres on. The speakers blared One dance, one dance, what one dance can do, what one dance can do... The crowd around her was a bundle of energy. She was not sure she remembered how to move, but she searched for the bass line, closed her eyes and followed its every turn. She became oblivious to everything around her except the bass line and the massaging vocals of Beres Hammond moving like coarse raindrops through her.

Then the selector took Beres away. She opened her eyes quickly, and saw Moet rocking gently and smiling patiently at her.

A harsh sound of cymbals crashed through the speakers, a deep thump of a drum followed and the crowd sighed audibly as Earth Wind and Fire went into their prelude to 'Reasons' that was without question, for Shirley, the greatest soul song ever recorded.

She watched Moet pause, widen the space between them and nod eloquently to her. He was giving her the choice to leave and wait for a less intimate song. Shirley hesitated slightly and looked up at him – big, black, strong, honest like the door of a bank vault. She shrugged her shoulders. He was kind of charming.

It was well over a year since she had held a man, and this one felt good. He was solid, hard and gentle. She closed her eyes, leaned into him, pressed her head against his throat and reached up to clasp her hands behind his neck. His hands fell and rested in the small of her back, locking her to him – making her feel safe. They found the slowest beat of the amazing rhythm and held ground there, on one tile, as if they had rented the spot for their very own for the rest of the night.

Chapter Nineteen

Next morning, the phone woke her up from a dead sleep. She crawled from the sofa bed to somewhere across the room and dragged it from its cradle.

"You have a wicked hangover, don't it?" A smile was in the strange voice. She made to hang up the phone. "You have the wrong number."

"No – Shirley this?"

"Who is this?" she asked tiredly. Whatever joy she had felt last night was in retreat and every part of her head was throbbing.

"I tell you, you shouldn't drink the champagne so fast. Is a creeper!"

And then he came back slowly to her: Moet "Oh," she said, with a dead voice, "could you call back another time?"

"Why?" he asked.

"Because I can't talk right now."

"Oh," he said, "is just the hangover, man. Don't bother drink no coffee. Lay-down no good for it either. What you need is some Alka Seltzer, or a hot lunch."

"Well, I have neither and I am going back to sleep. So see you."

"You can get lunch if you want, you know," he said.

And then he came fully back to her. Big and confident like the door of a bank vault. "I can imagine," she said.

"A sending the car for you. You bad friend can come."

"I think she's gone to work."

"How much time you want to get ready?"

"I did not say I was going anywhere. I'm going back to sleep."

"One hour. A give you one hour."

"For what? You are not listening to me." She pressed her hand against her head. The veins pulsed against the skin. "I have to go."

"Lay-down no good for it. Me will send Chef 'bout one."

"Suit yourself," she said, and slammed down the phone.

It seemed she had only returned to the couch a minute or so when the doorbell rang. She raised the window halfway and peeped out at the person knocking at the door. The man turned with a huge smile.

"Is me, man – Chef. Me kinda late but me did have to stop."

She pulled the hair from her face and looked again. He wore baggy jeans and a Tommy Hilfiger shirt. Behind him she saw a glistening black Lexus, as big as a house. She could not find the words to express her exasperation.

"You don' ready yet?" Chef asked.

"He said one o'clock!" was all she could find to defend herself.

"Is almost two now." Chef glanced at his watch. "Is all right. Me will wait in the car, take as much time." He turned and walked toward the large automobile.

Shirley fell back into the couch, raised her eyes to the ceiling and wondered what she had gotten herself into. There was no memory of what happened after the third or fourth song on the dance floor. Now there was a man at her door and a car waiting in her driveway.

Her head throbbed less, but a hollow pain gnawed at her stomach. She would have liked to go back to bed but she had a feeling that sooner or later, Chef would hammer on the door again. She looked around her. Cushions were scattered on the floor, shoes were strewn about, her handbag was under a chair near the kitchen. A huge burp escaped her lips and almost heeled her over. She admitted to herself that a good lunch was much better than lying around in that mess. She felt another burp coming and ran into the bathroom.

Shirley took her time bathing, ran the cold water through her hair till she felt almost faint. Then she dried it, pulled her hair back, and snapped it tight with a clip, so the ponytail flowed like a frayed rope onto her back. She chose a simple blouse and a jeans skirt that touched her knees, ignoring the sparse array of makeup on the dresser. If he wanted to see her, then he would – and be done with it. She found a pair of old comfortable loafers, pulled her bag from beneath the chair, then got her extra keys and headed for the door.

His apartment was north east of Hallandale in a secluded complex of beige, brown and glass. It had a security system with codes that reminded her of Coral Estates where she had worked for Nicole some heartaches ago. Chef ushered her into a living room of lacquer and glass lined with black, gold and silver. She stood in awe near a glistening, black-trimmed glass wall unit, while Moet and Chef spoke softly near the door. Chef left and Moet stepped down into the living room to smile broadly at her.

He was dressed casually in sweat bottoms, a large T-shirt, and black leather designer slippers. He was as big as she remembered and looked better than she expected: not handsome – more like a well-cut lawn. His skin was clean and cool, his hair perfectly barbered, mustache neat, small beard trimmed: perfect. He smelled fresh and clean.

"It's beautiful," she said.

"A no nothing," he said. "How the headache?"

"Still throbbing a bit. I thought we were going to lunch?"

"Yes," he said.

"You aren't dressed."

"You don't have to go out to eat lunch."

"You are going to cook!" she said with sarcasm.

"Yes."

He led her through the tastefully furnished living room to a spacious black and white kitchen that had a large counter in the centre of it. He offered her one of the four cushioned stools, checked the pots on the stove and flipped the switch on a white electric kettle.

"I goin' give you something for the hangover first. You headache will disappear in five minutes." He took a small packet from the cupboard and emptied its crystalline contents into a mug. Then he waited till the kettle gave a small beep and poured the hot water onto it.

"What's that?" she asked him.

"Come from China, work like magic." He offered the cup to her.

The contents smelled like herbs mixed with Alka Seltzer and made a thick steam that covered her face as she sipped it.

"You can take some fresh air," he said, and pointed to a wide glass door that led to a balcony.

She told him thanks and took her cup with her. Already the tea had begun to soothe her, and by the time she got outside, the headache was almost gone. The wide balcony looked onto a man-made lake that stretched out of sight on both sides of the apartment. Beyond was a large grove of trees. At one end of the balcony, she saw a small table set with beige linen, complete with cloth napkins expertly folded and wine glasses turned down. On the floor beside it was the inevitable bucket with the head of a champagne bottle sticking out.

She smiled to herself and turned toward the apartment. Her tea finished, she stood leaning against the kitchen's lacquered counter and watched him busy himself around the kitchen. He moved like an expert chef; bending to adjust the stove, tipping gravy into his hand to taste, his large white towel around his neck for the generous wipes he made after the several times he washed his hands. After a while he reached into the cupboard for two large dishes, brushed business-like past her and placed them onto the table.

"What's for lunch?"she asked.

He paused on his way back. "Curry shrimp."

"Oh!" He had surprised her again.

By the time they were ready to eat, her headache had completely gone. He allowed her to sit then moved to fill her plate with shrimp. There was bread, baked potatoes and a large salad. Her stomach growled. He sat, picked up the champagne, popped the cork and reached for her glass.

"You want my headache to start again?" She smiled at him.

"Is not the wine, you know – is how much you drink."

"Well, not too much," she told him.

He halved her glass.

"That's why they call you Moet? That's all you drink?"

He shrugged. "Them call me all kinda things."

"What's your real name?"

"Delroy."

The food was good. The shrimp was juicy, and the gravy thick and peppered. The only memory she had of such good curry was that of her father's cooking. But he was Indian and Indians invented curry food. "It's you they should call Chef," she told him.

He laughed gently. "Cho, people call people all kinda things for all kinda different reason."

"Well, you can really cook."

"A no nothing," he said.

It was his silences she liked – how calm he could be, allowing her her thoughts as she ate. Then how he listened keenly, giving her all the time in the world to compose herself and say what she wanted to say - picking up on her conversation as she ended, answering precisely as if he was onto her thoughts before she worked out what she had to say. So the afternoon passed. She ate more than she expected, laughed a little more than she thought she would have, wished she had worn more make-up.

When they were finished they sat and watched the afternoon push to evening and the sun move to four o'clock. Pigeons flocked the edge of the man-made lake, the long trees changed to copper and the distance beyond to deep azure.

"Thank you for lunch," she said.

"You say that already," he smiled.

"I know, but I think I have to go now."

"Why?"

"Why? I don't live here, and Queeny will come home soon. She will be worried."

He sat serenely. She knew he would see through the weaknesses in her argument. Nothing much seem to miss him. But it would have been unlike him to encourage or force her to stay.

"All right. You wan' freshen up?"

"I'd appreciate that," she said softly.

He pointed her through the bedroom to the bathroom. She walked past the large bed with its magnificent glass headboard, through the wide walk-through closet as neatly and well stacked as a small department store, into a spacious bathroom with Jacuzzi at one end.

As she stepped into the bathroom, she wondered why she felt a pang of disappointment that his dressing table was so well laid out and stacked with beauty products. There was a five-step facial treatment and manicure kit; a facial massager, chin massager and a plethora of beauty treatments and perfume. This was just lunch. In any event, she could not expect a man this rich not to have a wife – and as Queeny said, they all had a whole heap of women.

She reached curiously for a bottle - Clinique Skin Supplies for Men. She checked again in surprise and wonder, for every cosmetic on the table was for a man. There was more instruments, body-care equipment and hair treatments than in some beauty salons. She had heard of men who took care of themselves - but this one took the cake.

Shirley checked herself in the mirror and hated that she had not taken more care. Her face was like a grater, and black spots were scattered randomly across it. Her little blouse and cheap jeans skirt seemed like rags. Her hair was dry, the clip that held her hair little more than an elastic band. She washed quickly and dropped her eyes from the image in the mirror.

As she went back into the bedroom, he was there standing, with a large towel in his hand. "You all right?" he asked.

"I used one of those in the bathroom."

"A no nothing," he said.

And then he pulled her to him and kissed her long and hard. She resisted momentarily, but just like the night before, on the dance floor in Stingers, she reached for his neck and surrendered to whatever it was that made him feel so good.

She melted to him. He eased away and stared at her, nostrils flaring, teeth bared. Then he pulled her against his chest and groaned. When he lifted her face to kiss her again, she lunged at him, her mouth hungry, seeking deep, tasting champagne.

He pushed her toward the bed but she stuck to him and they moved together. As he laid her down, she instinctively spread herself to him. Her skirt rode away and her legs retreated till she almost halved herself into a T. His chest crushed her breasts and his torso rubbed against her unopposed.

His passion was like heavy steam, made them sweat just by kissing. He broke the strap of her blouse and laid her exposed. The worn snaps of her bra came away without resistance. His lips left hers and trailed a path to her navel and then back again and then his mouth descended again unto hers. They locked together, grunting like animals – his hands flayed around and his clothing fell aside till he was naked and she felt him hard and long against her legs – harder and longer than she had ever felt any man. His hands ran flat against her belly beneath the waist of her skirt and panties and stroked her from the top. She raised up against his hands, grinding madly, twisting and turning around his stroking finger.

And then he was in –filling every inch of her.

He pulled his mouth away and she looked up and held his eyes – matched his burning passionate stare. For an instant they just lay there, staring at each other. Then she lunged for his lips again, biting him, while her body quickened and trembled.

Then he moved.

There was no roughness in him. There was no jerky up and down. His body rotated against her– his organ stoking every inch of her around and around, circling gently like a rub-a-dub – only deeper and fuller. Then he pushed his hands beneath her waist so that her lower back was in his palms and her body was raised, freeing her hips to move. They tightened against each other, locked by the force of the turning, lost in the intensity. Orgasms came and went, limbs became tired, but the motion was a continuum in space with no force to stop it. Even when the sheets were soaked and the knees gave way, they still clung as if they lacked the force to disentangle or break the rhythm – till their motion gave way to spasms and gasps and contractions as the passion fused them.

When next she saw the time it was seven o'clock and he was pulling her tenderly to him to rest his chin in her hair. She leaned back against his chest as his hands played against her belly with the waist of her panties.

"I've got to go," she said.

She felt him begin to push the underwear down her hips. The worn elastic broke against his hand. A small tear of shame escaped her as he flexed his wrist so the other side broke and the tattered garment fell into his hand. He held her tightly – tenderly, his hardening member began to probe between her legs.

"Why?" he asked.

Chapter Twenty

When Moet dropped her home that night it was after eleven o'clock and Shirley wished to God he had not been a gentleman and walked her to her door. But the night took its own course and there was nothing to prevent the meeting at the door, and then the awkward moment as Queeny, frozen by surprise, blurted an ugly, "Eh, eh," then stormed away toward her bedroom.

Shirley was not sure why she should feel embarrassed, but she did. As Moet turned away, she closed the door, and passed through the small living room to the bathroom. She hoped that Queeny would remain in her room, but that was too much to ask, for Queeny was not the type to hide away at a time like this. When Shirley left the bathroom she was in the kitchen fussing over nothing at all.

Shirley began to remove the cushions from the sofa. She heaped them aside and pulled the bed flat. As she straightened the sheets she noticed that Queeny had settled on a coke and was sitting at the kitchen counter looking sourly at her.

She knew, Shirley thought as she sat on the edge of the sofa bed to face her. She knew. Two women living in such a small apartment the way they did, could hold no secrets from each other. Plus good sex had its own aura, and good sex after two years set off sirens. "You not going to work tomorrow?" Shirley made to stretch out on the bed.

But it seemed Queeny had no intention of moving. "You don' see that them boy there worthless."

"He called and invited me for a drink. What should I have done? Is just a drink."

"So that's why you go out with the ugly boy? You don't see is a druggist that? Boy can't even spell him name. You don' know them boys there. Is drugs them sell."

"Aw, come on," Shirley said with exaggerating tiredness. "You sleep with Mikey, and you are married."

"That is me. You different," Queeny said sadly. Then hastily, "Plus mi know them. And Mikey no wicked and ugly like the one Moet."

Shirley fell silent for a while. On the one hand she was ashamed for having somehow let Queeny down. On the other hand she was mad at herself for feeling any shame at all. She was her own woman and should be able to make her own decisions and Queeny had no right to be sitting there acting like her mother. "I'm going to bed," she finally said. "I'm going to sleep."

Queeny dropped the empty Coke tin noisily into the garbage and made to pass Shirley for the bedroom. Then she paused and hesitated. "I hope you really know what you doing. I know what I talking about." She then returned to the stool and sat in silence.

"Jesus Christ, Queeny! Is just a drink me have with him!"

"Just a drink, no. I never think I would live to see the day."

"You make it look as if I don't deserve a little fun."

"You must know," Queeny said.

"Jealousy is a hell of a thing," Shirley whispered beneath her breath.

"Me hear what you say, you know," Queeny said. "Me hear what you say. That's why I tell you before that you not a nice person. You should box me inna mi mouth. Box me inna mi mouth to rahtid, 'bout me a try help. You not even know when somebody looking out fi you."

"You don' worry," Shirley said. "I can take care of myself. Plus, how you know it's not just the one time?"

"You must know," Queeny said, and rose to leave the room.

The phone rang.

Queeny answered and then dropped the receiver like a piece of garbage onto the kitchen counter. "You one drink," she said.

"Hi, what happen?" he asked sexily.

"Hi," she said, as Queeny, who was standing a meter away looked straight at her.

"What you doing tomorrow?" he asked.

"Nothing."

"You want go shopping? I will pick you up 'bout twelve. Make we go buy you some things."

"OK," she said, matching Queeny's stare. "I have to go."

"Tomorrow," he said.

"Bye."

"What a piece a one drink!" Queeny cut her eyes dramatically.

"You know," Shirley said as she replaced the phone, "you know it's not your business what I do with my private life. I am having a telephone call and you standing there, looking down my throat like I am some teenager who broke some damn rule. You are not my mother. I am just cotching with you. Till . . . till . . ."

"Till what? Say it no! Why you don't say it?"

"Just leave me alone, OK? Just let me go to sleep."

"You damn right." Queeny finally swished her tail and turned toward her room. "You damn right. Make me leave you alone, yah. Next thing, you go say me want you ugly man."

Shirley fell silent and watched the silk nightgown ride up and down Queeny's figure as she stomped away toward her bedroom. Then she slumped against the bed. She was beginning to get angry. Not just at Queeny, but at all these people in her life who constantly expected her to live up to some imaginary standard in their minds, bear these impossible burdens, under these impossible circumstances, when they hardly understood the suffering and pain she felt. What was she to do? Sit around all day and not do anything, not go out - go mad with loneliness and desperation? What had she done that was so bad? It was all right for Queeny to talk. Where was Mikey with Shirley's money? Where was her green card and social security number? What would she gain by just lying down and watching TV every day? So a rich man wanted to take her out and buy her some drinks, and treat her like a woman – how long had it been since she felt that way? So what if she felt like sleeping with him? Whose body was it? Whose life was it anyway? And why did she feel so guilty and sad in the pit of her stomach?

She pressed her face into the folds of the sheets just in time for the tears to come.

Chapter Twenty-One

"I have something to take care of," Moet said, as he piloted the large car onto the 836, "so I goin' drop you off and pick you up later. About a hour or so. All right?"

"You are going to leave me alone?"

"Yeah man, plus I know onoo woman. Bet you by the time I come back, you don't even ready to start buy. Anyway, I know the store owner. She will take care of you." He reached into the pocket of his shirt and produced a wad of bills. "See some money here. Buy what you want."

"How much money that?"

"Bout a gran' or so."

He parked at a boutique that seemed to spill onto Collins Avenue. A tall skinny woman in an exotic green dress met them at the door.

"Take care of her for me, Cherry," Moet said. "Soon come back."

Cherry was pencil thin with an air of sophistication about her that suggested a good eye for quality; people as well as clothing. Shirley felt cheap and hesitant beneath her gaze, but her manner was becoming and she piloted Shirley graciously towards the centre of the store. She reminded Shirley of a grass squit – a tiny busy bird casing an ant hill.

"Do you have any special interest?" the woman asked politely.

"Do you have a Chanel collection?" Shirley asked.

The woman was too skilled to show her surprise at the correct pronunciation of the word, but Shirley detected a slight softening.

"This way," she said.

"I'll browse on my own." Shirley raised her hand. "I'll call you when I'm ready." She accessed the small landing to the next level, past a life-sized mannequin. Models were prancing through the store as if it were a catwalk, displaying garments to the few wealthy customers who perused them lazily with careful eyes.

Shirley picked a nice peach dress and found a dressing room. She dropped the dress onto the small seat and immediately began to count through the wad of bills that Moet had given her. There were fifteen hundred dollars there, consisting of mostly twenty and fifty dollar bills. She would not lose her cool, she would not forget herself... or where she had been yesterday. Fifteen Hundred Dollars!

Yesterday she had five. Today she had Fifteen Hundred. She would not forget herself.

She left the dress where it was and returned to the Chanel section. She got herself some facial treatments, tried a tiny summer dress and bought that too. She also bought a few undergarments – all the time making a mental account of all she had spent. Then she paid the bill of less than three hundred dollars.

Shirley had no intention of spending another cent of the money. She stuffed the rest into her bra and went outside to wait. If Moet did not show up within the hour she would find a bus and return home.

The car slid to her feet just as she began to feel impatient.

He alighted, big and cool, linen trousers crumpled, brushing the top of his Bally loafers.

"You finish already?" he asked.

"Yes, I am ready."

"Where the bag them?"

"Here," She showed him the single red Chanel bag she was carrying.

"Only that you buy?"

"Well," she stuttered, "that's all I need."

"You mad!" He sounded a bit annoyed. "Mi say buy clothes. Mi no mean one frock. When I say buy, I mean buy!" He held Shirley by the elbow, guided her back into the store and beckoned to the grass-squit woman. "Cherry, outfit her for me no. Give her about ten outfit, from top to bottom, inside out. Put it on the bill. You have any champagne?"

The woman clapped her hands and a man appeared from nowhere with a silver tray and two glasses with wine. Moet took the glasses, gave one to Shirley and guided her to a small area where there was a large sofa. He sat, stretched his legs and showed her the seat. "Relax man, have a drink."

In ten minutes Cherry returned with a model and the man laden with dresses on both arms. The model began to walk up and down before them, changing the dresses right there in their presence. Moet nodded, smiled and shook his head like a connoisseur. It took Shirley a while to come to terms with what was happening but slowly, like a blind person being healed by the hand of God, the scales lifted from her eyes; the years of poverty and want disappeared from her and she was once again Shirley Temple Brown – movie star. She straightened herself, sipped her wine and began to really shop. They left the store with enough bags to fill both the trunk and the back seat of the large car.

When Moet drove past her exit on the highway Shirley did not even flinch. And when on closing the door of his apartment he reached for her, she did not think to resist but grinded her body into him so he could know she was in a better mood than he could hope to imagine.

But later, much later, when he suggested she move in with him, she said she would have to think about it. For though she was happy and comfortable in Moet's company, as soon as she left it and returned to the apartment she felt ashamed and dirty for reasons she did not want to understand.

However, time and his constant presence wore her conscience down. The more time they spent together, the more she looked forward to his visits. And they got to timing it so that he would come just as Queeny left and drop her off just before she returned. When Queeny worked at nights, Shirley slept over at his place.

As the relationship grew, Shirley realized she would have to make a choice. Life with Queeny began to lose its appeal. Her apartment was not as cozy as before. The carpet now seemed old and frayed, the furniture worn and shiny at the edges, and the sofa-bed on which Shirley slept had a foul smell. The kitchen, all of a sudden stank, the bathroom was now tiny and uncomfortable and there was just not enough space to do anything.

Moet's place was a palace in comparison.

When Shirley finally told Queeny she would be leaving, Queeny looked at her sadly, screwed up her face, rolled her eyes, and said, "Me know you a sleep with him, all you try to hide it."

"I wasn't trying to hide it," Shirley said.

"Me wonder when you was going to make the final move."

"I wouldn't before telling you."

"You don't have to tell me, you know. You could just go on."

"I couldn't." Shirley was trying to contend with the shame she felt. "You have been a real friend, Queeny."

"Well," Queeny had dropped, "you a big woman, you mus' know what you up to."

"Queeny, you don't have to go on like that, you know."

"How you mean go on?"

"I know what I am doing."

"So you think," Queeny said to her, "so you think. You don' know Moet an' him frien' them. Them a druggist. Is coke them sell. Them kill people, and anytime them ready, them can just get up and get kill too. Man come shoot them, police come shoot them, them can shoot them one another. I hope you know what you doing. Plus Moet no fool, is not somebody you can just use."

"You going come by sometimes?" Shirley wanted to end the conversation. Moet would probably be by any minute.

"Me?!" Queeny said, making a face as if she had smelled something stinky and wet. "Me, ma? Me not coming to that dutty boy yard." Then she shut up and sat on the stool to wait on Moet so she could stare at him with more hate than Shirley had ever seen emanating from a human being.

Chapter Twenty-Two

It could have been a scene from an episode of Falcon Crest: the dim interior of the comedy club giving way to the subdued lighting of the foyer as they exit; Moet standing beside her in the half light - black in soft black on the grey of the moonlit night. And she in dusty silver leaning against him as the valet brings the Mercedes Benz to halt at their feet. He opens the door for Shirley and she slides inside while Moet tips him generously. Then Moet joins her and the car slips easily into the Fort Lauderdale night, its nose toward the beach and soft music gushing from hidden speakers to surround them.

"Want me to drop down the top?"

"Sure," she answered dreamily. "There is a moon. It is nice out."

The top slid back, opened the sky and the night, and washed her with the sweet cool breeze of the Fort Lauderdale intercostal.

"You ready to go home?"

"It's up to you."

"Make we cruise the beach little." Moet dropped a hand to find hers momentarily, then caressed her legs.

"Sure," Shirley said.

It was one thirty by the clock on the dashboard and all the shops and clubs were still open; people milled around, walked the long beach, and browsed the shops.

It seemed, Shirley thought, that the day was coming full circle as it closed. For the evening had started with them browsing the expensive boutiques of the Don Shula complex in upscale Miami Lakes. Later they had a quiet dinner at Don Shula's Restaurant and Steak House, then around nine or so they followed the mood of the night and took in a movie before finally getting to the comedy club. But there were too many Jamaicans there and the comedian was not as good as they expected, so they left early and now were cruising another fashion district, this time along the Fort Lauderdale strip, following the mood of the night . . . full circle, as it were, till it brought itself to a close.

"You want to drive?"

"Who, me?"

"Of course."

"You know I can't drive." The issue had come up before and Shirley had been somewhat embarrassed to admit that she had never had the reason to learn to drive.

"But you must learn one day."

"Well, not tonight. I am half drunk as it is."

He laughed. "Make we stop then." He maneuvered the car expertly into a parking spot along the side of the road, rummaged through the cooler in the back of the car, found a small bottle of champagne and two plastic cups, hid the bottle under his jacket. "Come."

She followed him through a chain-linked fence onto the silver beach to a spot off to the side where a large umbrella was stuck in the dirt. He poured two drinks and burrowed the half-empty bottle into the sand. They sat right there on the ground with the sea rippling ahead and Fort Lauderdale glistening to the side and behind them. Somewhere up ahead a club spilled on to the beach and reggae music drifted out to them. "Chris Garvey out there," Moet nodded as he sipped.

"When I come back, I goin' teach you to drive." Moet rested his head in her lap.

"You are leaving?"

"Tomorrow. No more than 'bout a week."

She tried not to think of him not being there, for she had never gotten used to him leaving in the dead of night and driving off in some old Honda or Toyota with Chef. And though he called at times, she would still begin to fear after the first hours. Queeny's warnings would come back to her and she would jump at each ring of the telephone or each thud near the door. One night she had even woken up in cold sweat at the insistent sounds of sirens, only to find she had left the TV on.

"Now if you could drive you could go out sometime when me not here."

"I'll be fine," she told him as she tried to press the half empty glass deep enough to stand in the sand. "I do go out sometimes, you know." She said this to quiet him, but also because she hated to feel she had no life outside of him.

"Can I ask you something?" The evening had given her courage, so she felt she could push further.

"What?"

"Did you ever hear from Mikey? What really happened to him? Do you think he ever got my documents at all?"

She felt him pause in his head – or rather, she felt his thoughts slow – so that when he spoke it was as if the words were being extruded slowly from him. "Me never even remember that." He took a long drag from the bottle. Then he began to roll the half-empty bottle into the sand so that the Champagne frothed from its mouth. "Is a long time, yes. Is really a long time now me promise you."

Shirley did not press him further. His tone told her it was a lost cause. And in any event he had already given her that money ten times over. She knew, however, that she would ultimately need her documents if she was ever going to achieve any sort of independence. So, though she dropped the subject for the time being, she planned to ask him about it again at another time.

The froth spilled from the bottle and Moet, who had fallen silent, emptied it. He then got up and began to look around for a garbage bin. He reached his hand down to pull her up. "Come," he said.

Next morning she woke to an empty bed.

She had hardly heard him leave, but suspected it must have been a few hours after they had gone to sleep. Snuggling down, she lifted the pillow to cover her head, and touched something: a small white envelope was resting beneath it. She shook its contents free and saw her face staring back at her from the laminated surface of her green card. She shook the envelope again and her social security card fell beside it on the white silk sheet.

Her first instinct was to run, to pack her things and go. That had always been the plan associated with the documents. First it was leaving Nicole, then it was leaving Queeny's to chase her dreams, now it was to walk away from this life and seek her American dream.

She rose from the bed and stood naked before one of the full length mirrors. She placed one laminated card on each breast and did a small dance.

She would forgive America today – for all the ills it had caused her.

Now she must leave.

But leave what? And go where?

She had a few thousand dollars saved. She had all the clothes she would need. But where would she go? Back to Queeny's drab apartment? Back to Tiny, whom she had not seen or spoken to in over a year? She took one look around her lodgings and realized that somehow she was trapped in a very splendid bondage.

When Moet returned a week later, she was soaking beneath a thick layer of the suds and fragrance of Chanel – her face deep beneath the mask of its six-step facial treatment – still contemplating the possibility of her departure.

Chapter Twenty-Three

"Is automatic man, all you have to do is steer. You don't even have to press the gas."

"But this is the middle of the street!" she squealed.

"How you think I learn to drive?" he laughed. "The middle of the road them start me. Everybody start in the middle of the road."

"But I should practice first," Shirley said.

"The light change."

"Jesus Christ!"

"Just lift you foot off the brake, mi right beside you."

Safe like a bank vault's door.

She lifted her foot and the car glided forward. Horns bellowed from behind her.

"Don't matter them," he said. "Them just trying to frighten you. Just go at you own pace and watch where you going."

She held the steering for dear life and crept slowly down University. Half a dozen stop lights later, she had the gauge of the gas and enough confidence to make the big vehicle glide down the half empty street at twenty miles per hour.

"When do I turn?" she asked as they halted behind a large bus.

"Whenever you want. Whenever you feel comfortable enough."

"Just drive straight so?"

"Why not?"

And so she drove. Pointed the large vehicle south on the University Drive. University turned to US9 and US9 emptied onto the US1. The road changed, got bigger, got smaller then bigger and she began to relax to the point where she changed to the middle lane to overtake an older slower car. Moet leaned his seat backward, dropped his designer glasses from his forehead to his nose and placed his crepe onto the dashboard.

He took his hand away from the emergency brake and clasped it with the other across his stomach.

"Go on, my big driver. You see that it easy?"

She smiled like a little girl. "It's not so bad."

"You like it?"

"Yeah," she said.

"Yeh," Moet laughed. "So we not turning back then."

"Just go on drive so?"

"Just go on drive," he said.

"But where this road lead?" she asked.

"The Keys where Florida done," he said.

"Just go on drive so?"

"Yeah man. Why not?"

By the time they left Miami behind, she began to feel enough confidence to try a turn, but the air began to change and the buildings were not tall any more, and her curiosity grew. Moet did not seem to care and she had nothing better to do, so she tilted her head forward as the white lines in the road sped faster toward her.

"Where is this?" she asked.

"About Homestead," he said.

And so she drove till the buildings disappeared and the road became two-lanes and cars whizzed around her at break-neck speed. There were marshes and swamps to the side of her now, and sea and beach sometimes. And then they left all of that for towns so small it took a minute to pass through them.

"Here so the Keys start," he smiled.

And she nodded and drove on till they landed at the sea. Now the only roads were bridges, high and arcing, flat and short, bridges seven miles long and six lanes wide – and sea: crystal blue and sparkling, rushing against coastlines, overtaking the distances, defusing the horizon, merging into sky.

"It pretty," she sighed. "I could stay here forever."

"A no nutten," he shrugged. "We can stay couple days if you want."

They stopped at the best-looking hotel on Key West. They had no extra clothing but they bought large T-shirts, bathing suits and broad-brimmed tourist hats.

They spent days lazing on the beach or partaking in every activity available: from parasailing and water skiing, to renting a boat for a whole day to fish and snorkel in the pink corals of a secluded reef. Then at nights they dressed in shorts and white flowing shirts to skirt the untamed nightlife around them. Finally they would retire to their room to make love on the carpet or to some desolate corner of the beach, in the sand – then exhaustion would take over and they would fall asleep till the sun would wake them to start paradise all over again.

They had been there a week and a day when the telephone rang to remind them there was a real world outside. And Moet's grunt to Chef on the other end, that he would see him late that night, reminded her that even paradise was for a time.

They left the Keys around three that afternoon.

Moet drove. He dropped the top on the Benz and pointed toward the seven-mile bridge.

Shirley leaned back into her seat and watched his serious face across the space – he was growing on her. She reached forward, selected a Garnett Silk CD, slipped it into the player, then snuggled into Moet as he placed a large arm around her. Everything was perfect that moment. Every feeling was good. And there was nothing to remind her of the warnings Queeny gave.

"Is drugs mi sell, you know."

She let the words pass because she could not believe he would have just said them like that; blow them into the car like a casual exhaling of cigarette smoke. "Is drugs me sell and me want you know up front. Me don' say it will go on forever. But me want you know the truth."

She was not sure how to respond to him. She could not pull suddenly away from him, and strangely enough, she did not feel to. He must have known she knew or had guessed by now. She was not a fool. So why did he choose to tell her now? At this moment, when he was growing on her?

"I'm not stupid, you know," was all she could manage.

He seemed to sigh deep inside. "Is America this, you know, man have to survive."

She did not answer immediately. She was unsure what words would best grace the space of the car... push the silence away.

"America make all kind a people do all kinds of things," she finally said.

They were halfway across the seven-mile bridge, the beauty of the Florida Keys on all sides of them. The evening was coming on. The car dipped towards the stretch of road in front of them. "True," he said. "Sometimes a man come to do one thing, and the vibes just push him certain ways."

"I think I understand what you mean."

"Yeah?"

"Yes."

"Is farm work me come for, you know."

"Yeah?"

"Yeah. Farm work me come. The second week after I come here, my brother come look for me in a brand new Honda. Right up near here too – Belglades, man. Old Belglades. Him just drive up, sit down on the bonnet and wait till me come to the gate, and start laugh. I can still see him on the bonnet of that Honda, just laughin'. Then him stop laugh and ask, 'How you love work so, man? How you love work so? Leave this and come, man.' So me leave it."

"Just so, same time, just like that?"

"Well, no. Me work till we get the weekend off and then leave with him. Go flea market and just don' go back."

"And he brought you into the business?"

"No." He shook his head. "Would you believe, even now, I don' know what kind of business him was in?"

"Was?"

"Yeah, was. Him drop me at him apartment, say him soon come and me never see him again."

"Wow!"

"That no nutten. The next night, me lie down sleeping. And all me hear was just gunshot a whistle all over the place."

"What you mean?"

"Man come shoot up the place. You should see me," he chuckled. "You should see me a run with me pants in mi hand. A run like mad. You would think is a man catch me with him wife. It wasn't husband, it was bullet I running from."

"Jesus!" She trembled visibly.

"Sometimes you see a man simple so, you don't know what him go through in this country. Is plenty things I go through in Uncle Sam country. Is under bridge me use to sleep, you know. Under the overpass." He kissed his teeth. "You think it easy? You have to learn how fi set cardboard layer by layer to keep off rain. You have fi get use to cold."

He was surprising her.

He was not a talkative man. Yet this evening, sitting with her in his arms cruising along, he seemed to have found a reason to open to her. She was not sure she wanted to hear much more. She made to adjust the radio and he slipped his hand away to let her go. She checked her face in the mirror and straightened her hair against the wind.

"You want me put up the top?"

She told him no and curled into her seat so that she was looking sideways at him.

"And all them time," he continued, "me still try fly straight, you know. Still fly straight."

"What did you do?" she asked softly.

"Wash pot. Wash pot and everything. First me use to go to the mall them and sit down near the wishing well and scoop out the money when people not looking. Yeah, man. Nuff things me go through, man. You see all them people who stand up a roadside and give out flyer? Me use to do that too, you know, they pay you by the amount of flyer you give out. Yeah man. I use to have two job. Live under the overpass and have two job. Use to wash pots a morning and give out flyer evening time. And it use to work. Things did start come together."

"Yeah?"

"Yeah. Is the one Chef mash up all a that."

"Chef?"

"Yeah."

"How come?"

He laughed. "Me shouldn't tell you all this, you know."

"You don't have to."

"A no nutten, really. You see, me and Chef use to live under the bridge, but while me work, him use to beg with a sign at the roadside. But I couldn' do that. Begging make more money, but me couldn' do that. Then I make the mistake and tell him 'bout the flyer thing – him say him nah wash no pot."

"But he is a chef!"

"That is another story," he said slyly.

"So what did he do?"

"Well. All right, might as well me tell you. You see, after you give out flyers for a while, it make you tired. And it no easy to wash pot, you know. So one day I get an idea. Me just collect the flyer them and drop them in a big garbage truck because the garbage company was right beside the bridge where me use to sleep."

"Jesus!" she cried. "But that was not right."

"I never say so," he said.

"So why did you do it?"

"Just the vibes, baby. Sometime me was just get tired. So when me tell Chef 'bout it, him use to do the same thing. Then him get greedy and use to go back three times a day for more flyers."

"So they got suspicious."

"How you mean! The man them a wonder how Chef could hand out fifteen hundred flyers per day every day."

She could not but laugh.

"So," he chuckled, "them trail him and catch him a throw them in the dumpster. And since it was me who did recommend him, them fire me too. All threaten fi bring police if we no give them back them money."

"So what you did?"

"Move to another underpass."

A sign said Miami Next Left. He angled the car gently, his fingers caressing the steering wheel. She tried to imagine him washing pots in some dark kitchen. It must have been a long way from those days to these manicured fingers and well-groomed designer look. He was as black as pearl, and in the lessening light his complexion seemed cool, his features soft. His thick lips gave his face the impression of one pouting halfway. His hair was cut low, and camouflaged his receding hairline. There was a gentleness about him – a self-made man reflecting and musing on his adventures. It was a side of him she had never seen and doubted she would ever see again.

"So why you come to America?" he asked, without taking his eyes from the road.

This caught her off-guard, but she was composed, and so paused only slightly. "A better life. Like anyone else."

"Everybody say that." He shook his head. "No better life not in America for black people."

"Maybe," she said. For she still believed that anyone could make it, given the right documents and circumstances.

"You know say, is when I come to America mi find out that me black."

"Me too," she said, though she was unsure what he meant. For she was several shades lighter than he was.

"Yeah man. Up here black is a different something from human being. Even when you rich you not anything."

"You plan to go back home then?"

"Me! Nothing no down there for me."

The mention of home made her a little sad. She had written her mother a week before, sent her some money and told her she was living alone and working at a bank. She explained that she had been in school all this time and had not been able to write because of the pressure. She was glad her mother did not have a visa to the United States. The thought of having to explain Moet to her mother – or anyone she knew, for that matter – made her shudder.

"You sure you don't want me put up the top?"

"It's all right." She hugged herself tightly. "Is so far we came? I did not even realize it."

"We have 'bout hour-and-a-half left," he said. "We not even reach Homestead yet."

"Wow!"

The car phone rang.

Moet spoke into it for a minute or two, then hung it up and shook his head in despair.

"Something wrong?"

"Is Chef," he said, "him too exited, man. I never see a man jumpy so. Me tell him me soon come and bet you him call me ten more time before ten o'clock."

"You'll be going away again tonight?"

He nodded.

"How come every time Chef calls, you have to leave?"

"Him don' really call me unless it important," he said. "Him won't tell me come, if it no necessary. Is just that him get excited sometimes. But him is bonafide."

"You two closer than batty and chamber to me."

"You go on, man," he said. "Is nuff things me and Chef go through. Nuff things."

"I can bet."

"Mi know you don' like him, you know. But I trust him with my life. You know say, if it wasn' for Chef, I wouldn' be here so right now. If him never sharp, I wouldn' be here right now."

"How come?"

"Is him start things, see certain opportunities, see certain move a go down and say make we move at this."

"Like what?"

He smiled, "Me caan tell you everything."

It was just as well, she thought.

Half an hour later, close to where the US1 joined the I-95, he slowed near the museum where the road forked toward downtown Miami and Key Biscayne. "Right there so mi use to sleep." He pointed to a criss-cross of highways and underpasses. "Sometimes when it really get cold we would go little further down so under the metro rail."

"Jesus!" was all she could say.

And as he pressed the gas and the car leapt forward, she could not help but feel some measure of respect for him. Pausing there on the edge of the thoroughfare, seeing the ugliness and the desolation from which he sprang, smelling it, tasting the moldy loneliness of it, made her sympathize with whatever he now did for a living. And somehow it all blended together, the beauty and the ugliness of him, the soft spoken and the talkative. She looked again across at him and thought she would be quiet for a while so the vibes would float across the car and he would bask in the satisfaction of having impressed her in his own way.

Later, at home, in the shower, as she rinsed herself to prepare for dinner and rest from the journey, he came to her. Slid away the frosted glass and peered in at her, naked under the fine sprays of water. "Make me wash you back no." Without a word she closed her eyes against the water beating down and handed the soap to him as he slid the glass door closed. He stood behind, held her against him and ran the soap up and down her body till she came alive and slippery in his hand. Somehow in his movements the soap fell from his hands. He held her waist firmly, pressed his mouth against her ear. "Pick it up for me." She bent forward, found the slippery bar. She found it awkward to come erect again as he had maneuvered expertly and she was now impaled by him. Her toes now barely touched the ground. So she tilted forward till she was pressed against the slippery wet tiles, found footing against a dripping edge, and with the water spraying down, pretended she was in a dancehall video and gave him what he wanted in a manner he could hardly have expected or dreamed of. She gave him till he crumpled... collapsed in the wetness around her, his slack mouth gasping against her back, "Shirley, me love you, we can married right now if you want."

Now the shower was like rain and the water on her face like tears, as his words gave fresh sobriety and a fear she never hoped to feel. She had slipped much further, faster than she expected and it was time to come awake, time to find Queeny and seek her friendship again.

Chapter Twenty-Four

Queeny came across the room looking tired. She must have worked that day, even though it was Saturday. She still looked good, dressed this evening in a beautiful blue blouse with a high collar and DKNYC splashed diagonally across it. She wore tight, well-fitted striped jeans and blue-and-white sneakers to match her top. But the powder showing above the top of the low-cut blouse was too much.

As soon as she said hi, and sat, Shirley knew she had to tread carefully that evening. For Queeny had the most eloquent mannerisms of anyone Shirley knew. A roll of the eyeballs, a flattening of the lids or a turn of the mouth, with the words pitched at the right level, could give a range of feelings from hot to freezing cold. Sometimes she did not have to say more than one word, like the hi she just dropped as she sat. Sometimes she did not even have to speak at all; just her body language alone could put a stop to conversation in the most crowded of rooms.

"Evening," Shirley said.

"What kind of emergency you have so?" Queeny went straight to the point.

"You going down any time soon? I want to send some money to Jamaica."

They were in Aunt I's on the edge of the 441, and the waitress was prompt and cordial.

Queeny regarded the woman casually. "You have any beer?"

"If you want you can get," the woman said.

"Beg you a cold one deh," Queeny said.

"You start drink now?" Shirley asked.

"How much money you want carry down?" Queeny spoke as if nothing had transpired since Shirley's original question.

"Two thousand dollars," Shirley said slowly. "When you going down?"

"Not for now."

Shirley ordered a soft drink and watched the waitress as she turned toward the interior of the restaurant. She had expected Queeny to be like this: distant, reluctant, a bit sarcastic. They had not spoken since that last quarrel when Moet took her away.

"Do you know anybody going?" Shirley asked.

"If is little money you sending for you mother, why you don't just mail it?" Queeny asked impatiently.

"It's not just the money, and it's not for my mother. It is to my friend in the bank and I have to send certain instructions. It is to open a foreign exchange account."

"No," Queeny said carelessly, "me not going down but I know somebody going Wednesday."

"Who?"

"You don't know her."

"You can trust her?"

"Is that I can't take with you, you know," she said testily.

"I'm sorry," Shirley said quickly. "I was just curious."

"Is mi cousin." Queeny still had not put her handbag away.

"You cousin?"

"Yes," Queeny said. "Say she can't take it no more. Some people think America easy."

Shirley ignored that. "OK."

"Nobody want to work, man. Come to America think everything easy. Nobody want work. That's why I have to keep to myself. Everybody want big life. And me don' want no friend."

Shirley moved to cut her short. "You are right, Queeny."

"And is not like say anybody did ask them to leave them fancy work and come. But them caan' do certain things."

Shirley sighed aloud and wished the waitress would return. "Queeny, I already said I am sorry."

"Me talking 'bout you? Is you me talking 'bout?"

"Well, I'm not sure, OK? I ask you one thing and you answer

something else."

"Is mi cousin. See yah! I can talk 'bout her all I want."

"But you said, you could trust her."

"Then no mi cousin? That don' mean a thing. She still go on hoity toity like some people."

The drinks came.

Shirley flipped the top of the Coke and sipped it gently. Queeny picked up the beer and took a large gulp of it.

"Queeny, I can understand if you are angry, but we don't have to do this."

"Don't have to do what?"

"Why are you drinking like that? I've never seen you drink beer like that before. Are you trying to make some sort of statement, Queeny? All right, go on and make it, but don' try to make me feel guilty, man. Don't try to make me feel like shit. It's as if – as if. . ." She ran out of words.

"You see it?" Queeny said. "All me doing is drink mi beer. I free to drink. How you know is you? You can make me drink?" She kissed her teeth. "How you know is not the work? Sometimes when you work whole day with them old people, you start smell like them, you know – old and stale. You know that? You think is you one have problem? How you know that is not why me powder up so? How you know me not drinking a beer to wash out them taste out a mi mouth."

"Is that?" Shirley felt rebuked.

"How you know is not that?"

"Then how you cousin come into it?"

"Is you ask 'bout her."

"Yeah, but all them other things. . ."

"Because she full a shit. Same like you. I get job for her and after two weeks she bawl say she want to go home. Like anything easy. Like she better than people."

"Oh. I thought you were talking about me."

Queeny ignored her and took another sip. "Is so you touchy, man?"

"So what kind of work you found her?"

Queeny's voice took on a cantankerous edge. "With one Cuban

woman, to take care of her place."

"So?"

"She say she caan take it."

"Just to clean the house?"

"Yeah, just clean the place and take care of the pet them and so. Damn stupid girl caan even clean dog teeth."

"What?" Shirley thought she had heard wrong. She checked to see if Queeny was trying to make a joke.

But the only thing in Queeny's face was disgust and anger. "Clean dog teeth. Clean dog teeth! The woman have a dog. Is America this. Is dog country. So what if the woman want her dog teeth clean every day? What can inna that?"

"Clean the woman dog teeth. Are you serious? I would leave too. Anybody would leave that."

Queeny huffed at her, and kissed her teeth. "Dog always a skin them teeth. I tell her make two quick brush, then make a quick rinse. What can hard in that?"

"You ever clean dog teeth yet?"

"No, but that no say."

"So she have a right to leave."

"Then she should leave from the first day. Now she damage the people them dog."

"What she do?"

Queeny smiled despite her mood and kissed her teeth again. "Sometimes you have to take bad things make laugh, you know. The stupid gal turn hose down the people them dog throat. I don' know if dog can gargle."

"Jesus Christ!" Shirley could not hold the laugh back. "So what happen?"

"The dog run her down, nearly bite her up. Run her round the yard. Is a tree them take her out of. Spend about two hours in there. All now the dog still can' bark again. Now she say she going home. Like she better than people."

"Oh God, Queeny man! You can't wrong the woman."

Queeny smiled her old smile. "But what she come up here for? What she leave big teaching job come up here for?" She chuckled and her breasts heaved. "Cho, is America this, man. She remind me a you and Grace and the shit-up."

There was a short silence and then they both broke into uncontrollable laughter. In the lightness of the mood Queeny beckoned to the waitress who was attending another table. "Darling, you may as well bring some food yah. Give me a curry goat."

"Oxtail," Shirley said. She could smile now. Laughter had come and cleared the air a bit. But she knew she could not relax; a lot had passed between them and Queeny was in one of her moods.

"And another beer and one more Coke there," she said, raising her eyebrows to Shirley.

Shirley smiled and nodded, then rolled her eyes. "Have your beer."

As the woman left, Queeny finally placed her bag on the table and sat properly on the chair to face Shirley. She picked up the bottle of toothpicks and began to play with her gums. "Out of fun and joke though, Shirley" she spoke through the pick, "What you really call me here for?"

"How you mean?"

"How me mean? Me look like me stupid? Me! I must believe, that you who work in bank, you, who was bank manager, want to send down two thousand dollars to Jamaica, and send come ask me. When you have FedEx and bank draft and all them things. Not to mention telephone and so. Is so me look stupid? I going watch you. Me going siddung and watch you, because I know that is not why you call me."

"He asked me to marry him."

It would have taken a market woman to beat the laugh that Queeny gave. "So tell me when is the wedding, make me leave town."

"Be serious," Shirley whispered urgently.

"Me! I look like I joking to you?"

"What must I do?"

"Me? You ask me, Shirley? I take you in like my sister, give you place to stay – give you job, put money in you pocket. But you caan wait. Me tell you say the ugly bwoy no good, but no, you leave go live with the piece a dog. You don't call me for six month because I tell you the truth. Now him want to marry to you and you come and ask me what to do . . . and telling me to be serious. Me! Don't bother with it this evening."

Shirley reached quickly for her bag, and began to leave. "I'm sorry I bothered you."

Queeny pointed at her. "You see you, is so you stay. That is you biggest problem. You don't like to face the truth. You run every time. You think I going stop you? Not me, baby. Run - go on. You think you can run every day?"

Shirley dropped back heavily into the seat. Queeny had spoken at more than a whisper and some patrons were glancing in their direction.

"Queeny, you mustn't go on so you know, man."

"How? How me go on?"

"You think this easy for me?"

"Yeah! So why you never just came and talk the truth and done?"

"All right Queeny, I'm sorry. But what should I do?"

Queeny relaxed and seemed to soften. If she had not extracted her pound of flesh, she had had more than a mouthful. "Anyway, is so man talk, all the while. Moet want married to nobody!" She kissed her teeth.

"He is serious," Shirley said.

"How you know?"

"Him dead serious. I know."

Queeny bit her lips. "What a thing. Can't say the ugly bwoy not ambitious. If you did have you green card, you could just leave."

Shirley could not pluck the guilt from the silence that ensued. So she reached into her bag for the documents and dropped them onto the counter.

"Jesus Christ, Shirley. You get them?" Queeny wailed. "Jesus Christ, then just leave him now!"

"And go where? You same one say him will find me."

"But him no must come after you."

"He will, I know him. You are right... him feel him in love."

"Bwoy, you really good," Queeny said as the food and new drinks came. "Why you don't just go home then? Go home. Take a break. Then go New York or somewhere."

"I don't have enough money."

"Money?"

"What would I do if I go home now, green card or no green card? Where would I go? Where would I live? How long it would take before him give up on me?"

"Well, married him then," Queeny said in exasperation.

"Oh Jesus."

"Lord Shirley, man, make me think little. All of a sudden you just drop something on me. Make we eat the little food."

They began to eat, but though Queeny ate healthily, Shirley hardly touched her oxtail. She watched as Queeny ate and drank, alternating the fork and beer bottle at her lips. Then suddenly Queeny stopped with both bottle and fork halfway to the table, the fork on its way down and the bottle on its way up.

"Hold on there. Which green card that?"

"How you mean?"

"Is the same green card?"

"How you mean, same green card?" Shirley asked.

"Me mean, you give him different picture or is the same one them that Mikey was working on?"

"The same one, I guess."

"The same one. When him give you that?"

"A couple weeks ago. I woke up and found them under my pillow."

"Jesus Christ! Is must him kill Mikey, you know."

"What?"

"Is must him kill Mikey!"

"Mikey is dead?"

"Dead, yes. Them find him in some bush with shot in him head – about six months now, 'bout the same time you malice me off and left. And them say is Moet them do it, but I never believe." Queeny was shaking her head.

"Mikey dead? But Queeny, Moet couldn't do that."

"But how him get the documents?"

"Remember we asked him for help," Shirley pointed out. "We asked him to get them."

"Then if Mikey dead so long, who give them to Moet couple weeks ago? Unless him did have them long time. Him must know something about it. It must be him or him dog friend Chef. It must be one of them or them must know something 'bout it."

"But Queeny, you have no proof."

"No bother defend him you know, Shirley." By this time, Queeny's nose was flaring like a mongrel's.

"I'm not defending him." Shirley whispered fiercely. Her hand began to shake and she had to drop the fork into the dish to stop it from chattering against its edge. "Jesus Christ, what this me get myself into."

She reached shakily for her bag and rose to go again. This time no word from Queeny could make her sit back down. The world was spinning around her. "I have to leave, have to get out of here." She was staggering toward the door, when she heard Queeny shout her name for the first time, but she ignored it and pressed against the glass. The door flung wide. The evening sun burst through and the piazza outside was white and hazy. "Shirley!" It was a distant sound. As she stepped out, she could hardly see in front of her, but it did not matter because the world was spinning faster, and she was falling to the ground.

Chapter Twenty-Five

"If me did know say is so you fainty-fainty, I wouldn' talk to you so hard," she heard Queeny say as she came to. Her head was resting on Queeny's lap. She looked around her quickly – she was on a hard bench, there were boxes stacked to one side.

"Where am I?"

"Where you expect? You faint right in front a the people them restaurant. Is them restroom this."

"I did what?"

"You fainty-fainty," Queeny said. "You all right now?"

"I guess so." Shirley felt tired.

"All right. Come, me take you home," Queeny said.

By the time the taxi dropped them at Moet's apartment, Shirley was strong enough to stand and search for her keys.

"I don' really want go in there and meet him, you know," Queeny said as Shirley pushed the key into the lock.

Shirley told her he was out of town.

They passed to the kitchen and Shirley made herself a cup of tea while Queeny walked around the apartment gaping. "Caan say the John Crow don' have taste," she whispered.

"Queeny!"

"Sorry, all right –is you husband-to-be. But him ugly same way."

Shirley smiled and shook her head. "Drink something no?"

"You have any beer?"

"Some wine."

"Moet Champagne, I bet you," Queeny said, with a hint of sarcasm.

"Yes."

"Him must be movie star. Old hypocrite."

Shirley handed her a glass of champagne and they walked to the patio. They sat at the little white table and looked out as the night descended on the man-made lake.

"How come you in America so long?" Shirley asked Queeny. "I thought you would have been back in Jamaica by now. Since when you start stay so long?"

Queeny shrugged. "Me goin' just work little money and see how it go."

"So what happened to your business?"

"It going on, but things slow down there."

"What happen to you children?"

"You know, I wish I did make one thing and get the green card and done. I would just take them here with me. Not even make sense go back sometimes."

"How you mean, Queeny? You don't have a husband down there?"

"Husband? The old dog breed woman down there!"

"Oh God! I'm sorry, Queeny. But you sure?"

"How you mean if me sure!" She kissed her teeth. "Sometimes life not even make no sense."

There was not much more to say right then. They just sat there as it got darker. The night came, the outside lights switched on automatically. The wine finished, the empty tea cup laid on its side. It was as if the silence turned a fresh page for them and their friendship was being closed and restored simultaneously.

"You know what my mother always say?" Queeny finally said.

"What?"

"If poorness is not a crime, white lice is not a disgrace."

"Life hard, yes."

"But the worst part is not just say it hard, you know. Is that we can sit down in a place like this, a drink wine and all kind a tea, and still a say it hard. That is the worse part."

"Yeah," Shirley whispered. "That make it hard."

"You know what me think?" Queeny said.

"What?'

"Me think you should just leave. Right now. Just pack up everything and walk through that door. Nothing not here for you."

"I've thought about it many times. But it is just so hard."

"How you mean hard?"

"It's not as if he has done anything to make me angry or unhappy. He has given me everything I wanted. Everything I ask for I get. Him treat me better than anybody ever treat me."

"But you know say you don't belong here."

"Tell you the truth, Queeny, sometimes I'm not even so sure any more."

"Me think you did wan' go school, turn bank manager."

"To get this," Shirley motioned around her. "To get this! But now I have it. I have it already." She rubbed her fingers through her long hair and brought her feet up to her stomach so that her chin rested on her knees. "Anyway, that is really how I think sometimes."

"Then why you call me? You happy?"

"Me ever happy? What happiness have to do with life?" Shirley sighed.

"Well, you probably right. I caan tell you bout that. So why you don' go look for your mother, Shirley? You no long fi see you mother?"

That brought tears to Shirley's eyes. And all the fears she had that were hidden deep inside her surfaced like smoke from a fireside freshly stirred. She had thought about it many times, and had accepted that she had to go back there and face her, see her, look on her face once more. But she wanted to return with the best possible Shirley that she could make. Yet every day her life became more complex and the forces in her more confused and the sense of what she wanted to be, less clear.

"I don't know, Queeny. It's just so confusing, you know."

Queeny probably would not understand what the answer had to do with the question, but it really did not matter to Shirley. She pulled her legs even tighter against her chest. Closed her eyes and tried to press the images from her head, of an old house on an ugly hill in Jamaica, half concrete and half wood, with a little woman with her Bible and her prayers, patiently waiting there.

One day, about a month and a half later, Queeny called to say she was returning to Jamaica. She had been in the United States for nearly two years and had grown tired. In any case, she had promised her little daughter that she would spend Christmas with her and she could not disappoint her again.

"Just out of the blue so?" Shirley asked. "Just going home so?" She had not realized how much Queeny's friendship had meant to her till it had returned. They had not resolved Shirley's situation but they had spent more time together. Shirley was glad to have her to talk to again, gossip on the phone and share laughs with and cuss men again. Sometimes she would come over and other times they would meet at Aunt I's or at a little steak house they had discovered on the intercostal.

"I caan take the place no more, man. Me want a break," Queeny had said in her careless way across the lines. "Plus mi promise Shereen."

"She's just five," Shirley had said. She'll understand. Is a living you trying to make for them."

"Lord, me tired yah, Shirley."

The sadness in Queeny's voice suggested she must have been harboring more pain than Shirley had imagined. Her husband had been unfaithful, her life was falling apart and her only sensible way to make a living was thousands of miles away. "Well, if you must go, you must go. How long you staying?"

"I don't even know," Queeny sighed across the line.

"Thought you were going to help me leave him."

"Lord, Shirley, you nah leave Moet. You not leavin' that life."

"How you know that?"

"Me know."

"You don't know everything... maybe is just time."

"Well, if is time we no will see?"

"When you gone to Jamaica gone kill off you husband." Shirley tried to make a joke.

"I will come back, man." Queeny's voice was sadder, if anything.

"So you say."

"Me, I caan stop come here. I just tired now... caan take the blasted place no more."

"I'll miss you though," Shirley said.

"So why you don' come too? You have you green card. Come! Come now! Leave the dog!"

"You think so?"

"When you ready, Shirley," Queeny said tiredly, "when you ready you come, and you come to my yard, make the dog come try look for you."

"Take care," Shirley heard herself saying. "Who knows, I may surprise you."

"Me gone."

"All right, later," Shirley said as she heard the click on the line.

PART IV

Place of Placelessness

Chapter Twenty-Six

Shirley strode ahead of the smiling orderly who dragged the trolley laden with her luggage. She pressed the large glass door wide, eager to pass the waving crowd and the anticipating eyes and enter the sweltering heat of Jamaica. Though no one knew she was coming and nobody was there to meet her, she felt an urge to run – to jog from the terminal to the streets and the sidewalk. Her heart jumped and missed a beat as she skipped into the heat and the atmosphere as she would the arms of a lover missed for years.

The orderly was at her side keeping stride with her as if they were travel partners. "Have a nice taxi for you." He waved ahead of him to where a young man leaned leisurely against the cafeteria wall. Shirley watched as the man pushed upright and moved quickly across the street toward a parked car.

"So why is he parked so far?"

"You no know, all kind o' grudgeful people deh 'bout the place."

"You mean he is a robot. He is illegal."

The orderly smiled and shrugged. "Daughter, you don' wan' go pay the whole heap a JUTA, money for government taxi. Is Camry this, you know!"

The large navy blue car began reversing into the channeled drive. Shirley watched, impressed. When she left Jamaica, she had travelled in an old Morris Oxford with no air conditioning and wheels as smooth as the asphalt they drove on. Now, on her return, her taxi was beautiful and seemingly new with glass tinted black.

"Are you sure this is a taxi?"

"Yeah man," he said.

The young man in jeans and white cotton shirt hanging loosely, with a dimpled smile matching the sun bouncing from his smooth head, came around the side and began to load Shirley's luggage.

"You don't look like a taxi driver."

"What does a taxi driver look like?"

"I don't know – crusty? You don't even talk like a taxi driver."

"Take care of youself." The orderly laughed, took his tip and closed the door firmly on the heat outside.

They were out of the airport and the Palisadoes strip was sliding beneath them; the sea was on both sides, the hue of the sun washed its blue to a whitish haze.

Jamaica again!

A week ago she had no thought of coming. But today she was here – upon a whim. An impulse influenced by a social security ad on TV : the best gift a child could give a parent. Just one ad, coming at a time when Moet was away and there was no Queeny to talk to . . . and she had decided on a whim, to surprise her mother, to surprise the old Jamaica; to just appear upon doorsteps so all could see the new Shirley - the Shirley that made it.

"Long time you haven't been back?"

"Yeah. Five years," Shirley sighed. Five years and several lifetimes. "The roads seem a bit better." She tried not to sound surprised.

"Where?" asked the driver with a sarcastic smile. "Here? Nothing gets better here!"

Shirley leaned back and sipped the familiar landscape through half-closed eyes as they cruised along the edge of the city and entered New Kingston from Trafalgar.

Once they touched Knutsford Boulevard, Shirley had to stop and see Dawn instead of firstly going to the hotel. She alighted from the taxi, lifted her eyes to across the street and almost fainted. Her bank was not there. Everything else was there: the little garden, once quaint, now nicely manicured; the old sidewalks where she used to sit and flirt with men in the after-work traffic – everything was there. But her bank, the one she knew with its blue, beige and delicate silver color, was not there.

National Commercial Bank?

But where is my bank – where is Mutual Security Bank? Where did it move to? Where would Dawn be?

Shirley stood across the street and mouthed the unfamiliar blue and gold words tastefully painted on the building before her. Somehow she had expected things to remain as she had left them. This was Jamaica, nothing happens here, nothing change here; yet everything from her ride with a clean-cut handsome man in his Camry for a taxi, to the two o'clock traffic jam crawling around her, to the face of the bank was different.

"You all right?" The taxi driver, Troy had spoken.

She looked at him suspiciously, Why would he care? What does he want?

"Is the bank name fool you, don't it?" he quipped. "NCB buy them out last year."

"I did not know," she said slowly. "I had a friend who would have been working there."

"Probably still working there. Only the name changed. I bank there. Same people... most of them."

"You sure?" She felt excited again, her manner tempered toward the clean-cut intelligent taxi man, who did not look like a taxi man. "Thank you."

"Is all right, I'll just wait on you."

Shirley hesitated. What if she went into the bank and returned to find him gone with all her luggage? She did not know this man. She paused halfway to the edge of the sidewalk. All her luggage was in that strange car. She felt stupid. Having made the decision to go into the bank, she was now wavering in mid-stride, not knowing how to resolve her dilemma. In Miami she would not have wavered; now in Jamaica she trusted no one. Five years ago she would not have wavered.

What is wrong with me!

She observed the taxi driver as he sat nonchalantly, reading an Observer. Jesus Christ, an Observer! When she left there was one newspaper, now there was another! So many surprises.

"Take care of my things, you hear?" Shirley stared at him squarely. "Soon come," she said and stepped unsteadily onto the pedestrian crossing of Knutsford Boulevard.

Shirley spotted Dawn the instant she entered the bank. She was giving instructions to a young woman at a small desk – she seemed to have gained a bit of weight. Shirley strode across the half-filled floor toward her but by the time she got near, Dawn had disappeared into an office to the side. She waited anxiously for her to emerge so she could see the surprise on her face. But after five minutes Dawn did not appear. Shirley finally beckoned to the young lady Dawn had been instructing.

"Could you call Dawn for me?"

"Who should I say?" the young lady asked.

"It is a surprise," Shirley said.

"I'm afraid I have to say who," she said.

"No man, it's a surprise," Shirley insisted.

"I wish I could," the young lady reminded Shirley of her old self, "but she gave strict instructions."

"What?" Shirley's mouth hung open.

"She gave strict instructions. I must say who, even her husband. I'm sorry."

"That's her office?"

The young lady squinted, her eyes drew close. "Who exactly do you want to see?"

"It's OK." Shirley felt a bit silly. "Tell her it's Shirley, Shirley Temple Brown."

Shirley understood that Dawn could not jump and shout, for this was a bank, but the surprise and joy in her eyes were genuine as she stood by the door of her office and waved her through. And when they were in the privacy of the large office, the hug was tight and real. And for the first time since Shirley touched Jamaica, she felt as good as she had expected to feel.

But it was still a different Dawn. Still beautiful, still with her head of hair, now creamed and set high and fluffing, still beautiful, though her hips came more squarely from her waist where once they curved voluptuously. She had a determined pout now, with stern and wiser eyes, a sharper more comprehensive glance.

"Shirley!" she said. "Jesus, Shirley! How you do, girl?"

Dawn forwarded the phone to her secretary and they sat together on the leather sofa and tried to recapture old times. And they did, for a few minutes at least, recaptured those golden early days when they ruled New Kingston. They covered years in minutes and for a while it was as if they had never separated. But time disappeared and brought the present to bear coldly on them when Dawn dropped her hands onto Shirley's lap and asked excitedly, "So what you doing with yourself, girl? Where you working now?"

Shirley looked down at the solid gold band on Dawn's left hand and felt something snap inside her.

"Don't bother go on like you don't see it!" Dawn exclaimed. "You don't see me trying show off on you?"

Shirley recovered quickly and held Dawn's hand, as if to inspect the wedding band. "I was just stealing a look."

Dawn kissed her teeth playfully and pretended to pull her hand away. "What's there to look at? It's just a little gold band."

"A big band."

"Well, it kinda broad."

"Broad gold is better than no gold. Is the best kind."

"Missis."

"Married woman!" Shirley exclaimed. "Married woman and big executive!"

"Mi dear," Dawn laughed sarcastically. "Turn bigshot, missis."

Shirley paused again and looked around the office in search of something to change the topic or broaden the conversation. But she could not find it. The subject of status had been raised, and there was no escaping it. "So, I know him?" she finally asked.

"Yes." Dawn smiled and rose to lean against her desk. "Know him yes."

"No!" Shirley said, reading the shyness in her eyes. "Don't tell me is

Barnes, no! Not Barnes."

"So what wrong with him?"

"To God?" Shirley screamed. "I know you did like him, you know, I knew all along!"

"Like what, missis." Dawn kissed her teeth. "Just a moment of weakness."

"Moment of weakness?"

"Really. One slip, I got pregnant... I was scared. I ready to leave him now. Wild like what."

"You got pregnant, you have baby?"

"Yes, a daughter, Jordan, she's three, soon three and a half. See her picture here."

Shirley took the small frame Dawn lifted from her desk. It showed the face of a bright-eyed child with Dawn's own smile.

"She looks just like you."

"So people say. Looks like her father to me."

"A little bit - the nose."

"The nose." Dawn laughed and slapped her leg.

"Barnes," Shirley laughed. "Mrs. Barnes - who would have thought?"

"Well, we taking you out tonight, you will see."

"Taking me out tonight?"

"How you mean! Taking you out, yes. I can leave the house for a change."

Shirley smiled. "Boy, you haven't changed."

"More than you would believe," Dawn said.

They paused again.

Shirley rose and stretched. "Anyway, let me leave you, till later."

"Where you staying?"

"Pegasus."

"Excuse me?" Dawn laughed. "Pegasus? Why you don't go and stay with your moth -"

"Maybe for a few days." Shirley smiled painfully.

"Then how long you staying?"

"A week or so. But we will talk tonight." Shirley turned to go.

Dawn drew close as if to escort her to the door. "So what happen to yours?" she asked. "You not leaving before you tell me 'bout that."

"My what?" Shirley asked.

Dawn kissed her teeth. "Lord, Shirley, is me this you know! Anybody can see the double ring mark on you wedding finger. Why you take off you ring? You planning to bad?"

But Shirley did not break her stride. She held Dawn's hand tightly, and glanced up at her. "Talk later?"

"Talk later," Dawn said. "Later we talk."

Chapter Twenty-Seven

There was no Moet in the hotel bar. Shirley had a bottle of something else sent up instead. When it arrived she did not bother to check the label but poured herself a drink and ambled to the balcony to look out over the sweltering sprawl of Kingston.

So what happen to yours; you not leaving till you tell me about yours.

Well, Dawn my friend, would you really like to know? There is nothing much to tell, but I will tell you anyway.

My man came one evening and with a big smile on his face said, "Mi buy the ring, you know - we can marry now if you want. Put on you clothes – we go down to the court now if you want. Chef can be best man."

And how did I answer? What did I say?

"I don't want Chef as my best man," that's what I said.

And he brushed it aside as he would anything that would litter our way. "That no matter, we don't need one. The court provide them own witness."

What did you say, Dawn when Barnes proposed? What were the words that passed between you? Were you trapped by the moment too? A wish that he had forgotten about the whole thing on one hand, and a massive diamond ring on the other?

Were you married like me without having really consented; well, in a formal way. Woke up the next morning hardly remembering – could not believe that it had not been a joke?

What about mine, what about mine?

Well, Dawn my friend, would you really like to know? Do you really want to hear about my husband; how handsome he is or not, how educated or not; or how he disappears in the wee hours of the night to stay away for days as he sells drugs to America's children?

Dawn, my friend, you don't really want to know.

The phone rang. It was Dawn.

"How you sound so, Shirley?"

"How, how I sound?"

"Well, you sound different from this afternoon - pensive, sad. I don't know, just different. Maybe you should rest after the flight - you know, do a cat nap or so."

"Maybe."

Dawn's voice softened a bit, yet held a certain assured edge. "I may not make it tonight, Shirley! Jordan is not well."

"Oh, what happened?"

"Her allergies acting up; I have to take her to the doctor before she gets an asthma attack or something like that. I am not sure how long the whole thing will take, and I wouldn't want to leave her after that. But tomorrow come by the bank and I'll take the afternoon off."

"Tomorrow?"

"Yes."

"I must go to Central Village tomorrow."

"I see." Then salience.

"Shirley, are you OK?"

Dawn, my friend would you really like to know?

"Look Carlton will take you out to eat tonight."

"Carlton?"

"Carlton Barnes, my husband."

She was tempted to refuse the offer to have dinner with Barnes, but Dawn was insistent. "Lord, man, is you first night. Go out enjoy yourself!"

"OK," Shirley said.

"Call me when you get back from seeing your mother." Dawn hung up.

Shirley hung up the phone, sat quietly on the bed, dug into her bag and placed her wedding ring on her finger. She reached for the TV remote and brought the dead screen to life. It was set on CNN. She flipped the channels and the first ten were American channels. The first Jamaican channel was fuzzy and the other was showing The Young and the Restless. She switched the TV off and threw the remote to the other side of the bed. I could have stayed in Miami for this, she thought, to be lonely in a room with America on TV.

Now she could not stay in if she wanted.

She pushed the bags with Dawn's gifts aside and stretched across the bed, slack and dead for a while, then she returned the dress she had laid out to wear, to the closet. She chose jeans and a white Donna Karan blouse instead. Halfway through her lipstick, the front desk called to say her friends were downstairs.

Barnes was the same old Barnes. He still had that arrogant, God's-gift-to-woman look about him. He had more weight: his belly bulged a bit and his rear was tight against the fabric of his pants.

But Orville was another matter.

Shirley did not recognize Orville immediately - a man of medium height, of smooth black complexion with eyes bright, alive and piercing – hair cut low, almost bald. He stood with the ease of a well-tuned athlete, shoulders broad, waist small, shirt hanging loosely against the cut of his muscles.

"Hi," he said, after Barnes introduced them. "I bet you don' remember me." His hand was strong yet gentle against her palm.

Shirley knitted her brow as she tried to remember. She would have remembered someone like him.

"Orville, man," Barnes said. "You must remember Orville. Him join the bank about a year before you leave."

She thought again. "Orville! You mean... no! Orville, who used to follow you around everywhere? Little Orville?"

"Same one," Barnes said as he ushered her through the door. "Same little Orville."

"But you look so, I mean, so different."

"And I have grown too," Orville chided. "I have heard that."

"But no." Shirley could not help her embarrassment. "Anyway, it's nice to meet you again."

"Even nicer for me." He took her hand and helped her into the car. "The pleasure is really mine."

They went to a little restaurant on Constant Spring Road called The Fish Place – Barnes said the best steam fish in Kingston was served there. The night was dry and crisp – cool against her skin, and the light of the candle on her table made everything soft. Shirley tried to relax, as the two friends finished ordering and tried to impress her with how rich Orville had become operating some strange cambio scheme of purchasing US dollars and selling them back to the government with money that Barnes advanced him through the bank.

Despite her mood Shirley tried her best to listen and every now and then chip in with a question or two.

"A cambio?" She held Orville's eyes across the table as he stuffed slimy okras into his mouth.

"The government run down the foreign exchange reserve. And the exchange rate is slipping out of control," Barnes explained. "They have no foreign exchange. So they license people to go out and buy foreign exchange wherever they can find it, and bring it in."

"So he buys US dollars for the government." Shirley looked across at Orville.

"In a way, yes. But our operation is at times more complex than that," Orville said.

It sounded to Shirley like an elaborate money-laundering scheme, but the food was good, the night was lifting her a bit and the two men seemed so happy together as they tried to impress her, that Shirley nodded and smiled as much as she could. Every now and then her eyes would catch Orville's across her glass. It was amazing how much he had changed. How handsome he had become; how strong and unapologetic his stare.

"So where you buy the money?"

"In the hills. Ganja money." Barnes slurped at a large okra. "Buy it at X, sell to the government at Y. Nobody ask no question, the man is a licensed cambio."

"With a two point mark up?"

"Two point minimum." Barnes twisted delicate flesh from the fish on his plate.

"A briefcase millionaire."

"A briefcase millionaire."

The waitress returned to her elbow and another Pina Colada was placed beside her plate.

"What do you do in Miami, Shirley?" Orville said.

"I work in a bank," she lied effortlessly. "I manage a small branch in south Miami."

"What bank?"

"Barnet," she said without thinking.

And all the time she felt Orville's eyes on her – felt the gaze by instinct even while she paid him no mind. Not the young, anxious stare that she remembered, but a patient confident one that rested on her like a shadow.

After goodnights at the hotel Orville held her elbow as she turned toward the elevators.

"How long you staying?" he asked.

Shirley shrugged. "Why?"

"I'd like to see you again."

"Why?"She repeated. She had not answered a man so stupidly since high school.

"I don't know. How you getting around?"

"I have a good taxi man," she said, remembering the feisty taxi man who had given her his card. "He is cheap."

"I'll take you around," he said softly.

"You sure you won't be too busy?"

"I'll find the time."

"No, it's OK. I have a taxi, but you can call me."

"You sure?"

"Yes," she told him. "Call me."

"I will."

He called her next morning and invited her to breakfast. They ate mackerel and bananas at Hot Pot. A day that began so beautifully deserved more than what Shirley gave. She was quiet most of the time and was glad he did not push. He wanted to see her that night, but she told him she had plans.

Today she would face her mother.

"Tomorrow night then?" he asked.

"Sure," she said, "but today I can't see anyone."

"I understand," he said.

But she knew he did not. He was just a predator on the prowl, deferring for a more opportune time.

When she got back to her room, she began to tremble visibly. She stretched onto the bed, grabbed a pillow and squeezed it tight against her stomach so her body could stop its tremors. The shaking slowed but a dullness remained in her stomach, and she knew it would not leave till she had faced her mother again after five years.

Chapter Twenty-Eight

It was the same old hill, more marl than rock, with white dust swirling to fall like powder on her shoes. The same old hill and the same old shacks on the road that climbed it. And the same old zinc fences that sucked the brilliance from the sunset and spat it back onto the street in dull ugly shadows.

The same old house stood there, modified somewhat – the wooden part had gone and all was concrete now – but it seemed the same even though the veranda where they once cooked had now been rebuilt. The same old place, the same little gate tied, the same barbed wire fence, and the same tiny, quiet woman sat there, hair combed in a bun, looking across her sewing, out at Shirley as if she had been waiting there for her, for seven long years.

Troy took the suitcase with her mother's gifts and placed them on the verandah. He nodded, and had he not turned back through the gate to leave her standing there, Shirley would have run back into the safety of the taxi. But the car engine was already revving behind her and her mother was already leaning against the column of the veranda, and calling her name. "Shirley?"

Shirley entered the veranda slowly, past the suitcase that Troy had placed there, and held the other side of the column. "Yes, is me."

They did not hug, but feelings surfaced, swam forth in the softness of watering eyes. "How you do?" Shirley said softly.

"Shirley," her mother whispered again. "Shirley."

"Yes, is me." And suddenly Shirley knew she should not respond but stand quietly, and revere the moment that would never come again, as her mother, molded by principles and pride, yet overcome by emotion, whispered her name. And with the one word, for the first and only time, told her how much she loved her. One word - a hundred times, a hundred different ways; Shirley, till the tears welled in Shirley's eyes and dropped like rain upon her blouse.

But the moment would not last and Shirley knew it had come too late – and now many of her tears were for that too. Because she knew how soon the moment would turn.

And it did.

The minute they sat down together and her mother saw the ring, held her hand and exclaimed, "But you married, Shirley!" she knew she had to begin to lie again. There was no escaping what she was. Her life was in that hard, glittering stone that bound her to a marriage of which she was so ashamed she had cut all links to the one real friend she could ever remember.

Suddenly she felt very tired, as if she had walked a thousand miles to get there to that veranda - a thousand miles on adrenalin and ambition alone. And now that she was here, her body was sagging onto itself. Tired! Soul too weary to fight, mouth too dry to say the next lie. "Tired," She sighed.

"Then you should rest," her mother said.

Shirley sniffed.

"I have some stew peas inside if you want some," her mother said after a short silence "Knowing you. . ." She caught herself. "You hungry?"

"OK," Shirley said, knowing her mother was granting her space to compose herself, or cry some more if she wanted.

She cried some more.

They did not speak again till after they had eaten.

After dinner her mother cleared the table and then went to pull the suitcase in. Shirley helped her put it into her old room and exclaimed audibly when she saw that the "palace" was almost as it had been when she left. The old bed was immaculately spread and the few things she had left behind were still there, neat and clean as if waiting for her return - waiting for her for five years.

They closed the door on her room and her mother began to search for something further to do. Shirley realized immediately what was happening. It would start all over again, just like before. They would now move around each other and find things to do to avoid the issues and face the truths before them. But Shirley had grown past that now. She had no intention of avoiding the issues this evening. Her heart was just too full and she knew that if she left as she came, the opportunity to talk would be lost forever.

"Lord, Mama, leave that for now. You not tired? Sit down little."

Her mother ignored her and began looking outside to where Shirley had left her shoes.

"Work going kill you."

"But they need to come in."

"But sit down little."

"I sit all the time, Shirley."

Shirley rose and left her as she fidgeted and passed her onto the veranda to sit sideways on the low wall. She looked down the drab hill till all she could see was marl swirling in the dying light. After a while she felt her mother standing beside her.

"You can go unpack now," she heard her say.

And that was another of Shirley's fears. All she had in the suitcase were gifts for her mother - unpacking would show she had not come to stay. Shirley sighed, there was to be no easing up that evening.

"I married him because he asked," she stammered out. "Because he asked and because he said he loved me."

"I never said I was against it, you know. Is your life. . . I would never tell you how to live it."

"I never say you did."

"I know you never say so. Me not saying you say so."

"Mama, I just trying to tell you say . . ." Shirley stammered again. "Mama, I just trying to . . . Mama, how it so hard to talk to you?"

"Hard, Shirley?"

"Yes, hard. How it so hard to talk to you – to tell you something?"

"Me never tell you to tell me what you don't want to tell me, you know. I never tell you to tell me anything."

Shirley felt exasperation coming on. She leaned forward desperately. "What you want me to do, Mama, you want me to feel guilty for everything? You want me to feel guilty for leaving and trying to make a life?"

"I don't want you to do anything. I didn't tell you to do anything."

"So what I must do?"

"You want me to tell you what to do? As if you would listen. You ever listen to me?"

"I listening now, Mama. You tell me what to do. You tell me."

"Satisfy," Miss Ivy said coldly. "Learn to satisfy."

Shirley stopped cold, as if stung by an open-handed slap. She knew her mother had waited a lifetime to say those words, that one venomous statement. She could have responded, but she could not find a way that would not be rude or open the chasm between them further, and she had not come for that. But to what end could she argue, when it all had gone so bad so long ago between them? Done gone bad already. Shirley sighed to herself. Done gone bad long time.

"If it bad is you make it bad."

"Mama," she said, "nobody not perfect, you know. I am not saying is not my fault, but nobody not perfect, not even you."

"I know you were coming to that." Miss ivy's voice fell. "Now everything is my fault."

"But how you mean fault, Mama? What you mean fault? Is not as if things turn out bad or so. I'm just saying, whatever must happen, will happen. I left though I knew you never liked it, I got married and never told you – or invite you – but it happen already. I'm just trying to be happy now."

"You don't look so happy to me."

"But how I must feel happy when you make me feel guilty from the minute I walked through the gate?"

Shirley watched her mother turn at that. Her eyelids made a quick and final flutter as if scales of shyness or reservation were falling from them. The dark brown eyes opened wide, with a barefaced honesty her daughter had never seen. "All right, Shirley. You want to talk, now? Let us really talk. You want honesty? Let us be really honest."

Miss Ivey took a deep breath and began: "From the day you drunkin' daddy left, him never give me a red cent to mind you."

"It is you who left him with you church."

"Let me talk!" Her mother's head shook so furiously, Shirley almost bit her tongue in shutting her mouth.

"For whatever reason him leave, is not you business. You were a child, you are still my child. You want know now? Very well. Is all the woman them that him use to have. And I never mind it till him bring disease in here and give me. But is not you business - you were a child."

"I never stop you from doing what you want to do. But you stay just like him. You know everything. You have you own way. I never stop you. But I work and make you comfortable. I clean people toilet, wipe them till me sore so you can go to school and get education. You go school, you get you subjects, you get good job, you make everybody proud.

"But you can't wait. You want everything one time. So you left go live a house with white man – why? God He knows. Tell me all kind a lie... like me born yesterday. I stop you? Is your life. What you want me to do? The most I can do is pray for you. For you have you own way."

"But Mama. . ."

"I say, let me talk! You think I love Central Village? You think I like this place, this old Sufferer's Heights? But is what I can afford, and I not hanging my hat farther than I can reach. I not putting myself out of the way, get in all kinda position because me craven. I know you hate the place, I know you wanted to leave, but you can't wait. You scorn everything, you even 'fraid to use the very toilet you grow up on. Is wonder you eat from me. You hate where you come from so much, you don't even want remember it. But you can't wait. You have fi get everything one time, and you don' stop fool youself. So you leave. You say you get visa, never ask me opinion, you just come and tell me. You disappear for nearly two years, then you drop one line here, write a note, then you send money. First you in school, then you working. I don't know what you up there doing, you don't tell me, you don't ask me. You send you money. I put it down for you.

"Now you come. Right? Now you come out of the blue, pretty and dress up, say you married. Say you want me to talk to you, say I stopping you from being happy because I don't want to talk to you. If you happy, what you want talk from me for, Shirley? What you want me to do? Heaven knows what in that suitcase, how much it cost, what you have to do to get it. But is your life. Is your secret them, is your whole heap a lie.

"So if you come to visit, visit. If you come to stay, stay. But don't come here and bother me this evening, 'bout done gone bad already. If it bad, is you make it bad. Don't come try put anything on me, you hear me! Don't come here come blame me. You never ask me nothing; don't come here with it."

It was like a game of cards – Strip Me. And somehow, her mother held all the high cards and she, Shirley, all the bush. And Miss Ivy was slamming them down onto the table one after the other – stripping Shirley of everything she had consoled herself with over the years. It was a game, she realized, her mother had been playing patiently, waiting for her to come home to throw the first card down. And now that the game had begun, Shirley knew she could not win – nor did she care to any more. For she was naked now. If she had hidden anything, it must have been through love and respect, because she hated the things she did so much she would have died if her mother should find out. But now her mother knew, she had the cards and she was playing them skillfully. And for the first time, Shirley realized how much better her mother was – how much more adept than her at everything: living, sacrificing, satisfying, hiding, everything.

Now all she wanted was to get away, before the rest of the cards were played, before her mother could reveal more of what she knew.

She pressed her hands against the wall to rise, to change position . . . to move. And somehow, though the movement was an upright one, it felt more like a crawl than a lengthening of stature.

"I'm tired," she said.

"Tired? You don't tired yet."

"Yes, but I am tired... tired of this."

"You not tired. Is the truth you can't take. Run, don't stop run, Shirley . . . run till you hear a voice say stop."

"No, you know, I'm really tired. Tired of the quarrelling and the fighting. I did not come for this. I did not come here for this."

"Is you start the argument."

"Because I want to talk, ma'am. Because I want to talk to you . . . even one time."

"I never stop you."

"But I just come to see how you do. See if you all right, you know. Just come look for you. And since I come, all we do is quarrel or don't talk at all. You not even ask me how me do. Five years you don't see me. I come look for you, you don't even ask how me do."

"I know how you do, Shirley – you don't have to tell me."

"But you don't know, ma'am. You don't know how I really do. Is like you sit here waiting for me to come back and stay. My room fix up and everything like me coming back. But I grow up now. I am a big woman. I'm trying to make life. What I really do? You care? I tell you I married and that I am trying to be happy. You don't even smile. You don't even happy for me . . . like you don't even care what happen to me."

"I know how you do, Shirley. I know; everybody know. Is you one fooling youself. You tell me what I must be proud of, and I will smile."

"But you don't even ask!"

"But I don't have to ask, I tell you." Her mother stood and almost stomped her feet. "I don't have to ask, Shirley. Look outside. See all the old nigger them walking up and down the hill? Is foreign clothes them wearing. Is higgler them. Them in Miami every day. Miami don't come like foreign any more . . . is almost Kingston. There are no secrets, Shirley. Everybody know everybody business. Is you one fooling youself. The only thing they probably don't know is that you fool enough to married to the damn drugs man."

Shirley staggered as if hit by a physical blow. Had she not quickly braced herself against the wall, she would have crumpled to the floor like an empty crocus bag. Her mouth worked soundlessly as she tried to come to grips with what her mother had said, how she said it and why. But the words did not come. And even if they did, Shirley knew there would be no pipeline to send them through. This was the end of it – the final statement – the one that had no answer. She sat slowly down again, unable to look anywhere except straight ahead – way out and down the hill where she expected her taxi to come any time now... to take her on that last journey away. For she knew right there and then, that she would never be returning to her mother's house before one of them died.

Chapter Twenty-Nine

The ringing of the phone panicked her. Too much wine had knocked her out the night before and now she was afraid that time had disappeared from her life again. Troy was on the line. When he told her what day it was, she realized she had only overslept.

She began to sob over the line.

"I'm going to Ocho Rios," he said. "You want to come?"

He must have heard her sobbing but he did not ask her about that and Shirley was grateful, just as she had been grateful for his silence as he drove her back to the hotel the evening before.

"I wasn't planning to go out," she said.

"Yeah, but when last you go Ochi?"

"I have never been to Ocho Rios."

"Then you must se it. Come, man. I'm dropping a tourist down there, and usually I would just spend the day. You can go Dunns River."

"What time you coming back?"

"'Bout three or so."

"OK," she said, "give me fifteen minutes."

"All right."

As she was about to leave, the phone rang again. It was Orville.

"Hey," he greeted her.

"Hi."

"Where were you last night?"

"I was here."

"I called."

"I must have been asleep. I was exhausted."

"How about lunch? I have reservations."

She paused and thought quickly. "I'm sorry, I am going to the country. But maybe later."

"Which country?"

"Ochi."

"OK," he said. "But what time later?"

"I don't know," she said. "I should be back by five."

"OK, tell you what, let me pick you up at eight so I can show you the place all over again."

"OK," she said. "I'd like that."

"Eight o'clock."

"Yes," she said quietly. "Later."

Shirley joined Troy in the lobby to find that he had lost his passenger. He was by the pool with some new friends he had met the night before and with whom he would head down to Ocho Rios later that night. But Shirley was already looking forward to the ride and so she offered to hire Troy to make the trip anyway.

"Gas money," he said, "just buy the gas. Might as well me just take the day too."

"Then you should buy half the gas," Shirley said, surprised that there was still some spirit in her.

"I will have to think about that."

The drive to Ocho Rios had not lifted her spirits as she had hoped, though the road was long and the countryside green and beautiful. Instead, the long ride made her pensive. There was only sorrow in her head. They stopped at Faiths Pen for lunch and she laughed once there. The ackee and saltfish and roast breadfruit made her feel at least a little better.

As they drove out of Faiths Pen, they made a bit of conversation and Troy had a chance to talk about himself.

He was a teacher who had walked out of the classroom one day when he decided the government was not paying him enough to take another insult from a student. He walked out because he was thirty years old and still lived with his parents. Now he drove a taxi and earned the annual teacher's salary in a month and a half. But he still kept his teacher's certificate in a little folder on his dashboard.

"Why?" Shirley asked.

"You know, to show people sometimes."

"Show who?"

"How you mean? Sometimes some passengers come in and want talk to you any way. You have to show them, you know. Show them that you are somebody, that you are not just a taxi driver."

But you are, Shirley said to herself. You are a taxi driver – a teacher would be in the classroom. But she did not have the guts to hurt him. "That's so sad," she finally said. But that was not the response he was looking for either, so he fell quiet and she was forced to be pensive again.

But it was hard to be sad in Ocho Rios, especially when it was her first time there. From Fern Gully to the sea, Shirley was enchanted. From the art and craft on the roadside to Burger King and Kentucky in the centre of the town. From the hustle and the bustle of the tourist traffic to the large cruise ship anchored in the rich-blue sea. She sat open-mouthed as Troy regained his composure and gave her the royal tour.

Dunns River Falls to her was the most beautiful thing she had ever seen and though she did not feel like changing into her swimsuit, she rolled up her pants legs, left Troy holding her bags, and climbed the frothing cascades for about fifty yards or so. Then she bought two T-shirts that said she climbed it all.

It was on her way back that she thought of Tiny.

Her name had occurred to her earlier that morning as she darted around the hotel room trying to find out what day it was. As she drove out of Ocho Rios and entered the rolling countryside of Moneague and Walkers Wood she began thinking how beautiful it was. This is what people remember most, she had said to herself. Maybe this is why we all come back. We dream of the misty green countryside, the rolling hills, the rich blue skies and the breeze gentle against our faces. Work in America for years, but in our heads we all have a place here , all have a home. We all have our Lot 44 Tamarind Place, Eltham Gardens.

Lot 44 Tamarind Place, Eltham Gardens. The Address came to her out of the blue.

"You know Eltham Gardens?" she asked Troy suddenly.

"Yeah man," Troy said. "Spanish Town, close to me. It's on our way to Kingston."

"I have a friend I want to see. A friend I want to surprise."

A large sign said, Welcome to Eltham Gardens, Drive carefully, We love our Children. As the car slowed for the turn, Shirley smiled to herself as she tried to compose the first words she would say when she saw Tiny. She was filled with excitement as Troy turned the car from the highway onto a well- paved road that led through dikes to the entrance of a large housing complex. She had not seen Tiny in years. After she had moved to live and work with Nicole, she had seen her probably two or three times, then she had heard by-the-way that Tiny had returned to Jamaica. And now she too was here and they would be meeting together in Jamaica for the first time.

"Tamarind Place," Shirley said.

"I remember," said Troy.

The small street had a slim green and white sign that said Tamarind Place. Shirley wished she had brought a present or something.

"Number forty - four," she said to Troy

"I know," he said, raising his eyebrows. "I know."

The small street ended quickly and though Troy said he knew, they had to turn back and cruise slowly in order to find the gate they were looking for. There was no house with 44 written on it. But they found 36 and counted forward until they got to what should have been Tiny's gate. They miscounted the first time and stopped in front of an abandoned house without a gate or fence. It was completely vandalized, with grass so tall, Shirley could hardly see the space where the door had been removed.

Shirley laughed and punched Troy playfully. "You can't even count," she said.

Troy reversed and picked up the count from the other end of the street. But they still ended up at the abandoned lot.

"You counting wrong." Shirley became impatient.

"This scheme must be different," Troy said.

"How you mean?"

"Well, every other scheme I know have even numbers on one side and odd numbers on the other. If this one is like that, then this is the house."

"Except that I have seen the house. I have seen the picture."

"Then if you know what it look like, why you have me looking at lot numbers?"

"I don't remember exactly what it look like," Shirley said. "I just remember it was built up and pretty. Maybe them just count straight."

"Or maybe you have the lot number and not the street number," Troy said, thoughtfully. "Let me try something."

They tried many things. They got out of the car and walked the length of the street. They drove through the entire housing project to see whether or not there was another street by the name – a Tamarind Avenue or a Tamarind Street. But always, they would return to the abandoned house.

"No one lives here!" Shirley finally exclaimed. "This could not be the place. But it is the number I remember."

Troy tried to be consoling. "Let us ask a neighbor."

"Ask them what? What they can tell us? That we in the wrong scheme, on the wrong street and the wrong everything else . . . just a waste of damn time."

He ignored her, put the car into motion and stopped at the gate they had estimated to be 46

After several knocks a woman came to the large French window, waved that she was coming and ducked inside. Shirley wondered how much money it had cost the owners to expand the basic three-bedroom concrete box into the elaborate modern residence in front of her. They had made a two-storey house out of it – complete with French windows, hip roof and a balcony.

The large door opened and the woman came through with a baby in her hand. She paused at the closed grill. "Yes? Can I help?" she asked.

"Yes, you live here?" Shirley asked the most stupid question she could find.

"No, I am just the helper. Everybody gone work."

"Oh." Shirley thought, not a stupid question after all. "What lot number is this?"

"Forty-six," the helper said.

"You know where forty-four is?" Shirley asked hopefully.

"Is that mash-up house over there. Mr. Salomon is forty-two and this is forty-six. Is buy you want to buy it?"

"Buy?" Shirley almost shrieked. "No! It's a wrong address! Somebody gave us the wrong address."

"Oh," the young lady said, "for from the other day all kinda people coming to look at it, say it selling in the newspaper and them looking to buy it."

"No," Shirley said, "we are not here to buy. Sorry to bother you. Come, Troy, I'm tired."

Shirley saw the form by the bus stop and might have ignored, it had Troy not curled his nose and uttered, "Jesus," painfully under his breath. They were about to clear Eltham Gardens, the houses had ended and they were now passing a large field with half-built structures, large prefabricated walls and construction equipment lying around.

She had barely glimpsed the small figure crouching in the prefabricated bus stop, but something caught her attention immediately.

"Stop," she said. "Turn back."

Troy stopped, swerved to the soft shoulder and began to reverse along the edge of the one-way street.

Shirley stared at the quiet figure through the glass of the window. Troy blew the horn.

"Why you did that?" Shirley almost slapped him. "Why you have to do that?"

Troy seemed exasperated. "You know her? Go out and talk to her!"

Shirley began to slowly wind the glass down. The small figure crouching on the concrete was so familiar it made the hair on the back of her neck stand on end. It may have been the way she moved as she lifted her head slowly, half-cocked to one side or the way she held her bag tightly as if to guard against whatever might pass and snatch it.

"Tiny!" Shirley wound the window further down, ashamed and frightened that the wasted bundle could have been her friend from long ago."Tiny, is that you?"

The head rose again; eyes filled with incredulity.

Shirley jumped from the car and stood in front of the crouching figure. "Tiny, is you this? Tiny, what happened to you?"

Tiny blinked as if she was waking from a long sleep in a dark room. Her eyes wavered madly as one trying to get accustomed to the light.

"Jesus, Tiny." Shirley was close to tears now, "Jesus, Tiny, if I didn't know better I would think you on drugs or something. Tiny, how you look so?"

She must have aged a hundred years. Her face was wizened and the skin hung around her wild unfocused eyes. She had a smell about her, a scent of mildew and unwashed aging flesh. Her steps to the car were weak, her walk a shy and hesitant shuffle – and when she got to the car she seemed to recoil with shame at its impeccable insides.

Shirley could not help the tears as the car pulled from the kerb, and she turned to look across the seat at her old friend. "Tiny, what happen to you?"

"Where to?" Troy's face was grave through the rearview mirror.

"Where you going, Tiny? Where is your house?"

Tiny did not speak. Troy stopped the car on the soft shoulder, looked around and spoke patiently. "Is Spanish Town you going? Eltham?"

"Eltham," she whispered. "Is Eltham."

"So we have to turn back here?" Troy asked.

"Yes. If you going, yes. If you going."

Troy pulled the car back onto the road.

"We spent the whole morning trying to find your house," Shirley said, attempting to pull conversation from Tiny and perchance discover why she looked like a madwoman and smelled as if she had not had a bath in years.

"You can leave me here if you want," Tiny said, as Troy paused at the four-way crossing that led into the various areas of the housing scheme.

Shirley said firmly. "I'm not leaving you anywhere till I find out what happened to you."

"But I all right here so, man."

"I not leaving you here! I'm taking you home."

"Why?" Tiny said. "Me say me OK."

"I don't care. You wouldn't leave me here."

"But I telling you to leave me," she insisted.

"Tiny, I don' care."

Tiny sighed, dropped her shoulders and sank some more into the seat. "All right," she said, pointing. "Turn here so."

"Where we going?" Troy asked.

"Phase Two," Tiny said.

"Same place we coming from," Troy said.

"You see, Tiny," Shirley said, "nothing hard in that."

"Is not every time you must force people," Tiny said quietly. "Not all the time."

"I don't know why you want me leave you on the street."

"You don' understand yah," Tiny said, looking down at her bag. "Me no live nowhere, you know, Shirley. Me no live nowhere."

Shirley watched as the tears dripped from her face. "How you mean?" she asked, trying to hold her own tears back.

"Me mean," Tiny used the dirty string of the bag to wipe her face, "me mean, where me live is not anywhere, you understand? Is not anywhere me live."

It was the same carcass of a house, overgrown with grass as tall as Shirley's head; the same deserted place they had kept returning to all afternoon. A house without windows or doors – bare and desolate – a building completely vandalized. There was no running water, no electricity. No telephone lines ran there. The paint had peeled from neglect. Shirley entered a stinking room onto bare and dirty floors, with dust and cobwebs clinging from every wall and dirt heaped to the corners where the wind had deposited it.

And the light shone through without stopping from vacant doorways, louvreless windows.

There was no sign of human habitation; but the largest of three bedrooms had a dirty sheet for a door and seemed to be the place where Tiny slept. Shirley saw a darker space inside with a bed and clothing strewn around.

And Tiny, wordlessly, shuffled around behind her, as empty and desolate as the place itself. As Shirley stumbled from the room to the hole that should have been the back door, an object slammed against the outside wall close to her face. "Madwoman! Hey, madwoman!"

Suddenly, two boys scampered through the grass. "A no she that!" one shouted, on seeing Shirley. The other looked around quickly and entangled with his friend. They fell in the grass as Shirley stepped forward, then both rose in panic and dashed away behind the property to disappear in an adjoining gully.

"Is so them stone me all the while." Tiny drew in beside her. Children can be very cruel. And when me come here, they was so nice. Then, them same ones thief away everything. It hard to believe that is the same people who use to be so nice to me... I don' even know." It was the most Tiny had uttered in one go all evening.

"Then where is you house, Tiny? What happen to the house in the picture, the one you show everybody in Miami?"

"Me don' know." Tiny began to cry. "Is this me come find. Same way so me come find it. But is how me fool so, eeh? Is how me fool so, Shirley?"

Shirley felt helpless as she looked at her friend standing there with the grass almost at her shoulders, with the disheveled hair and the tears streaming down, bag clutched in her hand as if she had not yet arrived where she was going. Shirley felt out of her depth. She looked around but Troy had stayed in his car. She reached toward Tiny. "Tiny, come here, come out of the sun."

And surprisingly she came – straight past her outstretched hands and into her bosom to press her face into the soft of Shirley's shoulders and sob there. Shirley held her, as much to balance herself as to comfort her. But Tiny had leaned into her with everything and the weight pushed

Shirley back till she found herself slipping down against the door jamb. She slid down gently, till she was seated in the doorway and Tiny was settled in her arms like a child. Every feeling in her transferred to the hand that patted Tiny's shoulder. "All right, Tiny, no mind, don't bother cry."

"Look what me come to, Shirley. Shirley, look what me come to."

"Don't mind, Tiny. Just don' mind now."

"An' you know mi friends in Miami did warn me. Is like them did know, you know – like they did know. You should a see the party them have fi me, Shirley. An' people all a crying for me, a cry say them a go miss me. Big party, Shirley. House full to the brim. People who I never even know come fi tell me how they wish it was them going home. And nuff food, Shirley, nuff, nuff food. And everything light up and pretty."

The wind gusted foul and dry through the long straw-colored grass. Flies hovered, blurred in the haze of the sweltering heat. Shirley felt her sweat beginning trickle down her armpits, but she was afraid to move. She was not sure what Tiny would do next. And she did not want to stop her from talking. She wanted to hear the story, she wanted to prod her on.

She shook her gently and whispered tenderly, "No mind, Tiny, don' mind."

"But mi friends use to tell me say go down and check, Tiny, go down and check. But me always tell them how I trust my sister."

The mention of family brought pain to Shirley's stomach.

"Everything different in Jamaica, eeh Shirley?"

"Yeah," Shirley said.

"The place change up, eeh? People don' say good morning again, Shirley. Nobody no help you like first time. Sometime it hard like America. Is not the same Jamaica, Shirley. Nobody kind any more, nobody no care what happen to you."

"It's hard to be kind," Shirley said. "We too busy now."

"I was one of the first person ever buy a house in this scheme. You know that, Shirley? Me was one a the first person. When me buy my house it never build yet. I come down for a few days to straighten out some business and heard about it. And just pay down 'pon it same time. I could a buy any house in this scheme you know? They show me the plan and say, 'pick any house you want. You are the first buyer.' Any house, any lot, you know, Shirley? Any one I did want. You know why I buy this house?"

"No."

"Because it perfect. Is the only perfect lot in the whole scheme. The only perfect square, and the house build right in the middle. You never know that? Perfect - and now them ban it. You know them ban mi house, Shirley?"

"Hush, Tiny. Nobody ban you house."

"Yes, them ban it. Water Commission, telephone company, public service. Them ban mi house. No more water, no more light, no telephone. You ever hear 'bout hundred thousand dollar phone bill, Shirley? You ever hear 'bout hundred thousand dollar for light?"

Shirley turned her head slightly to find Tiny's eyes. "But Tiny, you not making any sense to me. Just rest little, Tiny, just rest little man."

She felt her slacken in her lap, as if to relax more; her sobs had quieted and for a moment Shirley thought she might fall off to sleep like a child in her arms. But after a moment her voice came quietly and steadily into the afternoon. A voice seeking reason in itself.

"The evening I come back from Miami me come straight here from the airport. Me think me would jus' take the final flight and so. Them did send and tell me say the house ready and everything and that only mi sister did live inna one a the guest rooms. So me come straight. Me never did even wonder why nobody did come meet me. For they use to call me regular till me give them date that me was coming home. But I never put anything to that. I don' know why. Is mi sister. She would know."

Shirley listened in pain as Tiny recounted a search for her house, identical to the one she and Troy had just experienced. But she could hardly imagine the pain and confusion of standing in the middle of the night with her luggage all around her at the end of her dreams with no place to go.

"Is hotel me have to move into. But it come like it never really sink in, and for days I would take the taxi and come back and search to find mi house. And all the while I would end up back right here to this place. Till the taxi driver get tired taking me and start find excuse. And them ask me how me fool so. How me could be so fool fool. How me could live in Miami, so close to Jamaica and never come down and check for myself."

But Tiny must have known it was her house. She must have known from the first night, Shirley thought. But Shirley also understood that strange search for sanity. That tracing the path of falling dreams, that checking and back-checking the obvious... to hold tight the painful truths. Like checking her shadow to make sure it was hers, that it was not planted or stitched on.

Tiny fell silent and the rustle of the bending grass was all that Shirley could hear. She wondered if Tiny had fallen asleep again, but she did not check. She did not have the energy to move. She could not find the next question to ask, for though the story got more complex with each step, and though her curiosity was alive, she was not sure she wanted to hear the answers to the questions in her head. For somehow she felt that the story would get more horrifying as it proceeded and that the knowledge would taint her.

Then Tiny began to speak again.

"Them tell me to turn back right there so, turn back and go straight back to Miami - that's what people say when they use to talk to me, before children start stone me. But how? To what? When everything I own was down here on the wharf? Them say me should go back. But what me going to do – go clean people doodoo again, Shirley? Mi caan' go back to that."

"So what happened to your sister, Tiny? Where was she in all of this? What happened to her? You must have known where to find her."

"I don' know where she is."

"But how did you contact her while you were away?"

"Here. Right here."

"Here?"

"Yes! You don' understand? I tell her to live here. Stay with her children and so, jus' to keep the house and so, and that I would pay the mortgage. And after I finish pay for the house, since she was living here, I ask her to do the addition for me."

"And she added nothing."

"Not a thing, Shirley. You know how much money me send her?"

Shirley did not want to know.

"Remember when we was in Miami? They did send me picture to show that the house done. Is fifteen years I send them money, you know, Shirley. Fifteen years! When them send picture say the house done, them say me should send money come invest and so. Buy goat and cow and so, you know. Help pay the children school fee, you know."

"And nothing?"

"Not a thing, Shirley."

"Not a word since you come?"

"The lady cross the road, when they use to talk to me, said that some people lived here long ago. Say they come now and then to clear the mail box, but that they don' live here for long time now. Say they left after Public Service cut off the light."

"Light!"

"Yes. Is one whole heap of light bill owe on the house you know, Shirley. Telephone bill nearly $100,000. 00, water bill that mi caan' even count. All kind of bill. And they ban the house from getting light, phone or water, till me pay up the back amount and apply all over again."

"For her bills?"

"My bills, Shirley, everything in my name. Me not even have credit, Shirley, not even credit and me no live here for twenty years."

An animal, Shirley thought, a carrion and scavenger! That was the only way to describe a conscienceless human being who could live out a person's home like that – squat there, without paying the bills; live in it, use it down to the ground, then leave it like a parasite abandoning its prey once the resources were exhausted, leaving nothing to support or nurture life.

"Jamaica hard, you know, Shirley. Jamaica hard and expensive. And the people them tough and ginnalish and thief and wicked!"

"Not everybody, Tiny."

"The bank selling it, you know. I owe mortgage too. I send all that money to mi sister to pay and them spen' it off – never pay a thing."

"Come," Shirley said finally. For she had heard enough. She would not sit there a minute longer and listen to the story. Her belly was tight with a pain like severe hunger "Come." She rose, lifted Tiny with her and began to pull her through the house.

"Where we going?"

"Just come. I not leaving you here."

"But Shirley, is mi house. Is here me live – is all me have. . . is my house."

"I am not leaving you here."

"But where you going, Shirley? Where you taking me?"

"It matter, Tiny? Anywhere better than this. This is not a house – it is a garbage heap!" She turned around and tugged Tiny hard.

"Shirley!" Tiny screamed. "Me 'fraid." She sobbed quietly. "Where you taking me? Me 'fraid."

"Afraid of what?" Shirley paused again, exasperated and tired. "Afraid of what?"

"'Fraid of what me hear. Is not that me believe, is what me hear, Shirley."

"Now what are you talking about?" Shirley lifted her eyes. "You did not hear anything. We are alone in the house."

"Is not the house, Shirley. Is not the house. Is you."

"Me!"

They were staring at each other now and Tiny's eyes shone with what Shirley thought must have been her last vestige of strength. Me hear say you did involved in the drugs business. Shirley, is true?"

Now she would surely break down. For Tiny was adding guilt to the pain in her belly, and causing the air to rush through her lungs.

"Tiny, I am not leaving you here. Come with me."

Tiny became hesitant again and held back slightly. "Shirley, me 'fraid a the drugs business. And the drugs money and so. Shirley, me no able."

And shame too, shame was heavier than pain or guilt or sorrow. But combined they were like a loaded sack in Shirley's heart.

Shirley stopped, knelt in front of the little woman and shook her as she would a child. "Tiny, I am not getting you into any trouble! I am not giving you any drugs money. But I cannot leave you here. Trust me. You remember how you help me in Miami? Is my time now. Come!"

And so she took her through the desolate stinking house, through the tall grass and the wide, open space where a fence or a gate should have been, to the car where Troy waited patiently, resting in the reclined seat with his foot stretched along the ground through the open door.

"Come!" she said, for now it seemed the only word she could utter. Come! as if she was saying it not just to Tiny, not just to Troy, but to herself. As if it was part of a let's-go thing she did not understand. But it gave her strength, kept her on her feet, pushed back the tears. Troy closed the door, the engine came to life and they slipped away from the carcass of a house. Come.

Shirley tried to close her eyes as they drove through the housing scheme, with its variety of styles and designs: from large and immaculate to small and ridiculous. But even as she tried to close her eyes, she had to wonder just how many of the houses were built by the hard-earned money of some person toiling in America or England, or anywhere abroad for that matter. How many would receive a photo from some trusted relative in Jamaica representing a house that did not exist? How many returning residents, like Tiny, were there, walking the streets, half mad, hungry and dirty, with a picture of a house in their wallets – the fading picture of a house that was not theirs to have? The words escaped her lips. "How many?"

Tiny looked up questioningly at her. "You remember mi car?" she said suddenly "Me did bring it out here, you know."

"You brought a car?" Shirley began to straighten.

"Yes, me did ship it out, man, ship out everything."

"You have a car? So where is it?"

"It down a wharf, you know. As soon as me get money, me going clear it. Then I won't have to take bus any more."

How you mean down a wharf? Shirley almost asked her, to make sure she understood what Tiny was saying. But she remembered the scene in the house and was afraid Tiny would ask her again if she thought she was mad, so Shirley kept quiet.

But Tiny did not. She stared longingly through the window and continued to smile to herself, speaking slowly. "Sometimes, every now and then I see one like it on the road, one with the same color. But mine not so dirty... it always clean."

"What kinda car?" Troy looked through the rearview mirror.

"Dodge," Tiny said. "Dodge Avenger."

"Then what happened to it?" Troy was humoring Tiny and Shirley wished he would stop.

"Them have it, you know, have it down by the wharf, have it on storage for me. A went to clear it, but it was too much money. They wanted ten thousand US dollars to clear it."

"Ten thousand, is so them American car expensive." Troy nodded.

"But ten thousand?" Tiny said. "I buy it for seven. Them wanted more to clear it than I pay for it. And look how long I did have it."

Troy fell silent. The tone in Tiny's voice must have been too urgent for him, or he may have realized that in trying to lighten the mood, he had caused her to tell a truth which would only bring gloom and sadness to the car.

"Ship everything," Tiny said quietly to herself. "Ship everything and couldn't clear nothing more than the furniture. And what rain no wet them thief. Thief everything, you know, Shirley. Thief everything."

"All right." Shirley stretched out her hand. "You don' have to talk no more."

"But they keeping the car, though; have it on storage with the rest of the things me couldn't clear. And as soon as me get the money me going clear them." She gave a shrill laugh and slapped the seat. "You think this car pretty? You don't see nothing yet. You ask Shirley. My car pretty, don't it, Shirley?"

"Yes," Shirley said. "I remember."

Shirley watched her closely as she smiled almost like a child, lost in some fantasy. Tiny had gotten used to the American system, one that took care of people, in a place where buses worked, taxes gave returns, people were efficient and business like. Yet Tiny had spent her life there dreaming of a Jamaica that had begun changing the moment she stepped upon a plane to leave.

Shirley imagined her, lost, living in a hotel with a rate God knows how high, having to choose between paying off her house and fixing it, or clearing her car or furniture. What would a normal person have done? Clear the furniture with no house to put it in, or pay for the house with nothing to put in it? Clear a car and live in it while the house goes on sale – fix the house and lose it? What could she have done?

Shirley imagined her, alone, trying to come to terms with a country more foreign than the one she left. A distressed woman, old and saddened with a million decisions to make and a fading cash reserve. Desperate, desolate – alone, dreaming of goods that would have been auctioned off, sold, given away to friends, used and thrown out. Her car would have been driven, abandoned, sold and re-sold many times. Yet she sat in the corner of Troy's taxi, still hoping for the day she would get them back. Who would stand up for her and be her advocate, against the savagery of her family? What was left for her to do but huddle fearfully into a corner like a wet and frightened chicken, too scared to reach for the very sunlight that would make her better. She had no chance - no chance at all.

Silence came to the vehicle and Shirley was glad. They drove back through the housing scheme, through Spanish Town and its gallows and broken dreams, to Central Village and up the hill to the little gate, where a knock brought out the tidy little brown woman onto the veranda. Shirley brought Tiny, frail - spirit broken, through the gate she had promised herself never to cross again. She faced the stern figure and passed her friend's trembling arm across the space.

"Mama, this is Tiny," she said.

272

Chapter Thirty

That night, seated at the large dresser in her room, Shirley was having problems completing her makeup. She had barely applied a light base and reached for her powder when her hands began to tremble so much she had to put the container down.

Orville would be along any minute now. He had promised to show her Kingston all over again. But somehow the idea of leaving the room made her nervous and uncertain.

She had tried to rest but tossed all evening, as every time she closed her eyes, Tiny's wasted face appeared like a badly developed picture pasted against the back of her eyelids. She had showered but, try as she might, had felt she could not remove the stench of her friend's condition from her. It was as if Tiny's sorrow had become her own; she had caught her fear and was retreating.

But worse of all, Shirley knew that it was not just Tiny and her problems that made her shudder so. It was the feeling that had signaled to her from the very moment she stepped from the plane.

The feeling that she did not belong here.

From the changing face of transportation at the airport and the shifting profile of Knutsford Boulevard to the hard and painful conversation with her mother- everything; Dawn and her success and stable family; Barnes and Orville and their illegally legal briefcases of money; Troy, the fake taxi driver of a teacher posing with a certificate on his dashboard; and Tiny, her life wasted and destroyed by the very dream that created it. Everything had been showing her that there was no place for her here . . . in this country at this time.

And how could that be, when every breath she breathed, since the moment she had left an eternity ago, was to return? Jamaica was her home; returning had always seemed the natural thing to do.

But now she did not belong.

Suddenly she did not want to go out there did not want to experience what other differences there were out there, what other things had changed so much to bring further terror and dread to her. She did not want to see this new city. There was nothing but pain out there and loneliness, shame and disappointment.

And now Orville was due any minute.

There was a knock on the door.

She opened it and Orville stood there; beautiful and arrogant, in a silk shirt revealing breast. Jeans clung to a waist, slim and tight.

Why do we love you so, Jamaica? Why do we return to your arrogance and your beauty? Why?

Orville entered, smelling of French musk.

"You ready?" he asked.

"You know I'm a married woman."

"I know."

"I have a husband."

"I did not come to take him out."

"You don't understand. I am a married woman and I do not want to go out."

"I see. You want me to leave?"

"That's not what I am trying to say."

"What are you trying to say?"

"That I am a married woman."

"You said that before, Shirley. You are not making any sense." His presence, his beauty was overcoming her.

She was leaning into him now, tearfully leaning into him, her face was against the swell of his hard breast and she was hammering him lightly, as if to drive her words into him. "I am saying that I am a married woman. I don't want to go out, and I can't be alone tonight!"

The next morning, Shirley called Troy to tell him she needed a ride to the airport. She was going home. She did not call Dawn, did not go to see her. Did not answer the phone when it rang in her room. She did not care who it may have been. There was nothing for her in Jamaica any more. So she packed everything she had, even the undelivered gifts, and loaded it into the back of Troy's taxi.

Troy drove downtown and stopped near Parade where a Rastaman stood on the sidewalk beside a large tape recorder blasting music into the morning. Beside him on a box were huge stacks of cassettes with hand written labels.

As the car stopped, the man came over and smiled at Troy through the window.

"I want a Buju," Troy said.

"Yeah man," the man said, "mi have all kinda Buju. Which year?"

"Shiloh," Shirley heard Troy say. "You have Till Shiloh?"

"Yeah man."

The dread returned and pushed a cassette through the window. Troy paid him and slipped the cassette into the car stereo. The music of Buju Banton filled the car.

Shirley leaned back into the seat and wished he had not done that, as she did not particularly like Buju Banton. Troy must have been hearing her thoughts, because after ten minutes or so he reached forward to rewind and then eject the cassette from the stereo.

At the airport, as she told him goodbye and was about to enter the terminal, he held her hand suddenly and gave her the cassette. "Here," he said. "I bought this for you."

"You should not have," she said, almost impatiently. "I don't listen to that sort of music."

"Listen to this one," he said holding her eyes. "Listen to this one. If you don't like it, throw it away."

"OK." She took the cassette from his hand, a bit embarrassed by his generosity. "OK. Take care of yourself. Make sure you go back to teaching."

"You never can tell." He smiled, patted her hand and turned away.

PART V

Till I'm Laid To Rest

Chapter Thirty-One

Time... Shirley did not know or care how long she may have been sleeping, but when she opened her eyes, she could see her suitcase with its contents strewn across the room where she had left them some time ago. Some ages ago, when she had returned from Jamaica.

She remembered soaking for an hour in the bath, then going to bed and, waking some time later to find that over a day had passed. She had gotten up to try and tidy the place, but what did it matter if place was tidy or not; had tried to eat but had not gotten past a box of orange juice whose half-empty carton was somewhere outside on the kitchen table. She had switched on the TV but had crawled away from it seconds after its screen had snapped to life. Then on her way back to bed she had found the cassette Troy had given her and , with nothing better to do, had placed it into Moet's expensive stereo system. Shirley was not a Buju fan, but she lacked the will to rise again to switch it off. So she lay there, absorbing the words of the songs; till she fell asleep, only to wake up when the music stopped.

Suddenly she was anxious for her tape. She had never heard one stop in that stereo before; it had continuous play. She jumped from the bed. The ejected tape seemed fine, though a bit hot. She re-inserted the tape and pressed play. Buju's chant filled the room. On her way to the kitchen, Shirley recalled that Moet had said the stereo switched off automatically if the same tape continued playing for twenty-four hours... or thirty-six... It did not matter, this was Miami, time disappeared all the while.

She took a sandwich and a glass of milk to the patio and sat to watch the evening turn to night around her.

She had dreamt of a life like this – an expensive apartment in an upscale neighborhood with music filling every room, having all the money she wanted, all the food and clothing she needed – and a man, her own man -a husband. She had dreamt of a patio, too, like this where she would hold parties for her husband's friends -lawyers, doctors, professionals – and she would invite her friends from Jamaica to stay, to see and share her success. Then when she felt like it, she and her husband would visit Jamaica and do the country- grace the social scenes.

Now she had it all in a way she could not use. Now all she had was an empty evening with Buju on the speakers while her husband was somewhere far away selling drugs to America's children.

Murderer!

"Yeah, Buju, I know."

She raised her feet into a semi-lotus position so she could rest her chin on her knees. The evening was cool around her. The music hogged the atmosphere, engulfed her in its rhythms – filled her head. It was as if her life was written there, in those songs. As if Buju had discovered the very thing that moved her.

She almost ran into the house to stop the noise on the speakers – stop the testimony of her life. But she got as far as the fridge and a bottle of Moet Champagne . She held it to her head. The cold wine burned her belly and the bubbles filled her nostrils till she felt she would drown. Then she stumbled back to sit on the patio once more.

Till I'm laid to rest.

Was this not the secret vow she had made to herself from the first days in Central Village, when her father left, when she was no one else's movie star? Isn't that what she told herself: that she would make it, that she would rise to the top and be something, and that she would not stop, could not rest until she did?

Now they all wanted her to feel she had done something wrong. As if she had violated every rule – her mother's rules, Central Village's rules, Queeny's rules – everybody's rules. When all she did was try. *Satisfy!* Learn to *satisfy!* Yes, Mama, *satisfy!* But you ever *satisfy* with me? You must *satisfy*, Mama! *Satisfy* with me!

The almost empty champagne bottle fell from her hand and the liquid frothed onto the tile as she sank into the veranda chair. Her mouth fell open, and her bottom lip dropped away like that of a vagrant sprawled hopelessly in a gutter.

Chapter Thirty-Two

Moet must have found her there, for suddenly a fragrance of tangerine and spices filled her nostrils. And an aroma of delicious Jamaican food permeated her world. She was in bed, naked except for her underwear, and the sheets were pulled to her chin. And there was light in the bedroom – the soft, warm glow of sunlight reflecting through the cream and white drapery.

He came a few minutes later with food: tea of concocted mints, with boiled bananas and mackerel.

She watched him as he maneuvered around the suitcases and clothing strewn on the floor and came to sit at the edge of the bed as if he knew she would be awake.

"Sit up," he said, holding the large tray above her as she made herself comfortable against the bed head – then straddled her legs with it.

"Thanks," she whispered.

"Eat," he said. "Soon come." She reached for the cup as he moved away, back toward the kitchen. The food was good and exactly what she needed. And it frightened her – he frightened her. For he seemed to have a sixth sense about him that made him understand exactly what she needed or what she was thinking... almost like a woman's intuition. She sipped the tea.

She had already finished eating when he came again and she knew that the kitchen had been left in an immaculate condition, although the bedroom was in disarray, for he was like that. He took the tray from her.

As he sat at the edge of the bed and watched her quietly, she felt a tingle of fear, low, at the edge of her spine. He did not threaten her; the look on his face was as gentle as it had been that first night they met or the night of their honeymoon in Orlando when he tucked her in and walked to the balcony of the penthouse suite and stared outside across at Disneyland.

The same quiet look of settlement and finality.

The shiver in her spine widened a bit.

"You know say you pressure youself too much," he said.

They had been married now less than six months and had lived together before that for a much longer time, yet she still could not anticipate the next thing he would say or do.

On her wedding night she had dressed in the most expensive negligee that Victoria's Secrets had in stock – bought it from a catalogue, as if custom-built to her very measurements. But he had sat silently across from Shirley on the bed and looked quietly at her till she became nervous. Then he left her lying there in the large waterbed of the Orlando suite and went onto the balcony to look over at Disneyland.

He did not come to her, and she had lain there, confused and disappointed yet resigned. And when he did return, he curled up behind her and pulled her into him till she felt she had melded to his flesh. And they did not make love until the morning.

Those were the days, heady days, when she forgot the means and enjoyed the ends.

They lived a weird life. He was away half the time and when he was home he would watch TV and take her out to fancy restaurants and comedy clubs. Filling her life with toys, joys, frills and excitement like a whirlwind – everything to excite and tire her – everything except living. For she did not know him, was not sure how to move or excite him, did not understand how best to open the doors to his soul. And every woman should know that. She wondered, at times, if it was because she had neglected to care in those earlier days when all she wanted was his money.

He had surprised her one evening somewhere on Miami Beach when he had turned toward a tourist who had been interested in his car.

"I've never seen it with the steering on the left," the man had said.

"Benz is Benz," Moet replied.

"But the American is different," the man pointed out.

"Where you from?" Moet then asked.

"Australia."

"Ah, the Autobahn to an Ausie," Moet responded. "Now I understand."

"Yes," the man had said.

"They govern them over here, they can't go above say 85 or so."

"I know," said the man, "and make them heavier too. A left-hand drive Mercedes is not a Mercedes... really."

Shirley had expected Moet to be offended, but he offered the man and his wife a seat and they talked about cars and Australian wine way into the evening, while Shirley was having problems keeping up with the accent of the man's wife.

She had never forgotten that evening, and many times after that she had tried to engage in conversation with him. Speak on books or talk of foreign countries, but he seemed to close again and she gave up after a while. Maybe he had been drunk that night. Or maybe they had not lived.

But times like this, when he sat there quietly and sum up the circumstances of the room with just a glance that she wished she had tried harder to know what moved him. Then maybe she wouldn't be so afraid of him.

"I wasn't running away." She would not insult his intelligence.

"Who a talk 'bout run away?"

"Isn't that what you thinking?"

"I thinking say you too hard on youself. You take life too serious."

"I just wanted to see my mother."

"I believe you," he said.

This was a dangerous conversation. Just by the timing of it, the words. She had anticipated what he would be thinking and in doing so, had brought the possibility of leaving him out into the open.

"I just wanted to go and see my mother. I didn't even stay long, couldn't stand the place."

"You worry too much," he said, rising.

"If I had planned to leave you, I would not have married you."

"Mi tell you already, you know, you try too hard to prove too much things to youself."

"Moet!"

But he was already gone.

And just like that, just a few words of conversation had brought it all out into the open – that not only had she planned to leave him but that all along he knew.

And the fact of it stood before her in the silence of the room, like a third person.

Chapter Thirty-Three

When she awoke next morning, he was not beside her. She found him sprawled on the large couch in the living room, the remote control fallen from his hand and cricket was still showing on an international sports channel. Shirley left him there and went into the kitchen to fix breakfast. She hardly ever cooked, for he liked the kitchen more than she did and loved to pamper her. But today, she wanted him to awake to the smell of fried dumplings with ackee and salt fish.

She heard him stir as the dough touched the pan.

By the time the food was ready, he had cleaned himself and changed into comfortable shorts. She brought his food to him and he took it quietly. "Who playing?" she asked, nodding to the cricket that enthralled him on TV.

"West Indies and India."

"Who winning?"

"Who you expect?"

Cocky was good, she thought. Cocky was better than silent.

She got her breakfast on a tray and sat on the carpet beside his chair. And they watched quietly for a while.

"You can leave if you want, you know. I wouldn' stop you."

Shirley paused carefully so as not to choke on her food, but more so that the reaction on her face would not change because she did not know how to take what Moet had just said. She was not sure how to respond but knew she had to say something. She was aware that every sense in his body was tuned to her every movement and measured every word she spoke as they passed the edge of her lips. She wondered why he had to tell her that right now. And found that to be the only thing she could say. "Why?"

It caught him off guard, but he did not show it. "No that you want?" he asked.

"I told you that?"

"Every day."

"Yeah? I tell you that every day?"

"Of course. A no words alone say things, you know."

Now she felt she had a slight handle on where he was going, though they were walking on the edge of a precipice that she would not be able to navigate for long. "OK," she said, "let me tell you how it went. I went to visit my mother, I went to Jamaica and it just did not turn out right. I planned to stay a week or two but I returned after just a few days. I wasn't feeling good."

"What happened down there?"

"You wouldn't understand."

"Why? I have to pass exam? Or I never go the right school?"

"Jesus!"

"Moet, call me Moet." He rose, took his dish to the sink and stopped to pour himself a glass of champagne . Usually, he would have poured her one. She did not miss the message. He sat again to watch the TV.

"Do you want me to leave? Is that it?" she asked, sensing a chance to shift the advantage in the argument. "For if you want me to leave then that's a different thing."

He was quiet again, then he almost whispered to her, holding her eyes in a cold stare. "I don't want you to stay as if I have you in some kind a prison; I don't want you to stay if you don't want to stay – if you feel, say, well, you better than me. I am not no stepping stone. I don't want you to stay and to feel that you can use me."

"Thank you," she said. "Thank you for telling what you really think of me." She rose and almost slumped her shoulders.

"What me think of you now?" he asked.

"How do you mean?" She became angry. "I must be a whore or something, the way you talk. Some kind of dog or something who come to live you out and leave you."

"I did not say that."

"That's what you just say."

"I never mean it so."

"There's only one way to mean it."

"I mean that sometimes I don' know how to please you because you go on like what you want not here. That's what I mean, and you know that is what I mean, so don' try twist things on me. I don' like it."

"What I want! You never know what I want."

"You damn right," he said. "Nobody know what you want. All you do is go on like you better than people."

"I do not," she said vehemently. "I do not! Is just you think that."

"I jus' want you happy, you know."

"I am happy," she lied.

"Well, sometimes it don' look so."

"Women are moody," she said softly. "Men don't know patience."

He took a long sip from his drink and regarded the TV momentarily. "Well, cool off 'pon the mood them sometimes, man."

"I'll try." She sat on the edge of the chair. "I know I can be hard to live with sometimes."

"Sometimes I not even feel like I married," he said. "Like me jus' up and down same way."

"I could say the same thing," she whispered.

"Is just like nothing no change."

"I'll try." She found herself believing. "I'll try to change."

Shirley gave in to him as he sighed, placed his hand around her waist and pulled her down till she slid into the corner of the sofa beside him. She allowed her head to fall across his lap.

"Then that is it, man – and don't 'fraid to tell me what you want. You know I will give you anything."

They made love right there on the couch that morning, right there in the living room on the couch while cricket played somewhere in India. He felt different too, that morning, much more tender than she could remember. And she responded, she felt, with more of herself, though it took her a while to get there. For somewhere in the middle of it, as he groaned against her naked belly, it came to her that she was more fortunate than some – that she had all she wanted. So what if it was not packaged the way she had expected? The substance of it was much of what she dreamed. Maybe she was too hard on herself; maybe she should, as her mother suggested, learn to satisfy. She had pushed all her life, tried everything, and God had given her this: a man who worshipped her, gave her all she wanted in every way he could, with creature comforts to prove it and sexual ecstasy to enforce it. Here, she thought, was space to be happy. So halfway through, as his lips began to trace the lines of her waist, she decided that maybe this was it and that she would try for once to make it work.

When they were finished and lay entangled in each other's arms she felt she needed to ask another question.

"You really wanted me to go?"

"You mad!" he said. "But I was serious. I only react one way to pain. I would a prefer if you leave before it come to that."

The chill she felt at his response was momentary – the full force of the statement was to come to her much later, when it was almost too late. But now she nestled closer, thinking how not to disappoint him any more, thinking of how she would like to make her marriage work.

It was the small things, Shirley found, that changed a life and made a marriage better. Like listening when he talked or listening so he could talk. For he was a quiet man who had a lot to say – quick to recede if no one cared to receive his wisdom. Not that he was conceited, he just knew what he was saying. And Shirley realized that she had never granted that. So now they talked more. Where once they watched two different television sets, now she found she would nestle with him while he watched cricket on the one in the living room. And they would talk about the game and he would teach her about it with pride. Cricket took him home to Jamaica, he had said. When he was lonely or missed home, he watched cricket – bought every international sporting channel so he could.

Shirley found that the more she sat with him and the more they spoke, the less cricket he watched and the more she began to interest him in movies. He understood more than she had anticipated, for he was a master plotter and had a fine feel for intrigue. Soon they began going out to simpler things, to the movies, for walks in the park, to the flea market just to browse, or to the beach, just to sit and watch Miami happen around them.

Then she told him of her family and of her parents and of the trip to Jamaica and how it broke her heart, and he smiled at that, laughed even. For they were in the park that day, sitting under a tree near a small pond watching a couple jog along the man-made tracks. And she had told him and he had read it all along, for he understood her so well. And when she finished he had laughed and rolled on the grass. But that was all right; they were getting to be better together now.

"You can get a bank job here if you want," he had said after he had sobered.

"I know."

"Yeah man. Why you never try?"

"I don't know," she said.

"Well, go on now, get a job or something."

"You sure?"

"What kind of question that?" He sounded disappointed.

"I can get a job if I want, you know," she tried to counter.

"You get lazy man," he teased. "Too much good life."

"Maybe."

"Get one before I come back," he suggested.

"When you leaving?" she asked, a bit disappointed that he should still feel he needed to tell her skillfully, that he would be leaving.

"Tomorrow," he said.

"You know I don't like when you leave."

"I know, but is what I do."

"I know, but the place feel empty – lonely sometimes."

"Well, now you going get a job," he said. "Now you will have something fi tire you a daytime."

They were lying side by side on the grass watching a few ducks splashing about in the small pond. It was around five o'clock, so everything was cool and peaceful. Shirley wished secretly all her days could be like this, quiet and peaceful, just the two of them in their own world.

She sighed.

He ignored that, as if he could tell the nature of it and wanted it to slide.

Shirley knew she had a bad habit of not leaving well enough alone. It was the restlessness in her, a need to have things a certain way, a desire to know. She wished she was not like that.

"Moet?" she said. "Moet."

"What now?" he asked gently.

"I want to ask you something."

"What?" He spoke as if he knew already what was in her head – a what of anticipation like a batsman who has seen the grasp of the ball in the bowler's hand and already decided the shot he will take and the place on the field he will send the ball.

"I know it's your life," she tried to be tactful, "and it has given you everything... but you not planning to stop one day?" She paused. He did not answer. "I mean," she tried to be conciliatory, "I mean, is not that I feel it wrong or... Moet, you know what I am trying to say." She kissed her teeth against his silence and gave up.

"And do what?" he asked.

"How you mean? Open a store, a clothing store or something."

"Me?"

"Yes, you. Open a store."

"Me, who never go school? First you think me stupid – now, I can open store?"

"OK, forget it," she said. "I thought we could talk."

"Then no talk we talking?"

"But you can do anything you want," she said. "You are smart, you are calculated."

"When since?"

"Even if I never believe it, I know it now."

He rose and walked away. She did not try to stop him for she knew he just wanted to straighten the tangle in his mind. When he came, he began to tug at the edge of the blanket as if to tell her it was time to go.

"You said we should talk more." She looked up at him.

"I don' want talk no more."

"OK, but will you think about it?"

"Is drugs me sell. I tell you long time, is drugs me sell. Is that me know. I don' have no boss but the man who hungry for it. I work two weeks per month. America too hard fi black people. You don' have no other way for people like me to survive. You want me go open store, I caan' even open bank account. The first move you make, everybody wan' know where you get money from, where you get funding from... some things easy to talk."

"Where there is a will there is a way."

"Is drugs me sell."

"Just think 'bout it no, Moet?"

"I think 'bout it already. Three years now, me thinking 'bout it."

"But I wasn't you wife then."

That stopped him short. "How you mean? What you trying to say?"

"Now is not jus' you. You married now," she said desperately.

"But I tell you from the start."

"I know, but think about it again, just think about it, Moet. Promise me."

"All right. If you want... But I thinking about it for three years already. Come, make we go home."

She rose to meet him. "OK," she said.

Some would have said she should have left the evening as it was, but she was not like that. If she was going to have a life with him, she would have to have a say in it. And she did not see herself living as she did for the rest of her life. She had to speak her mind, and if that broke the relationship, that meant it would not have been strong enough to last in the first place. But she was gentle with him that night. And when he woke at the sound of the phone and headed to the bathroom, she got up too, and made him breakfast. She refused to feel like a housewife sending her man to work, but rather wanting him to know she would support whatever decision he made.

So for the first time since she knew him, she followed him outside to wait with him on Chef.

"Use one of the car," he said.

"I usually take a taxi."

"No, but if you going to look work you going need a car. Use the convertible – you handle it better."

"OK, if you insist, I will. But you know I hate to drive alone in Miami."

He pulled his cellular from his pocket and called Chef to find out how far from the house he was. She waited with him there, outside the complex, till Chef came to pick him up. He came in an old Toyota with fenders dented and color faded to nothing.

"Is Chef car that?" she asked.

"No man," he smiled, "Its the working car."

"That old thing?"

"Only the body old. Everything underneath brand new and suped-up."

"I see," she said.

As he slid into the car, she found herself waving at Chef who smiled and waved back with a slight look of surprise on his face. Even she was surprised as she realized just how possible it was to gain a smile from the worst of characters with a little bit of effort. She turned into the apartment complex as the shabby car turned toward the turnpike, and smiled to herself. Maybe he would change; maybe things would be OK. Maybe it would work out, after all. But, however it went, she thought. This is your life, Shirley Temple Brown, and you better make the best of it.

Chapter Thirty-Four

One day, about a week after Moet had left, Shirley drove to North Miami to drop an application at a new Nations Bank that had opened there. As she left the bank, she realized that she was only five minutes away from Queeny's old apartment. She did not expect to find Queeny there because, as far as she remembered, Queeny had left Miami months before she had gotten married to Moet. But a sense of nostalgia overtook her and she cruised by the complex wondering if fate would have been so strange as to allow her to see her friend again.

As she cruised by, she saw that nothing had really changed about the place, except that in front there was the semblance of a lawn now. The cheap apartment was as bare and dusty as the usual Miami day. She drove on but memories of Queeny flooded her; she thought of how special and strange their friendship had been, and then how it had just fallen apart like the links of a broken chain. Suddenly passersby began to look like Queeny. Everyone around her seemed to be dressed in a Versace shirt or large white DKNYC T-shirt, and sporting weaves of every color.

She bolted upright in her seat. Was it a fantasy or was it real? One of those women walking toward the complex might have been Queeny herself. Shirley spun the car around and returned, but there was no one in the yard of the complex and the apartment seemed as desolate as it did five minutes before.

She parked outside for a while and then decided to get out and knock. As she opened the car door, Queeny came around the corner from the bus stop. It was the strangest Shirley had ever felt in her life. Just like that, Queeny came around the corner in an oversized T-shirt and dark red jeans, with Mary Poppins shoes tied with a fancy bow on top. At first, Shirley did not recognize her because her hair was blond.

Queeny did not break her stride. She plunged her key into the door and spoke casually over her shoulder, "You can go on stand up there with you mouth open like you a idiot."

Shirley jumped from the convertible and chased after her. "Queeny!"

Queeny switched on the light, and searched quickly around with her eyes. "Who you expect?"

"Queeny, you are in Miami!"

"Same one. Same place." She found the bag she must have been looking for, picked it up, and turned to face Shirley. "Watch it deh," she said.

Shirley stood in her way. "I'm not moving, you know. I am not moving."

"Work me going, you know, is something me forget."

"I am not moving,"

"You can stay there," Queeny said. A smile began to wrinkle the corner of her mouth, "You can – ahh boy!"

"Ahh boy what?" Shirley asked.

"Ahh boy," Queeny repeated, a laugh gently falling from her. "You not easy, you know, you know you not easy."

"You couldn't tell me you in Miami, you couldn't call?"

"You did tell me you inna Jamaica?" Queeny sat back into the old sofa bed. "You couldn't call." She tried to mimic Shirley's tone.

"So that's why you vex?"

"Mi look vex to you? Mi no vex," she said earnestly, "but me really have to go work."

"But I can drop you."

"Then drop me," Queeny said, "drop me no?"

Now Shirley could hear the joy filling her voice the same way it filled her bosom. "Well, come no?"she said.

"Is you blocking the way," Queeny said.

Shirley rose from the sofa. "Let's go."

"I hope you can drive," Queeny said.

They drove together in silence for a while, Queeny staring purposefully ahead while Shirley negotiated their way along the road.

"Pembroke Pines me deh now," Queeny offered as Shirley began to change lanes for the exit that would take them to the beach.

"You not with Grace any more?"

"Lord, look how long Grace dead."

"She died?"

"Yes, nearly a year now."

"Grace died," Shirley mused to herself.

"Yes," Queeny said quietly, as if her mind had begun to process sad memories. "Dead in her sleep. One morning she just never wake up."

"So long I've not seen you," Shirley said, half to herself and half to Queeny.

The ride saved Queeny time so they stopped to eat at a little Burger King off Pembroke Drive. Queeny had an old man now. A little Jewish man, she said, who had prostate cancer. "Them say it turn back now," she told Shirley, as she spread her burger on the table. "They operate on him and cut it out. But you know them things, you never can tell. Just hope him live little longer. Just want one good year out o' him. I could finish mi house."

"I thought you had a house already. You left your husband?"

"No sir, lef' what? I putting on upstairs."

"Him start behave now?"

"Behave!" She rolled her eyes. "But where you going find better?"

Shirley watched as Queeny made a small ceremony of arranging her burger on the table. Preparing for the assault.

"So what you came and look for me for?" Queeny asked. "Me think you turn uptown girl now. Any time you come look for me is something you want."

"I don't want anything," Shirley said, annoyed. "I wasn't even looking for you. I was just passing, dropping off a resume."

Queeny kissed her teeth. "Passing. Yeah, right." She bit into the burger and her face sank almost to her nose. "Yeah?" Crumbs sprayed onto the table as she chewed heartily. "You looking work now?"

"Yes, I am looking work now. You have a problem with that?"

Queeny kissed her teeth again. "You can go on fool yourself 'bout you a look work. You want leave the ugly boy and you want me help you. Is that. 'Bout you a look work. Your problem is you don't know what you want."

"You don't worry about that; I know what I want. I am happy in my marriage." Shirley was defiant.

"Yeees?"

"Yes."

"You happy and you know what you want?"

"Yes." Shirley sighed and looked away. Realizing that it was futile to continue the conversation, the way it was going.

"All right then, tell me." Queeny laid the food on the table and gave Shirley her full attention. "What you want?"

"How you mean?"

"But you don't know. First you want one thing, then another and when you get it you can't satisfy because that not exactly what you want."

"I know what I don't want though," Shirley said after a slight pause. "I know what I do not want."

"But that not enough. You have to know what you want," Queeny said.

"But suppose you never have it. Suppose you never have what you want yet? How you going know what it is?"

"But you mus' know what it is. You mus' know what you want."

"You don't have to as long as you know what you don't want." Shirley was trying to be patient. Not just with Queeny but with herself. For the thoughts were coming to her as she spoke and she herself was trying to understand the words even as they passed her lips. "Maybe I'm not explaining it right." She sighed and swung her drink from side to side, glancing out onto the small garden. The chips of wood at the root of the plants glistened in the Miami heat. "Is like love," she said.

"Like somebody who never feel love and a try find it. Like sex, then, like orgasm, you know – when you friend them tell you 'bout it, how it nice and you never experience it yet, and you try and try, because even though you never experience it, never have it, you try and try because you feel that it out there, and is more than what you have."

"But maybe nothing out there. Maybe what you have is all that God give you. It just look greener on the other side, as them say," Queeny said.

"But how you know?"

"How you mean? Is not every woman can cum."

"But how you know that?" Shirley persisted.

"Doctor say so."

"But how you know that you are one of those who can't cum?"

"Then a how much try you going try so, missis, with how much different people, to find out that? Sometimes a man have to just decide on something, and just hold that, and move on. Just take what you have and make what you want."

"People should never settle."

"Yes, but sometimes life a give you message, and you mus' listen."

"I'm listening."

"You," Queeny said, and Shirley could sense the end of her patience, "you not listening, You not leaving that life. You going stay till it kill you."

"I know what I'm doing," Shirley insisted.

Queeny kissed her teeth. Ignored her and began to wrap the remainder of her lunch for the garbage.

"You know is jealous you jealous," Shirley said hotly.

"Jealous!"

And right away Shirley was sorry the words left her mouth. Queeny's voice rose till all in the Burger King turned to look at them.

"Jealous! You no see is a dutty murderer you married to? Is drugs you dutty husband sell. Is people him murder. Is him kill Mikey. You should a glad I even a talk to you! Jealous? But," she started to stammer, "but - you know what? Jus' come carry me go work before me tell you something, you hear? Come carry me go work. Cause me never send come call you."

And from the little Burger King to the large expensive apartment complex in Pembroke Pines, they never exchanged another word.

Chapter Thirty-Five

Shirley spaced the large white candles onto the ceramic tiles of her bathroom with movements that were almost ceremonial. There were a dozen of them, and she took her time to place them, as evenly as possible, so they covered the full area of the large room.

She took her time.

Jazz filtered into the space almost unnoticed to set the tempo of her breathing. Steam from the hot water flowing into the large Jacuzzi misted the large full-length glass on the wall and made her reflection ghostly and surreal as she moved.

Sometimes Queeny was a blessing and sometimes she was a curse. This time around Shirley was not sure what she was. Maybe she would have been better off if she had not gone looking for her that day. Now she felt confused again and lonely. And all of a sudden the old feelings about leaving Moet were upon her again, and this time they were so strong she wondered how she had ever suppressed them – how she had ever changed her mind.

One day in the real world – alone – had erased all the bliss and commitment that had filled her and now she was sure, more than ever, that she had to leave him to preserve her sanity.

The phone rang. It was Orville.

At first she did not recognize his voice. His words were quick and still had that sexy edge, but they were a bit hollow, a bit less persuasive than she remembered – or was it her?

"It must be my lucky day," she said.

"You gave me your number," he said.

The heat of the water tugged at her skin as she tested it with her hand.

"What?" she asked. "I gave you my number?"

"Yeah man."

"So how is Jamaica?" she asked, reaching for the matches.

"I'm not calling from Jamaica. I'm in Miami. When mi can see you?"

"When you want," she heard her voice tell him.

She struck the match and touched the flame to the tip of the stick; the incense sparkled like a starlight and settled to a dull burn. The smoke curled into the room. The aroma found its space and tone as the smoke of candle and incense mingled.

The phone call was distracting her.

"Now all right?" she heard him say.

"What?"

"Can I come now?"

"Come where now?"

"To check you."

"Could you hold a second," she told him. Her mind was on the meditation she was about to have. She had little time for conversation, especially from Orville. He was after only one thing. But she could handle that.

Large thick white bubbles began to form in the water. They rose quickly to the edge of the tub. Shirley tested the water and grunted with satisfaction. The room became misty and thick with the pungent mixture of scents. She let the robe fall from her, placed the phone on the floor and lowered herself gingerly into the warm bubbles. She reached outside to the controls of the bath, set the jets to medium and sighed as the pressure of the water forced against the several parts of her body. When she was settled she remembered he was on the line and picked the phone up again.

"So what happen, Orville?" She was more composed now.

"How you have me waiting so long?" She could sense in his voice that he was trying hard to be patient.

"I was doing something," she said.

"I want come check you now," he said.

"You are in Miami?" She sounded surprised.

"Yeah, I just tell you that. You said I could check you."

She remembered him now as she laid there. Recalled his strength, his finely muscled body... the night in her room at the Pegasus overlooking Kingston. But somehow he did not seem so inviting tonight. Tonight she had things to think about. But she still remembered him. Maybe tomorrow. . . "Maybe tomorrow," she said.

And then she heard the beep on the line that told her another call was coming in. She placed him on hold and switched the line.

"Is me, Queeny," the voice said.

"Yes?" Shirley said, as coldly as she could.

There was a short silence.

"Well," the voice continued, "me just call fi tell you say you business is you business."

"I know that," Shirley said quietly.

"Me never have to cuss or nothing. And me never mean nothing."

"Yeah?" Shirley asked.

"Well, is just that me call fi tell you," Queeny said. "Is your business. Is your marriage, and if you happy, you happy. But you still never have any right fi say me jealous."

"You can hold on?" Shirley asked. "Let me end this call."

She switched back. "Orville, I will have to call you back."

"But you just said I could come now."

"Me! When I said that?"

"You don't remember?"

"Let's do lunch tomorrow," she said, surprised at how easily she controlled the conversation. "I'll call and tell you when."

"You don't have my number."

"What is it?" she sighed.

"I'm in Fort Lauderdale." He spoke seven numbers haltingly into her ear.

"I'll call you," she said, and switched back to Queeny. "Yes, Queeny?"

"Well, me finish you know," Queeny said. "Me say what me have to say already. Me gone."

"Are you going to help me?" Shirley asked quickly.

"Help you do what?"

"Leave." Shirley spoke sharply. She felt suddenly close to tears.

"But how me going to help you?" Queeny sighed across the line. "If you wan' leave, just leave."

"You know I've been trying a long time to do that." Shirley tried hard not to sound too desperate.

Queeny's voice came haltingly across the line. "Next thing mi go help you and you change you mind and leave me one in trouble. Is one killer you married to, you know, Shirley. Him no 'fraid to do nothing, you know."

"Moet ever trouble you yet?"

"Him don't like me," Queeny said crossly.

"That shouldn't stop you."

"All right." Queeny gave in. "I know how you can do it but I can't tell you over the phone."

"Then come no, Queeny man. Come no."

"All right," Queeny said quietly, "I will check you tomorrow 'bout ten or so. After me wake up."

"OK," Shirley said.

And as the phone clicked in her ear she dropped her own instrument and settled into the bubbles. She closed her eyes and let the heat and aroma engulf her. The burning embers of the incense sticks seemed to hold their glow onto the insides of her eyelids and the pain and the uncertainties began to drain from her.

Chapter Thirty-Six

She was watching TV when Queeny came next day. Shirley let her in and went to the fridge to make her a drink. She already had half a bottle of Moet on the table beside a half empty glass.

"Jesus, you drinking nuff now, Shirley. Is so you drink now?" Queeny's consternation slapped her face with the cold of the open refrigerator.

"You start the mother thing again?" Shirley said testily.

"No, missis. But you no see you life a turn you inna alcoholic?"

"You said you would help and now as you come you start criticize. You apologize and now you start another quarrel – Jesus Christ!"

"But what I must do?" Queeny asked. "If I see something I have to talk 'bout it."

"But you can make some things rest, Queeny."

"And furthermore, I don't know what you call apologize. A just tell you something."

"Then you have to pick up on that too?"

"No, but is how you say things, man, Shirley. You know, is how you say things."

Shirley sighed, and did not bother to search for another drink. She just picked up another glass and poured Queeny some Moet spitefully.

Queeny smiled to herself, picked up the glass and headed for the balcony.

Shirley followed, waiting for Queeny's next outburst.

But Queeny played it cool.

They sat and sipped wine till Shirley's insides began to boil with anxiety. She could not wait to hear Queeny's grand plan. But Queeny was taking her time.

After a while, Queeny placed her glass upon the table, leaned back into the chair and spoke with a half smile playing across her lips."Woman, dog and pickney."

"What?" Shirley asked.

"Woman, dog and pickney," she repeated, "Man no have no rights inna this country."

"What you talking about?" Shirley asked again.

"You know, me tell you this plan already," Queeny said. "Me sure me tell you already, you know. Right here on this same balcony."

"You tell me a plan? In which world?"

"I tell you though, I remember."

"Well, tell me again. Two times better than one."

"You don't remember Dorothy?"

"Dorothy?"

"No, you wouldn't remember her," Queeny mused. "Is one time you see her, long time now, but you should see her now." Queeny raised her glass to an invisible Dorothy.

"What you talking 'bout?"

"Dorothy, man. Use to married to this druggist, name Palmer. Him use to sell all kinda drugs. Use to have a whole heap a woman too."

"So?" Shirley asked. "What that have to do with anything?"

"Then make me tell you no? You don' understand? The bwoy have a whole heap a woman and she always findin' out. But the one time she go have one little man with him, him find out and beat her up."

Shirley still could not understand the relevance. "So?"

Queeny kissed her teeth. "Him first lick was him first mistake. Her daughter call the police same time. Them jus' run him out a the house."

"And..."

"Him caan' go back. She get the house, everything. And all him get, is a one-mile restraining order. Him can't go near her, nor the house. And him still paying the mortgage."

"Are you serious?"

"How you mean? Is Miami this. One lick, that is all, one lick and him is at you mercy. Man no have no rights. The first rule: never lick a woman, never lick a dog and never lick a pickeny." Queeny shook her head. "That is the easiest way fi any man go jail inna this country.

Woman, dog and pickney... them rule America."

"You want me," Shirley spoke so low it was as if she whispered, "you want me to go out and find a man and bring him here, so Moet can find us together and beat me, so police can lock him up? Is you big plan that?"

"Where your plan deh?" Queeny asked indignantly.

"But no plan is better than that plan," Shirley laughed.

"Because you don' listen," Queeny said.

"But I must go get a man? Then Moet would kill me. I wouldn't have to leave him. Him would kill me."

"Who say anything 'bout man? You don' have to get no man. You no see how Moet big? Just make him lick you."

"What?"

"Just start a quarrel. Make him hit you. You no need more than one lick. Once him finger print out on you, and like how your skin red already, just one lick, once the police see him size, him done for."

"Just like that?"

"Men have no rights here." Queeny slurped her drink. "Once him lick you, they throw him out of the house... is the law."

"But what about bail? Moet will come back," Shirley said. "Then him would kill me."

"No! How him must do that? The law involve now. Him wouldn't do that. Plus them put restraining order on him and him have to stay away."

"Just like that?"

"Jus' like that," Queeny said.

"And what next?"

"You get everything: house and everything. And him still have to pay the mortgage and everything. Is America this. Woman, dog and pickney... we have all the rights."

Chapter Thirty-Seven

Sunday.

Shirley snuggled deep into Moet's large embrace and wondered what god could fool her into trying so hard to leave it. She was curled around a pillow while the rest of her body was pressed deep into him. He moved slightly and his large arm that draped across her pulled her even closer into him. There was a kind of timelessness about these moments when they would lie there in the darkness like this. The curtains would be drawn and the lights would be out, and though she knew it was Sunday morning she could not tell or care whether it be dawn or noon, for his huge frame was wrapped around her like a womb around a fetus – and all the dreams of what her life might be would lie far away – and outside.

She knew he would soon come awake and alive and wanting her – and he did. And as the passions swelled within her she could not help wondering if this was the last time. If this would be the day she made him angry enough to hit her so they could take him away from her forever – so she could have the life she dreamt of. She found she wanted more of him now – this morning. The crushing weight of his arm on her side squeezing her breasts into her chest could not be tight enough. His thrusts could not be deep enough; she felt she had to have it all then, all those sensuous fantasies she had, all those carnal dreams she wanted to come true - she felt she had to have them all then that morning, that day. And she found it was no wild thing she needed, no acrobatic positions, or personal pornography. It was the crush of his weight around her, the depth he reached inside her to make them one – and when climax raged and feelings rained inside her, there was no fear that they would end too soon, that he would not be there in full to drain every spasm from her, to hold her tight against the passions of the moment till all was spent within her.

The doorbell chimed. Shirley surfaced from sleep to check the face of the little clock at her bedside. It was almost one o'clock. Moet had already gone from the bed. She looked around sleepily to tell him to get the door, but she did not see him. She figured he was in the bathroom though she did not hear a faucet running – it was a big bathroom. She rose reluctantly to open the front door and invite Queeny and the rest of Sunday in.

"You no wake yet?" Queeny bellowed. "And me think me did late."

"Late for what?" Shirley asked, walking ahead of her into the living room.

"How you mean, you not going to Sawgrass again?"

Shirley dipped into the fridge for a large bottle of orange juice. "Sawgrass! Who going Sawgrass mall? I said I was going to Sawgrass?"

"You know you don' have no memory?"

Shirley began to vaguely remember wanting to go shopping at Sawgrass. She had promised many things to Queeny over the past weeks. Conspiracy had drawn them closer and they were big friends again. These days when they were not on the phone for hours they were together on the porch drinking Moet's champagne and refining their plot for her to leave him.

"Even if I wanted to go I changed my mind. I just want to relax today, just want to stay home," she finally said.

"Well, I don' like stay home with you." Queeny took the orange juice offered to her. "Me no like stay home with you. You too coward. And every day you change you mind."

Shirley almost spilled the juice she was lifting to her mouth. "How you mouth so big," she whispered.

Queeny kissed her teeth."What me must whisper for?" she scowled. "You man leave the house and you don't even know."

"Moet has left?"

"Two people caan' ugly so. Nearly bounce me down with him car."

"Well, I was sleeping."

"You think is was sleeping? You still sleeping and you nah go stop sleep till you really go sleep."

Shirley finished her drink and watched as Queeny made her way toward the patio. Less than five minutes into her apartment and Queeny had already changed the complexion of the Sunday. And all of a sudden the day and the feelings seemed to turn on their heads. It was confusing. She placed the glass upon the counter as she headed toward her bedroom. "Me a go bathe, soon come."

She was not sure if Queeny responded to her.

Shirley knew her indecisiveness was frustrating Queeny. One minute she wanted to leave Moet, the next she could not; another time she would be all for Queeny's plan, the next minute she could not find the courage to go through with it. And Moet did not make it easy, for there was very little to be angry with him about. And when he did do something wrong, usually Queeny would not be there to carry out her side of the plan.

But one thing remained. No matter how much fun she had, deep down she knew she had to leave him some day. Yet sometimes she wished that the day would remain as far down the road as possible, till she was strong enough.

As the first of the shower's hard spray touched her skin, she heard the door close outside. Either Queeny had gone or Moet had returned. The rustling in the bedroom told her the latter was true. He probably went to get the paper. She finished her shower, slipped into her robe and entered the bedroom to find him lying across the bed waiting on her.

As she passed the bed, he encircled her with his feet and pulled her down against him. "Send home you feisty friend," he whispered.

"Behave yourself." She tried to push him away.

"Send her home now," he whispered softer, more seductively.

"Why?"

"All right, she can watch then," he joked.

She shoved him off playfully and rose from the bed pulling her robe around her. It was then she saw his black travelling bag stowed in the doorway.

"You leaving?"

His feet were still wrapped loosely around her and he was by now sitting up on the edge of the bed. He pressed his face into the small of her back and spoke softly against her. "No fi long, we have a sort of emergency. We have to make a quick move."

"We were supposed to go somewhere tonight."

"Next time." He tugged her robe open. "Send home the little feisty gal no man."

She pushed herself free. "That's all me is to you, a sex stop?"

"What?"

She hardly believed the words as they left her. She had done the unthinkable – she was halfway into a quarrel. It was the opportunity they had been waiting for. Queeny was outside, there was the germ of a reason for a row. Now all she had to do was get angry enough. Her heart began to thump wildly.

"What happen to you?" he cooed. "Something happen to you?"

"You see something happen? What you take me for? Is that I want to know."

"How you mean, what kinda question that?" He reached for her – held her lightly.

She struggled against him. "Let me go, I say let me go! Is only sex alone you want?"

"How you mean? You all right, Shirley? Man leaving and man want a little catch-up before mi go. You know how it go."

"Catch-up! Could you please let me go." She pulled free. "You just let me go. If you want catch-up, you go look for some other woman. I am not for that."

She saw him pause, saw a calmness come to his face and knew his mind was working like a computer, sensing things: modes, nuances, inflections, matching them to words, actions, moments.

"Anyway, I'm not in the mood." She did not want him thinking too much.

"Is pregnant you pregnant?" Concern filled his voice. "Is pregnant you pregnant, don't it?"

Shirley almost rolled her eyes; he was so stupid he could not even see she was trying to pick a fight.

"That's all you men think about: everything have to do with sex, sex, sex. You know you not even tell me you leaving. People plan. You don't think I plan too? Now you leaving like say I don' matter. It's just sex. Like some stop at Burger King... just to eat and leave."

"Is pregnant you pregnant? You better check," he said this a bit more seriously, standing as he did, to hover over her as she tried to back away.

"I'm not pregnant. I'm just angry."

"Come here, man," he said and pulled her roughly to him. "Send home you ugly friend and give me two minutes and you stop vex right away."

"I said to let me go!" She screamed loud enough to fill the apartment.

"What happened to you?" He held her wrist tightly, pulled her to him and shook her as if to wake her from a daze.

But Shirley continued to make the quarrel come to life, to anger him, anger herself, so she could take the blow when it came. "You're hurting my wrist!" Everything she said was now at the top of her voice.

He released her and raised his hand in puzzlement.

"Yes man, lick me! Go ahead, hit me. Is all you men good for, hit me no?!" She slammed her fist into his chest. "Hit me, man!" But he stood there, his eyes bulging. "Hit me no!" she screamed again.

His eyes seemed to waver and his hand fell down lightly onto her shoulders, pulling her gently to him.

"Hit me no," she was begging now. "Hit me." She began to sob as he pulled her closer, pressed her face into his shoulders and held her tightly against him.

"Maybe is tired you tired," he whispered softly as he would to a baby.

"Oh my God," she sighed finally and fell from him onto the bed.

She felt his finger gently against her head as he pulled away the hair that had scattered onto the bed. "You all right?" he asked.

"Yes," she said.

"You sure? Let me get you something to drink."

"No, I'm OK, I really am," she insisted. But he was already leaving the room.

Even as he left her, she realized that she could not go through with Queeny's plan. How do you force a man to hit you, who loved you so? For his love was real, she knew that now. If she had not felt it before, she felt it when he pulled her to him and pressed her against his breast. That moment, that pull, that tenderness – as if his hands had disappeared and she was being hugged by feelings alone – she felt a tenderness she had never felt and she knew that no one in her life had ever loved her like this man, this big black ugly drug dealer she had married to. He really loved her. What was more, she knew in that moment also, that she had fallen in love with him.

She felt his weight upon the bed and turned to meet the glass of juice he offered. "I'm all right." She looked up at him; her eyes were misted over and her voice was soft against the space between them.

His eyes were nervous as he searched her face. "Boy, mi ketch mi 'fraid."

"I'm sorry. No, I'm fine."

"Drink you juice." He handed her the glass.

She sipped the juice. "Queeny out there? You send her home?"

"Me!" He laughed. "No, she out there on the patio."

"OK, let me call her." She started to rise from the bed.

"No man, no, is all right." He pressed her back into the crumpled blankets. "Just relax, man. Just relax."

His eyes were so warm she felt the heat against her face. She had to pull away from his stare or she was sure she would just explode into tears. "But suppose I want to?"

"Yeah, but you a mi wife, you know. You not going anywhere."

Shirley's own answer struggled against her tongue, caused her eyes to blink much too quickly. But the phone rang before her voice betrayed her guilt.

"Chef out a the gate," he said after a while. "Is a lucky thing."

"A lucky thing what? He would have to wait."

He laughed. "You not easy." And then he lifted her head and looked in her eyes. "Me have to leave. You all right? You sure you all right?"

"Yes," she said, "and I am not pregnant."

He rose to go. "Make Queeny stay with you no? Make she stay a couple days."

"Who, my feisty friend?"

He laughed and reached for his bag.

After he left, she was not sure how to face Queeny. So she stayed in her bed looking up at the ceiling and tried to gather her thoughts. She knew that sooner or later, Queeny would come to her.

It was much sooner than later, and even when Queeny sat beside her, she still had not come up with a way to tell her that the plan had failed.

"Then how you make him leave?" Queeny said as she sat down. The urgency in her voice brought Shirley's eyes immediately to bear on her. Queeny's face was anxious and her bag was in her hand.

"How you mean? And where you going?" Shirley asked.

"I leaving now. I have to go."

"So soon?"

"Yes. Him coming back?"

"No, he's gone out of town." Shirley was trying to read the urgency in Queeny's eyes.

Queeny sighed and dropped her handbag onto the bed as if it weighed a ton. "Jesus Christ, God know what him doing."

"What you mean?"

"Me jus' come fi tell you that me caan' stay and go through with this business. Me 'fraid. What we going tell the police when them come?"

"Me too," Shirley said, and then it hit her. "How you mean, when the police come?"

"How you mean? Then me no call them? As onoo start quarrel so, me call them."

"Quarrel! We never quarreled."

"Then me no hear you bawl out say him lick you."

"Quarrel! We never quarrel. When you call them?"

"Long time now." Queeny began to gather her bag again. "Them suppose to soon come by now. Me tell them say him beating' you bad bad."

"What?"

"But we can jus' tell them that is wrong number or something. Is me cellular mi call from that caan' trace."

Shirley jumped from the bed to find her slippers but they were nowhere in sight. How long? She imagined Queeny with her hasty self, dialing the moment she had raised her voice. And she knew that this was America, and when a woman called the police, they came. And when a woman was being beaten they would come even faster with sirens wailing and all. Sirens wailing!

Woman, dog and pickney.

And Moet was down there with a car full of drugs.

Jesus Christ!

"Jesus Christ! What have you done?!" She pushed Queeny and, without bothering to search for her shoes, she ran. Fear pounding in her chest, robe flying open, she ran like a madwoman for the door.

The door came open in her urgent hand. There was still a faint smell of his cologne, as if he was just in the corridor. She knew he could not be far, he had only left a few minutes ago. Maybe he was gone, maybe Chef had picked him up at the front of their building. They were gone by now, out of harm's way.

But her stomach was turning too hard for that. Her insides burned with the pain that premonition gave. She had to get to him, she had to warn him.

The elevator was two floors up. She ran for the stairs. Jesus Christ. Moet!

She took them two at a time; the last three she skidded down and landed half sitting, clinging to the rail.

"Moet - my husband. Where is he?"

The doorman was startled. He stared into her wide open robe as if he had been waxed there, with his mouth open and his eyes bulging.

"My husband!" she screamed, without even trying to close the robe. "Where is he? He left?"

"Who?"

"My husband – you saw my husband. He left in a car?"

"He walked."

"Where?"

"He walked. Only a minute, stepped out. You should catch -"

"Open the door."

"Your key?"

"Open the door. Open the damn door!" She ran. Slammed into the large glass door even as the buzzer sounded. "Moet!"

She looked left, then right. Which gate? Back gate or front gate? Left or right, which way? The road curved out and away from her on both sides, like the arms of a large horseshoe. She was in the middle. A gate was over a hundred yards around a curve in either direction. A long road. A damn long road.

And then she heard the sirens wailing in the distance, off to her right. Her choice was made. She began to run down the centre of the road that parted the polished lawns and glistening ponds of the complex. Dashing down the road, hair flying wildly, arms flaying about, robe open – oblivious of everything except the sound of that sirens and the hope in her, that when she turned the corner he would not be there, hearing it and thinking that they were after him.

He must not be there!

But when she turned the corner, she knew that fate would place him there. Way out near the gate, fifty yards from her. She had prayed too hard, too long for God to set her free. She saw him hunch down as he slid into the car, saw his head jerk around toward where the police cars were racing into view. Miami Police! When women called, they came. Women dog or pickney.

She knew she would not make it but she ran anyhow. She knew they could not hear her but she screamed anyway, not caring if she never spoke another word as long as she could warn them. "Moet. Moet, stop! They are not after you." But she knew it was too late. She heard engines roar and sirens wail, and now a chase was on.

She saw the old car jerk around. Saw it thrust itself forward against the red and white crossing bar, saw the bar splinter as the suped-up missile burst through into the complex and headed straight toward her.

Shirley stopped there in the middle of the road and closed her eyes so death would come to her.

But the chase went around her, with deafening sounds and swirling winds. And she did not have to open her eyes to know that death was somewhere down there – beyond the belly of the horseshoe. Death. In those sounds of wailing sirens, screeching tires, gunning engines, and staccato explosions of gunshots. And then a final sound – a large and agonizing crash.

Then silence sucked the sounds away, dragged her down into a crumpled heap, her robe falling somewhere around her, and Sunday pressed hot like pain against her skin.

Chapter Thirty-Eight

He was so dark, the room seemed dim around him. There was no life in his face. Had it not been for his lips' shining rim that prescribed his mouth, his face would have been one smooth, black, dead surface.

"Moet."

She had not expected to see him again. She thought the police would have buried him in some dark hole and left him there. That he would have become another statistic.

But now he was alive and sitting across from her.

And she could find nothing to do or say but to call his name.

Moet.

It was Wednesday now. Three days after Sunday.

She was not sure how she had gotten back to the apartment that fateful evening. She remembered though, that Queeny was not there when she had returned. And she remembered barricading herself inside to shut the world out, stacking every heavy thing she could move by herself, against the door.

She had been afraid the police would come to jail her and send her home with only the clothing on her back. She could not remember ever being so scared, so stressed out, so afraid to move.

Something had told her to pack her things and return to Jamaica immediately. But her fear said the police would be watching her house and would trail her when she left - trail her and lock her up in disgrace. So she had barricaded herself in the apartment, deciding that they would have to dig her out if they wanted her.

Tuesday she heard the phone ring. It rang incessantly but she refused to touch it. Then it stopped. She contemplated taking it from the hook but she feared that those on the line would realize she was there. But as soon as she dozed off, it began to ring again.

Then it spoke.

First a beep. Then a voice.

"Mrs. Stewart? This is Morgan Finlay. I represent your husband. Please call me. My number is... ... It is important that I speak to you." There was a pause and then the voice spoke again: "Mrs. Stewart? Things are fine. There is no need to be scared. Call me. It is very important."

She called him later that evening, when she had mustered the strength to go and identify the body.

"Your husband wants you to visit him," he said. "He is in the county jail at. . ."

But she did not hear the rest of the conversation. The phone fell from her hands.

Moet was alive.

That was all that mattered. He was alive. The news filled her with joy because she realized she loved him and was dying to see him again. But soon dread and fear overtook her, for Moet alive meant an angry Moet, who would wreak revenge on whoever betrayed him.

Now she was there at the county jail. They had given her fifteen minutes. At least five had already gone and Moet was sitting across from her, his face blank, a cast on his left had, and blood on his shirt.

"Moet!" She began to phrase her confession in her head.

He tilted his face to her. His eyes were steady with a strange calm in them. He seemed unable to blink and the dark brown balls seemed to be looking into her very soul.

"You all right?" he asked. His voice was as steady as his eyes were calm.

"Moet," she said, again thinking that he knew everything.

"Who a go cook the coke now that the chef gone?" he said suddenly.

"What?"

"That Chef use to say." He shook his head. "Now them kill him."

"Chef dead!" Her heart beat harsh with dread in her chest. The glass was thick between them. Now he would surely kill her.

"You all right?" Sometimes it seemed that that was the only phrase he knew. The only thing that mattered. His favorite phrase – his one concern all in one salutation: You all right?

"You ask me that already."

"Yeah, but you never answer."

"Yes, I'm all right."

"You sure you nah pressure youself. Nobody caan' come trouble you, so don't fret. Everything safe. You safe. You pressure youself too much. I tell you all the while. You understand? You understand when mi say everything safe?"

"I thought you were dead."

"Everything all right, man, everything all right."

His eyes moved from her face and roved in an eerie way. His face did not move but his eyeballs seemed to cover every inch of the room around her. From floor to ceiling from wall to walk. It felt weird sitting before him while his eyeballs roved like that.

"Moet - you all right?"

His eyes fell to hers again. And this time they were alive and urgent.

"All right, listen this," he said.

"What?"

"Listen this. You fifteen minutes soon done. I want you do something for me."

"Anything, Moet," she said, grasping at the chance for salvation. "Anything."

"You see the lawyer man. A want you give him something for me."

"What?"

"Listen!"

"Yes."

"You remember one long time we a come from the Keys and mi show you where mi use to live under the I-95. You remember?"

"Yes."

"Listen. Don't say yes so fast. Listen quick and understand."

"Yes," she said.

"All right. Where the I-95 done - the underpass - just climb up there. Right up under the road, you have a the incline; where the incline stop and the ground get flat, me have a black bag hide up there. Get it and give it to the lawyer."

"Black bag under the underpass?"

"Don't talk, the guard coming fi you."

"But where?"

"Where the 95 done. You will know where, just dig it up - it shallow, all right? A black bag, just give it to the lawyer man. Everything all right. Hush now. See the bwoy behind you."

"Next week again before visiting time. Next week before I see you."

"You going see me long before that," he said. "Just do what I tell you."

Then he was rising as the armed guard came to lead him away toward the large door and whatever hell lay beyond.

Chapter Thirty-Nine

Shirley took one look at the crisscross of roads at the end of the I-95 and realized immediately that she was in a lot of trouble. She had thought to stop there on her way from the jail, pick up the bag and deliver it to the lawyer. But she had miscalculated. The road was so busy that it was impossible for her to chance it by day. For she would have to park in the grass underneath the road itself and she knew that once she did, she would attract attention.

She would have to do it at night.

And she could not come alone. The place would be much too dangerous at night.

On her way home, she stopped by Queeny's apartment but Queeny was not there – or if she was, she certainly was not answering the door. Shirley parked and waited for nearly an hour, but she did not come. As soon as she got home Shirley began calling her but to no avail. The phone kept on ringing. Not even an answering machine came on.

By eight o'clock, Shirley was so nervous, she could hardly stand in one place.

She was dressed in black. Her hair was in a bun and her crepes were the Nike ones that Moet had bought some Christmases ago when she had said she wanted to go to the gym. She had dressed since seven and had spent an hour pacing up and down the apartment, dialing Queeny's number every five minutes. She wished she had spent more time socializing in Miami, going out, meeting people. But her whole world had been the apartment and Moet, and in any event she dared not socialize because her husband was a drug dealer. Now he was in jail and she was alone. And the realities of her life were facing her in a way she had never expected. The joyride was over; it was now time for her to make her contribution. And she was alone. She had to do it alone.

Alone!

She tried to drink some orange juice, then some champagne, but immediately her stomach turned and she raced to the bathroom to vomit into the bowl.

Jesus Christ.

She looked at the clock. It was five past eight. She tried Queeny's number once more. No answer. But Shirley knew that Queeny or no Queeny, she had to go. Moet needed her now and she had to get that bag and take it to the lawyer. She had put him in jail and it was up to her to get him out.

Her stomach turned and she raced to the bathroom once more.

Jesus Christ!

What to do? Who to turn to? No friends, no enemies. She would have given a million dollars to have anyone there right now. Anyone –even if they hated her, loved her, lusted after her. Anyone .

Orville.

Orville! Orville was in Miami. He called her the other day.

"Oh God," she exclaimed, and raced into the living room to find his number. But where had she written it down? Or had she written it down?

She stopped, began to think. Normally she could remember any number just like that. Just by linking the name, the conversation, the time, the number would just pop out. She had a memory for number - a photographic memory.

Think, Shirley, think.

Fort Lauderdale. She remembered he was in Fort Lauderdale.

She thought again, thought hard. What was the conversation? What did he say? What did she say?

She had been in the bath and Queeny was on the other line.

So you will call me? he had said.

OK, she had asked what the number was, then he had said it. She closed her eyes for the number to flow in on the tail of the conversation. Then punched the keys hard. "Wrong number" said a Hispanic voice.

She began to dial once more.

"Hello." The voice on the line was unfamiliar, but Jamaican.

"May I speak to Orville?"

"Just a minute."

"Hello." The voice sounded half awake.

"Orville!"

"Who this?"

"Shirley."

"Hey, Shirley, wait! What happen?"

Shirley sighed. Her hands trembled as she spoke. "I need to see you. What are you doing tonight?"

"Nothing," he said.

Shirley almost cried with relief. Ten minutes later she was heading north on the turnpike toward Fort Lauderdale.

Chapter Forty

The night was silver against the undersides of the highway. Shirley rode the banking and settled the car into the soft grass. Around her, vehicles flashed by on all sides. She looked up at the large column that supported a section of the road, at its sloping sides that ended at her feet. She followed the incline with her eyes to where the highway sat on its tip and focused on the spot of darkness underneath. She nodded to Orville beside her.

"There," she pointed. "Up there so."

"Up there so? What exactly up there, Shirley?"

"You helping me or not?" Shirley's voice was sharp.

"I will help you. That is why I'm here. But you don't think that at least I should know what I'm getting myself into?"

"You not getting youself into nothing." Shirley tried to brush his concern aside. She had no intention of giving a full explanation to Orville.

"Sure," he said sarcastically, "this come like some spy movie undercover business. Full black in the middle of the night – I mean, what is this? I need to know something."

"All right," Shirley said, wanting to get over with it. "Someone asked me to pick up something for them."

"Someone like who?"

"Someone who can't make it themself. Is only me them can trust. And is only you I can trust. Can I trust you?"

"How you mean? What kind a stupid question that, if you can trust me? But you must expect that I can't just enter a thing like this blind. Is America this, you know."

"Lord, America – so what?" Shirley was more frightened than angry. She just wanted to go up there, get the bag and leave this place as soon as possible. She began to climb the sloping side of the column. She heard the rustle of his feet in the grass behind her but did not look around. The surface was carved into large smooth squares so she had to bend and use her hand for support as she crawled. Her nails broke against the surface, her feet slipped and brought her to her knees several times, her breath became shallow and her chest heaved as she began to breathe the musty, foul air, but she did not stop until her hand touched the flat top of the concrete foundation where the large beam supported the underside of the highway. She pulled herself onto the flat and caught her breath and composure.

A minute later, Orville pulled himself up beside her. He was hardly breathless. "This come like somebody could live here," he said. "Whole heap a space. It stink though."

"Beggars live here sometimes," she said.

"Lived or live? This could be somebody's living room and kitchen." He flicked Shirley's flashlight on to expose the littered space. "So what now?"

"Lend me the flashlight." She took it from him and played the light around the area. There was an old car rim to the side, an old blanket rotten and discarded utensils of every kind strewn around, empty bottles, and a square of thick cardboard . . . but no bag.

She flashed the light around and down the slopes and along the joints of the large tiles that made the surface. She moved the light around for almost two minutes then dropped her shoulders and sighed. "Oh God."

"What?" Orville asked.

Shirley leaned against the side of the large beam and dropped the flashlight between her legs. "Nothing no up here."

"Nothing like what? What you looking for?"

"A bag," she said, "all right? I was to get a bag. He said it was up here."

"Who?"

"It matters? There is no bag."

"But I could tell you that from in the car. But you don't want tell me anything."

"What could you tell me?" She was at the end of her rope.

"Who could be so foolish to put bag up here?"

"He said it is here. If he did, it should be here."

"Up here! Where beggars and thief come when they ready? That don't sound right. So when he left it here? Yesterday or so?"

"I don't know."

"All right, so you don't want to tell me."

"I have told you all you need to know to help me," Shirley said angrily. "So just get off my fucking back, all right?" And suddenly the tears began to run down her face.

"All right." He spoke softly, trying to calm her. "Lend me the flashlight. I'm not really trying to know you business, just trying to get into the person's headspace. If somebody hiding a bag it different than if they leave it for you to pick it up. So if I was hiding a bag up here," he began to move around slowly, "I would bury it, but I don't know. . ." He began to play the light around along the concrete slopes that led up to the road proper. "Everything here is concrete."

"Maybe under the tiles," she said. "Under the square them."

"But how you know which one? He told you?"

"No, he said I would know."

"You would know?"

"Yes, that I would know or something like that." Her hands began to shake.

"You are sure this is where him say? You sure is this column?"

"Yes," Shirley said.

He was looking across her shoulders where the crisscross of roads sat on various slopes like the one they were on. "There are six or seven columns like this."

"He said the I-95."

"The 95," Orville mused. "Yes, but you don't see?" He pointed over their heads. "The road broad. It goes way over there so – you don't see there are three sets of columns; this, that massive middle one there – that make 'bout two of this – and that other one over to the right. How you know that this is the one?"

"I just know." Shirley began to lose her cool.

"You can't just know." He sat back against the concrete. "How you decide on this one?"

"This is where it end," she said. "He said where I-95 ends."

"End?" He rubbed his chin. "End or begin?"

"What difference?" she asked.

Orville kissed his teeth. "Ah boy. End different from begin. End mean done, begin mean start. I-95 goes straight to Canada. So the traffic that goes north begins it, and the side that go south ends it. You don't understand? So where? End or begin? What did he say?"

The light came on in Shirley's head and she pushed her mind back again to the jail though she knew what the answer would be. The underpass, remember where the 95 done.

"Where it ends," she nodded firmly. "He said where it done."

"Well then." Orville rose smugly and dusted the seat of his pants. "We on the wrong side."

Shirley slid down the column so fast she felt heat in her crepes and her palms were sore from friction. She began to race across the grass to cross the first section of road. Suddenly she felt him grab her and pull her to a halt. She began to wrestle her hand away.

"Slow down, take it easy. You want people think mi a run you down? You want them think mi a try kill you? Just relax, man. Just walk and take it easy."

He made sense. "Sorry." She began to walk as calmly as she could beside him while her heart thumped in her chest and her eyes were fixed on the column at the far side of the thoroughfare.

"Just relax," he said softly, almost nervously. "Is America this, you know."

The top of the second column was similar to the other with the same collection of garbage and the same foul smell. After a quick search, Shirley sat down exasperated and folded her arms to cry. She did not feel up to moving, did not care if the police came right now and jailed her. She was tired and frustrated and she wished the world would end right there and then as she sat.

Then Orville, who was sitting beside her, whistled in admiration. "A Susumber tree, to rahtid. What is a Susumber tree doing up here?"

Shirley came alert and followed the beam of the flashlight as he played it along the slopes they had climbed. There were shrubs along the edge of this incline, one particular tree spread as wide as a dwarfed lignum vitae – its leaves thick and dense, spreading like a tent, extending around the curvature of the column. It was on this tree that Orville kept his light.

"That is a Susumber tree?"

"Yeah, it look so, it short and spread out, but it look like a Susumber tree," he said. "A dwarf Susumber tree."

"You sure 'bout that?"

"How you mean?" he smiled. "And it makes sense too, if there is one tree in the world nobody would touch or bother is a Susumber tree. Who would pay it any mind? Think 'bout it. Only Jamaicans eat Susumber; fruit them small and bitter, smell like poison, and it look like bush. Haitians say is the devil's food and only their worse obeah man would even touch it. So if you have something to hide and want a tree to mark the spot, as a Jamaican; what better tree to use. A dwarf Susumber tree don't grow tall, leaves thick like carpet, stems filled with prickle, grows anywhere. And in the right soil, it uproot easier than carrot." His hand pulled at the edge of the underside of an extending limb. "Easier than carrot: a dwarf Susumber tree." The large tree came loose in his hand. Along with it came the edge of a large concrete tile, beneath which, in the dark earth, the black edge of a handle gleamed dully in the beam of the flashlight.

"See you bag there." He smiled at Shirley.

But Shirley needed no encouragement; she was already squeezing past him to drag on the handle of the duffel bag. It came easier than she expected, for the earth was soft around it and the concrete had been expertly broken and replaced so that everything fell away as the bag emerged.

Shirley tumbled back onto the slope as the bag came free and could not help but exclaim aloud. "Is only this?"

Orville dropped the tree to the side and looked at the bag. "That me wondering too."

They rummaged through the hole and searched the slope but the one bag was all that was there. It was just a small tubular nylon gym bag, with a large padlock at the end of the zip. It was fairly heavy but not much more than would have been the weight of an average carry-to-the-gym.

Shirley shrugged and began to descend the slope."Come."

"The bag small though," Orville mused. "A man so smart, have so much, must have more than that."

"What you say?" She was busy retrieving her key.

"We should check that column, you no know." He pointed the flashlight up the slopes of the massive central column."You see them trees there, I bet you any money that some of those are Susumber trees. Man like that must have more hiding places."

"Man like what?" Shirley was plunging the key into the door.

"How you mean?" Orville caught up with her. "You go on like is not your husband. No him them lock up the other day in the big shoot-out."

"What?"

"Cho, Shirley, man, is me this, you know."

"You drive," Shirley said calmly.

He jumped at the opportunity and eased the convertible onto the road expertly.

"So you thought I did not know all along. I just wanted you to admit it."

Shirley clasped the bag to her lap and looked at him. "Drive the fucking car, OK? Drive the car. This is America and everybody is here. This is America, the great equalizer, right? Everybody is the same. I don't ask whether you're on vacation – or whether you run away from Jamaica 'cause police after you for some bank fraud, because them catch you ripping off some bank or another, OK? You come and I accept you. You don't know what I do, or what my husband do and you don't know what is in this bag. So just drive, just chill and drive the fucking car, OK?

You want help, you help, but don't fucking judge me! You know nothing about me, all right?"

"Yes ma'am," he said, and pointed the car north along the moonlit surface of the I-95.

Chapter Forty-One

Shirley awoke early, feeling both nervous and excited. On her return she had searched every drawer in the apartment and tested every key she could find but none fitted the lock. She tried to feel its contents through the side but its fabric was of thick canvas and nothing felt familiar to her. So she worried and fretted through the night with dreams of the police banging down the door, seizing the bag and cutting it open to find enough drugs to put her away for a lifetime.

Shirley called the lawyer as the clock struck eight, but the message on his machine said his office opened at nine, so she had to wait another fidgeting hour. The time passed slowly. When she finally got him, he told her that his office was all the way in West Palm Beach.

She left immediately, trying hard not to drive too fast and draw attention to herself. In West Palm Beach she had to call him again for directions. She finally got into his office around eleven o'clock.

Morgan Finlay was a large white man with crisp, precise tones and an emotionless face. He locked the door behind Shirley and retrieved a key from his drawer that fitted the lock on the bag perfectly.

Finley took a clear plastic bag and emptied the contents out onto his desk. There were seven stacks of money and a smaller plastic bag with legal-looking documents. He went through the documents carefully, then selected one, nodding to himself. He then passed two stacks of bills toward Shirley along with two of the three documents from the bag.

"These are yours," he said. "the deed to your apartment and the car. This is all you need."

"What?" she said.

"This is for the Georgia property," he waved it at her. "This will do for the bail." He pressed his hand against the desk and made to rise. "Well, I guess that will be all. We will try to bring your husband to you today."

"What?" she repeated still dazed. "M-my money this?" She found herself stammering and out of sorts.

The lawyer sensed her discomfort and settled back into the chair – his eyes softening, his voice smooth. "Mrs. Stewart, Shirley. You have nothing to worry about. I will take care of everything. Just go home and your husband will join you soon."

"I understand, but everything is so sudden, so fast. I was told to bring the bag to you. I did not know what was in it."

"Oh," he smiled. "Oh. Well, those are the deeds to the apartment and the car." He spoke almost condescendingly. "See, they are in your name. And that's twenty thousand dollars. This fifty and the title for the property in Georgia is for bail."

"I... well, I gather that," she said. "But it is the speed of things." She raised the level of her conversation. "The dispatch with which you operate. It's a bit off-putting."

He smiled at that and she could see that he was hardly impressed. "It has been said of me before. I'm sorry."

"So when will I see him, Moet... my husband?"

"This evening or tonight maybe. That depends on how fast we get things to court, you understand. But tomorrow morning definitely. I would bank on the morning."

Shirley banked on the morning.

She thanked him and left.

Once in the car she locked it and went through the papers right there in the parking lot. The title for the car was registered in her maiden name – Shirley Temple Brown, it said. The deed for the apartment was more official-looking but it had the same name: deed made out to Shirley Temple Brown. There were no co-owners. Moet's name did not appear on either of the documents. They were hers and hers alone . . . all hers.

Try as she might, Shirley could not remember the trip back to Miami that day.

But when she got home, she began to clean it. Every inch of the house felt her touch. Every appliance and glass surface was washed and sparkling with Windex. She lifted the different components from the stereo system and cleaned under them, she pushed aside the TV and cleaned there too. She cleaned the fridge. She cleaned from bathroom to bedroom to living room to store rooms to guest room; and when she had finished each one, she backed out and closed the door as if she had no intention of entering again. She did not want the smell to escape.

It was like Sunday morning in Jamaica. Music on the stereo, the scent of disinfectant in the air, the vacuum cleaner buzzing and the windows flung open. She put Moet's favorite bed set on the bed, placed his choice CDs in the stereo; his favorite smell of lemon air freshener was in the air.

The kitchen she saved for last, for it was his room. She made sure that all the food he loved was in the cupboards – tenderloin steaks in the freezer and bottles of Moet set to chill.

Her man was coming home tomorrow.

Later, Shirley sprawled on the soft chair on the patio and let the broom slide to the floor. She squinted against the brown glare of the departing sun and watched as a large fly navigated the rim of dirt on the table where a wet glass had stayed too long.

Something was bothering her and she could not put her finger on it.

She removed a yellow working glove from her hand and sailed it lazily at the fly. The glove flew too high and landed on the floor at the other side of the table. She aimed the other glove and the fly zoomed high and pitched right on the tip of her nose; she squinted as it lifted off and circled the patio as if searching for a more interesting berth. After a while, it returned to the table and the ring of dirt. As it landed, Shirley hurled the glove but the fly jumped to the side and allowed it to pass then settled once more.

But something was bothering her and she could not put a finger on it. It had begun earlier today with a slow turn in her stomach and then it had spread. As night came, it began to swell into a burning ball in her stomach.

It was nearly seven o'clock, she had been cleaning for close to six hours and all that was left was the spot on the table where the fly enjoyed itself. She was exhausted, but she expected to sleep in an hour or so after she had soaked in Victoria's Secrets, and could take all the rest she needed, waiting for Moet.

She sprawled and watched the fly some more and wondered why her stomach burned with a sense of trouble. Something was wrong, she just knew it.

Moet!

She placed her mind on him, gave space to her intuition - but nothing happened. It was not Moet. It was not the prison thing. Maybe he was out and knew all she had done and was coming home to kill her. She left her senses there for a few minutes and went over the possibilities. But nothing clicked.

Queeny!

Was it Queeny? Where was she? What was she doing? She lifted the phone and called her number. It rang without an answer.

The lawyer!

She thought of him – the condescension in his eyes. Maybe he had double-crossed them – gone off with the money. But she recalled his opulent office in West Palm Beach and shifted her mind's focus. The problem was not there.

Ignoring the fly, she went into the bedroom, picked up the titles and held them in her hands. Nothing could touch her now. She was free. She could just leave if she wanted to. He had made her free.

He must love her more than anyone she ever remembered. He had given her everything she ever dreamed of – as if he knew, as if he trusted that she would not leave, even though she had her freedom.

And she discovered how she must have loved him too, though she pretended not to. He was not her ideal – he could not stand up to scrutiny, could not say what he did for a living in public – he was just Moet and he loved her.

You all right? he had said.

And now she wanted him to see that she would not let him down.

She could not wait to see him walk through the door – big and black and large in so many ways. She would confess to him. She would confess her actions, confess her love. A man who loved her so, would forgive her.

And look how smart he had been, keeping everything from her, planning for her so that even when he went to jail, she would have a roof over her head, a car to drive and money to live.

She fingered the two wads of bills. "Twenty thousand dollars." The words rolled off her tongue haltingly.

What did Orville say? Man like that, must have more hiding places.

She bolted upright. The pain in her belly swelled and burst like a bubble.

Jesus Christ. He was right - Orville was right, there must be more. Moet had no bank account. He had sold drugs for years, so there must be more. In the middle column. She was convinced of it. Moet had sent her to find only what was necessary. There was more money.

Orville!. She remembered the look on his face, his silence after the insult. He had been quiet because he knew he was going back. When they parted, he disappeared quickly without even making a pass at her. Because he was going back . . . going back to search the middle columns.

The pain in her stomach reacted like a warning signal on high. Maybe he had already gone. No, she thought. He did not have a car. The friend he was staying with, she would bet, was married with children, so he would not have left Fort Lauderdale at midnight last night. And Orville would not have gone in the day. He would be going tonight.

Yes, to Jesus.

She jumped from where she sat, all tiredness gone from her. She had to go there now.

Before Orville got there.

Jesus Christ, it was now that Moet would kill her. It was now that she would surely die. She had led a man to his fortune and he had stolen every cent.

She began to tremble uncontrollably. She needed help, she could not go alone. She dialed Queeny again.

This time she answered.

"Queeny!"

"Jesus, Shirley. What you calling me for? I don' know nothing."

"Queeny, you have to help me. Orville going to thief Moet money."

"Who name Orville, Shirley? What you talking 'bout?"

"A guy I met in Jamaica. He's going to steal the money."

"Listen, Shirley, is leave me leaving. I don' business with your mix-up. I not going near you man make him go kill me like how him kill Mikey."

"Queeny!"

But the phone went dead in her ear.

Moet had a bottle of tablets in the bathroom that he said he kept for Chef because he got nervous sometimes. Shirley searched quickly through the cabinet till she found the bottle in the back. There were no directions as to the dosage on the bottle. Just one word written in ink across the white label: Prozac. Shirley took one of the large tablets from the bottle and without hesitation swallowed it with a handful of water. She thought again and took another.

By the time she reached the bedroom to fetch a flashlight, her hands had stopped trembling and her head cleared as if she had slept for ten hours.

She found the flashlight and raced for the door. Then she halted, returned to the kitchen and selected the largest knife in the house. And this time as she left the kitchen she did not run but walked quickly and purposefully toward the door.

She would have to die tonight. He had to kill her first. If he touched that money, wherever in Miami he might choose to go with it, she would find him and he would have to kill her tonight.

Chapter Forty-Two

Shirley mounted the kerb onto the grassy divide and backed the car against the massive, sloping central columns of the I-95. The she leaned back into her seat for a while and took a deep breath. The outside of her head felt as if it was not there. She was so calm she had no sense of anything else other than the moment.

She did not know what the next minute would bring. Orville could come any time; the police could find her – question her, arrest her. Or Moet could come, think she was stealing his money, and kill her on the spot.

Any minute now could be her last.

And that was what it came to – all those restless suffering years in America, all those dreams and ambitions... this was what it all came down to.

Moments. Portions of time. And now a dime of time.

She left the top up on the convertible, stepped away from the car, put the knife into the back pocket of her shorts and with the flashlight in her hand began to climb the hard concrete slope.

Three quarters, up she knew she had hit pay dirt.

Directly in her path were the extended branches of a Susumber tree identical to the one they had discovered on the other slopes the night before. It was at the edge of a field of Susumber that covered most of the right corner of the slope's top. Shirley played the light in front of her and looked more clearly. It was hard to see so she had to lie flat on her stomach and look beneath the extended leaves. There were only four trees, but they were so well developed, their thick carpet-like leaves covered most of the area in front of her.

She heard a screech of rubber and looked down to see a car veer and twist as it came to a halt at a changing stoplight. Her heart thumped.

There was no time.

Move!

Shirley crawled on her belly to the root of the first tree and pulled hard against its stubby trunk. It came away into her hands and fell on her as if its top had suddenly gotten too heavy. The leaves were soft and pungent against her face; their thorns scratched her skin. She shoved and kicked in panic, and rolled the tree away noiselessly to halfway down the slope.

It was a large tree. Orville was right.

Orville!

She looked behind her down the slope. Thank God, her car was there, alone.

Shirley plunged her hand into the soft soil vacated by the tree and touched a bag immediately. She found the handle and pulled. The large duffel bag was almost as long as the span of her arms, as round as her hip, and bulging.

With a padlock at the mouth.

She was sure the lawyer did not have the key to this one.

She focused on the other trees ahead.

She moved, cold and calm on a dime of time.

When Shirley pulled up the second tree, it too fell on her but this time, earth flew all over her, blinding her for a minute. Jesus! She hated those trees. Then a thought struck her. Pushing the tree aside, she crawled underneath the third tree till she got above it and kicked it down the slope. It fell away from her but sprayed dirt in her face. The last one was better: it rolled away without any fuss.

Now she was out of trees.

All she had were the holes and the bags that were in them. Digging frantically with her bare hands like a bone-hunting dog, she tugged the bags free. In another minute she was sitting in the middle of four large black bags.

It was then she discovered that she had lost a shoe. The other one was practically off too, so she kicked her foot to dislodge it. Her foot caught a bag and before she could catch the handle, it rolled down the hill to thud against the rear of the convertible.

It was her cue. She nudged the other bags quickly down the slope.

Then she slid clumsily after them, her legs and thighs burning as they dragged against the concrete surface in her desperate descent.

Then she was there at the foot of the hill, her hand resting against the side of the car.

She reached inside and pulled the lever to open the trunk.

Her head began to spin, she felt exhausted and her legs crumpled beneath her.

Jesus Christ! She was breaking down.

Summoning all she had inside, she got up and threw the first bag into the trunk. It was much heavier than she had expected. She did the same with the second. The third would not fit. She tried to force it into the remaining space but it jutted halfway out. The trunk would not close.

Shirley realized she had no choice. The last two bags must go inside the car; one in the small back seat and the other forced upright in the front passenger seat beside her.

As she removed her head from the trunk, she saw Orville and another man trying to cross the highway to get to her. She almost felt relief with the surge of excitement that coursed through her.

Ignoring the badly fitted bag in the trunk, she lifted the one on the ground and heaved it into the convertible. It dropped right smack into the driver's seat.

Shirley raced around the car as brakes squealed on the highway. Through the corner of her eyes she saw that Orville had made his own break in the traffic. They were racing across. They were coming toward her at full speed.

She knew she would not make it. The bag was in her driver's seat, her keys were in her pocket and she was on the wrong side of the car. Not to mention the third bag sticking awkwardly from the open trunk.

Suddenly everything inside her quieted and she felt as calm as if she had taken a fresh dose of Prozac. As if all her anxiety had been centered around them getting there, and now with their arrival, all the fears in her had run their course. She stopped her running, took the knife from her pocket and held it in her hands even as she walked calmly to the rear of her car, removed the ill-fitting bag and slammed the trunk closed.

By the time Orville got to her she was fitting it neatly into the small back seat of the convertible.

"What happen, Shirley?" He was a bit out of breath. "You have to leave one of the bags, you know."

"Why?" she asked. "There is enough space in the car."

"Yeah, but I deserve some of the money."

"Deserve!" She settled the bag, walked to the front right-hand door and reached to pull the misplaced bag onto the passenger seat. "How you know is money in the bag?"

"No matter, I will take what I get."

"You put money in there? You put bag up there?" She turned to face him as she spoke, and leaned against the passenger door. They were a few paces away. To a passerby it would seem a casual conversation between friends.

"Don't let me have to take it, Shirley."

"You not taking anything, you know," Shirley said. "You have to kill me first."

His charm failed to come through, "What happen to you? Is how much bags? Four ... five?"

"See some Susumber there. Take that, go sell Susumber." She motioned to the slopes.

"How you craven so? Is two of us against you alone, you know."

"Yes, but you have to kill me first."

They were an arm's length away. The other man, short and stumpy, obviously had no idea that the issue would have gotten to this. Orville probably told him they were just coming to collect the bags. He seemed a little hesitant. He was a family man, Shirley picked that up immediately, an old friend who had offered Orville a place to stay. But one who would not mind stealing someone else's money if he could get away with it.

She brought the knife into the conversation casually. The man stepped back, but Orville stood his ground and smirked.

"What you going do with that?

"You have to kill me first," she said.

"All right." And in a flash he was onto her, clasping her wrist in grasps of steel. She felt her wrist turn past their limit, felt her back bend too far as her head crushed against the fabric of the convertible's seat.

"Leggo this," he said, panting hard, holding her down into the seat. "Let go this. How you so craven? Is just one bag mi want."

"You have to kill me first," she said even as the knife fell from her hands.

"Kill you! You don' see you can't move?" He motioned over his head."Pick up the bag, Johnno. Pick up one of the bags."

Johnno spoke hesitantly, "Boy, Orville..."

"Pick up the rass bag," Orville yelled harshly. "How long you want me hold her? You want come hold her? Pick up the one in the back seat."

She heard Johnno move, but she was pinned too tightly to do anything.

"Pick it up, put it in the van, and spin round and pick me up."

"You wife and you children going die for this, Johnno!" Shirley screamed.

"Stop the noise, man." Orville smirked and twisted her wrist some more. "Pick up the bag, Johnno."

That was when the tires screamed. And the lights hit them squarely. She did not see most of it because she was bent backward into the car. But she saw Orville turn his head, heard him scream, felt him release her as he tried to jump back. Saw him lifted and snapped away in the wake of the blur of a massive object. And then she heard a crash loud and heart-shattering – and saw, as she began to rise, a large car recoil from slamming into the base of the column of the I-95.

Orville was strewn on the grass near the wrecked car, and Johnno, without the bag, was running away and falling over himself on the grass. And Moet was stepping from the wreck, blacker than the night with a gun in his hand.

He moved as casually as if he was stepping from his house to collect the newspaper on a lazy Sunday morning. He turned toward the scampering Johnno and beckoned with the gun. "Hey man! Hoy, man!"

But Johnno kept on running

Then the night exploded around her as Moet raised the gun and fired twice. Shirley held her ears and screamed.

Johnno stopped and raised his hands.

In the air, he had only fired in the air.

"Hey man, come back, you caan' leave you friend!" Moet shouted.

Johnno returned slowly with his hands above his head, trembling. Even though Moet, by that time, had turned his back to him and was leaning casually against the wrecked car.

Shirley slid silently and gratefully to the ground. Not because Moet had come, but because she knew her dime of time had run completely out and all the struggles and pretensions of her life were finally over. She knew immediately that there was no way she could explain the circumstances to him, no way after all he knew and had gone through. Her time had come. And she was surprised at how relieved she was, how good it felt.

"You put anything there?" he asked casually.

She lifted her head. But he was speaking to Orville who was crawling away one side, obviously disabled.

It was his nonchalance that caused the fear; the way he leaned against the car, feet crossed in front of him; how he held the gun, not pointing at anything in particular, like a man would hold a hat he had just taken from his head because the wind was too high; the way he spoke casually as if he was asking the time of day.

"You put anything up there?"he repeated.

Orville did not answer, just dragged himself away, like a wounded dog. Then Johnno came into the picture and pulled him away hastily. As he dragged him, Moet smiled coldly. "No you friend, why you leaving him?"

"Don't kill me, don't kill me," was all Johnno could say as Moet turned his back on him and walked over to where Shirley was sitting on the ground.

Then it all came to her suddenly with every casual step he made: it all came to her, all that she had feared, had heard Queeny talk about ; all that Shirley had tried to suppress in her own mind. He was a dangerous and deadly human being, a man to be feared with her whole heart.

"Come," he said.

She lifted her face to him. He seemed like death itself - a smiling, casual death.

"Is only two bag you find?"

"Two more in the trunk."

"Come," he said again, giving her his hand.

"Moet, kill me right here so, kill me now."

"Come," he said again. "You pressure youself too much."

She did not know why he wanted her to go with him and not kill her right there. Maybe because she was his wife and her death could be linked to him. If he killed her here, the police would hear the gunshots, they would come and this time he would not be bailed. She looked up at him, saw him black and beautiful in the night, felt the last of her strength drain from her.

"You not coming?"

She closed her eyes and shook her head.

"All right," he said sadly. "All right, Shirley. Where the key?" She kept her eyes closed against him and twisted her hips. He reached and took the keys from her shorts. She felt him there, stooping beside her in the darkness. She took a deep breath and squeezed her eyes tightly.

"I will have to borrow the convertible," he said to her softly, softer than she had ever heard him speak. "That one mash up. Tomorrow pick up the car at Queeny. Something will be in it for you. Mi going home. Mi a go catch a ship. That's why them give you bail up here you know, so you can go home. So they don't have to pay to try you. So mi going home to Jamaica. You sure you don' wan' come?"

"What?" But she was sure he had not heard her, it was her mind reacting on itself.

She felt him rise.

"Is three million this, you know – three million and change." And then she felt him leave – heard the car door slam, the engine gun and growl, and his voice casual above and to the right.

"Lean forward, Shirley, watch you head."

The car was pulling away.

She looked around to see the receding tail-lights brighten as he paused to wait a break in the traffic. Queeny, car at Queeny, Queeny had told him everything - she must have. It must be Queeny who had sent him. When he did not find her at home he must have gone to Queeny, and she must have sent him here. He had come for her, to save her, not to kill her.

"Moet."

She rose quickly. The traffic was heavy, he would not make it yet.

"Moet!"

The wet grass stung her feet. She fell into its tangled green. She rose again and he was still there at the edge of the divide with the traffic standing still around him. It was as if the whole world was standing still... waiting on her. Waiting for her to join her man.

Moet!

She ran without looking, without thinking, without caring about anything but the convertible waiting on her with three million dollars and the man she loved... waiting on her for her final trip to Jamaica.

She had been such a fool.

The tail-lights of the car brightened then dulled as he slipped into the traffic.

"Moet!" A desperate scream now .

A large truck paused to give him way.

"Moet! Moet, wait. Don't leave me, Moet!"

The car stopped suddenly, and then it reversed and climbed back onto the grassy divide where Shirley ran to it.

Moet!

And then she was there and he was looking up at her as she fell against the side of the car, tears streaming down her face, her hair disheveled, her clothing dirty and her feet hurting from running without shoes.

"Moet. Is Queeny send you, don't it? Is me you come for, don't it?"

He looked up at her with a smug look on his face. "Me tell you, you pressure yourself too much all the while."

He reached across the large bag, to push the door open even as she ran around the car. "Fix the bag. Come in. Come quick."

The first siren sounded with her halfway into the, car trying to slide around the huge bag of money. She was halfway in and halfway out, and would have fallen out if he pulled away. And by the time she settled herself there was such a cacophony of police noises that she knew deep in her heart that the end had come.

Gunshots in the night; people running up and down with bags of money; a Lexus crashing into the base of the highway – only a fool would think they would not come…but so soon? Not now, on the verge of escape.

Moet turned the wheel quickly and pressed the gas; the car surged forward, but the gap in the traffic had closed and he had to swing hard to the right to avoid crashing headfirst into a minivan. He reversed hard toward the base of the highway, the wheels of the convertible skidding in the wet grass, sending dirt flying. He twisted and swerved the vehicle in an effort to access the other side of the highway.

Then a shape rose in front of them. Shirley screamed with fright. Moet twisted the wheel again and a policeman fell away from the glancing blow of the convertible as it decelerated to halt near the concrete base.

She saw him look right and left; looked frantically at her; reached for the gun and felt it in his hands.

"Moet!"

Her scream and the look on her face made him let the weapon go, allowing it to fall to the seat between his legs. He hammered the steering wheel hard with his fists, ran his hands over his head and leaned back into the seat with total surrender.

Suddenly the police were everywhere; harsh lights flashing blue and red; white lights trained on them; guns pointing at them and loudspeakers blaring, ordering them to leave the car with their hands in the air.

It all seemed so unreal to Shirley. Everything in one big blur – they being dragged from the car; Moet being shoved hard to the ground by big men in dark uniform with huge guns. And she too, being pressed hard into the ground; her face boring into the damp grass till she felt suffocated, then being hauled to her feet with the cold steel of handcuffs biting into her flesh.

The large policeman was speaking continuously to her, as he guided her forward. But she hardly heard him

"Moet!" She whispered his name with a voice trembling with dread.

But she was already passing away from him as the hand of the large policeman urged her on to another car a meter or so ahead. A policewoman pressed her palm into Shirley's chest to pause her as the door to the large car came open.

"Keep your head down," she said.

Shirley dropped her head till her chin rested tight against her chest and kept it there. And even as the door closed and shut the vision of Miami from her; even as the car slid from the grass and bumped down onto the US1, she did not move it. And through the sobs that rocked her Shirley doubted she would ever have occasion to lift her head with pride again.

PART VI

Deportee

Chapter Forty-Three

She came that summer into a Jamaican night wet and cold from July rain. It was twelve years almost to the day, that she had left her apartment in Kingston and sold her things to seek a life in the United States. Four of those years were spent in the custody of the United States' federal authorities. Now they had brought her home in handcuffs to deliver her to the place she had once forsaken.

All she wore was a white T-shirt and blue jeans. The rest of her possessions - the shorts and T-shirt they had taken from her that fateful night at the end of the I-95 - were in a little plastic bag held lightly in her hands.

She paused at the top of the stairs and pressed her face against the wetness of the night. Shirley could not remember Jamaica ever being so cold.

She shivered slightly, then caught herself. There would be no tears now. She had cried all of them an eternity ago when a judge's gavel sent her to prison for conspiracy and ensured that Moet would spend fifteen years in jail after Orville had cried and testified to things he could not have known or even imagined.

She had cried all her tears then. Bawled till her eyes ran dry and her sides shrank and sucked against her bones as if she was feeling hunger of a thousand years. Now from the void inside, all she had was a still cold face with distant eyes that had very few surprises left to see.

The hand of the US Marshal was firm against her back as she began to slowly descend the wet stairs. No one knew she was coming. No one was there to meet her except the uniformed policewoman waiting patiently on the tarmac.

At the last rung Shirley felt a final gentle shove as the American

Marshal nodded to the Jamaican Police woman on the ground.

"Shirley Temple Brown, deportee number 5975, she is all yours, Jamaica."

THE END